GOTCHA!

GOTCHA!

A MURDER IN WARRENSBURG

A MURDER MYSTERY BY

WAYNE HANCOCK

To order additional copies of this book, contact:
Xlibris Corporation
1-888-795-4274
www.Xlibris.com
Orders@Xlibris.com
65637

AUTHOR'S NOTE

THIS IS A NOVEL, and any resemblance between its characters and any persons living or dead is purely coincidental.

Warrensburg is a real town, however, with real, warm and friendly people. The university is real, and Dockery Hall still stands on campus. The Mules still play football in the same stadium. The courthouse is real, and the clock still strikes to remind people of the time. The dump was filled in long ago, and the old county jail is now used for other purposes. Shepard Park on north Holden Street is still used by the public.

Some of the buildings and businesses portrayed in the story, and all of the events, are figments of the author's imagination.

Don't expect accuracy concerning the trials and hearings depicted in the story. The author is not a lawyer, and many laws and offices have changed since 1936, rendering accurate research almost impossible for someone of the author's limited staff and means. The author accepts all responsibility for mistakes made in writing about a most important time in our nation's history.

ACKNOWLEDGMENTS

I WOULD LIKE to give credit to some people whose encouragement and expertise helped the author write this inaugural opus:

- First, June Hancock, my wife, who was the first to read the raw manuscript, and whose encouragement was vital.
- Sandy Fuller, who read the manuscript, gave me many good tips, and helped enormously with the punctuation.
- John Holland, whose wealth of legal experience helped me through the hearings and trials. Any mistakes in the procedures are mine, not John's.
- Bill Taylor, who labored hard to help me perfect the manuscript. His time, expertise and knowledge are greatly appreciated.
- And, lastly, all the folks who read the manuscript and encouraged me to have it published. Thank you.

CONTENTS

1

SATURDAY, MAY 16, 1936

THE PHONE JINGLED on Buck Pettit's desk and jolted him out of his daydream. He had been thinking about how hot and dry the last two years had been and was hoping this year would be better. As Police Chief of Warrensburg, Missouri, things just went better for him when it was cooler and they got some rain. The phone rang again and he took the receiver off the hook.

"Police Department."

"Chief, this is Ruby at the telephone office, and I've got a pretty excited woman on the line who wants to talk to you."

"Hi, Ruby, put her on."

"Is this the Police Department?" The woman's voice was quivering.

"Yes, this is Chief Pettit."

"He says he found a body!"

"Who found a body?"

"The young boy; he's right here in my living room."

The Chief sensed that she was about to go to pieces. "Let me talk to the boy, ma'am."

There was a pause on the phone, and a young man's voice said, "Hello."

"This is Chief Pettit, son, take your time and tell me what this is all about."

The boy's voice was shaky, and he talked like he was out of breath, but he seemed in better shape than the woman. "I . . . er, we were at the

1

dump looking for stuff we could sell to make some money, and I saw a body."

"What do you mean, you saw a body?" the Chief asked.

"I was poking through some old boxes, cans and stuff, and I saw a leg sticking out. At first I thought it was an old store dummy or something, but this leg had on a stocking and a fairly new shoe, and I didn't think a store would throw away a dummy and leave clothes on it like that."

"So then what happened?"

"I called for Johnny and Robert to come look."

"What's your name, son?"

"Irvin."

"Irwin who?"

"Irvin Hodges."

"Is that Irvin with a 'v' or a 'w'?"

"A 'v,' sir."

The Chief was taking notes as he talked to the boy. "And what did your friends say when they saw the leg?" he asked.

"They said they thought it was a real leg, too, sir!"

Buck leaned back in his chair, cradling the phone in his lap with his left hand as he thought for a minute. He was starting to get a sinking feeling in the pit of his stomach. There hadn't been a murder in Johnson County in over seven years, back when he was still a patrol officer. There had been two suicides in that time, but no murders.

"Hello."

The phone jarred him back to the business at hand. "I'll tell you what you do, son, go back to the dump and wait for me. I'll be there in a few minutes. Tell your buddies that you talked to me and that they are to wait for me, too. I don't want you guys to touch anything or move anything until I get there, okay?"

"Yes, sir."

"Okay, now let me talk to the lady."

"Hello."

"What's your name, ma'am?"

"Leona Roberts."

"You any relation to Harold Roberts?"

"Yes, sir, he's my husband."

"He's a fine mechanic, ma'am, works on our police cars all the time."

"Yes, sir, I know that." She was beginning to calm down.

"Mrs. Roberts, I'm going to have to talk to you later today, will you be home?"

"Yes, sir, I'll be home all day."

Buck glanced at the clock on the wall over Darlene's desk. It was 11:50. "It will be late this afternoon when I get there. What time does Harold get home for supper?"

"Usually about 6:00."

"Good, it may be as late as 8:00 when I get there, will that be okay?"

"Yes, sir, that would be fine."

"Good, I'll see you then."

Buck hung up the receiver and set the phone back on the desk. He sat back and studied for a couple of minutes. Darlene, his secretary/dispatcher, would be in at noon and would work until 10 p.m. His assistant chief, Clyde Burroughs, would come in at 10:00 and work until 8:00 the next morning. The department consisted of a chief, assistant chief, two patrol officers and Darlene, who acted as secretary and dispatcher, which was usually more than enough for a small college town of just under 6,000. The problem was that they only had two patrol cars. Clyde had one out at his house, and Clarence Slayton had the other one out on patrol.

He could wait for Darlene to come in, but sometimes she got delayed for one reason or another, or he could wait for Clarence to call in. He usually called in every hour on the hour, but even if he called in, it would take him another five to ten minutes to get to headquarters. The patrol cars had no radio, so he would usually call from a pay phone, and sometimes when he was out of nickels, he would just skip it, especially if it was really quiet.

I've got to get going, Buck thought to himself. Suddenly, he stood up, grabbed his straw hat off the wall peg and ran out the door.

Harry Foster would be just finishing his lunch at Dub's Café across the square. Sheriff Foster was a creature of habit. In his mid-50s and a confirmed bachelor, he was serving his fourth term as sheriff of Johnson County. He had taken care of his folks until they died, and still lived on the little farm he grew up on north of town. He had served as deputy sheriff while still farming with his parents, and ran for sheriff right after his mother died. He was the kind of man who would help his neighbors get their crops in if they were sick, repair the roof on the one-room schoolhouse near his home without charge, and always had a smile on his face. He was not a handsome man, just pleasant to look at. His tanned face was topped by a shock of steel gray hair that he parted in the middle, and he had deep smile wrinkles around his eyes and mouth. He was probably the most eligible bachelor in the county, and determined to stay that way.

Buck cut across the courthouse lawn to save time. He was starting to sweat and was panting by the time he reached for the handle on the screen door at Dub's. He vowed to himself to get in better shape. The Sheriff was sitting on his favorite stool at the counter sipping on his second coffee refill when Buck rushed up to him.

"I need your help, can you step outside with me, please? I'm in a hurry!"

Harry nodded, sensing that Buck didn't want to talk about it in front of the people in the café. He grabbed his hat off the stool next to him, threw a dime tip on the counter and followed Buck out the door. "Put that lunch on my tab, Lois. I'll pay you at the end of the month," he said over his shoulder as he stepped out the door.

"Sure, Sheriff," Lois said with a quizzical look on her face.

After they got out of ear shot of the café, Buck said, "I either need for you to take me someplace, or loan me your car." Buck briefly told Harry about the phone call he had received and the situation with the patrol cars.

"My car's right over there," he responded. "Get in and I'll drive you to the dump."

"We're in a hurry, but don't drive with your siren on; I don't want to attract any attention 'til I find out what's what."

Harry nodded and nosed his patrol car out onto Holden Street. He drove north to Gay Street, then west on Gay to Old Town hill. When they got to the corner of Water and Gay streets, Harry turned right for a short distance and then left into the dump.

It wasn't a planned dump, it just happened. Back in the 1800s, before the railroad came through Warrensburg, this was downtown, and Main Street was the main drag. The corner of Market and Main streets was the center of town. The street followed an old Indian trail along a ridge from what was now Federal Highway 50, south to the end of the ridge,

4

about seven blocks. From there, the ridge dropped steeply to dirt road that ran along the bluff.

At its peak, during the mid-1800s, there were two grocery stores, a dry goods store, a blacksmith shop and livery along Main, plus the Johnson County Courthouse. A tan stucco building, the courthouse was started in 1838, the year Johnson County was formed and finished in 1842. It was the site of the famous Burden vs. Hornsby trial in 1857. They were both farmers, and Hornsby had shot Burden's dog for trespassing on his property and killed it. Burden sued for damages, and Senator George Graham Vest of Missouri served as one of Burden's attorneys. It was during his closing argument at the end of the trial that Senator Vest made his famous "a man's best friend is his dog" tribute to "Old Drum," Burden's hound. The jury, all men, and most of the gallery were moved to tears by the speech, and needless to say, the jury found for the plaintiff and awarded him damages of $50, which was a princely sum in those days. Senator Vest's speech is still quoted to this day.

There was a small ravine that ran from near the intersection of Water and Gay streets in a generally westerly direction that got deeper and wider the further west it went. It terminated in a shady glen that was called "Cave Hollow" by the natives because of two caves, one in the north bluff and a larger one in the south bluff. There was a small stream that ran through it, which could become a torrent if it rained real hard. It was cool there in the hot summer, and several townspeople took their milk cows there to graze on the tall green grass that was plentiful.

Some of the townspeople had hauled some big rocks to the ravine and dumped them in to help stop the erosion, and that seemed to give everyone in town tacit permission to dump their unwanted trash in it also. This had been going on since the mid-1800s, and by 1936 a two- or three-acre lot had been formed by the city dumping dirt over the trash to keep down the smell as the trash was pushed over the edge. It had been officially designated as the city dump, and they had even built a metal building on the lot to house the city's tractor used to maintain the dump. This had been done after the railroad came to town and the city center of town was shifted ten blocks east. The county even built a new courthouse on a square platted at Market and Holden Streets, and the old tan stucco courthouse on Main stood vacant.

Harry stopped his car, and he and Buck got out. About ten feet from the edge of the ravine, three boys about ten years old stood by a coaster wagon loaded with assorted junk.

"Hi, fellows," Buck said in a casual attempt to put the boys at ease. "Which one of you guys did I talk to on the phone?"

"It was me, sir."

Irv's mother, Katie, had taught her children to always be polite. She had said, "We may be poor, but we can be clean and polite. Soap is cheap and manners are free."

"You're Irvin, right?"

"Yes, sir."

"I'm Chief Pettit, and this is Sheriff Foster. Who are your friends?"

Johnny spoke up, "I'm Johnny O'Reilly, and he's Bobby McKnight," Johnny said, pointing to Bobby.

The Chief took his notebook out of his pocket and was making notes as he spoke. "What's in your wagon?" he asked.

Again, Johnny spoke up, he seemed to want to be the spokesman for the group. "We were just gathering up junk to sell at Cohn's Junkyard," he said.

Just then the clock in the courthouse downtown chimed 12:00. The Chief made a note in his little book. "Irvin, since you are the one that discovered the alleged body, would you point it out to me? You don't have to go down there, just point it out to me, and the Sheriff and I will go down and take a look see."

Irv walked over to the edge and pointed to a spot about 20 feet from the top. "See the cushion and the Ivory soap box? There was a worn-out cushion from an old couch next to an empty cardboard box." The Chief nodded his head. "The leg is sticking out right beside that cushion. You can't see it from here because the box kind of hides it."

"Okay," the Chief said, "you go back with your friends and wait. The Sheriff and I will go look."

He motioned to Harry to follow, and he started wading down though the tin cans and other junk to where the cushion lay. When he got down to the cushion, he pushed the box to one side and, sure enough, there was a woman's leg showing up to the knee. Buck got that terrible sinking feeling in the pit of his stomach again. He motioned for Harry to come on down. They carefully removed the junk covering the body and found a woman in her mid-20s. She was pretty and petite and fully clothed except for a missing right shoe.

"Damn!" Buck muttered under his breath. "Harry, I'll stay with the body if you will go get the coroner, and tell those boys to stay put 'til I can get to them."

"I'll be back as soon as I can," Harold said over his shoulder as he struggled to the top. As he passed the boys, he told them that the Chief wanted to talk to them some more and to stay where they were until the coroner had picked up the body. Then he jumped into his patrol car and sped off.

Lester Phipps and his brother, Ellwood, ran the Phipps Funeral Home. Lester had gotten himself elected Johnson County Coroner mainly because he had the only body cooler in the county. He let it be known that if the County wanted to use his facilities to preserve a body for any purpose like an autopsy, or until some other agency could pick it up, he would charge the county $5 a day for every day they used his cooler, and if he was coroner, the fee would drop to $1 a day per body.

He was elected four times in a row. He appointed his brother, Ellwood, to the job of assistant coroner, and they had worked for the county for the past nine years.

The Phipps Funeral Home was on the northeast corner of Market and Holden streets, just across the street from the courthouse. It had been in the family for three generations and was the biggest facility in the county. Located in a well-maintained three-story red brick building, it had a reception area, offices and two chapels on the main floor. The second floor was used to store caskets and other supplies, and as a showroom for the caskets. They not only stocked caskets for their own clients, but wholesaled them to smaller funeral homes in the county. The third floor was divided into two spacious apartments for the Phipps brothers and their families. In the rear of the building there were two elevators—a passenger elevator and a larger freight elevator used mainly to move caskets and supplies from the loading dock to the second floor and back down to the main floor for funerals. There was a full basement under the building, and that was where the Phipps made a lot of their money. It was a well-equipped embalming room, where they embalmed bodies for their own customers, as well as doing most of the embalming in a two-county area. It was also well-equipped to do autopsies. In the back of the building there was a garage that housed their two Packard family cars, a LaSalle hearse and a Cadillac ambulance. They were doing well even in the hard times of the depression.

Harry's car slid to a stop in the driveway behind the funeral home, and he jumped up on the dock and frantically rang the bell by the back door. Mutt Bridges, their handyman, opened the door with a surprised look on his face. He had been expecting a delivery truck from the funeral supply company in Kansas City.

"What's up, Sheriff?"

"I need an ambulance out at the city dump right away," Harry blurted.

Mutt didn't say a word. He reached up and took the keys to the ambulance off the row of hooks inside the door and ran to the front to tell Lillian, their secretary, he was taking the ambulance and to get hold of Lester and send him out to the city dump right away. He ran out the back door and told Harry he would meet him there in about three minutes. Harry didn't wait for Mutt to follow him; he backed out into Market Street and headed back out to the dump.

By this time word was getting around town that something was up, and Harry could see two cars following him in his rearview mirror. As he pulled into the dump, he spotted the police patrol car that Clarence had been driving, and Clarence was talking to the boys. Harry pulled up beside the patrol car and got out. He waved to Clarence and pointed to the cars just pulling into the dump site.

"Looks like we are going to need some traffic control, Clarence," he shouted. "There's an ambulance coming!"

Clarence nodded and ran over to the first car. The driver started to get out, but Clarence stopped him with a gesture.

"Back out of here as quick as you can," he shouted.

He went to the second car and told the driver the same thing. His car must have had five people in it. The ambulance had pulled up behind them waiting to turn in. Clarence went to work and soon had the two cars back out on Water street and the ambulance backed up to the edge of the ravine. Before the cars could empty their passengers, Clarence rolled a couple of empty drums to the entrance and had set them in the middle of the driveway into the dump.

As people started to walk past them, he yelled, "Stay out of the dump and keep the street open for the ambulance!"

They looked shocked that mild-mannered Clarence would shout at them like that, but they could tell by the look in his eyes that he meant business. Clarence went over to the ambulance just as Harry was helping Mutt take the body cart out of the back.

Buck arrived at the top at the same time. He turned to Clarence and asked, "How did you find out I was here so fast?"

"Ruby at the telephone office caught me at the Tiptop Cafe and told about Mrs. Roberts' call. She must have listened in on the conversation, because she told me about the body. I rushed over here as soon as I could."

"That must be where all those other folks heard about it, too," the Chief snorted.

Lester Phipps pulled up and got out of his car. "Chief, I'll help you, Harry and Mutt, with the body if Clarence can handle the crowd. Those idiots will be all over us unless somebody takes charge."

The Chief nodded at Clarence, and he took his night stick out of his belt and started to the driveway. The courthouse clock chimed the half-hour.

After the body was loaded and Mutt had left in the ambulance, the Chief started to go back down to the spot where the body was found, when he suddenly became aware of the boys still standing by their wagon.

"I'm sorry, fellows, I plumb forgot about you. Listen, it's getting on to 1:00 and you guys must be getting hungry. I appreciate your waiting, but I've got your names and addresses, so why don't you go on home now and come up to my office around 3:00 and I'll take your statements then? Thanks a lot and tell your folks not to worry and that they can come with you when you come to my office if they want."

The boys started for the street with Johnny pulling the wagon. Clarence was still handling the curiosity seekers.

Buck turned to Lester. "Lester, I want you to go back to your place and check the body for me. Try to determine the cause of death without cutting the body open at this time. Look for stains, dirt, smudges, grass or any foreign substances on her clothing. Call Doctor Allen and have him check her for sexual assault. I'll try to get up there later today to go over what you find with you and to take a closer look at her myself. We've got to identify her so we can notify her next of kin. Harry, you got time to help me look for clues?"

Harry nodded his head.

"Okay, I'll go down where the body was found and work my way to the top, and you search the area up here."

"What are we looking for?" Harry asked.

"Anything that might give us a clue as to who brought her body here and dumped it over the side. I think that whoever did this also drug the body down to where we found it and covered it up with trash."

Harry looked around. "I doubt if we'll find any tire tracks that might help. There have been too many vehicles and people tramping around."

Buck looked disgusted. "Do the best you can, look for any jewelry, pieces of clothing, her purse, the other shoe, anything that might be a clue as to who she is and who killed her. I doubt if we'll find much, as it's obvious that she was killed somewhere else, but give it your best shot."

They searched for about ten minutes without finding anything, and Buck yelled at Harry, "I'm coming up, this is futile."

The Chief climbed to the top. There were sweat stains under his arms and down his back. He took his hat off and wiped his forehead with his handkerchief. "Man, it's hot down there. It's only the first week of May, and I'll bet it's already in the mid80s. I didn't find a thing. I thought at least I'd find the other shoe."

Harry shook his head. "I didn't find anything either." The courthouse clock struck 1:00, and Buck looked at his pocket watch.

"I'm going up to the funeral home, can you come with me?"

"Buck, I have to go by my office at the jail to make some calls and do some things; I will if I can."

The city didn't have a jail. It was closed when the county built its new jail at the southeast corner of Market and Washington just two blocks from the courthouse. The courthouse was built in 1897 out of sandstone quarried just north of Warrens-burg, and shortly after the turn of the century, the jail was built out of stone from the same quarry. A lot of the buildings at the college were also built out of the same stone. One day the workers blasted a little too deep and opened up a big underground spring which quickly filled the quarry with water. They say the workers barely made it out in time and that there is still a lot of abandoned machinery at the bottom of the quarry.

The jail had two floors and a basement. The main entrance opens onto Market Street, and the basement has a garage en trance on Washington Street because the lot slopes so severely. The Sheriff's Department parked their two patrol cars in the basement and could bring prisoners down from their cells and transport them to the courthouse without going outside.

Harry left the dump and Buck yelled at Clarence to come with him. There were only six bystanders left hanging around the entrance to the dump, as most of the curious had followed the ambulance downtown. They got in the patrol car, and Clarence drove them to the Phipps Funeral Home. They parked in back by the loading dock. There was a crowd of people in front of the funeral home, and when the police car drove up, they all ran to the rear of the building. Buck saw them coming, and he rang the bell and hoped they could duck in before he had to answer any questions. They didn't make it. Buck recognized the one in the lead as a reporter from the Star Journal.

"Chief," he yelled, waving his hand. "I'm Ross Ludlow from the *Star Journal,* and I would like to ask you some questions!"

Just then Mutt opened the back door, and they ducked inside. Mutt slid the bolt and locked it.

"It's been like this ever since we got back with the body. We had to shove everyone out the front door and lock it. They were even trying to go down to the basement to see who we had on the slab."

"Thanks, Mutt, we'll go on down."

The Chief and Clarence went down the steps to the basement. There was a smell of chemicals in the basement air, even though there was an exhaust fan pulling the air out into the alley behind the building. Up toward the front of the building was a long stainless steel table with a floodlight over it. There was a sheet covering the body on the table, and Lester sat on a stool beside the table writing on a clipboard. He glanced up when he heard them coming down the steps.

"Chief, I think I know how she died."

"Already?"

"Yup, I think she was strangled; come over here and look at the marks on her neck."

The Chief and Clarence moved closer while Lester turned the sheet back to her shoulders. Clarence let out a gasp when he saw her face.

"Chief, I think I know this woman!"

"What do you mean, think?" the Chief asked.

Clarence's hands were starting to shake a little. "I'm almost positive, let me take a closer look. Yup, that's her. I had her in a couple of my classes at CSTC a few years back. The last I heard, she was teaching at Reese School."

"What's her name?" the Chief asked.

"Margaret Wilson, she's from up in Carroll County originally. I think her folks farm in the bottoms south of Carrollton. Heck, I even dated her a couple of times before I got married. Man, this hurts to see a pretty woman like this murdered and thrown in a dump."

The Chief put his hand on Clarence's shoulder. "You're right about that, son. Now here's what I want you to do. Locate Hermann Glasscock, the county superintendent of schools, and tell him I need him to come see me as soon as he can. Tell him we want him to help us identify a murder victim, that we think she's one of his school teachers, and that we'll need her home address and phone number so we can notify her next of kin. Take the patrol car. I'll walk back to the station; it's only two blocks. Oh, and park the patrol car in front of the station and keep the people from pestering Darlene to death."

"Yes, sir, I'll go do it now. What should I tell people when they ask about what is going on?"

Buck paused for a moment, "Just tell them that there was a body found at the dump this morning and it's been taken to the funeral home to await identification. As soon as we find out who it is, we'll notify her next of kin and give a statement to the newspaper. That's all you need to tell them for now."

Buck turned to Lester. "Any Idea what time she died?"

"Not exactly without cutting her open."

Buck thought for a minute, "Don't do that, just give me your best estimate."

Lester scratched his head. "Judging from what decomposition there is, I d say between 12 and 18 hours. It's awfully hard to judge as warm as it has been."

Buck took out his notebook. "That would put it between noon and midnight yesterday. Thanks, Lester. Is there a phone down here I can use?"

"Right over there on the wall. I had better get this body back in the cooler until Dr. Allen can get away to come examine her."

Buck picked up the receiver.

"Number, please."

"Is that you, Ruby?"

"No, sir, this is Freda. Ruby got off at 1:00 today."

"Okay, give me number 22, please."

"Thank you."

The phone rang. The Chief's wife picked up the receiver on the second ring.

"Ann, this is Buck."

"Where have you been? The phone downstairs has been ringing off the wall. Darlene has been going crazy trying to keep up with it."

"Honey, there has been a murder, and I'm in it up to my ears. It's 1:30 now and I have to meet with some boys that found the body at 3:00 in my office. Could you fix me a sandwich of some kind and a cup of coffee? I'll sneak up the back stairs and grab a bite before I see the boys."

"I'll have it ready in five minutes."

That's what Buck loved about Ann. Not only was she beautiful and an accomplished musician, but also she was a genius at managing a home. They had been high school sweethearts, and he had never loved any other woman, except his mother, like he loved Ann. She had long blonde hair in high school, and often tap danced and played the piano at school assemblies. Every boy in their class had tried to date her. He had first met Ann Christian on a basketball trip to Clinton. He played guard on the team and she was a cheerleader. It was love at first sight, and neither one dated anyone else after that meeting. They graduated together, and he proposed to her at the graduation dance. She turned him down. He was devastated.

"Why?" he had sputtered.

She took him by the hand and led him out of the gym where the dance was being held. They went out the Grover Street entrance, and she sat him down on the steps and nestled beside him. They sat there for a few minutes. Buck was almost in tears.

Finally she said, "Buck, you know that I love you more than life itself, and if you believe that, then you know that I want to marry you. It's just that I promised my parents that I wouldn't marry until I had finished college. They want me to go to Stevens College in Columbia, and I promised I would."

"But that's a snooty girl's school, and I probably won't see much of you after you leave town," he blurted, tears starting to trickle down his cheeks.

Ann's parents were wealthy. They owned a lot of land south of Warrensburg and at two businesses in town. It was old money, and Buck was intimidated by it.

Buck's dad managed a chain grocery store on Holden Street, and with he, his two sisters and his mother to support, they did well to pay their bills every week. Buck was not ashamed of his family. His mother made sure they went to church every Sunday, and his sisters, both younger than Buck, sang in the church choir. The youngest was a sophomore at CSTC, and the oldest taught at Foster Elementary School. Buck, at 5' 11", had prided himself in the fact that he was the second tallest man on the basketball team, and still fast enough to play guard. A handsome young man with black curly hair and an athlete's build, all the girls in his class had considered him quite a catch, but they all knew that they couldn't compete with Ann, so they didn't try.

Ann took the hankie out that she had tucked in the bracelet she wore and dabbed at his cheeks.

"William Anderson Pettit, you know that I'll see you every chance I get. I'll be home almost every weekend, and we'll have summers to spend together."

Buck got himself together and gave Ann a big hug. He thought to himself, *Wow, I have to be the luckiest man in the world. She could have any man she wants, and she is willing to settle for a man whose highest ambition is to be a policeman.*

That fall Ann moved to Columbia, and Buck enrolled in a criminology course at CSTC. They both graduated in June 1916, and were married that month. Little Ann was born the next year.

2

INVESTIGATING THE CRIME

THE BOYS LEFT the dump and walked east on Gay Street until they reached Warren. They didn't say much as they walked. They were all three visibly shaken by the preceding events. They stopped for a minute, and Robert agreed to take the wagon on over to Cohn's to sell the junk, and they would all meet at the police station at 3:00.

Irv turned north on Warren St. It was just three blocks over to Lobbin Street where he lived.

He lived with his mother, Katie, his dad, Nate, a sister nine years older than he, Kathy, and a brother three years older, LeRoy. That was plenty for the four-room house. There was one big bedroom with two double beds. He and LeRoy shared one bed, and his mom and dad the other. The small back bedroom was reserved for Kathy, who at 18 needed more privacy.

There were two older brothers, Chuck, 24, and Louis, 21, who were away at a CCC camp near Higginsville. They had both enlisted in this "make work" federal program that was part of President Roosevelt's New Deal. Since the country was in the depths of the Great Depression, and there were no jobs to be had, this was a way for young men to earn some money, and it kept them off the streets where they were more apt to get into trouble. They lived in army-type barracks and worked on the roads mainly, cutting brush and mowing weeds.

Irv knew that there wouldn't be anyone home. Katie worked as a domestic in several homes around town. She had been approached at church by a friend who knew her circumstances and had told her that Professor Markham at the college needed someone to help his wife clean their home and to help with the cooking.

That afternoon, Katie went over to a neighbor's house to use their phone and had called Dr. Clyde Markham at his home. He had Katie talk to his wife, Elizabeth, and she hired Katie over the phone. She usually worked just a day and a half a week, which suited Katie as it didn't interrupt her own schedule too much. The pay was 15 cents an hour, which was generous considering farmers in the county were paying day laborers a dollar a day for 12-hour days. She also got some of her meals furnished. On Wednesdays she cleaned their house from top to bottom, and on Fridays she did some light dusting, some laundry and helped Elizabeth get ready for their weekly staff party.

Dr. Markham was head of the History Department at CSTC and had tenure. It had been his custom for several years to invite three or four of his colleagues and their spouses to his home on Friday evenings for drinks, hors d'oeuvres and cards. Sometimes they even included dinner. On those nights, Katie would stay until 7:00 to prepare dinner and help serve. Katie was a very good cook, and word got around the campus that the Markhams had a jewel in Katie. They often asked if they could "borrow" her for a special occasion. Sometimes Katie would consent, but only on a Saturday, as she had too much to do on other days.

Word around town was that the parties were Clyde and Elizabeth's way of "sucking up" to the board and President DeMint, and that's the way he got to be head of a department. Still, the professors and business swells around town looked forward to invitations from the Markhams, as it always meant a good time. Good conversation, good drinks, and sometimes an excellent meal, which was a treat, as really good restaurants in Warrensburg were non-existent.

Katie would be working for one of the Markhams' friends, Kathy would be with her friends, Maxine and June, up the street, and LeRoy would probably be at a Saturday matinee at the Star Theater. Irv went to the icebox and found a small saucepan with a good helping of brown beans, a bowl of apple sauce and some cooked carrots. He lit a burner on the kerosene stove and put the pan of beans on to heat. It was so warm out that he was tempted to eat them cold, but the fatback used to season them had congealed, so he had added some water to thin them out. He got a roll out of the bread box and smeared it with oleo from the icebox. He dished some applesauce into a small bowl and stirred the beans. In less than 15 minutes, he was sitting at the kitchen table eating his humble repast. He wished he had heated the carrots, too, as the oleo that Katie had cooked them in had congealed. They could never afford butter.

As he ate, he glanced over the *Kansas City Times* lying on the table. LeRoy had left it from his morning route. He usually had two extras from his route, and he always brought one home for the family to read. If he was lucky, someone would stop him on the street and buy the other extra copy, and he would have a nickel to spend that day.

He glanced at the headlines. Miss Colli, his fifth grade teacher, had encouraged her students to keep up on current events, and since Irv liked to read anyway, he usually scanned the headlines to look for a story he could talk to Miss Colli about. He liked miss Colli, and she could always depend on him to bring a news story to class that all the students could discuss.

Mussolini's conquest of Abyssinia complete! U.S.A., Britain, France protest to League! Since Miss Colli's parents lived in Italy, Irv wondered what she would have to say about this headline. He would read the story when he got home later and take it to school on Monday. There was only one week of school left in the year, and this might help him get a better grade.

He wondered what the Police Chief would ask him. He decided he would just tell him what he had seen and done. Then it struck him. He had forgotten the fountain pen. He'll surely want to know about that.

When he and his friends had pulled their wagon into the dump, he had walked over to the edge and looked down. His eye caught a glimpse of something shining in the dust at his feet. Someone must have dropped it while throwing trash over the edge. It turned out to be a silver-colored fountain pen. He had showed it to Johnny and Robert, and they both said it looked expensive. It was about five inches long with fancy engraving on its barrel. Johnny said it might even be gold. Irv said he thought gold was yellow, and Johnny said there was such a thing as white gold. Robert turned it around in his hand.

"Look, guys, there are initials on the top part!"

Johnny grabbed it, "Let me see," he said. Johnny squinted at the initials in the small rectangle on the cap. "TAB," Johnny read. "Do you know anyone with those initials?" Irv and Robert shrugged their shoulders.

Irv said, "I'll just keep it, and if nobody claims it, I'll give it to my mom, she writes lots of letters." He remembered dropping it in the bib pocket of his overalls and snapping the flap. He felt the pocket and it was still there. The old Seth Thomas clock that sat atop the secretary in the living room chimed 2:45. Irv quickly cleared the table and headed out the door.

He arrived at the police station at 2:55 and walked in. Johnny was already there sitting on a bench that ran along the east wall of the reception area.

Darlene asked, "Are you one of the boys that Chief Pettit wanted to talk to?"

"Yes, ma'am."

"Which one are you?"

"Irvin Hodges, ma'am."

"Good." She made a check mark on the pad that lay on the desk in front of her. "Just go sit with Johnny on that bench. The other boy, uh, Robert, hasn't arrived yet, so we'll just wait until he gets here, and then I'll call Chief Pettit. He's just upstairs, so it won't take long to get him here."

The courthouse clock struck 3:00. At 3:05, Robert and his mother, Lucille McKnight, walked in. You could tell she was looking for someone to confront. She and Robert, along with Robert's sister, Peggy, were living with her father in a big white two-story house on Gay Street, just two blocks from the station. Lucille had been a school teacher in St. Louis, and two years prior had divorced her husband for infidelity and moved her family back to Warrensburg to live with her father. Her mother was dead. She had been successful in landing the principal's job at Reese School her first year back. The current principal had resigned to marry a farmer and had moved to the country. Since Lucille had served as Reese's principal before moving to St. Louis, Superintendent Glasscock was more than happy to give her the job.

She strode briskly up to Darlene's desk and announced, "I am Lucille McKnight, and this is my son, Robert! I understand that the Chief wants to talk to Robert."

"Yes, ma'am, just have a seat. The Chief will be down in a minute." Darlene made another checkmark on her pad.

"I hope this won't take long. It has already disrupted my day," she snorted.

Irv got up so that Lucille and Robert could sit on the bench with Johnny. He didn't want to upset Lucille, because he was in the fifth grade at Reese and Lucille was the principal.

Darlene said, "I'll be right back."

She got up and walked through the door to the back offices. From the Chief's office along the East wall, a stairway led up to Buck and Ann's apartment. She didn't want to call Buck from her desk because she wanted to tell him something in private before he came down. She rapped gently on the door, and Buck opened it.

"Come in, Darlene, anything wrong?" She stepped into the kitchen of the apartment and closed the door.

* * * * *

The Warrensburg Police Department had gone through a big change since the depression hit in 1930. At its peak, there had been ten people in the department. Now they were down to five. Buck had made a deal with the county to house the city prisoners, and they had removed the two holding cells in the back of the first floor. They also took out the conference and interrogation rooms and moved the offices, lounge and break rooms downstairs from the second floor. The Chief had said they could use the break room or one of the offices for interrogations, and since there were only five people in the department, they could conference in his office, and if they had visitors, they could step across the street and use the conference room in the courthouse.

Buck and his officers had done most of the work, and all the city did was furnish the materials. Needless to say, Mayor Bob "Ike" Shannon and the Council members were pleased with the results, and especially pleased with the savings at budget time. However, when working on the 1935 budget in the fall of 1934, they still had a shortfall in their general operating budget, and had asked all city employees to take ten percent salary cut as of January 1, 1935.

19

Buck went before the council to plead his case for the department, but was turned down. The Mayor said that he was taking the cut along with the rest of them. Buck knew that it would mean that he and Ann would have to give up the big comfortable house they were renting on Broad Street, and he hated to break the news to her. They would have to start looking for an apartment right away. Then the thought hit him.

"Ike, I've got a proposition for you."

"Okay, let's hear it."

"The city owns the building that houses the Police Department, right?"

"Yes," the Mayor said with a quizzical look on his face, not knowing what to expect.

He and Buck had been on friendly terms ever since Buck had made Chief, but Buck had taken the cuts pretty hard, and Ike didn't quite know what he was driving at. Buck continued, "Since we have consolidated at the department, the whole upstairs of the building is sitting empty. After the pay cut, January first, Ann and I won't be able to afford the house we're renting, so how about shooting me a real cheap price on that space over the department, and we can move up there?"

The proposal took the Mayor by surprise. He was relieved. For a minute he had thought the popular Chief was going to resign and tell the Mayor where he could put the entire department. He knew Ann's parents had money and lived in a big house on South Holden Street. He wondered why they just didn't move in with them. A lot of young married people were doing that these days. He didn't know Buck and Ann. When Ann's parents had suggested it, she had told them flatly, "No." They doted on their granddaughter, Ann Marie, and longed to have her living under the same roof, but Ann would have no part of it. She loved her parents dearly, but she wanted the privilege of raising Ann Marie herself. She was Buck's girl, actually, and thought her "daddy" hung the moon. Buck was "bust your buttons" proud of her. She was 19 and finishing up her sophomore year at Stevens College in Columbia, the tuition and board being furnished by her grandparents at their insistence.

That was the only concession that Ann had made to her parents. They were paying Ann Marie's board and tuition at college.

It was a family tradition that all the women in Ann's family go to Stevens, and Ann and Buck just couldn't afford it. Buck had suggested she go to his Alma Mater, CSTC. That way she could live at home and Buck could keep an eye on her. Buck was out numbered four to one, so he conceded.

Mayor Shannon had talked it over with the attorney that did the city's legal work, and he gave it his blessing. He then polled the council members to get their input. There were six—one from each of the four wards and two at large. The Mayor's vote made seven to avoid a tie. In fact, Leland Grimes, Fourth Ward Councilman, reminded Ike that Chief Pettit had been in line for a raise, and they were cutting his pay instead. He suggested that the city rent the space to the Chief's family for $1 dollar a year and that the city furnish the utilities. The Mayor and the rest of the councilmen had concurred, so that's why the Chief and his family were living over the Police Department.

The city had furnished the materials, and Buck and his men did the work. Soon they had finished a lovely three-bedroom apartment. Ann bought material and made curtains, and it was real homey. There was a back door from the dining room that led down to the small staff parking lot in back of the building, and a door that led from the kitchen down to the Chief's office.

Darlene said "Chief, the boys are all here. Robert brought his mother, or rather she brought him. She is in a kind of a dither, so could you talk to him first?"

"No, I want to talk to the Hodges boy first' he's the one that found the body."

"Okay, but it's your funeral," she said as they walked down the steps.

Buck plopped down in his desk chair, and Darlene went up front. There was a note on his desk from Clarence saying that Superintendent Glasscock would meet them between 4:00 and 4:30 today at the funeral home. "Irvin Hodges," Darlene said sweetly, trying to avoid the icy stare from Lucille McKnight.

She motioned for Irv to follow her and ushered him into the Chief's office. Buck indicated a chair beside his desk and Irv sat down. The Chief took out his notebook and pencil. "Now, son, don't be afraid, you're not in any trouble. I just want you to tell me everything you and your friends did from the time you pulled your wagon into the dump until the time I got there."

"That was Robert's wagon," Irv said softly.

"I know, son, just tell me everything that happened."

Irv cleared his throat, his mouth was dry. "I was in front, and I walked over to the edge to look down at all the junk to see if I could see anything from the top."

The Chief was taking notes.

Irv knew he had to tell him about the fountain pen. "I looked down and I saw something shining in the dirt by my foot. I almost stepped on it."

The Chief perked up. "What did you find, son?"

Irv unsnapped the bib pocket of his overalls and pulled out the pen. He handed it to Buck, who took it carefully and examined it for two or three minutes before saying anything. Finally, he looked up with an amazed look on his face.

"This is an expensive pen, son, I'm glad you found it. It may be just the clue we've been looking for. Go on with your story while I look it over some more." He unscrewed the cap to reveal a solid gold point.

"I picked the pen up and showed it to Robert and Johnny. They both thought it was an expensive pen, too. Johnny said it had somebody's initials on the top. I said I would keep it, and unless somebody claimed it, give it to my mother. She writes a lot of letters and postcards."

"Who is your mother, son?" the Chief asked.

"Katie Hodges, sir."

"Is she the one who cooks and does work for Professor Markham?"

"Yes, sir."

"She's a great cook. Ann and I have been to a couple of their dinners and they feed well. Go on, son," the Chief urged.

"Well, then I walked down a ways looking for stuff to sell. I moved that box and that's when I saw the leg." Irv was staring at the pen and forgot what he was going to say next. Buck motioned for him to continue as he turned the pen in his hands to examine it. "I yelled at Johnny and Robert to come look. They both said they thought it was a body, too. We ran out of there as fast as we could. They decided that I was the one to call the police, so I ran around to that house on Gay Street on the other side of the dump, and she called you."

"She?"

"The lady who came to the door."

"Why that house? There are houses right across the street from the dump."

"Well, sir, colored people live in those houses, and I didn't know what they would think about a white boy running up on their porch and asking them to call the police. Besides, I didn't know for sure if any of them had a phone. I looked over at that other house, and I could see a phone line running into it from the pole."

Buck's eyebrows went up. "You're pretty smart for a boy your age," he said. "I'm going to keep this pen for the time being. I think it might be a clue in this case. If nothing comes of it, I'll see that you get it back. Of course, you know I'll be looking for the owner."

"Yes, sir."

Buck took out an envelope, dated it and wrote on it, "Fountain pen found at the dump. Possible clue to murder," and locked it in the middle drawer of his desk.

"Then what did you do?" he asked.

"I ran back to the dump, and we just waited for you to come," he said.

As Buck walked Irv up front, he told him to come in or call him if he thought of anything else the police should know about what happened this morning. He said he would.

Buck told Darlene to send Johnny back. Lucille McKnight glared at Darlene as she escorted Johnny back to Buck's office. Irv didn't even look at her as he went out the door. Back in Buck's office, Johnny told the Chief almost word for what Irv and said, including the part about Irv finding the pen. Buck made notes, then walked Johnny up front and told him what he had told Irv about contacting him if he had any additional information. He motioned for Lucille and Robert to come back. After he had seated them in his office, Lucille lit into him.

"You did that deliberately!" she fumed.

"I'm sorry, but I took the boys in the order that I had talked to them this morning," he said.

"Oh, no, you didn't! I watched you, and you kept Robert and me waiting just because I said that I was very busy today."

"Mrs. McKnight, it has only been 30 minutes. Why don't you leave Robert with me and I'll send him home as soon as I have finished talking with him? That way, you won't waste any more time."

"Oh, that's as good as you would want, isn't it, so you can put words in Robert's mouth? Accuse him of saying things he doesn't say!"

Buck had had enough. "Have it your way, Mrs. McKnight. I just need to ask Robert a few questions."

"Yes, I'm sure you do," she snorted.

Buck turned to Robert.

"Robert, I want you to tell me everything that happened after you and your friends pulled your wagon into the dump."

Lucille interjected, "I have told Robert to stay away from that dump, but he persists on going there. It's dirty, and he could get hurt. He only goes there because those 'so-called' friends of his insist. Oh, I suppose that Johnny O'Reilly is all right, but that Hodges boy is nothing but trouble."

"Oh, how is that?" Buck asked.

"Well, for one thing, they live next to a colored woman and they go to that church on Washington across from the jail. I think it's some kind of a cult."

Robert stared at the floor and didn't say anything. He was plainly embarrassed by his mother's tantrum.

"Mrs. McKnight," Buck said, "why don't you let Robert tell his story. Then I can let you go, and you can get done some of those things you're so anxious to do."

Lucille glared at Buck again. He nodded at Robert and Robert told him almost exactly what the other two had said, including Irv finding the fountain pen.

"Aha!" Lucille interjected, "I'll bet that Hodges boy didn't even tell you about the pen, did he? It's an expensive one, you know."

Buck didn't answer; he just unlocked his middle drawer, took out the envelope and held it up. "It's in here," he said.

Lucille fell silent and moped while Robert and Buck finished up his deposition. Buck escorted them out the front door, turned and rolled his eyes at Darlene. She snickered and went on with her work.

* * * * *

Clarence parked his patrol car in front of the station and had been fending off reporters and curiosity seekers. He had located Hermann Glasscock, the county superintendent of schools. He was at his office in the high school getting the information on Miss Wilson. He told Clarence he would meet him and Buck at the funeral home between 4:00 and 4:30. He hoped the Chief had gotten his message.

Buck had gone back up to the apartment and filled Ann in on everything that had been going on. She remarked that she was glad Ann Marie had stayed in Columbia instead of coming home this weekend. She was cramming for her finals and needed the weekend to work on a paper for her English Lit class. Buck was glad, too, because he knew he would be spending long hours on this new homicide case, and he hated neglecting his family. He wouldn't feel quite as guilty with Ann Marie staying in Columbia.

The courthouse clock struck 4:00. Buck looked at his watch. It read one minute after. Buck carried a Hamilton pocket watch. It had been given to him by his grandfather who retired as a switchman from the Missouri Pacific Railroad in 1930 at age 65 when Buck was only 14. He died suddenly two years later of a heart attack. Buck loved his grandfather, and put the watch away in his dresser drawer after the funeral for safekeeping. It was Ann who convinced him to use it every day. She had said, "Every fine machine needs to be used and kept running, or it will just deteriorate." He took her advice and was glad he did, as it kept perfect time.

He squeezed her hand and said, "I'll be back as soon as I can; it might be as late as 10:00. I have to talk to some people out by the dump after I leave the funeral home." She smiled and squeezed back.

Buck went down the back stairs and walked over to the funeral home. He went around to the back door and rang the bell. Mutt let him in, and together they walked down to the basement. Dr. Allen was just finishing up with the body, and Hermann Glasscock was standing back watching. He looked up when he heard Buck and Mutt coming down the stairs.

"Hi, Chief, it's her, all right." He shook his head. "How sad," he said. "Such a pretty and talented young woman."

"Yeah, I know," Buck said. "I've got a daughter just a few years younger than Miss Wilson, and it gives me the shivers to think about it".

"Oh, Ann Marie," Hermann said as he smiled at Buck. "Is she still at Stevens?"

Buck nodded.

Hermann Glasscock had been a classroom teacher and a high school principal before being appointed by the Warrensburg District School Board to be superintendent of schools in 1928. Taller than average with a kind face and snowy white hair, he looked older than his 52 years. He and his wife had four children, and they had all gone into the field of education. Three daughters were teachers in various school districts in mid-Missouri, and their son was assistant journalism professor at the University of Missouri at Columbia.

Despite his kindly demeanor, he was a good administrator. He handed Buck a slip of paper with Miss Wilson's home address and her parents' phone number on it. Buck had that sinking feeling in the pit of his stomach again. He turned to Dr. Allen.

"Any sign of sexual assault?" he asked.

The doctor nodded. "I'm afraid so," he said. "There are bruises on her forearms and thighs where she tried to fend off her attacker. There are vaginal abrasions indicating forced entry, and she was apparently trying to scream, and that's why he choked her, to shut her up. In my opinion, that's what caused her death."

Buck just nodded. He went back to the station and called her parents from his office. Her mother fainted while she was talking to Buck on the phone. While he waited on the line, he could hear her husband talking to her, trying to revive her. Finally, he came on the line and asked Buck to call him back in a few minutes. Buck said he would and hung up.

He had to go through Freda to get a long distance line, probably out of Kansas City, and then go through an operator in Carrollton, and when she rang the Wilsons' number, he heard two long and one short ring. This meant that they were on a party line. He knew the news of the murder of Margaret Wilson was traveling like wildfire through Carroll County, and Lord knows where else. He shuddered. "Lord help them," he muttered. He had really dreaded making that call, and now he felt like he was going to throw up. He waited ten minutes and called back. Mr. Wilson answered the phone.

"This is Chief Pettit again, is your wife all right?"

There was a pause, "She's awake, but she's taking it pretty hard," he said.

Buck could tell he was almost in tears himself. "Mr. Wilson, your daughter was a well-thought-of school teacher in this town, and believe me when I tell you that we're going to hunt down her killer and bring him to justice. I'm going to give you the phone number of the coroner who has charge of her body, so you can make arrangements to have it transported home. Both the coroner and the doctor that examined her body are sure she was strangled, so I'm not going to order an autopsy."

"Mr. Wilson, I'm so sorry this has happened to your daughter, and if you need any more information that I can furnish, or if my department and I can be of any help, please call us." He gave the Mr. Wilson the department's phone number and hung up.

Buck called Darlene back to his office, and between them they composed a statement to give to the papers. Just the bare facts. Her name, hometown and where and when body was found. They didn't mention who found the body, because the Chief didn't want reporters trying to pump information out of some nine-year-old boys. They did say that there were no suspects at this time, and that more information would be released as it became available. Buck asked Darlene to call it into *The Warrensburg Star Journal, The Kansas City Star/Times* and the St. Louis papers, the *Globe Democrat* and *Post Dispatch.*

* * * * *

Buck went out front to talk to Clarence. He was sitting in his patrol car talking to a couple of curious citizens. The thermometer had reached 84, and it wasn't even the middle of May yet. Word had gotten out that the police weren't giving out any information, so the crowd had thinned out.

In 1936, there were only five ways to get news. Word of mouth (commonly called gossip), newspapers and magazines, radio and newsreels at the theaters. There was no television. There was, but it was in its infancy with transmitters in New York and Chicago and very few receiving sets. The picture was round and about the size of a softball. The reception was only good for a few miles, and the broadcasts were in fuzzy black and white.

The fastest of the news media was gossip. It seemed to travel at the speed of light. Radio was next, but it didn't carry much news in those days; it was mostly for entertainment. Next fastest were the daily newspapers. The newsreels at the theaters were probably next. They were usually changed twice weekly, and you didn't have to read them. They were brought to you on the big screen in living black and white. The weekly magazines were popular then. They sold for ten cents and usually were distributed by young boys and some girls who were sent out by local distributors to sell them door to door or on the street corners downtown. Chief among them were *Colliers* and the *Saturday Evening Post*. There were others like the *Ladies Home Journal* and *Good Housekeeping,* but none of them sold like the *Saturday Evening Post.*

Buck's biggest problem was dealing with the fastest medium, gossip. He opened the patrol car door and slid into the passengers side. "Crank her up, Clarence, and let's take a little ride," he said.

"Where to, Chief?"

"Just go around the square and down on Pine Street and back. Drive slow, I want to talk to you."

Clarence started the car, pulled out from the curb and turned left on Maynard Street. He drove along the west side of the court house to Hout Street, turned left to Holden, turned right and headed south on Holden to Pine. Buck turned to Clarence. "What are people saying?"

"About finding a body at the dump?" Clarence asked.

"Yes, what are the rumors?"

Clarence thought for a minute, "Chief, a lot of them think some colored kid did it."

"Colored kid?"

"That's what they say."

"Where did they come up with that?"

28

Clarence nodded at Bob White (everybody called him Quail), at the intersection of Pine and Holden streets as he turned right onto Pine. Bob was the other patrol officer, and he usually patrolled downtown on foot, especially on Saturdays. Bob waved at them and wondered what was going on. Clarence chewed on a toothpick. Darlene had run over to Dub's and gotten Clarence a pork tenderloin sandwich at 2:30 and had taken him a Coke out of the machine in the break room. Clarence made a clucking noise with his tongue and teeth like he was trying to suck a piece of tenderloin from between them.

Buck turned in his seat toward Clarence. "Well!" he said.

"Well, I was just listening to what they said, and Charlie Shanks, who lives right across the street from Reese on Market Street, said that a bunch of nigger kids were playing baseball on Reese's playground Friday after school. He said he thought they were all from Howard School on West Culton, you know, that nigger school, and that they had no right to be playing on the Reese playgrounds."

They drove out to the Roberts' house across from the dump. Harold wasn't home yet, but it was Leona that Buck wanted to talk to anyway. She repeated what she had said over the phone, and had very little to add. Buck asked if she had seen or heard anything over at the dump the night before. She couldn't recall having seen or heard anything unusual. She said that she did hear something rummaging around in the tin cans right after dark, but that was not unusual, as stray dogs, raccoons and opossums frequented the dump at night. Buck put his notebook back in his breast pocket and thanked her. He and Clarence drove back to the station. The courthouse clock struck 6:00 as Buck walked in the front door.

* * * * *

The Warrensburg elementary schools, grades five and six, customarily held a baseball tournament the last week of school at the college baseball field. There had always been five teams. The four ward schools, Foster, Pershing, Reese and one called commonly, Fourth Ward School, plus the school on the campus of CSTC that was primarily where the seniors did their practice teaching. It was simply referred to as College Elementary. The tournament usually took place after the last class of the year and grade cards had been given out, which was on the Wednesday of the last week.

On Thursday of the last week, the children went to school for a half-day and the mothers would bring a covered dish at noon, and the schools would have a picnic on their respective playgrounds. The fathers were usually at work, but this gave the teachers a chance to talk to the mothers who were able to attend. Some mothers worked also, and some had pre-school children to care for, but there were usually at least half of the mothers in attendance, and there was always more food than needed. After the picnic, they would all go to the college to watch the first day of the games.

The college had a varsity field and a practice field, so they could play two games at once, and the spectators could watch the game of their choice. On Friday morning, there would be the last preliminary game, and in the afternoon there would be a finals double header with the number one seeded team getting a bye and playing the winner of the first game for the championship. It was a carnival atmosphere, and everyone seemed to have a good time at these events. The various school PTAs would have booths and sell pies, cookies and crafts to make money for their treasury to start the next school year.

This year, Superintendent Glasscock had invited Howard School to participate, making a total of six teams. He had known that this would not be a popular decision with some in the district, but in the name of fairness had decided to go ahead with it anyway. He knew he had at least one school board member on his side, Doctor Funston, a prominent local dentist, whom he was sure could persuade the rest of the board to go along. At any rate, he had made the decision and gone ahead with the plans, and if they didn't like it, they could always fire him. He was ready to retire anyway. He had given the Howard School boys permission to use the Reese playground to practice on at times when the Reese boys weren't using it. Reese School sat on half a city block, and the west end of the playground had been made into a ball diamond.

Reese usually had a pretty good baseball team, mainly because they had such a good place to practice. Herman Glasscock had told Lucille McKnight about the arrangements, but didn't see any need to notify anyone else. The collage was going to use their practice field that week, so the games had been extended to Saturday, with one preliminary game on Thursday afternoon, one on Friday morning and two games on Friday afternoon, one preliminary game and one semi-final game. The team that had gotten the bye would then play the winner of the semi-final game in the championship game at 2:00 p.m. on Saturday. Some members of the Warrensburg Cubs, the local semi-pro team, would act as umpires and base line coaches for the games. It was to be quite a tournament.

3

THE SUSPECT

MILTON O. STEVENSON was 15 and already out of school for the year. In fact, he really didn't go to school, which was not unusual for colored boys his age, but his circumstances were different. Milton's mother, Thelma, had been an educator before she had married his father, who was a Methodist preacher. In fact, she had been the Latin teacher at the Negro College for Women at Sedalia when she met and subsequently married the Reverend George W. Stevenson, who had taken over the Methodist Church where she attended. She resigned her position at the college when her husband was transferred to Iowa. Not long after they left Sedalia, the college mysteriously burned to the ground. The Methodist Church group that sponsored it never built it back.

While in Iowa, three children were born—two older daughters and Milton. Milton had gone to colored elementary schools in Cedar Rapids, and in Salina, Kansas, where his father had been transferred at the end his fourth grade. He had just finished seventh grade in Salina when his father came back from a church convention in Kansas City, Missouri, to announce that he had accepted a challenge to start a new church in a rural area of Missouri, near a small town by the name of Slater.

After the Civil War, a group of about 30 freed slaves had migrated to Missouri from Georgia looking for some cheap land to buy. As luck would have it, when they arrived at St. Louis, there was a big demand for dock hands to unload paddle wheelers coming up the Mississippi from New Orleans and down the Ohio from Cincinnati with goods destined for the railroad workers, miners, farmers and the army further west. The men in the group got jobs on the docks, and the women set up what shelters they could on the shore, and they stayed there through the winter of 1865-66. By spring they had accumulated enough money to buy supplies and food for their trip to mid-Missouri, where they had planned to buy a few acres of land to start their farm.

Their former master had told them when he freed them that as many as wanted to could stay, up to 20. He had told them that he would pay the prevailing wage for field hands up to that amount, but couldn't afford to keep them all. He said the war had almost broken him, or he would have tried to keep them all. They could live in their old slave quarters rent free until better housing could be built. He owned 51 slaves when the war ended. The other 31 would have to find work elsewhere. The Negroes had worked it out among themselves as to who would stay and who would go, and on the day the 31 left the plantation there were many tears among both groups. They had tried to keep families together, but there were a few exceptions, and they had all promised to keep in touch as much as possible. Thomas Roy, the owner, had handed the lead man, Josh, his former foreman who had a wife and four children, a pouch containing some gold coins.

"Josh, I know you have talked about getting some land and starting a farm for your group to live on. I sold some livestock and some family jewelry that we no longer need, and here is a little money to help you get started."

Josh's eyes were welling up as he tucked the pouch in his bib pocket without even looking in it. He and Tom embraced, and Josh got up on the seat of the wagon and team of mules that Tom had also given them, and they started down the dusty road to Missouri, most of them walking. Tom had actually given the group two wagons and four mules. The excuse he gave Josh was that since he wouldn't have as many hands, he wouldn't need as many wagons or mules to pull the plows. As Tom and his wife watched the band wend their way down the road toward Tennessee, he turned to Beth and said, "I was going to free them all after the war anyway."

Beth smiled and said, "I know, Tom, I know."

The 30 left St. Louis in early April 1866. One baby had died during the winter. Following the south bank of the Missouri River, it took them a little over two weeks to reach Booneville, Missouri, where Josh decided they would camp for a few days to rest and inquire about any land that might be for sale. They camped on the south edge of town, and the first morning they were there. Josh and old Ned walked downtown to the Cooper County Courthouse to inquire of the County Clerk if he knew of any land for sale. The clerk told them no, but that he had heard there was a tobacco farm for sale over in Saline County. His sister lived in the little town of Slater, and she had mentioned it in one of her letters to him. Josh asked him how to get to Slater, and the clerk told him to take the Boonville Ferry across the river into Howard County. He said that there was a pretty good road north from the ferry landing to Glasgow, about 25 miles. Then he told them to take the ferry from Glasgow over into Saline County, and go west on that road a distance of about 13 miles to Slater. "Ask around Slater," the clerk had said. "Someone can tell you where the farm is."

Josh and Ned walked back to camp and told everyone the good news. The next morning they set out for Slater. They arrived at Slater on April 18th and set up camp about a half-mile from town. The next morning they found out that the farm was just about four miles north of town, and they set out to find it. A Negro the townspeople called Thistle, who had been a freeman before the war, was in town for some supplies when they pulled in. There was quite a stir in the little town of Slater when that many Negroes came walking into town, and the Town Constable sent Thistle to see what they wanted. He walked up to Josh and said, "Howdy, where y'all be goin'?"

Josh looked him over and asked, "And who you be?"

Thistle grinned. "They call me Thistle," he said.

"How come they call you that?"

"Well," Thistle said, "I got a round head and hair that sticks up, and one day the constable said, 'Boy, if your hair was purple, you'd look like a thistle,' and they been callin' me that ever since. That be 20 years ago."

Josh put his big hands on his hips and glared down at Thistle. "Tell your constable that we be lookin' for a farm round here that's for sale, and can he tell us where it is?"

Thistle grinned at Josh "I know where that farm is," he said. "I live out that way. I got a little farm not two mile from there."

"What you doin' with a farm? You don't look like no gentleman farmer."

Thistle grinned his widest grin. "That farm been in our family for 35 years. My daddy and momma homesteaded that land, and when they passed, they left it to me. I got 40 acres. Nice little farm. I raise pigs and grow corn. Got me a garden. I raise nearly everything we eat, my wife and I."

Josh softened his voice a little, "Can you show us how to get to the place that's for sale?"

Thistle grinned again, "I'll take you pert near there," he said.

They started north out of Slater, and the constable breathed a sigh of relief. The war was just barely over, and he didn't want any of the local Southern sympathizers going up against that bunch. At least not in his town.

The farm was owned by August Kruise, a German immigrant who had learned tobacco farming in Virginia before coming west to Missouri. He was 73 and had outlived his wife and four of their five children. He had a son who had gotten a law degree at Washington and Lee University in Virginia and was practicing law in St. Louis. He longed to be with family and had made up his mind to sell the farm and move to St. Louis so he could see his grandchildren more often.

He couldn't get dependable field hands anymore and couldn't farm it by himself. Along came Josh and his group. Josh walked up the door of August's house and rapped as loud as he could, while the rest of them waited in the road out front. It was almost noon, and it was starting to look like rain. Josh rapped again, and a third time. No answer. He turned to go when heard a, "Helloooo!" Josh looked out toward the barn, and past the barn about 50 yards he saw a horse galloping toward him. He had never seen such a big barn in his life. August Kruise pulled his horse up in front of his house and dismounted.

"My name is August Kruise, and who might you be?" he asked.

Josh took off his hat and offered his hand, "My name's Josh, and this here is Ned." Waving his hat toward the wagons and the rest of the Negroes, he said, "These other folk are our families."

"What brings you to these parts?" August asked, still holding his horse by the reins.

"We been lookin' for a farm to buy. We heard this place might be for sale," Josh said, waving his hat toward the barn.

August was a German, and known to be careful with a dollar. "You got any money?" he asked.

Josh pulled the leather pouch from his bib pocket and rattled it towards August. He hadn't even opened it to look inside. Master Tom said it was to buy them a farm and he had believed him. Master Tom had never lied to him.

"How much money you got?" August asked.

Josh was no fool. "How much you askin' for the farm?"

August took his hat off and scratched his head. He had planned to ask $20 an acre for the 80 acres, including all improvements, which he had figured would bring him $1,600, and if they wanted his machinery, household goods and livestock, that would bring it up to $2,000. He could plainly see that there couldn't be $2,000 in that leather pouch.

"I'm asking $2,000 for everything," he said, "but maybe we can work some kind of a deal. You folks are welcome to spend the night in my tobacco barn yonder and we'll work something out."

August was a shrewd businessman. He could tell an honest man by just looking him in the eyes. He liked Josh's eyes. It was past noon, and he invited them all to have lunch with him. He opened the double gate to the road that led to the barn, and the Negroes pulled their wagons into the tobacco barn and unhitched the mules. August told Josh that he had plenty of smoked ham and flour, and if Josh would have two or three of the women to come to the house, they could fry the ham and make biscuits. He got four one-gallon jugs of apple cider out of the spring house for them to drink. He got some of the men to help him bring some two-by-twelve planks from the barn to the front yard along with some sawhorses, and they set up two long tables. By 2:00 that afternoon, the Negroes were eating the best meal they had tasted in weeks. August smiled as they devoured two of his biggest hams and two big platters of biscuits.

That evening, around the dining room table, August, Josh and Ned worked out a deal. The pouch had contained $210 in gold coins. August took it as a down payment. He agreed to stay until Christmas to help them plant the tobacco and to show them how to shade the tender plants with tobacco cloth he had stored in the barn. At harvest time, he would show them how to hang the tobacco in the barn, and when dried properly, he would help them get the crop to the St. Louis tobacco auction. Their half of the crop would be used to pay off their note on the farm. For subsistence until they got the farm paid for, August would leave any canned goods, dried fruit in the cellar, and any other supplies on hand. There were two

36

apple trees, a pear tree and two cherry trees on the farm and a big garden area behind the house. By not having to hire any help, he figured the Negroes could have the place paid for in three years, barring any disasters such as floods or damaging winds. He planned to move to St. Louis by Christmas, but would be available to help them if needed.

Josh beamed from ear to ear after he and Ned had put their "Xs" on the note that August had drawn up. August wrote their names under their "Xs" and signed his name. He, Josh and Ned went to Slater the next day and had the bank notarize the note.

It took Josh's group four years to pay off the note. They had one rainy year and had a rather poor tobacco crop, but the next year was a bumper year, and after the tobacco was sold, August went back to the farm with Josh and Ned, and they celebrated with a note-burning and feast.

* * * * *

Through the next 50 years the clan increased and bought more land surrounding theirs. Josh, before he died in 1910 at age 72, had lived to see his extended family prosper and multiply. There were over 70 of them to celebrate Josh's passing. They were split into 14 families, and Josh had made sure that each family had enough land to support them. The only thing that puzzled the white folks in the surrounding area was that the families all had the last name of Roy. Also, there were a lot of boys named Thomas and a lot of girls named Beth.

As time went by, some of them moved to Kansas City, St. Louis, and a few moved Chicago to find jobs in industry. Still, there were over 80 of the Roy clan still farming in the area when Reverend and Mrs. Stevenson moved there to start a church. They had no church of their own, and Josh's grandson, James Roy Jr., had gotten the group together one February in the big tobacco barn to decide what to do about building a church. They decided that if they all got together and built a church building, then James Roy Jr. would find them a pastor.

James had been in Slater to buy some kerosene a few days later and ran into the grandson of Thistle. Thistle had died just two years after Josh's death. The grandson's name was Henry Curtis. James had talked to him on several occasions before. "Henry, are you a church goin' man?" he had asked.

Henry took his hat off, scratched his head and looked up at the sky like he was trying to figure out if it was going to snow or not. "Well, yes and no," he drawled.

"What you mean by that?"

"Well, my granddaddy always said we was Methodists, but we never went to no church while he was livin'. I heard there was a Negro Methodist Church in Marshall, and one Sunday last year my wife made me load everybody up in the wagon and drive 'em there for church. We had to leave at 7:00 in the morning to get there by 10:00. It's near on to 16 miles from my house. It had rained the night before and the road was so muddy, them mules was plum winded by the time we got there. It was in late July, and they had dinner on the grounds after church. All the ladies had brung food and there seemed like they was plenty to eat, but Jessie, that's my wife, said we didn't bring nothin', so we couldn't stay and eat. We was gittin' in the wagon when the preacher come over and said we had to stay for dinner. Said the ladies of the church would think we didn't like their cookin' if we didn't, so we stayed and et."

"What did you think of their church?" James asked. "Well, the food were good. Piles of fried chicken, green beans, little potatoes and the best water melon I ever et. The church were about a mile out of town. Sat on top of a hill, kind of in the woods. When we left, the preacher took our address down on a piece of paper, like he may be goin' to write to us."

"Did he?"

"Did he what?"

"Write to you?"

"Well, not for a long time, but I just now stopped by the post office, and they had this letter for me. The man at the window said it came in about a week ago. I haven't been to town in over a week. I think it's from that preacher."

"Have you opened it yet?"

"No, I thought I'd wait 'til I got home and let Jessie read it to me."

"Mind if I look at it?"

"Can you read?"

"Of course I can read. One of my aunt's mother that came west with our family had lived in the big house at the plantation. She had learned to read and cipher from a teacher that came to the big house to teach the master's children. The master's wife let Penny, that's what they called 'cause she weren't dark like most of us. Her skin was kind of copper-colored, so they named her Penny. Anyway, she taught all us kids to read and cipher."

"Then you read it to me," Henry said, handing the envelope to James. James tore the envelope open and took out the letter. It was just a mimeographed notice of a Methodist Church conference to be held in August 16, 17 and 18th, 1933, at the big Negro Methodist Church in Kansas City. James read it to Henry.

"Is that all there is to it?" Henry asked. "Hell, I ain't goin' to Kansas City to no church. Marshall's fer enough for me."

"Yup, that's it," James replied. He thought for a minute and held the letter out to Henry. "Do you mind if I keep it?"

"I guess not. What you want with it? Henry cocked his head as if to say, "What's goin' on here?"

"I just might go to that conference," James said.

"What fer?"

"Just 'cause I want to." James tipped his hat and walked down the street to where he'd parked his Model A Ford.

* * * * *

James did go to the conference. He drove to the city in the Model A and stayed at the home of a nephew who worked at the stockyards. He went to the conference for two days. He got an appointment to talk to the Chairman of the Governing Board on the second day about a preacher for the new church they had built. The chairman liked the idea of a new church in his district, so he took it before the board. They asked James how many members he thought they would have in their new church. James said he thought he could get at least 60. The new church was approved, and when the board asked for a volunteer to accept the new church as pastor, George W. Stephenson stepped forward. He had been wanting to get out of Salina for some time. The church was small and the town was about 90% white, which offered him and his family little in the way of a social life. He was approved. In late April of 1936, the Reverend Stevenson and his family had been at the "Holy Word of God Methodist Church" for a little over three years. Their membership had started out with 54 Roys. The district chairman and four preachers from the Kansas

City District had come to the church one Sunday in early April 1936 and baptized all 54 in one day. They had been given membership certificates, and they all went out the front door waving their certificates. It was a proud moment for James Roy and Preacher Stephenson. By April of 1936, their membership had risen to 73. The members had built a nice parsonage for the preacher's family, and there was even talk of building a school on the same grounds so all of the Negro children in the area could learn to read and write. James Roy Jr. and his family had given eight acres of land for the church and cemetery, so there was plenty of room for the parsonage and school. The church sat on a hilltop a half-mile north of James Roy Junior's farmhouse, in the middle of the Roy Enclave.

* * * * *

Thelma Stephenson had been tutoring her children at home since moving to Missouri. The Stephensons had acquired quite a library through the years, so there was no lack of material. The closest Negro school was at Marshall, and that was just too far to drive every day. There was no rural bus service for the children. Thelma didn't mind. Her children were bright and learned quickly. In fact, Milton, although only 15, was doing senior high work. He had mastered algebra, plane and solid geometry, and was working on trigonometry. All three of the Stephenson children had mastered French, and Milton was into advanced Latin. She had named him Milton after the English author.

One morning, at the breakfast table in mid-May 1936, she announced that it was time to go see Grandma Belle. They had been back in Missouri three years and had only been to see her twice. Grandma Belle was actually Belle Reed, Thelma's grandmother. She lived in Warrensburg, in a little wood frame house on Warren Street, just across the alley from the Hodges. Her house faced Warren, and the Hodges house faced Lobbin Street.

She had been born into slavery in northeast Arkansas on a big cotton plantation near Rector, on the St. Francis River in 1856. After the war, her folks moved to Warrensburg, where her father got a job as a section hand on the railroad. He bought a two-story house on Railroad Street that backed up to the tracks so he could walk to work. Belle, her two brothers and her sister used to go along the tracks with bushel baskets and pick up coal dropped by the coal tender after the trains went by. Their mother cooked on a coal stove, and the coal was also used to stoke the big Warm

Morning heating stove in the living room that heated their house in the winter. They seldom had to buy any coal.

When Belle was 16, she married William "Willie" Reed. Willie worked for the railroad, too. They lived with her folks for two years and then rented a little house just down the street from them, where William Junior was born in 1872. Belle had almost died when he was born, and the midwife who delivered him said she didn't think Belle could have any more children, and she didn't. William Junior Reed married Thelma Smithson when he was 18, and little Thelma was born a year later.

William Junior had rented a house on Madison Street until 1901, when they bought the house on Warren. When little Thelma finished the sixth grade at Howard School in Warrensburg, her parents made arrangements for her to live with a sister of Willie's in Sedalia, where she could attend Lincoln High School. She did so well at Lincoln that she was awarded a scholarship to Lincoln University in Jefferson City. She had graduated at the top of her class. At Lincoln, she did equally as well and graduated cum laud-de 1912. The Lincoln year book for 1912 said, "Thelma Louise Reed is an outstanding Latin scholar." From there, she moved back to Sedalia to teach, where she met George Stephenson.

Belle and Willie Jr. still lived in the little house on Warren Street. Willie Jr. died in 1931, and Belle continued to live there 'til she died in 1946 at age 90. After Willie Jr. died, she took up smoking his old corn cob pipe. She said it reminded her of him. Nobody, not even Thelma, dared tell her to quit.

Saturday, May 9, at about 10:30 a.m., George, Thelma and the children drove into Belle Reed's Yard. She was sitting in her rocker under the elm tree by her back door smoking her corn cob pipe and rocking with her eyes closed. When she heard the car drive up, she struggled out of the rocker and headed for the front of the house.

"Grandma," the children shouted as they got out of the car.

There were lots of hugs and kisses. Thelma and Belle busied themselves with fixing dinner, while George and the children did little things around the place for Belle. They weeded her garden, pulled some weeds along the back fence and knocked down the mud daubers' nests in the outhouse.

After a big meal, they sat in the back yard in the shade and just rested and visited. About 5:00 in the afternoon, when it was time for the visitors to head home, Milton begged his mother to let him stay with Belle for the summer.

"I've got all my school work done, and I'll be bored at home with nothing to do," he had pleaded.

"You've got plenty to do at home," his mother countered, "like hoeing in the garden, running errands and helping your father around the church."

Milton won the argument and was allowed to stay until the sixth of June, when they would come after him, if it was all right with Belle. Belle had been listening and shaking her head yes the whole time. As they were getting in the car to leave, Thelma tried to press a $5 bill into Belle's hand. Belle shook her head and made Thelma take it back. Thelma stuffed it into Belle's apron pocket with a stern look on her face.

"Don't be a fool, Grandma, that boy can eat that much food in a week," she insisted.

Belle finally relented, and the car pulled out onto Warren Street and headed home, with the girls hanging out the window waving goodbye.

* * * * *

On Sunday morning, Belle and Milton went to church, and that afternoon Milton strolled around town to see the sights. He went by the college and longed to go in the buildings to look around, but knew that it would not be allowed. He vowed to go to college somewhere, somehow.

On Monday, May 11th, he happened by Reese School as the Howard boys were practicing baseball. He stood and watched them for a while. He could see that they needed some help. His father, George, had been quite a baseball player in his youth and had coached Milton into a being pretty good pitcher. He had organized a church team, and they were good enough that it was hard to find teams willing to play them. A few white teams had played them at the fair grounds in Marshall and hadn't fared that well. The games had attracted good crowds, but when the white teams lost, the mostly white spectators had thrown bottles and booed the Negroes. They just didn't like to see their teams lose to those niggers.

Milton walked out to the pitcher's mound, and play stopped. He was a tall boy for 15, almost six feet, and stood more than a head taller than the ten and eleven-year-olds. There were a couple of twelve-year-olds on the team, but they weren't any taller than the rest.

"Who are you?" the boy on the mound asked.

"My name is Milton Stephenson, but you can call me Mac. That's what all my friends call me."

"You a baseball player?" the boy on the mound asked.

"Well, yes and no. I have played some baseball, but since I'm only 15, my father's team won't let me play in any of their games."

"Where you from?"

"I'm from near Slater. I'm visiting my great-grandmother here in Warrensburg."

"My name is Abraham. Will you be our coach?" the boy asked.

"Don't you have a coach?"

"Nope, just us boys."

By now, the boys had all gathered around the pitcher's mound, begging Milton to be their coach. He was flattered and readily agreed. He rolled up his sleeves and hit fly balls to the outfield and showed the boys how to follow the ball with their eyes and run under it to make the catch. He hit grounders to the infield and showed them how to get in front of the ball so it wouldn't get past them, and how to make the throw to first base. He worked with the catcher and the pitchers, and they soon began to show improvement. They practiced until the courthouse clock struck 6:00; then the boys all scattered for home. They took all of their equipment with them, except for a catcher's mitt lying on homeplate. Milton spotted it and went over and picked it up.

They'll need this on Wednesday, he thought to himself.

He took it home to Belle's house for safekeeping. On Tuesday, Milton helped Belle around the house, sweeping her front porch, trimming some bushes and planting some more of her garden. By evening, he was tired and really dug into the meal Belle had fixed. While he had working in the yard, Belle had taken an empty bushel basket and had gone to her favorite hunting places and brought back a mess of greens, which she washed at the pump and cooked with some bacon grease left over from breakfast. She baked some cornbread and fried some of the ham left in the icebox from Sunday. Belle smiled as her great-grandson ate like a threshing hand.

Wednesday morning, after the morning chores were done, beds made, breakfast dishes done, etc., Milton and Belle sat in the shade of the big elm tree in her back yard. Milton helped her bring her favorite rocker out of the house and one of the kitchen chairs. Belle sat and rocked with her eyes shut, as she puffed on her corn cob pipe while Milton read to her from a book that he had brought from home. When the courthouse clock struck 3:00, he told Belle he would be home around 7:00, and headed for the baseball diamond at Reese School, taking the catcher's mitt with him.

He worked with the boys until almost dark. When he left, they made him promise that he would be at their game on Friday, and if they won that he would practice with them Friday evening for the semi-finals on Saturday morning. If they won it all, Milton promised them that he would take them all to the picture show on Saturday night.

The Reese boys were eliminated on Thursday afternoon by the Foster team. The Howard boys won their preliminary game. In fact, they won three games straight, and won the city championship. Hermann Glasscock presented them with a nice trophy at home plate Saturday after the championship game. There was cheering and some booing in the stands and much celebrating in the colored part of town. Milton accepted the trophy on behalf of the team and bought them all ice cream bars.

Later they went to the Star Theater together to watch cartoons and a double feature. Even though they had to sit in the back of the balcony with the rest of the colored folks, they were a happy bunch.

It was midnight when Milton got home, and Belle was getting frantic. He had told her he would be late, but she had had reason to worry. During the evening, a car had driven slowly by her house three times. They turned out the lights and went to bed, but Belle did not sleep.

* * * * *

Monday morning at 8:50 the phone in the police department rang. Buck was sitting at Darlene's desk and picked up the receiver.

"Police Department," Bucked snapped.

"Wow, are you grouchy this morning" It was Lester Phipps.

"I'm sorry, Lester, I didn't get much sleep over the weekend."

"I know what you mean, I didn't get much sleep either. Hey, Marshall Funeral Home in Carrollton just called me, and they have charge of the services for the Wilson family. They want to come over this morning with

44

a casket and pick up the body I'm holding. They said the services are planned for Wednesday. Is it all right if I release the body to them?"

"I guess so, can you think of anything we've missed?"

"No, Chief, I took pictures of the neck area, for arms and thighs where the bruises are. I took notes, Doc Wilson took notes, and I know you took notes. I think we've got everything covered. Her family drove over yesterday afternoon to view the body. I had fixed her up as best I could, but I was afraid I was going to have to bury her folks. They really took it hard. She has a sister living in Columbia and a brother in Jefferson City, but they couldn't make it. Some neighbors drove them over."

"Yeah, it's real sad. I keep thinking, what if it was Ann Marie?"

"Yeah, I know. Okay then, I'll call them back and tell them to come get the body. I'll get a receipt in case there are any problems."

Just as Buck hung up, in walked Charlie Shanks.

"You got a minute, Chief?" he asked.

Buck motioned to a chair by Darlene's desk.

"Sit down, tell me who you are and what I can do for you." Buck was a little impatient this morning.

"My name's Charlie Shanks, and I live right across the street from Reese School. I'm pretty sure I seen who done the killing."

"Are you talking about the body that was found at the dump Saturday?

"You know what killing I'm talking about. The one that was in this morning's *Kansas City Times*. The school teacher."

"What makes you think she was a school teacher? Her name hasn't been released yet."

"Hell, Chief, it's all over town. It was that Wilson woman that taught first grade. Pretty little thing, too."

"Tell me what you saw." Buck took out his notebook.

"I seen that nigger kid going into the back of the school Friday evening about dark. He's the one that killed her, I'd bet my last dollar on it."

"You actually saw him go into the school building?"

"Well, not exactly, but he went behind the building and disappeared. I watched for several minutes, and he never came out."

"There's no back door to that building."

"Oh, yes, there is, there's steps that comes up out of the basement where the furnace is. That's where old man Swenson brings the coal in and takes the cinders out."

"How did you happen to be on your front porch at that time?"

"Well, I run a milk route and I'm usually through for the day by 9:00. I get up at 4:00 every morning, and I got my truck loaded and I'm out on my route by 5:00. My wife works at the overall factory, and she's usually gone when I get home. I fix me some breakfast, and after I eat, I take a nap 'til about noon. Then I get up and go down to Dub's or Hearts and get me a sandwich. My wife takes her lunch. In the evening when my wife gets home, we have supper. After supper, usually about 6:00, I fix me a glass of cold buttermilk and go out on the porch and just sit and sip buttermilk and watch what's goin' on. That's exactly what I was doin' last Friday evening."

Buck looked up from his notes. "How can you be sure it was a colored boy?" he asked.

"I know a nigger when I see one. How could you miss that wooly hair, and this one was as black as night. What you gonna do about it, Chief, arrest him?"

"I'll try to locate him and talk to him. Do you know where he lives?"

"Naw, just go down to that nigger school. If the teacher is still there, she'll know. He was with them nigger baseball players. You better hurry, Chief, he may be out killin' another white woman right now. Them other niggers might be helpin' him."

"Okay, I'll take care of it. Don't worry, and don't be mouthing this around town, or he might get scared and run before we can catch him." Buck had had about all of Charlie Shanks he could stand. He was tired and irritable anyway, and his conversation with Charlie had really upset him. All he needed now was for Charlie Shanks to run around town stirring up whites against the Negroes.

The phone rang again. "Police Department," Buck growled.

"Who you mad at, Chief?" It was Clarence.

"Charlie Shanks. Come on in and pick me up, and I'll explain it all to you. We've got to go talk to some people."

Buck was waiting at the curb when Clarence pulled up in the patrol car. He opened the door and slid in beside him and motioned for him to turn left.

"Where are we going?"

"To Howard School. Drive slow, I want to talk to you."

The courthouse clock struck 10:00.

* * * * *

It was a little over four blocks to Howard School from the station, and Buck was still relating to Clarence the morning's happenings when they pulled into the school yard. They sat in the car for a few minutes talking.

"I'll tell you what set Charlie Shanks off," Clarence said.

"What?"

"It was those Negro kids winning the baseball tournament Saturday."

Buck had been so busy Saturday that he hadn't even thought about the tournament. "They won, huh?"

"Three games straight, won the whole shootin' match."

"Yeah, that's probably what did it. I don't think Charlie is too fond of Negroes."

There weren't any cars parked around the school anywhere, so Buck wasn't sure there would be anyone to answer when he knocked on the front door. He had never been inside the building, so he didn't want to just barge right in. He heard steps inside, and the door opened. A pleasant-looking Negro woman in her late 40s smiled at the Chief.

"Hello, I'm Grace Johnson, principal of Howard School, what can I do for you?" she asked sweetly.

"Hi, I'm Buck Pettit, Police Chief, and this is Officer Slaton. We would like to ask you a few questions."

Grace Johnson had taught in colored schools ever since she had graduated from Lincoln University in Jefferson City. In her years of experience, when a white policeman came to a colored school to ask questions, it usually meant trouble. She hid her fear well.

"Won't you gentlemen come inside, we can talk better in my office." She led them down a hall to the back of the building, where she had a small corner office. She borrowed a chair from one of the classrooms, and they all sat down. "Is there a problem, Chief?" she asked.

"No, not exactly, Miss Johnson, I just have a couple of questions."

"It's Mrs. Johnson, but please, call me Grace."

"Yes, ma'am. By the way, congratulations on your team winning the city baseball championship. That is something."

"Yes, Chief, it is something." She picked the trophy up from her desk and handed it to Buck. "Milton brought that to church yesterday and gave it to me to keep for the boys. I plan to get a lot of use out of that trophy in years to come as an inspiration to our students."

Buck looked the trophy over and handed it to Clarence. Clarence admired it briefly and handed it back to Grace.

Buck took his notebook from his breast pocket. "Speaking of the boy, Milton, I think that was his name, do you know where he's staying? I understand he is from out of town."

"Is that what this is about, Chief? You really don't want to talk to me, It's Milton you want to question, isn't It? Is he in some kind of trouble?"

Buck tried to be as diplomatic as possible. "No, ma'am, we're trying to keep him out of trouble. He has been accused of being near a possible crime scene, and we just want his side of the story."

"Are you talking about the murder of that white teacher, Chief? Because if you are, I'm certain Milton had nothing to do with it. He was too busy with the baseball team to do anything like that. Besides, he's a fine, upstanding young man. Did you know that he speaks Latin and quotes Shakespeare? Not a very good candidate for a murderer, is he?"

"No, ma'am, all the more reason for us to talk to him. I'm sure he'll have a good alibi for the time of the murder. If you know where he is staying, please tell us, it will save us some footwork."

Grace sensed their urgency and told them where Milton was staying. They got in their patrol car and drove over to Belle's house. It was another hot day. Buck didn't like the way this year was starting out. When they got to Belle's house, she and Milton were in the back yard under the big elm tree. Milton was reading to Belle, who sat in her rocker with her eyes closed, puffing on her corn cob pipe.

"Howdy," Buck said, as he and Clarence walked around to the back of the house.

Belle sat up and Milton closed his book. They both sat silently as Buck and Clarence came to where they were sitting.

"Hot, isn't it?" Buck mused.

"Yes, sir," Milton offered not too enthusiastically.

"I'm Chief Pettit of the Warrensburg Police Department, and this is Officer Slaton. Do you folks mind if we ask you a few questions?" Buck tried not to look too stern.

Milton glanced at his great-grandmother. Belle nodded to him, and he said, "No, sir, we'll do our best."

Buck took out his notebook and started to ask Milton questions like, "Did you go into Reese School at any time on Friday afternoon or evening of May 8th?" Milton had answered, "No," and explained to Buck that on that Friday evening from about 5:00 until about 7:00 his team had been practicing near the school, and that on two occasions the ball had gotten away from the catcher and had rolled up the alley almost even with the school building, and he had chased them down and tossed them back to the pitcher.

Buck asked him if he had a roster of the team with names and addresses of all the players. Milton told him that he didn't, but that he could get one from the school principal if needed. Buck asked a few more questions, then turned to Belle.

"Mrs. Reed, do you mind if I call you Aunt Belle? I remember you now. Your picture was in the paper back in January, I believe, when your church group celebrated your 80th birthday. Everybody referred to you as Aunt Belle."

"No, sir, I don't mind, that's what all the neighbors call me."

"Aunt Belle, what time did Milton get home Friday night?"

"It was just after dark, he had been practicin' ball with those boys, you know."

"Yes, I know, but I wanted to hear it from you. Everybody in town says you are an honest person, so I know you wouldn't lie. Would you say it was around 7:00 or 7:30?"

Aunt Belle looked worried. She scratched her head with the stem of her corncob pipe and studied.

"Let's see now," she muttered to herself. "It was right after that last car went sneakin' by that Milton came in. It was after dark, and I had just come in the house, as the mosquitoes were eatin' me up. I heard the courthouse clock strike 7:30. Yes, sir, Chief, it was right at 7:30."

"You mentioned that a car went sneaking by. What did you mean by that?"

"Just that, Chief, three of 'em went by here 'bout 15 minutes apart. The last one went by just before Milton came in."

"Did they do, or say anything?"

"No, sir, they just went by slow and stared at the house as they went by. There was one sedan-lookin' car and two pick-up trucks. Two white men in each one. They didn't go 'round the block, just went straight on by."

Buck glanced over at Clarence, then back to his notebook. He made a few notes, then turned to Clarence.

"Clarence, it's almost noon, and Bob has been holding the fort down by himself. Aunt Belle, Milton, thanks for your time.

It might be wise for you to stay close to home for a few days until we get things sorted out. We'll be talking to you folks later. Thanks again."

Back in the car, Buck took his notes out and looked at what he had written.

"Clarence, did you hear what Aunt Belle said about those cars driving by the house?"

"I sure did, Chief, and do you know what's up in Murphy's pasture less than three blocks from her house?"

"Yeah, and I hate to think that that bunch are still around."

* * * * *

In the late 19th century Warrensburg was known as somewhat of a tourist attraction with its springs that were said to have healing powers. Electric Springs operated up until the '40s before giving way to other attractions. It was located at the junction of Federal Highway 50 and Warren Street. It was primarily a campground where tourists could camp by the night or the week to bathe in its healing waters. Diagonally across the intersection, on the southeast corner, was a tourist court built of logs. It also had a spring that attracted people, plus a grocery store, gas pumps and a tavern. In the summer, their outdoor beer garden was well attended, especially on Saturday nights. Around the turn of the 20th century the proprietors had built a dance hall up on the bluff overlooking the intersection. It was in the middle of the west end of a pasture known locally as Murphy's Pasture, which was bounded on the west by Warren Street, on the east by Washington, and on the north and south by U.S. 50 and West Oak. It was low and swampy on the Washington end, and it went uphill all the way to Warren, where it was about 30 feet above the roadbed. You couldn't see the dance pavilion from either Warren or the highway, so the owners had built a wooden stair from the tavern up to the top of the bluff to provide access to it. There was also a driveway from Oak Street that led to it.

The pavilion did pretty well, especially on Saturday nights when they would have live musicians. It was a wooden frame building about 40 feet by 60 feet, with a hardwood dance floor and a raised platform on the north end used for a bandstand. There was a front door on the south end and a back door on the north end. The sides of the building were screened, with window covers that were hinged at the top and could be swung out and propped up to let the breezes flow through in the summertime. In 1920, when prohibition went into effect, their business dried up and they closed it.

A few years later, rumor had it that the Ku Klux Klan had bought it and turned it into the headquarters for their Mid-Missouri chapter. The wooden staircase was torn down, and there was a padlock on the gate. Buck had climbed the fence one time when he still a patrolman, and pried a window cover open enough that he could flash his flashlight in. The dance floor was still intact, and there was a pulpit-like structure up on the bandstand. Along the east and west walls, there were what looked like benches or seats below the windows with hinged lids. Buck figured that's where they stored their sheets and pointed hats. Other than that, the building was empty. Buck hadn't stayed long. His curiosity satisfied, he climbed the fence and left. He never went back.

* * * * *

The courthouse clock struck 12:00, and the fire station's siren went off just as Clarence pulled the patrol car into the parking space behind the station. The fire station blew their siren every day at noon, except Sunday, and since the fire station was right next door to the police station, the Pettits always knew when it was lunch time.

Buck dashed up the back stairs to his apartment, and Clarence went into the station to relieve Bob for lunch. For the first time in days, Buck and Ann sat down to eat lunch together. Ann had fixed Buck's favorite sandwich, ham and cheese on whole wheat bread with lots of mayonnaise, and had it in the refrigerator waiting for him to come home. She made a fresh pot of coffee while he was washing up, and put the pear and pineapple salad she had made on the table.

For the next hour, they ate and talked. That was one of the things Buck loved about Ann. She was easy to talk to. Sometimes in the evening, when he wasn't too busy with police work, they would leave the radio off and sit at the kitchen table and talk and drink coffee or hot chocolate until bedtime. He would tell her what he had been doing at work, and she would tell him about a concert she had been to at the college, or a lecture she had attended. On the weekends when Ann Marie was home, they would go over to Ann's parents' house for dinner on Saturday evenings. After dinner, they would play cards and talk. Buck and Ann loved having Ann Marie at home, and missed her when she was away.

Buck valued Ann's opinion, and when he told her about his fears concerning the Klan, she looked worried.

"Honey, why don't you go talk to Harry Foster, and see what he's heard?" she had said. "Two heads are better than one."

"That sounds like a good idea," Buck answered. "I think I'll do that right now."

* * * * *

He kissed Ann and sort of galloped down the stairs to his office, the way he usually did when he was in a hurry. He picked up the phone and gave the operator the jail's number. One of Harry's deputies answered.

"Hi, this is Police Chief Pettit, is the Sheriff there?"

"No, Chief, he's at the courthouse. He arrested a kid in a stolen car on South 13 last month, and they're having the hearing this afternoon. It won't take long; his lawyer will probably plead it. Do you want me to have him call you when he comes in?"

"No, I'll just run over to the courthouse and see him there." Buck hung up the phone and walked across the street to the courthouse. The court room was on the second floor, and Buck took the steps two at a time. He started to open the courtroom door when it opened and Sheriff Foster walked out. They almost bumped.

"Harry, just the man I want to see," he said.

"I've been wanting to talk to you, too. What say we go over to Dub's and have a cup of coffee, and we can talk?"

"Too many ears in that place to suit me."

Harry chuckled, "We can get a corner booth, it'll be okay."

"I guess, let's go.

They settled in a corner booth and Lois automatically brought over two coffee mugs and a pot of coffee.

"Who's minding the store?" she laughed as she poured the coffee.

"Nobody," Harry said, "why don't you go rob a bank?"

"Seriously, Sheriff, is there anything new on that teacher killing?"

Harry glanced over at Buck, "Not yet," he said, "but we're working hard on it. The minute we get any leads, or anything important pertaining to the case, we'll call the paper, and they'll print it, okay?"

Lois looked disappointed and started to walk away, when an out-of-town reporter came in looking for Buck. He came over to the booth and introduced himself. Lois hung around to listen in on the conversation. He pumped Buck for a story, but Buck assured him that there was no story to tell. He told him what Harry had told Lois, that when anything broke, he would call the newspaper. The reporter handed him his card.

"I'm staying tonight at the Martin Hotel, if anything breaks between now and about 3:00 tomorrow afternoon, please call me," he said.

Harry stood up and threw a dime on the table for the coffee. "You were right, Buck," he said, "let's get out of here."

They went across to where the Sheriff had parked his car and both got in. Buck didn't say a word as Harry drove them north on Holden street to Shepherd's Park and turned in. He drove to the east end of the park and pulled into place with a picnic table. They both got out and started to sit down, when the reporter drove up behind their car.

Buck said, "Let me handle this." He walked over to the reporter's car and leaned on the open window. "You know, he said, "I haven't shot a reporter in quite a while. Harry, do you think a jury would convict me if I was to shoot this man?"

"Not in my county," Harry said. "Of course, they would have to find the body first."

The reporter started his car and drove off without a word. Buck sat down and took out his notebook, the courthouse clock struck 2:00.

Buck studied his notes. "Have you heard anything about any Klan activity around here lately?' he asked.

"No, what have you heard?"

Buck told him about his conversations with Charlie Shanks and Aunt Belle.

Harry took off his hat and ran his hand though his hair. "You know that old building where they used to meet is still standing, up there in Murphy's pasture."

"I know, and it's just about three blocks from Aunt Belle's house. Maybe I'm a little premature about this, but I think the Klan is going to try to blame the murder of the teacher on that colored boy, and I don't think he had anything to do with it. Another thing, Harry, could you spare a man to help with the investigation? We need to go through the whole area around the school and talk to people. Surely there are other witnesses besides Charlie Shanks."

"I'll help, I'm through at the courthouse, and I have a couple of hours this afternoon."

"Good, take me back to the station and I'll pick up Clarence. We'll meet you at the school in about ten minutes."

Both cars pulled up beside the school yard along Warren Street. The three men got out.

Buck gave the instructions. "Clarence, I want you to take Gay Street from two houses east of Warren, all the way west to Chestnut. Clarence took his notebook out of his pocket and nodded. Harry, if you'll take Market street east for a half-block on both sides, I'll take Market on the south side opposite the school. Let's meet back here in an hour to see how we are progressing. Be sure to ask if anyone saw anything unusual or out of place last Friday evening between 5:00 and dark."

By 3:30 all three men had drifted back to the car and were comparing notes. Clarence had talked to a lady over on Gay Street who had been watering some plants in her back yard, and she claimed she had seen a colored boy that looked to be about 16 or 17 run up the alley a couple of times. When Clarence asked her if she saw him go back to the group, she had answered yes.

"I kept a pretty good eye on those colored boys," she had said. "You never know what kind of mischief they're up to, but by and large, they behaved themselves pretty well."

54

Harry had talked to a woman a couple of houses up on Market who had seen a dark blue sedan circle the block a couple of times. She had been to the bakery up on Holden Street to buy some rolls, and while she was walking down Market from the square, she saw it go by, and before she reached her house, it went by again. She said it went past the school and turned north on Chestnut. By that time she had reached her house and gone in.

"I asked her if she recognized the driver, and she said no. I asked her what kind of car it was, and she didn't know much about cars, but said that it wasn't a Chevy or a Ford, she was sure of that. She gave me a description of the driver; she said the car was driving slow, so she got a pretty good look at him. It was a man in his mid-20s with dark hair and a ruddy complexion. She said she thought at the time that it must his parents' car, because it was too big and fancy for a young fellow like him to be driving. I asked her if she could describe the car, and she was sort of vague. It was a four-door sedan, she said, dark blue with a sort of odd-shaped radiator, probably only a year or two old. I asked her what time she saw the car. She said she was hurrying home to make supper for her husband, and he usually got home around 6:30 or 7:00. He is working on that new state park at Knobnoster and has to drive home after he gets off. She said the courthouse clock struck 6:00 just as she was coming out of the bakery, and it took her about ten minutes to walk home, so it must have been about 6:10."

"Great," Buck said. "I've got another job for you if you don't mind." He didn't want to wear out their friendship by asking too much from him all at once, but this was urgent.

"Sure, I'm as anxious to solve this as you are."

"I know, and I'm very grateful for your help. She said she knew Chevrolets and Fords. What I would like for you to do is go to the local auto dealers, look in the *National Geographic, The Saturday Evening Post* or any other source you can think of, and find pictures of the front end of cars. Look for Hudsons, Lincolns, Chryslers, Cadillacs, LaSalles, Packards, and any others you might think of. She said it was a late model, big fancy car. In my book, that makes it a Cadillac, Chrysler or Packard."

"You're right, It's probably a Cadillac or Packard. I only know of two big Chryslers in town, and I know who owns both of them."

Buck looked at his notes again. "I talked to two young ladies in one of the houses right across from the school playground. They're sisters, one about 19 or 20 and the other one a year or two older. Their parents operate a clothing store on Holden Street. They both attend CSTC and get out about the same time. They usually walk home together. Their routine is to do a few chores around the house, you know, do the breakfast dishes, make the beds, do some dusting to help their mother out. She works at the store with their dad. After chores, they like to go out on the front porch and do homework, read or listen to their phonograph."

Harry interrupted, "If you're talking about the Rutledges, I know them pretty well. I buy most of my clothes from them."

"Me, too," Clarence chimed in.

"That's who I'm talking about. Anyway, they both saw basically what your folks saw. They saw Milton run up the alley a couple of times chasing balls, and they saw the blue car go by. They don't know the make or model of the car, but they did get a good look at the driver, because he stared at them, waved and grinned as he went by. The oldest girl, Janet, said he gave her the creeps."

Harry grinned as he put his notes in his breast pocket and tucked his pencil away. "I've got to get back to the courthouse before the judge gets away. We're sharing a Circuit Judge with Henry County now, and I have some more cases to discuss with him before he goes back to Clinton."

"Thanks, Harry, let's get together tomorrow sometime and compare notes again."

"See you later," Harry said as he waved and drove off.

"Looks like we've got a little something to work on," Clarence said as he got in the driver seat of the patrol car. He dropped Buck off at the station and went back out on patrol.

Darlene was busy on the phone when Buck walked in the door. He stood for a couple of minutes, and when it looked like she was going to talk for awhile, he went on back to his desk. He unlocked the middle drawer and took out the envelope that contained the pen. He took the pen out and examined it closely. It was an expensive pen, all right. He took the cap off and looked at the gold point. Then he noticed some small lettering on the barrel just above the tip. He got out his magnifying glass and looked. He could barely make it out. "Tiffany's," it said. *Very expensive,* he thought to himself. *That makes it rare, and easier to identify.*

Just then Darlene walked in.

"I'm sorry, Chief, I was trying to get rid of another reporter. That was about the tenth one today. I keep telling them the same thing, nothing new to give out at this time."

"I know, Darlene, thanks for handling it for me. Right now, I've got a very important job for you to do."

"Sure, Chief. What is it?"

"I want you to take the Warrensburg phone directory and go through it to look for the initials TAB. You'll probably only have to look through the Bs." He could have done it, but he wanted Darlene to feel like she was one of the team. That was Buck's long suit, working with people and making them feel important.

"Chief, I don't even have to look through the phone book, I already know who that is. That has to be Thomas A. Breckenridge, president of the Breckenridge State Bank. He comes from a long line of Breckenridges."

"Well, I'll be darned, see why we keep you on our team—you have a terrific memory. Where did you come up with that?"

"It was easy, Chief. I bank at Breckenridge, and when you walk into the lobby, his name is on the door to his office in gold leaf, 'Thomas A. Breckenridge III, President.' If he wasn't married, I'd go after him to be my Sugar Daddy. He is loaded with money."

Buck chuckled to himself as he dropped the pen in his breast pocket. "Hold down the fort, I'm going down to talk to our Mr. Breckenridge," he said, as grabbed his hat off the coat rack in his office and headed for the front door.

Darlene stopped him before he got to the door. "Chief, the bank closed at 3:00, and it's almost 4:30 now."

Buck stopped and pulled out his watch and looked at. "Darn, you're right. I guess I'll just have go out to Mr. Breckenridge's house."

"On a day like today, he might be out at the golf course."

"Is he a golfer?"

"I don't know, Chief, but you know how bankers are," she laughed.

The phone rang, and Darlene picked up the receiver. "Police Department. Oh, hi, Clarence."

Buck reached for the phone, "Let me talk to him, Darlene."

"Clarence, how soon can you come pick me up?"

"I can be there in ten minutes, Chief. I'm out on the highway. Why, is something up?"

"I want you to drive me out to see a banker, I want to ask him a few questions."

* * * * *

They drove up to the Breckenridge mansion on South Holden at 4:50. There was no car in the driveway, but Clarence said he was sure they kept their cars in a garage in back of the house. They went up to the door and rang the bell. In less than a minute, a colored maid opened the door.

Buck spoke first, "Good evening ma'am, I'm Chief Pettit from the Warrensburg Police Department, and this is Officer Slaton. We're here to talk to Mr. Breckenridge if he is available."

"Yes, suh, if you gentlemens will just wait right here, I'll see is he available." She was gone about a minute, and ushered them to a poolside patio.

The Breckenridges were having a drink by the recently filled swimming pool. Tom Breckenridge introduced his wife, Elizabeth, and offered Buck and Clarence a glass of wine or a highball, but Buck refused for both of them. The maid pulled out two chairs, and they sat down.

Buck pulled out the fountain pen. "Mr. Breckenridge, do you recognize this pen?" he said as he handed the pen to Tom.

Tom's eyes got wide, "Why, y-yes," he stammered. "Where on earth did you find it?"

Buck explained how it was found at the murder scene. "Are you sure that's your pen?"

Tom glanced at Elizabeth, who looked surprised. "I'm absolutely certain, it was a gift from Elizabeth a year ago last Christmas. See, it even has my initials on it. I cherish it dearly."

Buck was satisfied. "How do you think you lost it?"

"I'm almost certain it was taken from my desk in the bank, probably by a customer inadvertently."

"How could that happen?" Buck asked.

"Well, Chief, I approve all loans, and I always talk to each prospect personally before I approve them. They sign the loan forms right at my desk, so I can witness them. I keep some advertising fountain pens in my desk drawer with the bank's name and logo on them. If the size if the loan warrants it, I give them a pen as a souvenir. I guess, when I went to get some customer's check, he or she took the pen, thinking it was a gift from the bank."

"When did you miss the pen?" Buck queried.

"It was just last Friday. I made a couple of loans right at closing time, and as I was straightening up my desk, I noticed the pen was gone."

"Do you remember who those late customers were?"

"No, Chief, but I can check our loan applications for last Friday and tell you. I made several loans Friday. This is the time of the year when a lot of farmers borrow money to buy seed corn so they can get crops planted."

"Can we check them now?"

"Is it that urgent?"

"Yes, it is, sir. I need to make an arrest soon, or I'm afraid there is a certain element in this town that might want to take things into their own hands. I've seen signs already."

Tom followed them to the bank and unlocked a file cabinet and took the loan applications. There were seven for Friday, May 15. They sorted through them and came up with the two that had been made just before the bank closed. One was to Margaret Wilson, and the other one was to Russell Wilhelm.

"Do you remember making those loans?" Buck asked.

"Yes, I do, Chief, I remember very distinctly now. Miss Wilson came in about 2:30. She was closing out her classroom at the school and was going home on the bus. I think she said the bus left here at a little after 8:00. She said she had to finish the final report cards and have them on the principal's desk before she left, so she was going back to the school to work until about 7:00. She told me that the janitor often stayed late on Fridays to wash all the blackboards and clean out the chalk trays, things like that, so he would be there with her until she left.

"She borrowed the money for her dad, who farms over in Carroll County. He needed it for seed corn. She told me that he had exhausted his credit at the Carrollton bank where he did business, and since she has banked with us for three years and has made similar loans before with no problem, we loaned her the money. You can see, it was only for $200. Of course, that will buy a lot of seed corn."

"If she was leaving town for the summer, I wonder where her luggage was?" Buck asked.

"She told me that her rent was paid up until the end of the month, and that her folks would drive her back to help her close her apartment and get her things then."

"You had quite a chat with her."

"Yes, I did, and not just because she was such a pretty woman. I do that with all loan applicants. I try to get an idea of their background, and whether they will be able to pay the loan back."

"What do you know about this Russell Wilhelm?"

"He has banked with us for some time, and his father before him. His parents had quite a bit of money. They owned half a section of land northeast of town. They just died two years ago. It was sad, too. They had just gotten to where they could travel and see some of the country, with Russell to tend the farm, when they both died within two weeks of each other. He dropped dead of a heart attack, and right after she buried him, she started feeling real bad. She died two weeks to the day of his death. They said she died from grief, but when they did an autopsy on her, she was eaten up with cancer. Too bad, they had just bought a new car to travel in."

"What kind of car?" Buck asked.

"Strange you should ask," Tom said. "I drive a Packard 120, and one day it was sitting in front of the bank when August Wilhelm came in and asked me if that was my car. I told him yes, and he asked me where I bought it. I told him in Kansas City because there wasn't a Packard dealer in Warrensburg. He wanted to know the address, and I gave it to him. I take mine in once in a while for service, so I even told him how to get there. The very next day he went to Kansas City and bought a brand new 1934 Packard 120 with everything on it. I'll bet he paid $1,100 for it."

"What color was it?" Buck was starting to get excited.

"Dark blue, same color as mine."

"Where is the car now?" Buck's heart was pounding.

"I'm pretty sure his son Russell drives it now. When his folks died, they left the farm and equipment to him, and split their cash and bonds with their two daughters. The girls are both married and live out of town. Neither one wanted to come back to Warrensburg, and since Russell had stayed on the farm with his folks when he graduated from high school, they left it to him. I helped him settle the estate."

"How old is Russell, and do you have his address handy?"

Buck was really getting antsy.

"I think he's about 23 or 24," Tom said as he wrote the address down for Buck. "You know, you just go out that road that runs by the poor farm about three miles and you'll see his name on the mail box."

Buck stood and put the pen back in his pocket, "Mr. Breckenridge, we really appreciate your help, and we would ask you not to tell anyone about our conversation, or anything about our investigation of this case, please. We sure don't want the papers to get hold of any of this until we are ready to release it. It's only been three days, and already the rumors are flying. I'm going to have to keep your pen as evidence for awhile. I'll return it as soon as possible." He motioned to Clarence, and headed for the door.

When they got back to the station, it was 6:30 in the evening, and Buck was tired. It had been a long day. He told Darlene he was going upstairs to eat, and not to disturb him unless it was very important. He smelled Ann's meatloaf when he got to the top of the stairs.

4

TROUBLE BREWING

CHARLIE SHANKS PULLED his old pick-up into the drive to Murphy's pasture and unlocked the gate. He drove up to the old dance hall and got out. He lit a cigarette and waited for the other men to arrive. They were instructed to drive by Aunt Belle's slowly and then drive up here. All day they had been watching Buck and Clarence drive around town. When they went to Aunt Belle's, he had parked on Oak street, just up a little from Warren Street and watched.

It's now or never, he had thought to himself. If the police or sheriff picked that nigger up, he was sure they would try him and turn him loose. Probably escort him out of town, and they never would get him. He had contacted two Klansmen he knew in town, and had called a fellow Klansman in Clinton who worked for the same dairy he did. He had been promised four men, but only three showed up.

Charlie smoked his cigarette and waited. Just after the courthouse clock struck 9:00, a 1933 Ford sedan drove in. Two of the men from Clinton got out. There was a 12-gauge shotgun in the back seat. Not long after, another pick-up drove in with the two more men. They unloaded two cases of beer. Charlie unlocked the building, and they all went in.

Aunt Belle had fixed an early supper for Milton and herself. Her instincts told her to get supper out of the way just in case something bad happened. She had seen the trucks and the car go by slowly, so slowly that she could see the hate in their eyes. After supper, she and Milton sat in the living room with the kerosene lamp in the kitchen turned down low. She had opened some windows to let in what little breeze there was. The front door was open, but the screen was hooked so no one could get in without knocking, or breaking in. She told Milton she was afraid the night riders would come tonight.

She said, "Child, if they do come, I want you to go out the back door and run for your life, 'cause it's you they're after, not me."

"Where will I go, and what will happen to you?" he asked. He was starting to shiver.

"Never mind about me," she said, "I'm an old lady. They may slap me around some, but they won't kill me 'cause they're cowards. It's you they want."

"When do you think they will come?" Milton felt like he was going to throw up, and his hands were shaking.

"When they get drunk enough, child. Probably around midnight. I want you to go over to the Hodges house. There's a crawl space under their kitchen where you can hide. Just open that little door and go in and be sure to close the door behind you. They spread their walnuts out in there to dry after they hull them. I've seen them do it lots of times. The Klan won't think to look for you there. You can come back when it's over."

A few minutes after the courthouse clock struck midnight, Aunt Belle could see the vehicles slowly coming up Warren street with their lights off. There wasn't much of a moon, but she could make them out.

"Quickly, child, out the back door, now, scoot!" she said in a loud whisper.

Milton was torn. He didn't want to leave Belle, but he knew in his heart that she was right, they were after him.

Belle gave him a little shove. "Go now!" she whispered urgently.

Milton ducked out the back just as a brick came crashing through the screen on the front door. The vehicles had stopped right in front of Belle's house, and the Klansmen had all gotten out dressed in their white robes and pointed hats. Two of them lit torches, and a third one loaded the shotgun. They were all drunk. The three with the shotgun and torches came up on the porch while the others stood in the front yard.

The one with the shotgun yelled, "Come out here, nigger boy, we want to talk to you!"

No answer from inside.

"Did you hear me, nigger boy, I said come out here now, or we'll burn you out!"

Still no answer. Belle was stalling them as long as she could. The man with the shotgun motioned for the men with the torches to come up on the porch. Just as they reached the doorway, Aunt Belle appeared at what was left of the screen door.

"He ain't here," she said as calmly as she could. "You gentlemens had best go on home now."

"Don't you sass me, nigger woman," the man with the torch said as he jerked the screen door open and slapped her across the face.

* * * * *

Assistant Chief Burroughs was sitting at Darlene's desk reading the newspaper when the phone rang. He picked up the receiver.

"Police Department," he said matter-of-factly.

"You had better send somebody to old Aunt Belle's house right now, or they're going to kill her."

"Who is this?"

"Never mind who this is, but you better get there quick."

"Where is all this supposed to be happening?"

"On Warren Street between Lobbin and Oak." The caller hung up.

Clyde Burroughs grabbed his hat and ran out to the patrol car standing at the curb. He opened the trunk, grabbed a shotgun and a box of shells and threw them in the back seat. With red light blinking and the siren wide open, he sped out Market Street past the jail, hoping that one of the sheriff's patrol cars would follow him. He skidded around the corner at Warren and turned north toward Aunt Belle's house.

He reached her house just as the three vehicles were pulling away in the opposite direction he was going. They sped south on Warren. They had heard his siren coming down the street. Clyde skidded to a stop and rushed up to the house. There were two torches burning in the living room where the Klansmen had thrown them. Just as Clyde came in the door, Aunt Belle was getting up off the floor. Clyde grabbed the torches and threw them into the front yard. He and Aunt Belle folded the living room rug over the flames to smother them. Clyde literally picked Aunt Belle up and took her out to the front yard. He sat her gently down on the grass and got a blanket out of the trunk of the patrol car. He started to spread the blanket over Aunt Belle, but she was struggling to get up.

"Are you hurt?" he asked as he looked her face over. He could see her left eye was starting to close. "Do you want me to call a doctor?"

"No, suh, I ain't hurt. Just help me up, and I'll be fine," she said as she held her arms up to him.

Just then, Sheriff's Deputy Larry Jackson pulled up and got out of his patrol car. "What's going on?" he asked.

"Looks like she had a visit from the Klan," Clyde said as he helped Belle to her feet.

"Klan? They haven't been active around here in years, what do you think brought this on?"

"I think it has to do with that school teacher's murder. According to the Chief, they think Miss Belle's grandson did it."

"He's my great grandson, and he had nothin' to do with it," Belle said indignantly.

"Where is he now?" Clyde asked.

Belle didn't say a word, she just stood there.

"Miss Belle, I think you should have a doctor look at that eye," Clyde said as he looked her over carefully. She seemed okay, except for her left eye.

"I'll be fine," she said. "Just y'all never mind about me."

Clyde and Larry stayed around for a few minutes more to see if Belle needed any help. The living room rug was ruined, so they dragged it out the front door and took it out to the road so the city could pick it up. Clyde made a note to tell the sanitation department about it. Larry had a hammer and some brads in his trunk, and he put the screen door back together as best he could. The smoke had cleared enough from the house that Clyde thought it would be safe for Belle to go back in. They both told her that they would be back from time to time during the night to check on her, and left.

* * * * *

Irv woke up about 7:30 Tuesday morning. He had been up half the night. His whole family had been awakened when Clyde pulled up to Belle's house with his siren on. They stood at the kitchen window with the lights off and tried to see what was happening. All the windows were up because of the early season warm spell, but they couldn't hear enough to tell what was going on. As near as they could tell, Aunt Belle had had a fire, and the police came to put it out. When everybody left, they all went back to bed just as the courthouse clock struck 2:00.

Irv was the only one home. Katie had gone to the Markhams to clean, Nate was painting the interior of a shoe store downtown, Katherine had gone to visit her girlfriend up the street, and LeRoy hadn't gotten home from his paper route yet.

He had just sat down to his usual bowl on oatmeal when he thought he heard a sound coming from under the kitchen. He didn't think much about it and went on eating. He missed the morning *Times*. LeRoy was usually home by this time with a copy. Then it happened again—tap, tap, right under his feet. It scared him for a minute, and a tingling sensation went through his body. A dog, or wild animal, maybe a coon, or a possum, he thought. Tap, tap, tap, it went again. Irv slipped out the back door and sneaked around the screened-in porch and peeked around the corner. There was the kitchen window where they had all stood and watched last night, and directly below the window was the door to the crawl space, but it was closed. *If it was an animal, wouldn't the door be open?* he asked himself. He slowly approached the door. It was about three feet square. He heard the tapping sound again.

"Who's in there?" he asked. Irv's mouth was so dry he could hardly talk. Not a sound. "I said who's in there?" he repeated—still no sound. Irv reached down and grasped the wooden spool with a nail driven through the hole that served as a knob and slowly opened the door. He peered into the semi-darkness. The lot the house was on sloped from front to back. The crawl space varied from only inches under the front porch to over three and a half feet in back. The house sat on a brick foundation. The back porch was on six-by-six posts enclosed with lattice work. Under the back porch was a cistern that provided water for washing clothes and bathing. That's where Irv had first thought the sound was coming from.

There was still no sound from the crawl space, so Irv bent down and slowly stepped through the door. As his eyes got accustomed to the dim light, he saw someone lying between the floor joists toward the front of the house.

"Who are you and what are you doing under here?"

Slowly the form crawled back toward the door. When he got close enough for Irv to get a good look at him, a look of surprise went over his face.

"Aren't you the one that's staying with Aunt Belle?" he asked.

"Yes, I'm Milton Stevenson, and I have been staying with my great-grandmother, Belle," he said, enunciating clearly as he had been taught to do by his mother.

"What are you doing under here?"

"I'm scared."

"Scared of what?"

Milton explained to Irv what had happened the night before and that he was afraid the Klan would come back and try to kill him and hurt his grandmother, or even kill her." He seemed genuinely frightened to Irv.

"What was that noise I heard?"

"I was hungry, and saw these walnuts. I cracked some with these two bricks, I hope you don't mind."

He talked so distinctly that Irv was amazed. He had never heard a Negro talk like that before.

"Come up to the kitchen and I'll give you something to eat if you're hungry."

"No, thank you, I'm afraid to leave here until after dark. They might see me. I think they are watching for me right now."

Irv peeked out to see if he could see anyone. There was no one in sight. "I don't see anyone. Why do you think they're watching you?"

"I just have a feeling I'm being watched, and it scares me. I'm worried about my great-grandmother, Belle. Would you check on her for me?"

Irv was puzzled. "Yes, I'll go see if she is okay, but I had better not go over there right now. If I do, and they're watching the neighborhood, they might see me and figure out that you're hiding in here. I'll go over there in an hour or two."

Milton was quiet; it was obvious he was scared. He was almost a hundred miles from home in a hostile environment. He was an educated, sensitive, colored boy in a town where "uppity niggers" were targets of white rednecks, and even some blacks.

"Hey, I've got an idea!" Irv's remark jolted Milton back to reality. "I know the perfect place for you to hide."

"Where?"

"In the courthouse!"

"Courthouse? That place is probably swarming with white men who would want to kill me. I'll bet half of them belong to the Klan."

"No, I mean in the clock tower. Nobody goes up there except the janitor, and he only goes up there once a week to wind the clock. You could hide under the stairs while he is up there. It only takes him about 15 minutes to wind the clock. Besides, what better place to hide while the Klan are looking all over town for you?"

"I need to figure out a way to get home, to get away from Grandma Belle so they will quit harassing her, to get out of town. I can't stay in Warrensburg any longer, I've got to leave as soon as possible."

"You could stay up there a couple of days while I get you come help, couldn't you?"

"What would I eat, what would I do for a toilet?"

"I hang out in the furnace room sometimes, and I know the janitor real well. In the wintertime, he even lets me shovel coal into the furnace sometimes. There used to be two janitors, but a few years back when the depression started, they had to cut down to one. There is another set of keys to every door in the courthouse hanging on a nail by the door going into the basement from the furnace room. I could take those keys without old Gus even missing them. I could take the keys to the furnace room door and the clock tower down to the hardware store and have duplicates made. Then I could take the whole set back and hang them where they belong. Then at night you could go down to the basement and use the men's restroom. There's a drinking fountain down there, too."

"What would I eat?"

"Hey, I know!" Irv was getting excited. "There are a lot of commodities stored in a locked store room in the basement. You know, the government buys up surplus stuff from the farmers and sends it out to the counties to give out to the poor. There's a whole room full of raisins, prunes, dried beans, flour and cornmeal, and stuff like that."

"I can't eat flour and cornmeal raw," Milton was getting exasperated.

"You can eat raisins, can't you?" Irv asked. "Hey, they have boxes of cookies, canned goods and things like that, too. Besides, you'll only be up there for a couple of days until I can get you some help."

That afternoon while the janitor was up on the second floor working, Irv took the keys and had duplicates made of three keys, including the one to the commodity storage room. He had an extra key to the clock tower made for himself. That night after dark, he slipped Milton into the courthouse, handed him two keys. "I'll be back tomorrow night and let you know how Aunt Belle is doing, and what I've gotten done."

5

THE ARREST

WEDNESDAY MORNING, MAY 20. Sheriff Harrison Foster was in the courthouse at 9:30 on his way up to the judge's chamber to talk to Judge Emerson Whitfield about a case, but before he got to the steps to the second floor, Gerald Essex came out of his office and grabbed his arm.

"Harry, I need to talk to you," he said in his usual sarcastic way.

Gerald "Red" Essex was the youngest prosecuting attorney in the state. He had just graduated from Law School at the University of Missouri's Kansas City campus when he had been swept into office in Roosevelt's big win over Hoover in the last election. He was running for re-election this year, and was feeling pretty cocky about his chances of winning, because Roosevelt was picked to win by a large margin over Alf Landon for a second term. He had no competition in the primary, so was considered the automatic winner in November. Only 5' 4" tall, with red hair, he reminded Harry of a bantam rooster.

"Sure, Red, what about?"

"How many times do I have to tell you people not to call me Red? My name is Gerald Essex. You can call me Gerald, but don't ever call me Red again!" His face was getting about the color of his hair.

"Yes, sir, Your Honor," Harry said with a grin on his face. He knew it wasn't wise to irritate the prosecuting attorney that way, but he couldn't resist.

Gerald got right up in Harry's face, even rocking up on the balls of his feet to reach it, "I'm not a judge either," he said through clinched teeth,

70

his face flaming red by now, "But I am a damn good prosecutor, and you had better understand that!"

Harry acquiesced. "I'm sorry, I didn't mean to upset you," he said, "what can I do for you?"

"Come in my office, I need to talk to you," he said, beginning to calm down a little.

Harry walked into his office and sat down. He knew better than to irritate the prosecutor that way. Actually, it was dumb, because he knew that Gerald had been hand-picked by the Pendergast Machine to be Johnson County's prosecuting attorney, and everybody knew that Tom Pendergast ran Missouri politics. He could even get Harry's job.

"I want you to arrest that colored kid; his name is Milton Stevenson."

"On what charge?"

"First degree murder, I've got a warrant being drawn up right now."

"Don't you want to impanel a Grand Jury and do some investigating first?"

"Don't try to tell me how to run my office, I said arrest him."

"Have you been talking to Charlie Shanks?" Harry was finding it increasingly hard to control his emotions.

"Yes, and that's not all. I've got three witnesses that can put him at the scene of the crime. One of them practically saw him dump the body. Go on up and do whatever business you have with the judge, and stop by here on your way out. I'll have the warrant ready."

Harry picked up the warrant and walked across the street to the police station. He had never been so exasperated in his life. Buck was sitting at Darlene's desk when he walked in. He laid the warrant on the desk in front of Buck.

"Good morning, Mister Police Chief, take a look at this." His disgust showed in his voice.

Buck picked up the warrant and read it. "What in the world is he thinking about?" he said incredulously. "We don't have any evidence on that boy."

"The prosecutor thinks he does." Harry couldn't even bring himself to say his name.

"Are you going to do it?"

"I guess I'll have to, I sure hope he has left town. That would let me off the hook if he can't be found."

71

* * * * *

Irv walked south on Washington Street. He walked slowly as he tried to think what he would say to Rudolph Eisenstein when he got to his office. As he crossed Market Street, he glanced up at the courthouse clock, it was 10:15. He didn't have an appointment; he didn't even know if he would be in his office, but he just knew he had to try.

* * * * *

Rudolph Eisenstein and his older brother by two years, Wilhelm had come to Warrensburg in 1898. Rudolph was 35 at the time and Wilhelm was 37. They were born in Furstenwalde, Germany, the youngest of the five children of Heinrich and Freda Eisenstein. Furstenwalde is about 60 kilometers East of Berlin, about halfway between Berlin and Frankfurt. Not the Frankfurt in Hesse, but the one right on the Polish border. Heinrich and his brother Joseph owned a small bank in Furstenwalde. They were not wealthy, but comfortable. They enjoyed living in a small town, and there was less anti-Semitism there than in the big cities like Berlin.

Heinrich and Freda's three eldest children were girls. Heinrich had dreams of a son joining him in the bank, but it was not to be. When Wilhelm and Rudolph were born, neither boy wanted to be a banker. Instead, after high school, Wilhelm went to dental school at the University of Berlin. He liked it because he could catch the train home on weekends and be with family. Two years later, Rudolph talked his father into letting him go to Heidelberg University to get a law degree. He liked being with Wilhelm, but his sisters drove him crazy, so he enjoyed being so far from home. His sisters talked too much to suit him. His oldest sister had married, and her husband joined the bank as a teller trainee, and that seemed to please Heinrich, so he quit pressuring Wilhelm and Rudolph to join the bank.

After Wilhelm graduated from dental school, he set up a practice in Berlin, but was never satisfied. When Rudolph got his law degree, he joined a law firm in Berlin, and he and Wilhelm would take their vacations together, but they both longed to leave Germany. In 1891 they took a train to Paris where they transferred to another train that took them to

Le Havre. At Le Havre they took an ocean going vessel to New York and never looked back.

While in New York, they got a letter from their father telling them that their mother was gravely ill, but while they were trying to book passage to France, another letter arrived telling them of her passing. Although they grieved her passing, all they could do was send their condolences to their family, and go on with their lives. Neither one of them liked the neighborhood in Brooklyn where most of the foreign Jews lived. It was too crowded and dirty to suit them, so two years later, almost to the day from their arrival, they boarded a train for Chicago.

They liked Chicago better than New York, as it was not as crowded, and the people seemed friendlier. They rented an apartment on West Madison not too far from the loop. Wilhelm opened an office over a clothing store on West Madison not far from their apartment and Rudolf joined an all Jewish law firm in the Balaban-Katz Building right down in the loop. He could catch the EL a block from their apartment and be at his office in ten minutes. They were happy at first.

Then one day in April 1898, they got a cable from Fritzie, their oldest sister, telling them of their father's passing. Again, there was nothing they could do, but send their condolences. Four weeks later when they got a letter from a Berlin lawyer with a copy of their father's will, they were not surprised to learn that his estate had been divided between their three sisters, and that Fritzie's husband was now president of the bank. They felt like they no longer had any ties to Germany, so they decided to go west to seek their fortune. Wilhelm was 37 and Rudolph was 35. Wilhelm closed his office and Rudolph gave his employers two weeks' notice, they settled all their bills and packed their bags.

One beautiful Spring day in May, they took a taxi to Union Station and bought train tickets to St. Louis. They stayed there for a week, looking around, but decide to go farther West. They bought train tickets to Kansas City, but when it stopped at Warrensburg to change crews and take on water and coal, they got off and walked around. They liked what they saw, and tipped the porter to unload their bags and got a double room at the Martin Hotel, right next door to the station.

The next day they went up to the Breckenridge Bank and opened up an account. They wired their bank in Chicago to transfer their funds to

Breckenridge and went looking for office space. By the end of the month, they had located a building down on Pine Street that was for sale. The ground floor was rented to a weekly newspaper, but the second floor was empty. They were surprised at how much cheaper real estate was in Warrensburg than in New York and Chicago.

It took them three months to have the second floor built out to suit them, but in late August 1898 they opened for business. Wilhelm's dental office was in front overlooking Pine Street, and Rudolph's Law office was behind it and across the hall. They had built a two-bedroom apartment in the back with a door leading to a landing and stairs to ground behind the building. There was a door beside the newspaper in front that led to the stairs up to the offices. It had a frosted glass window with gold leaf lettering that read "Wilhelm Eisenstein, Family Dentistry," and right below that, "Rudolf Eisenstein, Attorney at Law."

They prospered until 1930 when the great depression hit. In 1933, Rudolf had let his secretary go to save on overhead. Their building was paid for, but their income had dropped dramatically.

* * * * *

Irv opened the door and started up the stairs. He was going to ask a stranger for a big favor, and he didn't know how to go about it. Wilhelm had done the dental work for his family for several years, so he felt like he knew him, but he could only remember seeing Rudolph two or three times in his entire life. His mouth was dry as he opened the door to his office.

Rudolph was sitting at his former secretary's desk reading a law book. The room was sparsely furnished. There were two windows in the front of the room that looked out over Pine Street with the shades pulled about a third of the way down. A well-worn Persian Rug covered most of the wooden floor. Four straight-back chairs lined the west wall and two on the east wall, with a square library table between them. It was covered with old magazines. A single light dropped down from the ceiling with a hobnail milk glass shade. The big oak secretary's desk was in front of a partition separating the reception room from the offices behind. An ancient Remington Typewriter sat on a stand to the left of the desk. There was another straight-back chair at the right of the desk. A desk lamp and a telephone completed the furnishings. Rudolph looked up from his book.

"Come in, young man," he said in a soft low voice with a trace of German accent.

Irv took a hesitant step toward him.

"Come, come," Rudolph beckoned as he stood and pointed to the chair beside the desk.

Irv sat down. His mouth was dry and he was so nervous his hands trembled.

"You want a glass of water?" Rudolph asked.

"No, sir, I'm fine," Irv finally managed to say.

"Now, what can I do for you, young man?" Rudolph asked softly.

Irv told Rudolph his name and began to relate to him what had happened over the past five days. He ended with a plea for help for his new friend, Milton. Rudolph closed his eyes to think. Irv took this gesture as a rejection and started to get up from the chair.

"No, no," Rudolph said as he opened his eyes and took Irv's hand. "I was just thinking to myself. I have been following this story in the papers. Can you take me to see this boy?"

"Yes, sir, but I don't have much money. How much do you charge?"

A twinkle came in Rudolph's eye. "My fees are so outrageously high that even I can't afford them," he said, "but for you I'll make a special deal. How much money do you have?"

Irv emptied his pockets on the corner of the desk. In addition to a pocket knife, that had been a Christmas gift from his brother Louis, he had 28 cents. "Not much," he said softly.

"That's enough to retain my services, but I might have some expenses," Rudolph said as he brushed the money into his hand and dropped the coins into the middle drawer of the desk.

"Expenses?"

"Yes, all lawyers have expenses. That's another way we have of getting more money out of our clients. I might have to buy a new pencil, for example, and where you might be satisfied with the penny variety, I always insist on at least a three-cent one," he said with a trace of a grin at the corners of his mouth.

He patted Irv on the head. "Come, take me to your friend."

Irv explained that Milton was hiding in the courthouse tower because the Klan was after him, and also the police, he thought.

"Ingenious," Rudolph muttered to himself, "hiding in plain sight."

It was only three blocks to the courthouse, so they walked. The Eisenstein brothers owned a 1929 Buick sedan with very few miles on it, but they kept it in a garage they rented from a widow woman up on Madison Street and rarely drove it.

At the courthouse, they went in the south door, and after looking around to make sure no one was watching, Irv unlocked the door to the clock tower and they went up.

"Mac," Irv called. Milton had told him to call him by his nickname. "I brought you some help."

They found Milton cowering beneath the steps that led up to the clock. He didn't know what to expect, and was relieved to see just the two of them. He was afraid there might be police with Irv. Rudolph put him at ease immediately.

"You must be Milton," he said, extending his hand to him. "Do you mind if I call you Mac?"

Milton shook his head no.

"Good, Mac, then we can get down to business. My name is Rudolph Eisenstein. I'm a lawyer, and I like to think I'm a good one. Master Hodges here has retained my services in your behalf."

"I told you I would get you some help," Irv chimed in.

The clock startled the three of them as it loudly chimed 12:00.

Milton looked tired and dejected. The clock chiming every 15 minutes had kept him up all night. That's something neither he nor Irv had thought about when he hid in the tower. Now, it was obvious that he couldn't stay there.

"Mac," Rudolph continued, "I'm going to try to tell you what, in my mind, is going to happen in the next few days. If you continue to hide, the sheriff and police will continue to look for you. Eventually, you will be found. If you try to leave town, you will, most likely, be spotted and taken into custody by the police, or the Klan."

Milton broke down and started to sob. He thought of the trouble he had caused Belle by his presence, and now he was being suspected of a horrible crime he didn't commit. He missed his family and wondered if they knew the trouble he was in. He hoped not. His body shook with sobs.

Irv stood with his mouth open. He didn't know what to say. Tears were starting to form in his eyes.

Rudolph laid a gentle hand on Milton's shoulder. "Now, now," he said, "things aren't as bad as they seem. First of all, from what I read in the papers, they don't seem to have a case against you, and if it comes to trial, I think we would win. Secondly, I may be able to talk the county prosecuting attorney into calling a Grand Jury to investigate the murder, and if so, they might not even indict you."

Milton looked up, tears streaming down his cheeks. Rudolph offered him a handkerchief, and he started wiping away the tears.

"I'll tell you what I'll do," Rudolph said emphatically. I'll go down right now and talk to the prosecuting attorney. I'll also talk to the Police Chief and Sheriff; then I'll come back up here and we'll plan our strategy. How does that sound, Mac?"

Milton nodded yes; he was too upset to talk.

Rudolph opened the door a crack and peeked out. When he was sure no one was watching, he eased out into the foyer. He knew exactly where the prosecuting attorney's office was, having been there many times. It was on the same floor, on the north end, west side. He paused for a moment outside the door to think about what he was going to say, opened the door and walked in.

The receptionist looked up from the crossword puzzle she was working. "Yes," she asked.

"I have an urgent matter to discuss with Mr. Essex." Rudolph knew how this office was run; it came from the top down. The people were curt, unsmiling and unaccommodating.

"Do you have an appointment?" she asked in a brusque manner.

"No, but I think he will want to talk to me." Rudolph smiled a big smile trying to disarm her.

"And what makes you think that, Mr. Eisenstein?" she said sarcastically.

Rudolph didn't know that there was a warrant out for Milton, but he was sure that this was the place to start.

"Because I represent someone who might be of interest to him." Rudolph could see back into the prosecutor's office, and could see Gerald Essex on the telephone.

"I'm sorry, you'll have to make an appointment and come back later!" she snorted.

Rudolph smiled and thanked her, but instead of leaving, he simply walked back into Gerald's office and closed the door. The receptionist yelled after him, but it was too late. She knocked on the door and opened it just as Gerald hung up the phone.

"Mr. Essex, I tried to stop him, but he came on in anyway." She glared at Rudolph.

The prosecutor jumped out of his chair, ran around his desk and got right up in Rudolph's face.

"What are you trying to pull, Mr. Eisenstein?" he sputtered, his face turning scarlet.

"Please calm down. I have some information that would interest you very much, and it can't wait."

"Well, it will just have to wait. It's 12:10 and I'm on my way to a luncheon. I'm already late." He started for the door.

"I know where Milton Stevenson is."

Gerald Essex stopped in his tracks. "I could have you arrested for harboring a fugitive." By now his face was the same color as his hair.

"Fugitive?"

"Yes, fugitive! I swore out a warrant for his arrest at 9:30 this morning."

"On what charges?"

"On first degree murder charges, that's what!"

"I don't remember you calling for a Grand Jury investigation, what evidence do you have?"

"I've got at least three witnesses to the crime. I don't need a Grand Jury to investigate!" Gerald was standing on his tip toes with the index finger on his right hand almost up Rudolph's nose.

Calmly, Rudolph pushed his hand away. "Witnesses to the crime, or hearsay witnesses?"

"You'll find out when it comes to trial!"

"There hasn't even been a preliminary hearing yet." Rudolph had had all he could take of Gerald Essex. He had made a mistake even coming to him. He started for the door.

"Come back here!" Gerald shouted. "I want to know where that boy is right now!"

Rudolph kept on walking, out the prosecuting attorney's door and out the north door of the courthouse with Gerald trailing behind screaming at him to stop or he would have him arrested. By this time the noise of Gerald's screaming had started to attract a crowd.

Rudolph walked across the street toward the police station. When Gerald saw where he was headed, he stopped. When he looked around and saw how many people were watching him, most of whom worked in the courthouse, he dashed back up the steps into the courthouse, went into his office and slammed the door.

Rudolph walked into the police station and was greeted by Darlene, "Hi, Rudy." Darlene had a nickname for everyone.

"Is the Chief in?"

"He just went upstairs for lunch, he was a little late getting away. Do you want me to get him?"

"If you don't mind, I have something to tell him that is urgent and confidential."

Darlene hurried up the stairs to the Chief's apartment and rapped lightly on the door. She knew Buck would be in the kitchen having lunch with Ann. Ann opened the door.

"Hi, Darlene, what's up?"

"Would you tell the Chief that Rudolph Eisenstein is downstairs and wants to talk to him. He says it's urgent and confidential."

Buck came up behind Ann. "Send him up here, Darlene. We can talk while we eat. Tell him he is invited to lunch."

Ann nodded her head, "Yes, by all means, tell him to come on up."

Rudolph hadn't realized he was hungry until he reached the apartment and smelled Ann's Yankee pot roast. She had made it the day before for dinner, but always made enough for two meals. And as usual, it tasted better the second day.

While they ate, Rudolph related to Buck and Ann what had happened in the hours preceding noon, and what had happened in the prosecutor's office.

"He is probably watching the station right now waiting for me to come out so he can follow me and find out where Milton is hiding." Rudolph had a touch of regret in his voice.

Ann was more concerned about the boys being up in that hot courthouse attic with nothing to eat or drink.

Buck thought for a minute. "I have a plan that I think will work. It involves Clarence, so I'll have to get hold of him."

Gerald Essex stood at his office window with his arms folded watching the police station across the street. He stood to one side so he couldn't be seen from the street. His assistant prosecutor had pulled his car about halfway up the driveway that went to the furnace room. It was normally used to haul coal and other supplies to the furnace room. It ran along the north side of the west entrance. It was parked facing the street, so they could pull out onto Maynard Street and go in whatever direction their quarry might take them. He waited in the reception room for orders from his boss. Gerald stiffened as Buck and Rudolph came out of the front door of the police station and turned east on West Market Street. Gerald watched them for a minute, then dashed out to the door of his office.

"Come on quick," he said to his assistant, they just left the station on foot, so they must have him stashed nearby."

They went out the east entrance of the courthouse and paused on the steps to give Buck and Rudolph a chance to make the jog on Holden Street, and then go on east on East Market. East Market ran right into the courthouse, so the two men had a clear view of Buck and Rudolph as they walked hurriedly up the street. They started following at a discreet distance.

Rudolph, at age 73, managed to keep up with Buck, although he was starting to pant. They crossed College and Maguire, still on a steady pace. For the next four blocks, there were no side streets. Gerald and his assistant were still a block behind them. Neither Buck nor Rudolph looked back, pretending they didn't know they were being followed.

"Where in the hell are they going?" Gerald was running out of breath.

* * * * *

Harry Foster got in his patrol car, drove to the courthouse and parked it in front of the south entrance. He dashed up the steps and turned right to the clock tower door. He rapped lightly, and Irv opened it a crack.

"Come with me quickly," he said as he motioned them to follow.

They went down the south steps and jumped into the patrol car. Harry sped away with the boys crouched on the floor behind the front seat. He

80

went straight to the jail and into his office with the boys in tow and locked the door behind them.

* * * * *

Just as Buck and Rudolph got to the corner of East Market and North Mitchell Street, Clarence slid to a stop in the patrol car, heading south on Mitchell. Buck and Rudolph jumped in, and Clarence sped away.

Gerald knew that he'd been snookered. "Shit," he said almost under his breath, his face getting fiery red. "Let's go back to the courthouse and get the car. We've got to find those SOBs."

They ran back to the courthouse as fast as they could, and both were out of breath when they reached the car. They sped east on Market Street, and just after they crossed Holden Street, Clarence drove up Holden past the courthouse, turned west on Gay, then south on Maynard to the back of the police station and parked the car. They all got out, smiling from ear to ear. Clarence went in the back door of the station while Buck and Rudolph walked down to the jail.

Harry was filling out booking papers on Milton when Buck knocked on the door. He let them in, and Buck told him their plan had worked as smooth as silk.

"Let me tell you what I'm doing here," Harry said. "I have officially arrested Milton in compliance with the arrest warrant. I have filled out the arrest papers, and I am in the process of booking him into the jail now. Once I get him locked up in back, he'll be safe. We have a separate juvenile cell, away from the rest of the convicts, and I'm going to post a deputy outside his door just to make sure. Rudolph, as soon as that happens, I want you to go with me to see the judge so we can get a hearing date, the sooner the better."

Irv went back to the cell with Milton, and after he had been settled in, Milton thanked Irv for his help, and made him promise he would tell Aunt Belle where he was. The Sheriff had already promised him he would try to get word to his parents. The problem was that they lived 90 miles away and had no phone. They weren't to pick him up until June 6th. Irv went back to Harry's office with the jailer. He thanked Harry, Buck and Rudolph, and started to leave when Ann walked in with a picnic basket.

"Sheriff," she said, "I would like permission to visit one of your prisoners, and I want to visit with you, too," she said, pointing to Irv.

"Permission granted," Harry said with a grin. He escorted Ann back to Milton's cell, and she set out a meal of pot roast, fresh cornbread, iced tea and chocolate cake for a hungry, grateful and frightened young man. Then she went back to Harry's office and set the same up for Irv. He hadn't eaten that well in weeks. The clock in the courthouse struck 3:00.

Harry and Rudolph hurried up to the courthouse to try to catch the circuit judge before he went back to Clinton, where he lived.

Judge Emerson A. Whitfield served both Johnson and Henry Counties. At age 60, he appeared much younger because his coal black hair had not turned gray, and his face did not have as many wrinkles as most 60-year-olds. Of average build, he was mild-mannered, but stern. He had the reputation of being a fair and honest man. His case load in Johnson County was heavier that in Henry County for some reason, so he was spending a lot of time in the Johnson County Courthouse.

Harry and Rudolph were starting up the steps to the second floor courtroom, when Gerald Essex came bursting out of his office waving a sheet of paper at them.

"Rudolph Eisenstein, I'm having you arrested," he blustered, his face already beet red. "How dare you pull what you pulled this afternoon!"

Rudolph struggled to remain calm, "Oh, what was that, Mister Prosecutor?" He emphasized the Mister.

"For obstructing justice, that's why! You're harboring a felon, and I have the Arrest Warrant right here, and as soon as the judge signs it, I'm having you arrested and throwing you in the county jail!"

His bluster was attracting attention, and a small crowd of county employees and courthouse loafers was starting to collect.

"What felon are you referring to?" Rudolph asked.

"You know exactly who I'm referring to!" he shouted. "That nigger murderer, that's who!" When he realized there were several Negroes looking on, his face got even redder.

Harry interrupted him. "If you mean Milton Stevenson, he's in my jail right now."

"Wh . . . what's he doing in your jail?" Gerald stammered.

"You gave me a warrant for his arrest this morning, remember?"

"Well, keep him there, I want to talk to him." Gerald's voice was much calmer as he tried to save face.

Rudolph reached over and took the paper from Gerald's hand, tore it in two and handed it back to him. Without a word, Gerald turned on his heels and marched back into his office and slammed the door. Rudolph and Harry grinned at each other as they went up the steps.

After hearing the circumstances of the case from the Sheriff and Rudolph, and after talking to a very upset prosecuting attorney, Judge Whitfield set Friday, May 22, as the preliminary hearing date.

By the time Harry and Rudolph got back to the jail, there were already four men sitting in two pick-up trucks in front. They glared at both men as they walked up the steps to the front door. *News really gets around fast in a small town,* Harry thought to himself.

Buck and Ann had gone back to the police station, and he and Clarence were on their way out to see Russell Wilhelm.

Irv had gone down to the room under the drugstore at Holden and Pine to help LeRoy carry his afternoon *K.C. Star* route. The room faced the railroad tracks, and the papers came in on the 3:15 Colorado Eagle from Kansas City. Harry caught up on his paperwork, while Rudolph went back to talk to Milton.

Clarence and Buck pulled into the lane at the Wilhelm farm at 4:00. Russell was on his way up to the house on his tractor. He had just finished planting the last of his seed corn, and had waved at them as they passed by on the road. It took him a few minutes to park the tractor at the barn, with the corn planter still attached, and walk up to the house. Clarence and Buck waited for him on the front porch.

Russell recognized Buck. "Hello," he greeted them as he came around the house. "What brings you guys out here this time of day?"

The Wilhelm house was an imposing structure. Built around the turn of the century, it was a two-and-a-half-story Victorian with the usual towers with their pointed roofs, lots of gables, spindles and lattice work. It had been well-maintained, and looked almost new, although it was nearly 40 years old. Russell had a woman come in two days a week to clean and do laundry. He did his own cooking.

Buck spoke first. "We came out to talk to you and to admire this fine old house."

Nothing like a little flattery to break the ice, Buck thought.

"Thank you, my grandfather built this house just before he passed on."

Russell was about six feet tall, with a stocky build. His ruddy face was topped by a thick shock of dark brown hair. He had the stout hands of farmer used to milking cows by hand and bucking bales in the hayfield. Buck and Clarence were sitting in the porch swing, so Russell sat down on the steps and leaned against the side of the porch. He took his hat off and laid it on the porch.

"I've got my corn in the ground," he said, "but if we don't get some rain soon, it won't come up. If you guys are religious men, you might pray for some rain to help us farmers out." He grinned a big grin. He wasn't a bad-looking man, especially when he smiled.

Buck stood up. "Russell, we're holding a young man in the jail on suspicion of killing that school teacher, but we're still running down leads to make sure we have the right man."

"Yes, sir, I read all about that killing in the paper."

Russell took a red bandanna out of a rear pocket in his overalls and wiped his face. He didn't seem the least bit nervous. He wiped the sweatband in his hat off, and put the bandanna back in his pocket. Buck studied him carefully while this was going on.

"Do you own a dark blue Packard sedan?" Buck was trying to rattle him.

"Yes, sir, I do. It was left to me by my dad, when he passed away two years ago." There was no sign of nervousness.

"Do you mind if we take a look at it?"

"Not at all, if it will help solve that case, it's parked out in the barn."

Russell got up and started for the barn. Buck was amazed at how calm Russell was as he and Clarence followed him to the barn. Russell rolled the barn door open and pointed to a big car under a white duck tarp.

"I keep that tarp over it to keep the chickens and the cats from climbing all over it and scratching the paint. Also, there's pigeons in here, and they like to poop all over everything. It's just like new; it's only got a little over 3,000 miles on it. I just drive it when I want to show off," he said with a grin.

He pulled the tarp off and revealed a beautiful shiny blue Packard Car. "There she is," he said proudly, "my pride and joy."

Buck sent Clarence back to the patrol car for a flashlight and started looking the car over. When Clarence returned, he went over the interior, shining the light under the seats and in the glove box. He had Russell unlocked the trunk and looked the inside of it over very carefully. He didn't find so much as a stray hair.

Buck handed the flashlight back to Clarence and took out his notebook.

"Russell, I need to know where you were last Friday evening between about 6:00 and 9:00," he said, looking Russell in the eyes to see if he could pick up any kind of emotion.

Russell stood with his thumbs hooked in the bib of his overalls, his head cocked to one side as if deep in thought.

Finally, he said, "I went to the bank about 3:00, and from there I went down to elevator on Pine Street and bought some seed corn. Let's see, I brought the seed corn home and unloaded into that metal granary you saw as came down here to the barn, to keep the rats out of it. Then I decided I was thirsty, so I cleaned up, changed clothes and drove the Packard down to Walker's cafe on Pine at about 6:00 and had a chicken fried steak dinner and a beer. That took me 'til about 7:00; as a matter of fact, I heard the courthouse clock strike 7:00 as I walked down the street to George's pool hall. I left the car parked up by Walker's. You know how hard it is to find a parking space on Pine Street on Friday and Saturday evenings on account of the theater across the street."

"Were you alone?" Buck was taking notes and trying to picture all this in his mind.

"Chief, I don't have a steady girlfriend any more. You know, I got married right out of high school, but she didn't like living on a farm, so she up and left. She moved to Kansas City right away and said she didn't want to see me any more. That was five years ago, and the only time I've seen her since I was up at the courthouse when the judge granted us a divorce."

"So you went down to the pool hall, how long were you there?"

"Well, let's see, I played a couple of games of eight ball with a fellow that works up at the feed store, and I think I had maybe two more beers."

"Then where did you go?"

"I got in my car and drove around a little bit, 'til about dark, then drove home."

"Did you happen to go by Reese School while you were driving around?"

"Yes, I did. I drove around that block a couple of times. There's two real pretty girls that live right across the street from the school. I spotted them as I drove by the first time, so I went around the block again, but they stuck their noses in the air and went in the house. I said, 'To heck with them,' and drove on home."

"Did you see any cars in that neighborhood while you were driving around?"

"No, Chief, I didn't."

The Chief put his notebook back in his pocket and shook hands with Russell. "Thanks for your time," Russell he said, and motioned Clarence back to the patrol car.

On their way back to town, Buck took out his notebook and, tapping it with his pencil, turned to Clarence.

"What did you think about our little interview? His story seemed awfully pat to me, almost like he'd been rehearsing it?"

"Yes, and that car had been cleaned from top to bottom, just in the last day or two."

"I know," Buck said, "either he is completely innocent, or he has done a great job of covering his tracks. Why don't you go down to Walkers' and the pool hall and see in you can find any witnesses to corroborate his alibi for Friday night? I want to go back to the jail and talk to Milton some more."

"Do you want me to drop you off at the jail?"

"Yes, and tomorrow morning, I think Ann and I will take our car and drive over to Saline County and talk to Milton's parents. They need to know what's going on."

"Can't you call them?"

"No, they don't have a phone. Besides, there is no phone service in that part of the county."

When they pulled up to the jail, there were three pick-up trucks and two cars parked along the curb, and Buck counted 12 men around the steps leading up to the front door of the jail. When they saw Buck, they started yelling for the sheriff to bring that nigger out so justice could be done. Harry Foster stepped outside the front door and glared at them as he and Buck went in. He closed and locked it. They went into Harry's office to talk.

"Harry, Clarence and I just came from Russell Wilhelm's place, and he didn't deny anything. He does own a dark blue Packard, and he admits he drove around Reese school in it a couple of times last Friday evening just before dark."

"What time was that?"

"Well, he says he came to town about 6:00, right after chores. He had supper at Walkers' Cafe, then went down to George's pool hall just down the street and had a couple of beers. He says he shot a game or two of pool, then drove around town a while, and went home. He said it was just getting dark when he left town."

"We don't have anything on him, do we?" Harry said, scratching his head to try to recall something they could use.

Buck was thumbing through his notes.

"Wait a minute, here's something!" Buck held his notes so Harry could see. "That lady you interviewed Monday said she saw him in the blue car at 6:10 on her way home from the bakery."

Harry pulled out his notes and studied them for a while.

"By golly, you're right. She did say 6:10. Well, now, if he's lying about that, maybe he's lying about something else."

Buck pocketed his notes and stood up.

"I need to go talk to Mr. Wilhelm again. I'll do that tomorrow. Right now, I have a dinner date with a beautiful lady, care to join us?"

"I'm sorely tempted. I know that beautiful lady you're referring to is also a good cook, but you two deserve an evening together by yourselves. I'll take a rain check."

Harry stood and followed Buck to the front door. He wanted to see if those idiots were still out front.

They were, and they jeered at Buck as he picked his way down the steps to the sidewalk and headed up Market to the police station. He didn't look back until one of the drunks yelled, "Nigger lover!" at him. He stopped, turned and slowly walked back to the Klansman who had yelled it. The small mob fell silent as Buck got right up in his face. He could smell stale beer on his breath.

"Yes, I do love niggers, although I prefer to call them Negroes. I even love stupid drunks like you. Do you know why?"

Suddenly, it got very quiet. Harry watched intently from behind the slightly open jail door, his hand resting on butt of the Smith and Wesson 38 police special in his holster.

"I'll tell you why, because my Lord Jesus requires me to, so I can obtain salvation. He tells me to love everybody, including my enemies, like you."

The drunk put his hand on the front of Buck's shirt as if to shove him backward. That was all Buck needed. Quick as a wink, he grabbed the hand, turning it so the palm was facing the drunk, and taking two fingers in each hand, bent the hand back toward him. Wrist bones snapped as the drunk went down to his knees howling in pain. The rest of the mob started toward Buck until they heard the jail door swing open. Harry stepped out on the porch with his hand on his pistol.

Not a word was spoken as the mob slowly moved to their vehicles. Two of them helped the drunk to his feet and into one of the pick-up trucks. He whined as he held his right wrist to his stomach with his other hand. Buck turned and walked to the police station. Harry smiled and closed the jail door.

That evening Buck and Ann dined on spaghetti and meatballs with tossed Caesar salad. Ann had lit some candles and poured two glasses of red wine. They listened to a new record on the phonograph that Ann had bought that day at the music store. It was a brand new love song, and they held hands as "That's the glory of, that's the story of love" wafted through their apartment.

* * * * *

Thursday morning, just as the courthouse clock struck 8:00, Ann and Buck pulled out of their parking space behind the jail and headed for Saline County. They were driving their new 1936 Studebaker President, an early 20th anniversary gift from Ann's parents. Ann was at the wheel. Buck felt intimidated by the expensive car; therefore, he only drove it to church on Sunday, and only then because Ann insisted.

It had been given to them in January, although their anniversary wasn't actually until late June. Buck had resisted, but her parents were very insistent. Buck had been racking his brain, trying to think of an appropriate anniversary gift for his beloved Ann, and now he had been completely upstaged by her parents. He was angry at himself for being so resentful, because he really did love the Christians. After all, they had given him Ann.

They drove up Missouri Highway 13 to U.S. Highway 40 and headed east to Marshall Junction. At Marshall Junction, they turned north on U.S. 65 toward Marshall. The new Studebaker came equipped with a wonderful Philco car radio, and they passed the time listening to everything from local news to farm market reports. Buck and Ann joked that they would have to start raising some hogs so the farm reports would be more meaningful.

They drove through Marshall, and about two miles north of town took County Road C east to Slater. The trip had taken less time than Buck had figured, as it was only 9:30 when they reached Slater. They stopped for coffee at a little cafe downtown. Slater was what was known as an inland town, because it was not on a railroad line or major highway. It was strictly a farm community of about 2,500 people.

Heads turned when the new Studebaker pulled up at the Slater Cafe and the handsome couple got out. They ordered coffee and struck up a conversation with the waitress. It was a small cafe, and only three people were seated at the well-worn tables with red-checkered oilcloth covers.

"Where you folks from?" the waitress asked as she poured their coffee.

Buck had worn civilian clothes, so there was no way the waitress could know he was a police officer.

"We're from Warrensburg," Ann said pleasantly.

"What on earth brings nice folks like you to this little burg?"

Buck explained that they were on their way to Columbia to visit their daughter, and thought they would stop by and say hello to some friends while they were in the area. It was just a little lie, because they had intended to drive on to Columbia to visit with Ann Marie if they got through with the Stevensons in time.

"Who are you visiting in Slater?"

Ann smiled, "We're looking for the Holy Word of God Methodist Church. The minister and his wife are friends of ours." Another little white lie.

"That's a colored church!" The waitress sat the coffee pot down on the counter as if she was going to drop it.

Ann smiled her sweetest smile, "And isn't it nice when we can count such lovely colored people among our friends?" she said as pleasantly as she could. "Could you direct us to their church, please?"

The waitress stammered a bit, but finally told them to stay on County Road C and go about three miles out of town. They couldn't miss it.

Buck paid for the coffee and left a dime tip, which was generous, because the two cups of coffee only came to a dime. He thanked the waitress, and he and Ann got in the Studebaker and headed north out of town.

They found the church without any trouble. Ann pulled into the gravel parking lot beside the church, and they went through the front door into the foyer. It had hat shelves and coat racks along both sides. There were double doors leading into the sanctuary, which was plain but neat. There was a carpeted main aisle that ran from the doors to the altar. There were neat rows of oak pews on both sides of the aisle. Secondary aisles ran along both sides of the church between the pews and the windows. On the raised platform in front, there was an altar, a lectern, and behind that were two rows of chairs for the choir. There was a fairly new piano on the left side of the platform, and a rather plump colored lady was seated at it. She wasn't aware of the visitors. She hummed softly to herself as she thumbed through a hymn book, picking out hymns for Sunday's service. She was obviously the music director.

"Hello!" Ann called.

The startled lady looked up from her hymn book. When she saw who it was, she grinned.

"What can I do for you nice folks?" she said, closing her hymn book.

"Hi," Buck said, offering her his hand, "I'm Buck Pettit, and this is my wife, Ann."

She stood up and shook hands with them. Buck explained that they needed to talk to the Reverend Stevenson and his wife.

"He's back in his study, I'll go fetch him for you." She flashed a big friendly smile and disappeared through a door behind the piano.

The Reverend George Stevenson soon appeared. He was taller than average, with a slender, athletic build. In his early 40s, he appeared younger. His hair was clipped short and graying slightly at the temples. He had a very engaging smile and greeted them warmly.

"I'm George Stevenson. Miss Emma said you wanted to talk to Thelma and me. She has gone over to the house to get her. It's just next door, so she won't be long." He offered his hand.

Buck and Ann shook his hand.

"My study is rather small, or I would invite you folks back there to talk. Would it be all right if we just sat on this front pew?"

Buck assured him that it was fine. He could see the fear creeping into the Reverend's eyes. He could also see where Milton got is precise diction and wide vocabulary. Just then the front doors opened and Thelma Stevenson walked down the aisle. She was an attractive woman in a printed cotton dress and low heels, a couple of years younger than her husband.

She laughed. "I was out in the vegetable garden when Emma found me."

She shook hands with the Pettits; her smile belied her fear. They all sat down in the front pew, the Pettits facing the Stevensons.

Buck spoke first. "We're here about your son, Milton." He tried to keep his voice as calm as possible.

There was a gasp from Thelma. "Is he all right?" Her voice was breaking.

"Yes, he's all right, but he's in jail." Buck tried to assure her.

Thelma almost fainted. George put his arms around her. "What happened?" he asked, his voice starting to crack.

Ann slid over and took Thelma's hand while Buck related all the events that had taken place since last Saturday.

Thelma started crying. "They'll send him to prison for the rest of his life!" she wailed.

Buck assured her that everything was being done to keep that from happening. He told her that Milton had a lawyer, and that his preliminary hearing was tomorrow at 10:00. He said he had another suspect, and even if Milton was brought to trial, that there was a very good chance he would be acquitted. He knew he shouldn't have told her all that, but he just couldn't help trying to ease her pain.

George was stoic. He knew in his mind that anytime a black man was accused of murdering a white woman, the Klan would always be there to cause trouble. He assured Buck that he and Thelma would be in Warrensburg tomorrow at 10:00. He was already planning to bring a caravan of Negroes with them. He thanked them for making the trip all the way to the Roy community to tell them the news. They said their goodbyes out by the car, and Ann pulled out onto Route C. She headed south to Slater.

* * * * *

It was 11:15 when Buck and Ann left the church. They took Missouri 240 over to Rocheport, where they hit U.S. Highway 40. From there it was only 15 miles in to Columbia. They arrived at Ann Marie's sorority house at 12:40. From the girl at the desk they learned that she had had a snack earlier and had gone to the library to study. They found her in the library studying for finals. She was a biology major with a minor in music.

They strolled the campus and talked. Ann Marie was in a good mood. She felt good about her grades and had been asked to play a piano solo at the graduation services. She had a 3:00 class, so they said their goodbyes in front of the library at 2:45, and Ann and Buck headed back to Warrensburg.

They pulled up in back of the police station at 4:15. Ann went up to the apartment, and Buck went looking for Clarence. He found him sitting on a corner of Darlene's desk eating an ice cream cone. He was minding the phone while Darlene went to the restroom. As soon as Darlene came back, they got in the patrol car and headed out to the Wilhelm farm.

They found Russell out in his machine shed beside the barn welding a tine back on his cultivator. He was getting ready to cultivate his corn.

"Hello!" Buck yelled as he beat on the door of the shed to get Russell's attention.

Russell stopped welding and raised the welder's hood he wore over his face. When he saw who it was, he turned his torch off and stood up.

"You're all dressed up, Chief, what's the occasion?"

"I just got back from Columbia. Ann and I went over to visit with Ann Marie." He didn't tell him about the visit with Milton's parents.

"Can I get you a beer or something?" Russell took off his welding gloves and shook hands with them.

"No, Clarence and I are on duty, and besides, we just have a minute."

"Shall we go up to the house and sit on the porch?"

"No, we can talk right here." Buck took his note book out. "You told me the other day that the day Miss Wilson was killed you came to town about 6:00. Is that right?"

"Yes, sir, that's right."

"You also said you went right straight to Walker's Cafe and ate, is that correct?"

92

"Yes, sir, what's wrong?"

"Russell, we have a witness who says she saw you drive by Reese school at 6:10 that Friday afternoon. Do you have anything you want to add to your statement?"

Russell's face turned redder than normal. He looked down at his shoes.

"Yes, I guess I do. I did get to town at 6:00, but I had seen that school teacher when I was at the bank earlier that afternoon. She was so pretty, and I overheard her tell Mr. Breckenridge that she would be working late that night, so I drove by the school to see if I could see her."

"Did you go in?"

"No, I couldn't get up the nerve, so then I went up to Walker's and ate supper. It was about 6:15 when I got to Walker's. You can ask Delta, she's the one that waited on me. I sat in that booth up by the front door." Russell was scared, he knew that he'd been caught in a lie.

Buck looked him right in the eye. "Did you kill Margaret Wilson?"

Russell's knees almost buckled, and he dropped the welding torch in his hand.

"No, sir, I did not." His mouth was so dry, he could barely manage to get it out.

Buck persisted. "Come on, Russell, get it off your chest, you'll feel better. You did kill Margaret Wilson, didn't you?"

Russell sat down on the frame of the cultivator he was repairing and covered his face with his hands.

"No, no, I didn't kill her!" he sobbed. "I wanted to meet her, I wanted to be her friend, and now she's dead, and I'll never get to be her friend," his voice trailed off into a whining sob.

"That's all for now, Russell, but stay close to home. We'll probably want to talk to you again."

"Yes, sir," he said weakly.

On the way back to town, Clarence said, "I thought you had him for a while there, Chief. I expected him to break down and admit it any minute."

"He didn't do it. I can tell by his eyes."

"He looked guilty to me, Chief."

"No, I think he was telling the truth. I can tell when someone is lying by watching their eyes."

"What about the witnesses? Why did he go by the school, not once, but two or three times?"

"The witnesses saw what they saw. They didn't see him go in the school, or witness the actual killing. As for going by the school, I think he was smitten by a pretty woman and wanted to get better acquainted with her. I think he's lonely out on that farm and wanted some female companionship."

"Will we be talking to him again?"

"We'll see."

GREAT CHIEFS
OF THE
AMERICAN WEST

Ouray
(Utes)

Cochise
(Chiricahua-Apache)

Geronimo
(Apache)

Little Raven
(Arapahos)

Sitting Bull
(Hunkpapa Sioux)

Rain-In-The-Face
(Sioux)

Chief - Joseph
(Nez Perce)

Quanah Parker
Comanche

GREAT AMERICAN INDIAN CHIEFS

DONTOM, Inc., P.O. Box 272, Manitou Springs, CO 80829
www.dontominc.com

Ouray
(Utes)

Cochise
(Chiricahua-Apache)

Geronimo
(Apache)

Little Raven
(Arapahos)

SPACE BELOW RESERVED FOR U.S. POSTAL SERVICE

267 PC9   0910-11

0 34504 40002 8

6

THE HEARING

FRIDAY MORNING AT 9:45, Harry Foster and two deputies took Milton to the courthouse. Harry didn't handcuff him, as was customary. He didn't see a need. He put Milton in the back seat of the patrol car with a deputy on each side. He figured that if the Klan made any trouble and Milton was forced to flee, he would be better off without handcuffs.

They went in the west entrance, and up the stairs to the second floor courtroom. A few Klansmen were waiting at the north entrance, but Buck had Milton in the courtroom before they realized their mistake. The Klan knew the judge wouldn't allow them in the courtroom, so they went around to the west entrance and waited for Milton to come out.

Gerald Essex and his assistant prosecutor were already there, sitting at the prosecution table. Rudolph Eisenstein was visiting with George and Thelma Stevenson. He had been sitting at the defense table trying to ignore Gerald, when he saw them come in. He insisted that they sit in the first row behind the rail on the defense side of the courtroom, so they could be near Milton.

Judge Whitfield had given Harry specific instructions not to allow any Klansmen in the courtroom. Likewise, he didn't want the courtroom overloaded with Negroes. He had ordered all men to be frisked for weapons and any large purses searched. As a result of his statement and the Sheriff's deputy's actions, there were very few in attendance other than the principals. Three colored men and two suspicious-looking white men were in the gallery. Buck and Ann sat on the front row next to the Stevensons. There were three reporters on the front row behind the prosecution—one each from the local *Star Journal, The Kansas City Star Times* and *The Independence Examiner.*

As Harry and his deputies came in the side door by the jury box with Milton, Thelma let out a gasp and tried to go through the gate to get to him, but one of the Sheriff's deputies acting as assistant bailiff stopped her. Rudolph took her back to her seat, but she would not be placated. When Milton heard her trying to get to him, he caught her eye and smiled to reassure her, although he was frightened nearly out of his wits. This is exactly why Harry had avoided the handcuffs. He had seen mothers react to their sons being in handcuffs before, and he wanted everybody in the courtroom to be as calm as possible.

Finally, George and Rudolph got her settled enough so Rudolph could take his place at the defense table, just as the bailiff called for everyone to rise.

"Oyez, Oyez, Oyez!" he said in a loud voice. "The Circuit Court of Johnson County, State of Missouri will now be in session, the Honorable Emerson Whitfield presiding! All rise!" Everyone in the courtroom stood.

Judge Whitfield took the bench. He had the reputation of being a fair, but firm judge. He lived in Clinton and served as Circuit Judge in both Henry and Johnson Counties. He had a full docket, so he didn't waste any time.

"You may be seated," he said. "You will notice that the jury box is empty. This is not a trial. It is a preliminary hearing, to find out if there is enough evidence against the defendant to bind him over for trial in Circuit Court. I will be the one to decide. I will allow each side to call up to three witnesses. I expect this to be over by noon. In case it's not, we will adjourn for lunch at 12 noon, and convene again at 1:30 p.m. If all this is clear to both attorneys, we can begin."

He looked over his glasses at both lawyers, and when neither one said anything, he banged his gavel.

"The prosecutor will go first."

Gerald stood and straightened his tie. He wore a new blue seersucker suit that looked like he had bought it just for this occasion. He picked up a yellow legal pad from the table before him and came up on the balls of his feet to appear taller than he was.

Judge Whitfield had seen Gerald's strutting and preening in court before. He would allow it as long as it didn't slow the proceedings.

"Your honor, the prosecution will prove without a doubt that the prisoner before the bar, one Negro (he was prone to use the word 'nigger,' but caught himself just in time), by the name of Milton Stevenson, did willfully, and with malice in his heart, murder and rape Miss Margaret Wilson."

The judge banged his gavel. "Mr. Essex, we know the nature of the crime, just how do you intend to prove the accused did it?"

Gerald's face started to redden. "We plan to call three witnesses who will testify that the accused was not only at the scene of the crime, but was seen leaving the building where the crime was committed, with the body."

You could hear a gasp from Thelma. "No, no!" she cried.

The judge banged his gavel. "No outbursts in the courtroom, please!"

Rudolph was taken completely by surprise. He looked over at Milton as if to say, "Where did this come from?"

Milton shook his head no. He leaned over to Rudolph and whispered, "I don't know what he's talking about, I didn't even see a body."

Rudolph tried to remain calm, so as not to frighten Milton or his mother. He didn't know exactly what Gerald was going to pull, but he knew that he was devious and would do anything to get publicity.

Buck was surprised, too. He looked over at Harry Foster, who was just shaking his head as if to say, "This is ridiculous."

They had both canvassed the neighborhood around the school, and also around the city dump. They had run across no such witness.

Judge Whitfield banged his gavel and motioned to Gerald. "Call your first witness."

"The State calls Charlie Shanks." Gerald had tried to lower his voice to sound more authoritative.

The bailiff went to the witness room and got Charlie. He sort of swaggered over to the witness chair where the bailiff swore him in. The smirk on his face said, "We missed you Monday night, but we got you now."

He testified that about 7:15 on Friday evening, May 15, he had been sitting on his front porch, right across the street from the school, and just about dark he had seen Milton come from behind the school pushing a two-wheel cart. The cart had what looked like a 50-gallon drum on it, and he saw a woman's foot sticking above the rim of the drum.

"How did you know it was a woman's foot?" Gerald asked.

"Because it had women's shoe on it," Charlie said with a grin on his face. "In fact, it was Miss Wilson's shoe, 'cause I had seen her wear it around the school before."

Gerald looked over at the defense table with a smirk on his face. "No more questions, Your Honor."

Judge Whitfield looked over his glasses at Rudolph. "Does the defense have any questions for this witness?"

Rudolph stood. "Yes, Your Honor, I do." He paused for a moment looking at his notes, then turned to Charlie.

"Mr. Shanks, you say it was about dark when you say you saw the accused come out of the school with the body of Miss Wilson?"

"That's what I said."

"How far, would you say, your front porch is from the back of the school house? A hundred feet, 150 feet, 200 feet? How far?"

Gerald jumped to his feet. "I object, Your Honor. Counsel is leading the witness!"

Judge Whitfield peered at Gerald over his glasses. "Overruled, Mr. Shanks is a witness for the prosecution, and the attorney for the defense is allowed to lead the witness. If you were paying attention when I was giving my instructions, you would know that this is not a trial. This is a hearing, and I intend to let the witnesses talk with as few interruptions as possible. Answer the question, Mr. Shanks."

Gerald's face was beet red when he sat down. He was angry at the judge's remarks.

Charley Shanks was mad, too. How dare this long-nosed Jew question his testimony. To him, Jews were worse than niggers. He interlaced his fingers and put his hands in his lap to keep from taking a swing at Rudolph.

"Mr. Shanks, you may answer the question now," Judge Whitfield insisted.

"Uh," Charlie stammered, "it was about that."

"About what?" Rudolph remained patient.

"About a hunnerd feet."

Rudolph went back to the defense table and got a pad and pencil. "Let's see now, your house is about ten feet from the street, the street is at least 50 feet wide, there is another 30 feet from the edge of the street to the front door of the school, the school is about 75 feet deep. That's about 165 feet. Does that sound about right, Mr. Shanks?"

"Uh, I guess so." Charlie was really getting angry. His nostrils flared and his jaw muscles tightened.

"Okay, the accused was about 160 feet away, and it was getting dark. Are you absolutely sure that it was the accused you saw, or just a person that looked somewhat like the accused?"

"It was him, damn it, I know it was. Don't try to tell me who I saw and who I didn't see."

"Also, at that distance, and at that time of night, are you sure you could see well enough to tell that the shoe you saw was even a woman's shoes, much less Miss Wilson's?"

"Yes, I'm sure!" Charlie glared at Milton when he said it.

So much hate in that man, Rudolph thought as he dismissed Charlie with a hand gesture. "That's all I have for this witness, Your Honor."

Gerald Essex called two more witnesses. One was a lady that lived over on Gay Street who said she saw the same man go by her house pushing a two-wheeled cart with a metal drum in it. She said he had a hard time pushing it up Old Town Hill because there was so much weight on it. Even though it was almost dark, she swore that it was Milton.

Buck nudged Ann. "I know that lady. Her husband works down at the feed mill on Pine. Rumor has it that he is a member of the Klan."

The last witness was a man who claimed he was coming out of the grocery store on the corner of Gay and Main Streets just in time to see the same man wheel the cart into the dump.

Rudolph knew they were all lying, so he didn't cross-examine the last two witnesses. Instead, he called to the witness stand the lady that lived on Gay Street who was watering flowers in her back yard that Friday night.

She said she saw Milton go from the baseball diamond almost to the school and back twice, both times chasing a baseball. She said she didn't see him go into the school. Rudolph pointed out that this witness was much closer to the scene than Charlie Shanks. Gerald tried to object, but was immediately gaveled down by Judge Whitfield.

Rudolph's last two witnesses were the ones who had seen the dark blue Packard circling the school. He was trying to let the judge know that there was at least one other suspect out there, and that it was an ongoing investigation.

Gerald had decided not to cross-examine any of Rudolph's witnesses. He was confident that he had given the judge enough evidence to bind Milton over for trial.

Judge Whitfield banged his gavel and called for a 15-minute recess while he made his decision. He went back to his chambers, but no one left the courtroom. He poured himself a glass of water and studied his notes. He really wanted to throw the case out for lack of evidence, but he knew the Klan would be furious. He finally decided to bind the defendant over for trial. As much as he disliked the prosecuting attorney, he decided it was best. Like Rudolph, he knew in his heart that the prosecution witnesses were lying. He figured that by calling for a trial, it would serve three purposes. It would give the police more time to look for other suspects, it would give Rudolph time to investigate Gerald's three witnesses, so he could discredit them in open court, and finally, it would give Milton the opportunity to clear his name completely.

"All rise," the bailiff said in his usual loud voice.

Judge Whitfield took the bench and banged his gavel. "This court is back in session." He paused and studied his notes one more time. "It is my decision that the suspect be bound over for trial in Circuit Court on the charge of first degree murder."

Thelma gasped, but Milton turned and smiled to reassure her. Buck and Ann looked at each other in sheer disbelief. Harry Foster just shook his head.

Judge Whitfield continued. "Trial will be set for Monday, June 22., at 10:00 a.m. The prisoner will be remanded to the Johnson County Jail to await trial. Bailiff, take charge of the prisoner." He banged his gavel. "This hearing is adjourned."

When Harry and his deputies took Milton out the west door of the courthouse, the Klan was waiting. There were about 30 of them, and they tried to shove the deputies aside to get to Milton. It was four against 30. Harry took his pistol out and fired in the air. "Back off," he yelled, "or somebody's going to get hurt."

They all backed down about two steps. Charlie Shanks wasn't among them as he had just testified in court, but there was an out-of-town Klansman in front of the group who looked to Harry as if he was in charge. He wore a white shirt and a tie. *Probably a union organizer from*

St. Louis, Harry thought. He took a step up toward Harry to confront him. Holding his revolver high in his right hand away from the crowd, he put his big left hand in the man's face and shoved him as hard as he could. The man staggered backward all the way to the bottom of the steps and took five others with him.

Just then Clarence pulled up behind them in the police cruiser and hit the siren. The men jumped, as it was pretty loud, and they weren't expecting it. Clarence got out and drew his revolver.

"Need any help, Sheriff?" he asked in a loud voice.

"Not right now, Clarence, but I might in about three minutes if these men don't clear out of here and let us pass with our prisoner."

Just then Buck walked out of the courthouse to see what was going on, and another Sheriff's patrol car pulled up from the jail with two more deputies in it. Now, it was eight armed men against 30, and since cowards usually can't stand anywhere near even odds, they began to disperse.

Harry and his men stood on the steps until the mob had all gone to their cars; then they took Milton back to the jail and locked him in the same holding cell they had him in before.

* * * * *

Buck got in the patrol car with Clarence. "Let's go to Reese School and see if the janitor is still there. We haven't questioned him about the murder yet."

"Do you know his name?"

Buck pulled out his notebook. "I've got Amos Swenson written down."

Clarence pulled the patrol car around in back and parked near the steps that came up from the furnace room. Amos' old pick-up truck was backed up to the big cinder pile next to the steps, and he was using a pitchfork to load the cinders into the truck. When he saw the patrol car drive up, he stopped to wipe his forehead with a big blue bandanna from his hip pocket.

Buck waved at him as he got out of the car. "Kind of warm for May, isn't it?"

"Ya, it sure is," Amos replied in an obvious Swedish accent. He was a medium-built man in his mid-60s with white hair and big walrus mustache to match. He had come to the United States in 1878 at the age of seven with his parents. They were farmers and didn't like New York, so they had settled in Missouri. Amos was the eldest child and had met and married a Johnson County girl in 1890. When his parents, along with his younger siblings, moved on to Lindsborg, Kansas in 1895, he stayed in Missouri and moved his little family into a small frame house on West Gay Street. He and his wife still lived there. Their three children had families of their own.

"Cleaning up the cinders from the winter's coal burning, I see. Why don't you use a scoop shovel?"

"I do ven I get to da fine stuff," Amos replied.

"Looks like your coal pile is about gone."

"Ya, de bring da coal in da fall und pile it here." He indicated the small pile of coal left over from winter. "All vinter da coal pile goes down und da cinder pile goes up. After school's out in da spring, I bring my old truck and haul da cinders to da county barn. Dey mash 'em up und put 'em on da roads."

Buck took his notebook out. "Amos, I'm Chief Pettit, and this is Officer Slayton. We would like to ask you some questions about what you saw or heard here the night Miss Wilson was killed. It was a week ago this evening, do you remember that night?"

Amos leaned on his pitchfork and shook his head. "Oh ya, dat vas terrible vat he done to dat young voman."

"I want you to think back and tell us what you did and what you saw, from the time Miss Wilson got back from the bank, until the time you locked up and went home."

Amos stuck his pitch fork in the cinder pile. "Come, I show you."

He took them around to the front doors and unlocked them. They were big double doors that opened into an entrance area. To the left and right were classrooms. Ahead, on the left side a stairway went to the second floor. Along the right side, a wide hall led to a big double classroom across the back of the building. In front of that classroom was an open area with three doors. One door, directly under the stairway, led down to the basement and the girls' restroom. Along the west wall was another door under the stairway leading down to the boys' restrooms. To the right of that was a door leading to the furnace room.

Amos took them into the classroom on the left. "Dis is Miss Vilson's classroom. Ven she come back from da bank, I check to see if she is okay. Dis vas about 4:00. She vas sitting right dere at her desk vorking."

Buck and Clarence looked around the room. There were no signs of a struggle. Her desk and chair were in the north, or front end of the room in the northwest corner. All it had on it was a small Mason jar full of assorted pencils, a stack of report cards and a writing pad with a pencil laying across it. There were blackboards along the north and east sides of the room, and windows along the other two sides.

All of the student's desks and chairs were where they were supposed to be. Buck turned to Amos. "Did you clean this room after Miss Wilson was killed?"

"No, I clean it while she vas at da bank. She told me she vould be back about 4:00. She said she had to catch a bus downtown at 8:00, and vould leave here about 7:30. I say I will stay 'til you leave and then lock it up."

Buck opened the top left drawer of the desk. All it contained was a half-used box of Kleenex. He opened the big drawer below it. There was her purse, right where she had left it. Surprised, Buck looked up at Clarence. When he opened it, there was $200 in $20 bills in a bank envelope. He also found a bus ticket to Carrollton and a small coin purse containing $6 and some change. Clarence and Amos stood silent while Buck went through it. In another compartment of the purse, he found a lipstick, a small box of face powder with a powder puff in it, a small round box of rouge, a comb and a few bobby pins.

"Well, we know the motive wasn't robbery," Buck said to no one in particular. He handed the purse to Clarence. "Let's take this down to the station when we leave. I want everything in it catalogued; then I'll lock it up in my desk and figure out a way to get it to her parents."

Clarence put the handles of the purse over his left arm so he wouldn't lose it.

"Whoever killed her took the time to straighten things up before he took her out of here," he said.

"I was thinking the same thing," Buck said as he looked at the writing tablet on the desk. "This looks like she was writing a note to the principal, Mrs. McKnight. It looks like she was listing some of the children who had made low grades, and her plans to correct it next school year. She must have taught the second grade, too."

"Ya, she did. She vas a good teacher," Amos interjected.

Buck turned to Amos. "When did you last see Miss Wilson?"

"Ven I go upstairs to clean."

"What time was that?"

"It vas about 5:00."

"Are you sure?"

"Ya, I'm sure. I stick my head in the door and tell her I go upstairs to clean, und if she need me to yust holler. I tell her I vill stay 'til she leave to catch da bus. Ven I start upstairs, the courthouse clock strike 5:00. I take out my vatch to check, and it is right on the money." He took out his gold pocket watch and proudly showed it to Buck and Clarence.

"Dis vatch is solid gold. It belonged to my father. It vas made in Germany. It keeps very goot time."

Buck fondled the watch, admiring the engraving on the case. On the face was printed 21 Juwel in tiny letters. "Yes, it is a very good watch," he said.

"Tack," the old man said, reverting back to the Swedish word for 'thanks.' "Come, I show you upstairs."

At the head of the stairs there was another open area to match the one downstairs, then double doors opening into a big classroom. There was a wide hall leading along the stairway to the two classrooms in the front of the building. They were exactly like the ones downstairs.

"Dere is only one teacher up here. De big room dey use for singing practice. Miss Yonson teach in dis room." He indicated the classroom on the left. "De other room is use for storage. Ve used to have six teachers, but now ve only have four. Ven de depression come, ve have to cut down."

There was a heavy rope dangling down from a hole in the ceiling between the two windows that looked down on Market Street.

"Dis is vere I ring de bell," Amos said with a grin. He gave the rope a tug, and a big bell clanged overhead. "All de kids can hear it for blocks."

Amos took them into Miss Johnson's room. There were two windows looking down on Market street and four along the Warren Street side. Buck walked over and looked down on Warren Street. He had a thought.

"Amos, when you were cleaning up here last Friday, did you happen to see any cars parked around the building?"

"Cars? Ya, I see a big blue von. It vas parked right down dere." He pointed down to indicate it was parked next to the building on Warren Street.

104

"Did you see anyone get in or out?"

"No, I vasn't vatching it, I vas too busy vorking. It vasn't dere ven I go home though."

"What time was that?" Buck asked.

"Vell, let's see. I tink it vas 7:30. I finish up, up here, und de courthouse clock strike, und I look at my vatch. It said 7:30, so I say to myself, 'It's time for Miss Vilson to go catch her bus.' I go downstairs und look in her room, und she vas gone. I say to myself, 'She has already gone to get her bus,' so I lock de door und go home."

"Was the car there when you left?" Buck's heart was pounding.

"No, it vas gone. It vas getting dark out, but I didn't see it."

"Could you have seen it if it had been there, considering that it was almost dark?"

"Oh ya, dere is a street light at de corner."

"One other thing, Amos, did you ever see a two-wheeled push cart with a colored man pushing it go down the alley in back of the school?"

"Oh ya, dat's Villie Cates."

Buck's heart skipped a beat. "Willie Cates, is he colored?"

"Oh, ya, he goes down de alley twice a veek. Tree of de ladies who live over on Gay street save dere garbage for him. Dey put it in a slop bucket mit a lid on it to keep de flies out und set it out by de back fence. He feeds it to his swine. He buys baby pigs in the spring und feeds dem all vinter. Ven dey are fat, he keep one for meat, und sells de rest. He make a little money dat vey."

Buck glanced at Clarence, who was nodding his head yes. "What days does he collect from those ladies?"

"Every Tuesday und Friday. He vorks days, so it's usually 6:00 or 7:00 ven he comes by. On other days, he has other houses he collects from. Some evenings, he gets a whole barrel full. He feeds six or eight swine at a time."

"How do you know him?"

"He vorks for the city, mostly at de dump, but sometimes on de streets, spreading gravel und tings like dat. Sometime ven I have a broken desk dat I can't fix, I just trow it avay. I give him a nickel und he takes it to de dump for me. De school gives me my nickel back. Sometimes, in de vinter, I see him trow a few lumps of coal on his cart as he goes by de school, but I don't say nothing. He has a vife und tree or four little ones, und they need to keep varm, too, ya? I like Villie, he is a hard vorker."

"Do you know where he lives?" Buck was furiously taking notes.

"Oh ya, he lives in a little house close to de dump. It's yust off Main Street. I don't tink he has an address. About where North Street ends, dere is a lane dat goes back a vays off Main Street. His house is down dat lane. He has his back yard fenced in for de swine."

Buck thanked Amos profusely and put his notebook in his breast pocket. He nodded to Clarence, and they left the school. As they passed the jail on the way back to the station, they were jeered by the same men who had caused the problem at the courthouse. Clarence cruised right by them, and neither he nor Buick made eye contact with any of them. There was no need to antagonize them.

Buck started to get out of the patrol car, then turned to Clarence. "I think the best time to talk to Willie Cates would be this evening when he makes his rounds. This is Friday, and if, as Amos said, he comes down that alley behind the school to pick up garbage this evening, we could get a first hand view of the man and his cart."

"We sure could, do you want to go with me?"

"Yes, I do, and I think we should take Rudolph Eisenstein with us. He'll probably want to line him up as a witness for the defense."

"What time do you want to go?"

"You're off at 6:00 today, aren't you?"

"Yes, but I don't mind working a few hours overtime if it will help the case. I'll pick you up here at 5:55. Will you call Mr. Eisenstein?"

"Yes, if he's free, I'll have him here."

The courthouse clock struck 1:00 as Clarence drove off. Buck locked Margaret Wilson's purse up in his desk, then dashed up the stairs to have lunch with his sweetheart.

* * * * *

Harry Foster was sitting in his office at the jail when Elsie Reed came to the door. Elsie was Harry's secretary, daytime dispatcher, booking officer, and anything else that needed to be done around the jail. Sort of like Darlene at the Police Department. The door was open, so she knocked on the frame. Harry looked up from the file on his desk.

"Sheriff, Lois Huff is up front wanting to talk to you."

106

"I wonder what she wants?" He looked at his watch, it was 2:15. "I don't know, I think she has something for you." "Send her back." Lois had come directly from her job as waitress at Dub's Café. She was an attractive woman in her early 30s. Divorced and the mother of a ten-year-old boy, she lived with her widowed mother, who took care of the boy while she worked. Although she had lots of male admirers, she never encouraged any of them. She was serious about her job, because it supported her, her son and her mother. She was also serious about her future, and for the past three years had been taking night classes at CSTC toward a degree in education. She figured she was about two years away from a teacher's job if she could find one. Meanwhile, her $7 a week salary plus the $2 to $3 a week in tips was keeping the family going. She worked six days a week from 6:00 a.m. to 2:00 p.m., and considered herself lucky. Lots of waitresses worked longer hours than she did for less money. Dub was good to his help.

"Hi, Sheriff, I bring a peace offering," she said sweetly.

"Peace offering?"

She set a cardboard box on the chair by his desk. "Yes, I know I was the reason you and Chief Pettit left the café the other day. You wanted privacy, and I kept butting in. I'm sorry." She opened the box and set two beautiful home-baked pies on his desk.

"Wow!" Harry was starting to salivate.

"First, let me explain how this came about. Effie Banks is the colored woman who helps Dub out in the kitchen. She washes the dishes, but most of all, she bakes pies."

"I know that, the main reason I eat at Dub's is because of Effie's pies."

"Well, we were talking early this morning, before we got busy, and she asked me if I knew how the colored boy was getting along in jail, and did he need anything. I told her I didn't know very much, but I did know you well enough, I thought, to come over here and ask you."

"It's okay, Lois, I don't mind. You didn't need to bring me anything."

"She wanted to know if it was all right for her to bake him a nice fresh peach pie, and I told her that would be fine, and if she didn't mind, to bake you your favorite . . ."

Buck interrupted with a grin. "Lemon meringue!" "Yes," she smiled. "I offered to pay Dub for them, but he wouldn't have it. So, the peach is for the colored boy, uh." "Milton Stevenson."

"Yes, Milton Stevenson, and the lemon is for you, compliments of Dub's Café."

Harry stood and picked up the peach pie. "Come with me," he said. He took her back to Milton's cell.

"Milton, I have a surprise for you."

Milton was sitting on his bunk reading a book that Aunt Belle had brought him on Wednesday. He stood up and smiled at Lois and Harry.

"Milton, this is Lois Huff, and she has brought you one of Effie Banks' famous peach pies from Dub's Café." He held our the pie for him to see.

"That's very nice of you and Miss Effie, but I can't eat a whole pie. Would you and the sheriff care to join me?"

Harry snapped his fingers. "That's a great idea. Let's go to the break room and make a fresh pot of coffee, and Elsie and the men on duty here can join us." He unlocked Milton's cell, and the three of them went up front.

The break room was in the northeast corner of the building with a window facing Market Street. There were heavy lace curtains at the window, so you could see out, but people out on the street couldn't see in. Elsie cut the pies in fifths so every one could have a slice. She found some paper plates in a cupboard left over from a birthday party and got out some forks. Word got around the jail that there was pie in the break room, so in addition to the four of them, Hal Griggs, the jailer, and his deputy came up front, along with the trustee from the basement.

Ed Grafton, the trustee, had received a year in jail on a domestic battery charge, and since he was an experienced mechanic, he was given the task of maintaining the county's four patrol cars. He worked in the basement garage in the day and was locked up in his cell at night.

They were enjoying their pie and coffee when a shot rang out and a bullet crashed through the window, narrowly missing Harry and burying itself in the opposite wall. Everybody ducked, and pie and coffee went flying.

"Is anybody hurt?" Harry asked tersely. No answer. "Okay, everybody stay down!" He crawled on his hands and knees until he was out in the hall; then staying low, he ran back to stairs leading to the basement. His intention was to go out the basement door and slip along the retaining wall to the front to see if he could spot where the shot came from. Just as he reached the side door, Ed Grafton came in.

Harry was angry. "Where the hell have you been?"

"I . . . er . . . went out to see where the shot came from."

"Lay down on your stomach on the floor, I'll deal with you later!"

Harry dashed out the door, and keeping low, he ran to the front of the jail. He heard tires screeching on the pavement as he ran along the retaining wall. When he got to the front, there was no one there. Two cars were speeding west on Market, but were too far for Harry to see who was in them. A pick-up truck was turning north on Maynard Street, and that was it. All of the Klan was gone.

Harry went up the steps and in the front door. "It's me!" he yelled as he went into the break room. "Somebody fired a rifle at us, then they all took off."

Elsie and Lois started cleaning up the pie and coffee mess. Harry told the deputy jailer to take Milton back to his cell. Milton was visibly shaken as he was led to the back. Harry motioned for Hal Griggs to follow him, and they went down the basement steps. Ed Grafton was still lying on his stomach.

Harry was still angry. "Hal, this man is a traitor. He ratted to the Klan about our little coffee break, and probably told them that Milton would be there, too."

"Oh, no, sir, I didn't tell anybody," Ed whined.

"Shut up, I wasn't talking to you!" Harry never talked to people in that manner, but he was making an exception for Ed. "Hal, look there on the work bench. There's his pie and coffee.

While we werc enjoying our break, he slips down here, deposits his pie and coffee on the bench and then goes around the side and signals the Klan that this would be a good time to get Milton."

"Oh, no, sir. I wouldn't do that!"

"Hal, take this vermin to his cell, I can't stand the sight of him any longer. When I cool down, I want to talk to him."

Hal reached down and hand cuffed Ed's hands behind him, then rolled him over and angrily told him to get up. Ed knew his trustee days were over.

* * * * *

109

Harry went back up to the break room. Elsie and Lois had cleaned up the mess and were beginning to calm down.

Lois said, "Harry, I'm sorry, I probably started all this by bringing those pies over."

Harry was standing on a chair digging the spent bullet out of the plaster with his pocket knife. He got down with the bullet in his hand. "Don't blame yourself for the actions of a bunch of idiots," he said softly, as if to make up for the harsh treatment of Ed Grafton. "Tell Effie the pies were delicious, and that we appreciate her thoughtfulness."

"I'll do that, Harry," she said rather hesitantly, suddenly realizing that she had called him Harry instead of Sheriff.

Harry picked up the phone and called Buck Pettit. "Did you hear about our shooting?" he asked.

"No, what happened?"

"We were in our break room having a little pie and coffee, and someone fired a rifle shot through our front window."

"Anybody hurt?"

"No, I think it was just meant to scare us, or for revenge for you breaking that guy's wrist, although it could have hurt, or even killed someone."

"How long ago did it happen?"

"About ten or fifteen minutes ago. I dug the bullet out of the wall. It looks like a 22 caliber to me. That's what makes me think it was meant to scare instead of kill. If whoever did this meant to do a lot of harm, they would have used a 30-30, or a 30-06 deer rifle, and fired off more than one round."

"They probably wouldn't have done it in broad daylight either."

"You're right, Buck, but what concerns me is, I've got a Klansman, or Klan sympathizer, in my jail."

"Oh, who is that?"

"Ed Grafton, do you know him?"

"Oh, yes, he used to work or our patrol cars when he worked at Bill Harris' Garage. I think Bill fired him because he drank too much. I didn't like him because he was sneaky. Always trying to cheat somebody. What's he in for?"

"He came home drunk one night and beat the hell out of Susie. The judge gave him a year in jail and fined him $50. I made him a trustee so he could work on our cars, but I may put him in solitary after what he pulled."

"What did he do?"

Harry told him what had happened at the jail. "I think he slipped out the basement door and told the Klan boys out front that Milton was in the break room, and it would be a good time to scare him into a confession or something."

"Can you prove it?"

"No, but I'm convinced that's what happened. What have you been up to?"

Buck told him about their plan to stake out the school to see if they could actually see Willie Cates push his cart down the alley behind the school. "If it's like Amos said, he would make a powerful witness for the defense in Milton's trial."

"He sure would," Harry mused. "Need any help?"

"No, there'll be three of us. I think that's enough, but thanks anyway."

* * * * *

At 5:45, Buck drove the Studebaker around to the front of the police station. He didn't want to use a patrol car to do the stake-out, as he didn't want to arouse any suspicion from the neighbors, especially Charlie Shanks. He had called Rudolph Eisenstein right after lunch, and he had said he would like to go with them.

It was still early, so Ann invited them up to the apartment for coffee. She and Buck had eaten supper at 5:00, and she had some cinnamon rolls left over. She had baked them that afternoon, so they were still fresh. She, Buck, Clarence and Rudolph sat around the kitchen table and discussed the murder case.

None of them thought Milton was guilty, but there was a vigorous discussion about who else could, or would have done it. Clarence thought the Klan had killed her so they could blame it on a colored boy. Buck and Rudolph both leaned toward Russell Wilhelm. Ann had her doubts about either of their theories. She still thought that someone they didn't even suspect at this time had done it, and that if they kept looking a clue would turn up that would divulge who the real killer was.

* * * * *

At 6:15, the Studebaker pulled up in front of the Rutledge house. The girls were sitting on the front porch listening to boogie-woogie music on their phonograph and working on school lessons. They were having tests all week. Their parents were already home from the store, and their mother was fixing supper.

Buck walked up to the porch. "Hi, I'm Buck Pettit, Chief of police, and out in the car is Officer Slayton and an attorney by the name of Rudolph Eisenstein. We will be parked in front of your house for about an hour. Don't be alarmed; this has nothing to do with you good people. We're just observing the neighborhood for a while. We'll be gone in about an hour, maybe a little longer. Do you have any questions?"

The girls shook their heads, gathered up their books, turned off the phonograph and went into the house without saying a word. Buck went back out to the car and a couple of minutes later, he saw Jim Rutledge peeking out the front door at them.

Two houses up the street Charlie Shanks came out of his house and sat in his porch swing sipping a glass of buttermilk.

The courthouse clock struck 7:00, and still no Willie Cates. Buck was beginning to wonder what had happened to him. Rudolph enjoyed a good cigar occasionally and asked permission to light one up. Buck asked him not to, so he put it back in his breast pocket. It was almost dark at 7:20, when they saw a lone figure come down the alley behind the school pushing a two-wheeled cart. He stopped at a back yard fence, just past the children's slide, reached over and picked up a five-gallon garbage can. They watched him dump it into his barrel, put the lid back on the can, put the can back where he found it, and proceed on down the alley. Three houses down, he stopped again and repeated the procedure.

Buck started the car and drove down to Chestnut Street and turned right. He pulled up and blocked the alley. After his third stop, Willie looked up and saw the car. He stopped, not sure what to do. Buck and Clarence both got out, and Willie started to run.

"Willie, it's me, Chief Pettit!" Buck yelled. "We just want to talk to you!"

Willie didn't recognize the car and was still afraid, but Buck's voice was reassuring. He went back to his cart. There was a hickory club about five feet long and two inches in diameter sticking out of the barrel. Willie used it to stir the slop before he fed it to his pigs. He took it out of the barrel and stood defiantly as Buck approached him.

"Willie, we're not here to harm you. We just want to talk to you," Buck said calmly. Willie lowered the club. "Do you know about Milton Stevenson?" Buck continued.

"Yes, suh, he be in jail fo killin' dat teacher."

"Would you like to help him?"

"Yes, suh, I would, but how can I do that?"

Buck told him about the testimony of the witness for the prosecution who testified he had seen Milton leave the school with a cart and that he saw a woman's leg sticking out of it.

"I think what he really saw was you picking up your garbage. Did you go from here to the dump?"

"Yes, suh, I did. Miss Mattie Shivers, that's one of the ladies in this block that leaves me garbage for my pigs, she left an old suitcase for me. She's always leaving things she thinks I might can use. She knows I got a big family, and is always tryin' to help. Well, Chief, I didn't have no need for a suitcase 'cause we don't go no place 'cept home. Besides, it were pert near wore out. I didn't want to hurt Miss Mattie's feelins, so I took the suitcase and took it to the dump on the way home."

"What about a shoe, did you have a shoe with you last Friday night when you came down this alley?"

"Yes, suh, it sho is strange you should ask me about a shoe. Miss Mattie's husband is an engineer fo the railroad. He got a good job and anytime Miss Mattie wants somethin', he generally gets it fo her. She got sugar diabetes, and the doctor had to cut her right foot off, jes below the knee. She won't wear no wooden leg, so she jes walks round with one crutch. My Jennie got blood poisonin' in her left foot four year ago from steppin' on a board with a nail in it, and the doctor had to take it off jes below the knee. Miss Mattie, she know about my Jennie, 'cause the same doctor did both of them, and every time Miss Mattie buys a new pair of shoes, she give me the right one to take to Jennie. They wear 'bout the same size."

"Did she give you one last Friday night?" Buck could hardly contain himself.

"Yes, suh. She left it right by the garbage can."

"What did you do with it?" He was taking notes as fast as he could write.

"Well, suh, I didn't want it bouncin' off my cart on the way home, so I tied it onto the end of the big stick in my barrel."

"Willie, will you testify to that in court?" Buck was really excited now.

"Would it help that colored boy?"

"It sure would, Willie, it sure would. In fact, it could even get him acquitted."

"Then I'll do it," Willie said with a grin.

Buck and Clarence got back in the car. Rudolph had been sitting in the back seat with the door open, taking notes on a yellow pad. He was grinning from ear to ear.

"If Willie testifies, his testimony will take care of all three of the prosecution's witnesses," he said excitedly.

Clarence dropped Rudolph off at his office down on Pine Street and drove to the jail. Buck wanted to visit with Harry for a while to let him know about Willie. Clarence drove back to the station to check out for the night. It had been a long day.

As Buck dashed up the steps to the front door, the Klansmen who were sitting on the steps parted to let him by. They glared at him, but no one said a word.

Harry had been receiving complaints from some of the town's citizens about the Klansmen whistling at women and yelling at cars. Harry knew they had beer, but had never seen them drinking publicly. He had simply gone out on the front porch of the jail one evening when they were getting too rowdy and announced that if anyone was caught drinking in public, especially on County property, they would be given free lodging in his hotel. Also, harassing women, yelling at cars, and otherwise being a public nuisance, would earn them lodging in his establishment.

When the union guy in the white shirt and tie made a crack about their right to be there, Harry walked over to where he was sitting on the steps, reached down and grabbed his tie. Lifting him up so that his feet were on the first step below the porch, Harry leaned down until their noses almost touched.

"Other people have rights, too," he said calmly but firmly, "and I intend to protect their rights as well as yours, understood?"

The Union man nodded his head, and the Klan had been fairly peaceful since then.

Harry was out at his farm, so Buck walked to the police station. He would call him in the morning to set up a meeting. This couldn't be discussed over the phone; the operators had big ears. There was not a word said as he walked down the steps from the jail.

* * * * *

Saturday morning, the 24th of May, Irv got up early and helped his older brother, LeRoy, with his paper route. On Saturday, the Kansas City Times was small, sometimes as few as 12 pages. They were through by 7:30. They went home and ate breakfast; then LeRoy went looking for the boys his age that lived in the neighborhood. Clarence Slaton's little brother was one. They liked to go down to George's pool hall and play eight ball.

After checking on Aunt Belle to see if she was okay, Irv went out to the golf course on West Pine to see if he could get a job caddying.

It was a private, nine-hole, sand greens course, and the only one in town. It cost $50 to join and $25 a year in dues to belong. Therefore, it attracted the dentists, doctors, lawyers, bankers and college professors as members. Twenty-five dollars was two weeks' pay for most people in those days, so the yearly fee kept the riff-raff out. Also they had a board that voted on new members, so they could screen their members carefully.

The only non-members allowed on the grounds were the maintenance staff and the boys who came out to caddy. There was a bench just outside the pro shop door where the caddies were supposed to sit. Irv took his place on the bench and waited.

The boys were all supposed to be at least 12 years old to caddy, and Irv wouldn't turn ten until July, but he stood half a head taller than most 12-year-olds, so no one questioned his age.

A foursome came out of the pro shop, and all wanted caddies, so that left Irv and Brad Swifton on the bench. Next out were a dentist, Larry, and his banker friend, Tom. They hired Irv and Brad and played 18 holes. When they were through, in addition to the 50 cents for caddying, they each tipped the boys 25 cents. They had done a good job caddying, and the banker took their names and said that if they were at the golf course next Saturday morning they would hire them again. The boys thanked them and assured them that they would be out and would like very much to caddy for them. The banker gave Irv his business card; then he and the dentist got into the banker's car and drove back to town for drinks at the banker's house.

It was just after one as Irv and Brad started walking up Pine Street toward town. Irv took the banker's card out and looked at it. It read, "Thomas Breckenridge, President, Breckenridge State Bank, Warrensburg, Missouri. Phone #17."

Irv turned to Brad, "Wow, he must be rich; he's the president of the Breckenridge State Bank! No wonder they gave us big tips."

Irv stopped at the Vernaz Drug Store and bought a Snickers candy bar for Milton and took it to him at the jail. Milton was delighted. Irv assured him that Aunt Belle was getting along just fine, and that she had had no further trouble from the Klan.

"I know," Milton told him. "She comes to see me almost every day."

Irv told him he would see him again soon, and left to go home. He knew his mother would be at the Markhams, so he planned to fix himself some lunch, then with his newly acquired wealth, would get a haircut and take in a Saturday night double feature at the Star Theater. That would still leave him 35 cents to give to his mother to keep in a safe place for him.

7

DISASTER STRIKES

WILLIE CATES WOKE up about midnight. A noise from just outside their bedroom window had roused him. It was hot, and the window was open. It sounded like someone had hit the side of the house with a stick or something. He got up and pulled his overalls on, trying not to wake Jennie or the children. He got his old single shot 12-gauge shotgun from under the bed and tiptoed to the back door in his bare feet.

He thought he heard movement outside the back door, so he took the safety off the shotgun and cocked it. He unhooked the screen on the back door as quietly as he could and gently pushed it open. Not a sound, except for the pigs grunting as they were aroused in their pen. Wham! A two-by-four came crashing down on his head. As he slumped to the ground, he pulled the trigger on the shotgun.

The blast woke Jennie and the kids.

She screamed for Willie and grabbed her crutch by the bed. The blast also woke some of the colored folks that lived back up the lane on Main Street. Lights came on in two of the houses. The one Klansman left to guard the three old pick-up trucks parked along Main flashed his light down the lane to Willie's place and whistled for the four other men.

Two of the men picked Willie up and threw him over the fence, where he landed face down in the muddy pig pen, blood streaming from a gash in the top of his head.

Jennie came out of the house on her crutch, swinging a large butcher knife in her right hand and screaming, "Don't you hurt my Willie!"

The kids were crying, and in the confusion the four Klansmen ran back up the lane toward Main Street, one of them with a severe limp.

Just as they were climbing into their pick-ups, a big colored man by the name of Ed Wheeler came out on his front porch with a double-barreled shotgun. In an instant, he figured out what had probably happened. There was a shotgun blast, and four white men came running out of Willie Cates' lane after midnight. He lowered his shotgun and fired both barrels at the last truck pulling out on Main. The first blast smashed the rear window of the cab, and the second one blew out the left tail light and punctured the tire. The truck went careening down Main Street with the rear tire flop-flopping, causing it to fishtail, but they succeeded in getting away.

Ed and another neighbor went down to Willie's house and found Jennie in the pig pen trying to revive Willie. The kids were standing in the kitchen doorway crying. The two men managed to get Willie into Ed's Model T touring car, and he took Willie and Jennie to the clinic on Market Street just east of the courthouse.

Ed's wife went to Willie's house to look after the kids.

The nurse on duty cleaned the wound on Willie's head, but she knew by looking into Willie's eyes and taking his vital signs that he had severe head trauma. She just wasn't equipped to handle such a severe wound. She told Jennie she wanted to transfer him to Research Hospital in Kansas City, where they had a head trauma team on duty. She convinced Jennie that they had to act fast to save Willie's life.

The nurse made two calls—one to the doctor on duty and got his permission to transfer the patient to Research Hospital, and the other one to Phipps Funeral Home for an ambulance. Phipps was just across the street, so the ambulance was there in three minutes. Ed went back to the Cates' house to get some clothes for Jennie. They loaded Willie and Jennie into the ambulance, and it went speeding north on Holden Street toward Highway 50 with red lights flashing and the siren blaring. When they got to the intersection of Main Street and Highway 50, Ed met them and handed Lester Phipps, the driver, a paper sack with Jennie's clothes in it. Lester handed them over to Mutt, and they sped off toward Kansas City.

* * * * *

Clyde Burroughs, assistant chief, was sitting at Darlene's desk when Ed's Model T went by. The square, as usual, was deserted. He had heard the courthouse clock strike 12:00 some minutes ago, so he felt something was up. The movie crowd from the Star had already gone home, so there wasn't even any traffic on Holden Street. He walked out to the sidewalk in front of the station and looked around. He couldn't see anything unusual or out of place. He crossed the street and looked down toward the jail. Not a car or pedestrian in sight.

Clyde liked an occasional cigar, but Darlene wouldn't let him smoke them in the station; she said they stunk up the whole building. He was toying with the idea of lighting one now and smoking out on the sidewalk when he heard Phipps' ambulance pull out of the garage. He walked toward Holden Street to get a better look, but when he heard it stop so soon, he figured something was wrong at the clinic.

He went into the station and tried to call the clinic, but the operator couldn't get through to them. She said their line was busy making a long distance call.

Clyde grabbed his police cap, locked the front door and went out the back where his patrol car was parked. He got to the clinic just as the ambulance was pulling away. The nurse filled him in on what had happened, and he went looking for Ed Wheeler. He stopped at the station long enough to wake Buck and tell him what had happened to Willie Cates. Buck got up to answer the phone while Clyde was out.

* * * * *

The man in the white shirt and tie was waiting for the five clansmen when they pulled into Murphy's pasture. He wasn't pleased with the way things had gone. He told Charlie Shanks to park his old Ford truck around behind the building to hide it. It had a flat tire that was almost off the rim and a smashed rear window. One of the men from Clinton had buckshot in his right leg and needed medical attention. He could hardly walk on it, and blood was running down into his shoe.

They went inside and lit a lantern. They didn't dare raise the window covers, so it was hot. The union man took the Clinton man's shoe and sock off and poured whiskey on the wounds. One of the men took his white undershirt off, and they used it to bind up the wound as best they could. Mr. White Shirt was obviously in charge.

"I'm going to take this man to Kansas City to get his leg tended to. We don't want him to get blood poisoning in it."

Charlie Shanks was worried. "How you gonna do that without gettin' the cops all over us?"

"I'll take him to the union hall. They can get him treatment without raising any suspicions. They have a doctor that works in the emergency room at the county hospital who's on their pay roll. Besides, the police in that precinct are pretty friendly, too. I'll take my car. We should be back by tomorrow afternoon. Let's all be here at 9:00 tomorrow night."

"I'll need a ride home," Charlie Shanks said. "I don't know what I'll tell my wife about the truck."

"Hell, Charlie, don't you think she already knows what you've been up to?" White Shirt was getting angry with Charlie; he blamed him for tonight's fiasco.

"Just be damned sure she keeps her mouth shut. We'll figure out what to do with your truck later."

* * * * *

Sunday morning just before 8:00, Buck, Clyde and Clarence met in Buck's office and went over the previous night's events. Buck took notes and would have Darlene transcribe them into some semblance of a report for their files later. Buck had called Research Hospital, and the report on Willie Cates was not good. His brain was swelling and he was in a coma, but still hanging on. Clyde had gotten statements from Ed, his wife and two other neighbors of Willie and Jennie. They had all seen the trucks, but it had been too dark to get license plate numbers. One man was limping when they left, according to Ed, so Willie might have shot him.

The facts were these: Willie Cates had been assaulted and was in the hospital in Kansas City in a coma. The assault was probably carried out by the Klan in an effort to keep Willie from testifying in the Wilson murder case. Ed Wheeler had hit one of the trucks used in the assault with his double-barreled shotgun, breaking out the back glass, the left tail light, and puncturing the left rear tire One of the assailants had probably been wounded, possibly by Willie Cates before he passed out. All of the witnesses said they thought that there were five of them, all told.

Buck stood up, a signal that the meeting was over.

"The first thing we need to do is find the pick-up truck that was hit. As near as we can tell, it was about a 1929 or 1930 black Ford Model A. Clyde, you need to go home and get some sleep, Clarence and I will look for the truck."

"You didn't get much sleep last night either," Clyde retorted.

"I know, but we need you fresh for tonight. Clarence and I will get our sleep then."

As they were breaking up, Ann yelled down the stairs, "Are you going to church with me this morning, Buck?" She knew about Willie and doubted that he would be able to, but asked just in case.

"No, sweetie, too much going on. I'll check in with you this afternoon and bring you up to date."

"Okay! We'll pray for Willie!"

"Thanks, honey, please do."

* * * * *

Buck and Clarence went looking for the Ford pick-up. Their first stop was Charlie Shank's house. When Buck knocked, his wife came to the door in her chenille robe. They could smell bacon frying when she opened the door.

"We want to talk to Charlie." Buck didn't mince any words.

"I'm sorry, but he's in bed asleep. I usually go to church on Sunday, but he sleeps 'til noon as a rule."

"Well, ma'am, we need for you to get him up. It's urgent that we talk to him right now."

Buck's tone was so persistent that she didn't say a word. She just nodded and went back to the bedroom.

In a few minutes, Charlie came to the door rubbing the sleep from his eyes, clad only in a pair of jeans and a white undershirt. He was barefooted and had a three-day growth of beard.

"Mr. Shanks, I'm Police Chief Pettit, and this is Officer Slayton," he said, pointing to Clarence.

"I know who you are," he snarled. "You don't remember me, do you? I talked to you in the police station just last Monday."

"Oh, I remember you, Mr. Shanks. That's one of the reasons we're here."

"Why is that?"

121

"When you came to see me, you were driving a Model A Ford pick-up truck. We would like to see that truck right now."

Charlie's knees almost buckled. "You can't."

"Why not?"

"Because I loaned it to a fellow," he lied.

"Who did you loan it to?" Buck had his note pad out, pencil poised.

The only name he could think of that Buck might not know was White Shirt. "Uh, uh, Joe Versano."

Buck wrote the name down on his note pad. "Who is he, and where is the truck now?" Buck looked him in the eyes to see if he was lying.

"Uh, he works for a union in St. Louis. He had to do some business in Kansas City, and didn't have a car, so I loaned him my truck." Charlie was starting to sweat.

"What was he doing here in Warrensburg?"

"Uh, he was doin' some union business."

"When will he be back with the truck?" Buck could tell he was lying.

"Uh, I don't know, he may be gone several days."

"Listen carefully, Mr. Shanks." Buck could barely hide his disdain for Charlie Shanks. "We will probably need to talk to you again soon, so don't leave town without telling me or Officer Slaton where you are going and how long you will be gone. Is that clear?"

"Yes, sir." Charlie closed the door.

* * * * *

Back in the car, Buck and Clarence drove around aimlessly looking for suspicious pick-up trucks.

"He was lying as sure as I'm sitting here." Buck was disgusted. "He knows that we're on to him, too, so we had better watch him close. Also, I want you to go down to the overall factory and talk to his wife when Charlie's not around. She may know something she's not us telling in front of him."

Clarence pulled over to the curb and put the car in neutral. "He probably won't do anything until after dark. That's how those people operate."

"You're right, Buck said. "Let's drive over to Murphy's pasture to see if there is any activity around there."

They drove by Aunt Belle's house.

"She'll be in church," Clarence volunteered.

"You're probably right, drive on up to Murphy's pasture, let's see if we can spot Charlie Shank's truck."

Clarence pulled the patrol car up to the locked gate that blocked the drive to the Klan building. They both got out, and Buck climbed as high as he could on the gate to get a better look. He could just barely see the roof of the building. It was too far back from the road and at a higher elevation to see anything.

"We'll need a search warrant to do a thorough search of this place, and it will be tomorrow morning before we can get one," Buck said rather dejectedly.

"I've got an idea that might work."

"What's that?"

"Let's go down to the grocery store and tavern on the corner. You know, the log building that has the tourist cabins and the spring? I think the Klan building is only about 30 feet from the back fence. We could climb up that steep bank behind the log building and maybe get a better look."

"That's a good idea; maybe we could spot the truck, and not even have to climb the fence." Buck's face brightened a little. He was tired from very little sleep.

It was quite a struggle, but they managed to reach the top of the bluff. By standing on their tiptoes at the fence, they could barely see the top of the cab of a pick-up truck parked in back of the building.

"I'll bet a dollar to a doughnut that that's our truck," Buck said, a little out of breath.

"I'm tempted to climb this fence and have a good look."

"No, Buck said, "let's do it legally."

* * * * *

By 9:00, only six Klansmen had shown up in Murphy's pasture, including the one with the patched-up leg. Since there had been some shooting and the shooting had come from the colored and not the Klan, some of the out-of-towners had gone home. Charlie Shanks showed up, but he didn't want to come. He was scared, but he was also very concerned about his truck, and how White Shirt planned to get it fixed up so he could drive it again. It didn't take long for him to get his answer.

The very first thing White Shirt said was, "We've got to get rid of that damned truck!"

"What do you mean, get rid of it?" Charlie was starting to get angry.

"It's evidence they can use against us, so we need to take it over to Waverly and push it off that bluff into the Missouri River. The water is about 30 feet deep there, and the State Police will never find it."

"Sounds like you've done that before," one of the Klansmen said.

"Never mind about that. Now, who wants to drive it over to Waverly?"

Charlie Shanks was furious. "What about just puttin' in a new back window and fixin' the tail light? I can put the spare tire on it; that way you wouldn't even have to buy a new tire. It's a good truck, and I need it."

"There's buckshot dents all over the back end, you idiot!

How long do you think it would take some policeman to spot that?"

Charlie bit his tongue and sat down. He knew White Shirt was right, but he was still mad.

"First we'll get rid of the truck, then we'll go after those niggers that shot at us last night. We want to put the fear in their hearts, so when the trial comes up the jury will know we mean business."

The lookout at the gate came running in. "I blinked my flashlight to warn you guys, but nobody saw me, I guess. There's a police car at the gate wanting in."

White Shirt walked down to the gate. Three of the men followed him. Charlie and the guy with the bandaged leg stayed in the building out of sight.

Buck and Clarence were there to greet them; the motor in their patrol car was running, and the lights were on.

Buck spoke first. "Hello there. I'm Police Chief Pettit, and this is Officer Clarence Slayton. We would like to look around your place if we may."

"No, you may not!" White Shirt was belligerent. "This is private property, and there is nothing going on here that would interest you guys anyway."

124

"Okay, we were just following up on some complaints we had received. I guess they didn't amount to much. Thanks anyway."

Buck and Clarence got in the patrol car and drove off, smiling to themselves.

Buck looked over at Clarence and grinned. "That should keep them from moving the truck until I can get a search warrant. Let's go home, I'm tired."

Their little ruse worked. White Shirt was in a highly agitated state.

"Well, that cancels our trip to Waverly," he said sarcastically, looking right at Charlie. "We'll have to leave that truck where it is for awhile. Those damn cops will be watching this place like a hawk. Somebody get a tarp and cover the truck up for now. We'll just have to sit tight while I think about our next move."

* * * * *

Monday morning, May, 25th, Buck went to the prosecuting attorney's office to get an application for a warrant to search Murphy's pasture. Gerald Essex was out of town, and his assistant tried to delay the warrant until he got back. He told Buck that he didn't have authority to give him an application and that he would have to wait until Gerald got back. Buck knew better.

"I can't wait until he gets back, I need it right now, and if you won't cooperate, I'll go directly to Judge Whitfield. He'll issue a warrant for me. I was just going through your office as a courtesy anyway."

Buck had had so many problems with the prosecuting attorney's office that he'd made up his mind to stand his ground.

"Wa . . . well, don't be that way," the assistant stammered. "I'm sure one day won't make that much difference."

"I'm afraid it will," Buck said, and turning on his heels he walked out of the office and up the stairs to the judge's chambers, leaving the assistant prosecutor standing behind the counter with his mouth open.

Just as Buck walked out of the courthouse with the search warrant in his hand, the fire truck pulled out of its stall next to the police station and started west on Market. Buck got that sinking feeling again. He stuck his head in the firehouse door and yelled at the back-up driver.

"Where's the fire?"

"One hundred block of west Oak," he yelled back.

Clarence skidded to a stop in front of the fire station just as Buck turned around. He had heard the siren, and it was the Police Department's duty to furnish crowd and traffic control at fires. Buck jumped in beside him, and they sped off to the fire.

Oak Street formed the south boundary of Murphy's pasture. The one hundred block was the east end, or the swampy part of the pasture. When Buck and Clarence got there, black smoke was billowing up from a spot about halfway between Oak Street and Highway 50. The fire truck was sitting in the street with its lights blinking, and the firemen were standing along the fence talking to a man in a white shirt and tie.

Buck walked over to the fence. "What's going on, Charlie?"

Charlie Yokum was the fire chief. "I don't know, Chief. Somebody phoned in an alarm, but when we got here, the man in the white shirt stopped us and said they were just burning some brush, but there's more than brush burning there. I smell an accelerant, like gasoline, and it looks like there is a vehicle burning."

White Shirt spoke up. "I don't know who turned in the alarm, but this is private property, and all we're doing is burning some brush and trash. Why don't you all go back to the station? We're not breaking any law here."

Charlie turned to Buck. "I think I'll take the truck back to the station. There's nothing we can do here, unless the fire gets out of hand."

"Yeah, you're probably right," Buck said disgustedly as he turned to go back to the patrol car.

Clarence cleared the street so the fire truck could get out, then drove Buck back to the station.

Buck was getting a little dejected by recent events. "This fire renders my search warrant useless. That truck was going to be exhibit A," he said.

Back at the station, Buck called Sheriff Harry Foster and filled him in on what had happened. Harry told Buck that the Klan seemed to be laying low for a while. None had been at the jail since Saturday.

"They're not gone though, they're just regrouping. Buck also told Harry he thought someone in the courthouse had warned the Klan that he was coming with a search warrant. "I didn't have that warrant in my hand ten minutes until that fire broke out. I think it's someone in the prosecuting attorney's office."

126

"Was it the assistant prosecutor, Jim Sartin?"

"I think so, either he or the receptionist. They're the only ones that had time. I was in their office about ten minutes, and then spent about 45 minutes in the judge's office getting the warrant. By the time I walked out of the courthouse, the fire siren went off."

"That would be my guess; I've had my eye on Jim for some time. He hates Negroes and is always doing something to harass them."

Buck also called Rudolph to tell him the bad news. Rudolph was actually quite cheerful. He had been investigating the background of the prosecution's witnesses and didn't think he would have any trouble disputing them on the witness stand.

"That's great," Buck said, "but watch your back. Remember what happened to Willie Cates."

* * * * *

Buck spent Tuesday morning, May 26th, going over his notes on the Margaret Wilson case. He knew in his mind that Milton Stevenson didn't do it, so that meant that a killer was still on the loose. He went over his conversations with Russell Wilhelm, the talks with the boys who found the body, the coroner and Dr. Allen. There had to be something he was missing. He had talked to Ann about the case, and she still maintained that Russell Wilhelm didn't do it. Buck tended to agree with her. In his interviews with Russell, he had watched his eyes. He didn't think he was lying.

At 11:45 the phone rang. It was the coroner, Lester Phipps.

"Buck, Willie Cates just died, and the hospital wants me to come get the body."

Buck was stunned. He sat for a minute gathering his thoughts.

"Buck?"

"Yes, I'm here, I was so in hopes that Willie would make it. Not just because he would have made a good witness, but because of his family."

"Yeah, me, too."

"When are you leaving for Kansas City?"

"Right now."

"Have a good trip, and call me when you get back."

"I will, bye." He hung up.

Buck called Harry and Rudolph and gave them the news, then went upstairs to tell Ann and try to choke down some lunch.

* * * * *

After lunch, Buck went next door to the firehouse and borrowed their bolt cutters and a rake. He got hold of Clarence, and with the search warrant in his pocket they went back out to Murphy's pasture.

Buck knew the Klan did most of their mischief at night, so he didn't anticipate a confrontation with any of them, but he was prepared. He had called Sheriff Foster just before they left the station and told him of their plans. He asked him to swing by the gate in half an hour just to check. Harry said he would.

There was no one around when Buck and Clarence pulled in the drive in front of the gate. They got out, and Buck yelled for someone to let them in. There was no answer, so Clarence cut the chain, and chain and padlock clattered to the ground. Buck swung the gate open, and they drove up to the building. It was locked, so Clarence pried it open with a big screwdriver he kept in the patrol car.

They opened some of the big window covers to let in some light and fresh air. They found some white robes and pointed hats in the hinged seat boxes that lined the walls. In one of them they found several ax handles and two baseball bats. There was nothing else of interest inside.

Out back they found an empty gas can and the makings of a wooden cross. The pieces were all there; they just hadn't put it together yet.

"I wonder who their next victim is going to be?" Buck pondered.

Clarence poked around in the grass with the rake. "I wouldn't be surprised if they went after that big colored guy, you know, the one that fired his shotgun at them."

"You're probably right. Let's be sure to patrol that neighborhood as frequently as possible, especially at night."

"I'll tell Chief Burroughs what we found when he comes in."

Buck started back around to the front of the building. "Come on, let's go down to the other end of the pasture where they burned the truck," he said, motioning for Clarence to follow him.

* * * * *

128

The truck was still smoldering, but had cooled enough that they could get close enough to poke through the rubble. Everything flammable was reduced to ashes—the tires, upholstery and what few wooden parts it had on it, such as the floorboards. The glass in windows and headlamps had melted into shapeless blobs. It had been a hot fire. The gas tank had ruptured and added fuel to the inferno.

Clarence scratched around in the burned-out hulk, not really knowing what he was looking for, until he spotted something under the springs of what had been the seat. He pulled the springs away with the rake and scratched something out on the ground. It was a 22 caliber rifle minus the stock.

"I think we know who fired the shot into the jail now," he said as he took his hankie out and held it up for Buck to see.

"That just confirms what we already knew," Buck said, motioning for Clarence to follow him back up to their patrol car. "Take that thing back to the station and tag it for evidence, and come back later when it has cooled off and get the number off the motor. We can run down the owner that way."

Just as the courthouse clock struck 4:00, the phone on Darlene's desk rang. It was Lester Phipps. He told her he had just gotten back from Kansas City with Willie Cates' body. Jennie had ridden back with him in the hearse. He asked her to tell Buck he was back, and that the funeral had been tentatively set for Friday morning.

Darlene walked back to Buck's office and found him with his elbows on his desk and his head in his hands. He had apparently been doodling on a yellow pad in front of him.

"Anything wrong, Chief? Are you all right?" The Chief looked tired and drawn; Darlene was worried.

"I'm okay, Darlene. This murder case is about to get me down. I'm being frustrated at every turn. Every time I get a good solid clue, something happens to it."

"How long has it been since you had a good night's sleep?"

"Too long, I'm afraid."

"Why don't you go upstairs and take your shoes off? Put your feet up and relax before dinner. Clarence, Bob and I can handle things, and Clyde comes in at 8:00. Go to bed early and get a good night's sleep, so you can get a fresh start in the morning."

"I think I'll do just that, Darlene. Thanks." He trudged wearily up the stairs.

* * * * *

"Friday dawned hot and dry. Willie's funeral was scheduled for 10:00 at the same colored church Belle attended. The Phipps brothers handled the arrangements at no charge. The only thing Jennie was charged for was the casket. The little life insurance policy on Willie just barely covered that.

An agent from a reputable insurance company had gone through the colored community in the early '30s selling a new product. It was strictly a burial policy, meant to cover just the minimum expenses of a funeral. The longer you lived, the more it paid. Jennie had talked Willie into buying one on each of them in 1931.

It was a large funeral by any standards. The church was full, and the crowd spilled out into the yard. The preacher was a kindly man in his late 60s. His white hair contrasted sharply with his dark skin. There were a number of white folks in the crowd, mainly city employees. Buck and Ann were there, as well as Harry Foster and Rudolph Eisenstein.

The preacher read the obituary, and the choir sang two numbers. It was hot inside the church, so the preacher skipped his usual two-hour sermon. He summed up Willie's life as a life of service to his family and community. There was a lot of sobbing and "Amen's" from the mourners.

They adjourned to the colored cemetery, and Willie was laid to rest.

The local churches set up a fund for Jennie and the children at one of the banks, and in two weeks the people in the town had contributed over $500. That was more money than Willie made in two years. Ann Pettit had been the driving force behind the fund.

* * * * *

Friday was also Ann Marie's last day of school until the fall semester. A student at the University of Missouri who lived in Kansas City had offered to drive her home. Ann Marie had dated him a few times and felt she knew him pretty well. She called home the night before to tell Buck and Ann not to come to Columbia to get her, and that she should be home about 3:00 in the afternoon.

Their rooms at the sorority house were furnished, even their towels and linens, so all she had to pack was her clothing.

At noon Friday, Jerry Whitman picked Ann up at her sorority house. He put her bags in the back seat with his, and they went downtown to a drugstore and had sandwiches and Cokes. At 12:45, they headed west on Highway 40 in Jerry's '34 Ford convertible, a high school graduation present from his parents. His father was a prominent Kansas City surgeon.

At Marshall Junction, they turned south toward Sedalia on highway 65. They would pick up Highway 50 at Sedalia. It would take them directly to Warrensburg. At 2:15, they were driving down Ohio Street in Sedalia with the top down, waving at people and really enjoying the trip. Jerry found a parking space right in front of J.C. Penney's, and they walked across the street to the Crown Drug Store for Cokes.

After their refreshment stop, they drove on south on Ohio Street to Broadway, which was 50 Highway, and headed west to Warrensburg. West Broadway was a beautiful street, with huge elm trees along each side of the parkway that almost met overhead. Sedalia had a new radio station that played contemporary music, and it didn't take Ann Marie long to find it on the dial. They hummed along with the tunes as they motored west out of town.

At 3:05, an eastbound car, driving too fast, swerved into their lane in an attempt to miss the back end of a truck that had slowed to turn off of the highway at the little town of Dresden. In a matter of seconds, three people were dead. Ann Marie was thrown from the car and died of a broken neck.

A resident of Dresden, who happened to be in his car right behind the car that struck Jerry's convertible, called the Sedalia police from the filling station across the highway. They, in turn, called two funeral homes to send ambulances and the Missouri Highway Patrol. The first policeman to reach the scene was a big patrolman from the Missouri Highway Patrol.

The bodies had already been taken to two different funeral homes. Jerry and Ann Marie's to one and the driver of the other car to another. After examining the accident scene, talking to witnesses and taking notes, the patrolman asked for some help. Onlookers helped him gather the luggage and personal things scattered along the right-of-way and put them in his car. He took them to the Sedalia police station for safekeeping. He then went through the victim's personal things looking for identification and found Ann Marie's driver's license.

The patrolman went through Warrensburg information and asked for Ann Marie's home phone number. Every operator in the Warrensburg exchange knew that Ann Marie Pettit was the daughter of the Police Chief, so she connected him to the police station. Darlene answered the phone.

When Buck heard a loud wail from Darlene, he rushed up front to see what was wrong. Something was terribly wrong. He had lost his precious Ann Marie. Buck sank into a chair and sobbed. Darlene somehow found the strength to go upstairs and tell Ann.

The small caravan left Warrensburg just as the courthouse clock struck 5:00. Clarence was driving the Pettits' car with Ann and Buck in the back, both of them too upset to drive.

Following them was Lester Phipps and Mutt Bridges in the hearse. They brought the body of Ann Marie home, and the funeral was set for Tuesday, June 2, at 11:00 a.m.

Beautiful young Ann Marie was dead. The homecoming queen with the long blonde hair and sparkling blue eyes, the image of her mother, was gone. The love of her father's life, and the heart and soul of her mother was gone. The talented musician with so much promise was gone. Her wealthy grandparents would have given everything they owned for another moment of her life, but she was gone. The whole town mourned.

The funeral was the largest in Warrensburg's history up to that time. It was held in the high school auditorium to accommodate all the people who wanted to attend. Her white coffin was draped with a blanket of yellow roses, Ann Marie's favorite color. The high school choral group sang two of Ann Marie's favorite hymns, and her grandfather gave a stirring eulogy. The Methodist minister gave an inspirational talk especially addressed to the many teenagers in the assembly. He talked about the wonderful life Ann Marie had led, and held her up as an example as one who was ready to meet her Maker when she was called home.

There were many tears as the mourners filed past the open casket. Ann Marie was laid out in a yellow chiffon dress, her golden hair tied with a yellow ribbon. She held a small bouquet of white lilies of the valley. After a brief gravesite service, beautiful Ann Marie was laid to rest.

* * * * *

For the next week, Buck did nothing but wander aimlessly around the police station. He couldn't eat, he couldn't sleep; the least little thing would send tears streaming down his cheeks. Ann was the same way. She closed the door to Ann Marie's room and never went in. She couldn't bear the sight of the bed where Ann Marie had slept. When trying to prepare a meal, her mind would go back to Ann Marie's favorite food, and she would sit down and weep. Fortunately, people were constantly bringing dishes of food to the station for them, so there was plenty available, but neither she nor Buck had any appetite. Ann usually sent the fried chicken, green bean casseroles, loads of pies and cakes and other food home with the staff to keep it from going to waste. She even sent some home with Sheriff Foster.

It was a bad time for everyone. Darlene would start crying for no reason. Clarence was in a bad mood, and even he would have an occasional tear run down his cheek. The whole town was affected. First Margaret Wilson, then Willie Cates, then Ann Marie. How much more could they take? They were soon to find out.

* * * * *

Wednesday, June 10, was another hot, dry day. It had been over a week since Ann Marie's funeral. The town was slowly getting back to normal after all the tragedy they had experienced. Jimmy Hardesty's family would change all that.

Jimmy Hardesty had grown up in Warrensburg. Jimmy's parents had always wanted children, but had no success until Jimmy's mother was 41 years old. The doctor told them he was a "change-of-life" baby. Jimmy's family ran a butcher shop down on Pine Street. From the time he was tall enough to see over the counter, he worked in the shop part-time. He was a big kid for his age, and while he was in high school his father taught him how to break down carcasses into the various cuts of meat. He worked in the shop after school and on Saturdays. He learned fast, and by the time he was a senior in high school, their customers actually preferred his cuts over those of his father.

His father always expected him to come to work full-time for him after he graduated, but that was not Jimmy's plan. Jimmy wanted to go to college. In those days, less than 10% of the high school graduates went on to college, but Jimmy was determined. His parents couldn't afford to send him, so he went to the personnel director at CSTC and talked him into letting him work part-time in the storehouse until they had a full-time opening. He told the director he would take his wages out in schooling if they didn't have the money in their budget to hire him.

That pleased the director, so he hired him to work part-time as needed. Soon word got back to him that this big kid was a good worker. After only three months on the job, he was hired full-time in the purchasing department.

Jimmy was happy. He had a good job and was taking college courses at night. He soon met a girl student on campus, and they started dating. She had a part-time job, too, so the only time they had together was at the movie on Saturday nights. They would see each other on campus once in a while and would occasionally eat together at the cafeteria, but they both lived for Saturday nights.

Her name was Eleanor Bates, and she was from Michigan City, Indiana. Her mother had graduated from CSTC and had always wanted Eleanor to go there. She was Methodist and Jimmy was Baptist, so they seldom saw each other on Sunday. There was always homework to do for Monday classes, so Eleanor spent many a Sunday afternoon in her room at the dorm studying.

Eleanor graduated in June 1932, and she and Jimmie were married the same month. Jimmy continued to work at the college, and Eleanor got a part-time teaching job. When Little Jimmy was born in July of the next year, they rented a little two-bedroom house on North Street and moved out of their cramped apartment. Eleanor quit her job to take care of little Jimmy. Jimmy got a salary raise in January of 1933, so in spite of the extra expenses, they got along fine.

When little Ellie (Eleanor after her mother) was born in September of 1934, Jimmy had to quit college, even though he had only a few hours to go for his bachelor's degree, and took a part-time job at the Safeway store up on Holden Street as a butcher. Safeway had advertised for an experienced butcher to work part-time and were glad when Jimmy applied for the job. It was a perfect fit for both of them, as the store's busiest day was Saturday and that was Jimmy's day off at the college. They got along fine until the long depression deepened in 1936.

* * * * *

Since 1930 when the depression first took hold on the nation's economy, everybody expected things to get better soon. Just when people thought things were as bad as they could get and were starting pick up a little, the economy would sag again, and there would be more layoffs. The people blamed the depression on Herbert Hoover, but Roosevelt's New Deal wasn't working either. The nation was depressed.

In November of 1934, Jimmy's mother died of cancer. After Christmas of that year, his dad was forced to close the butcher shop. The big chain stores could sell meat so much cheaper than he could that he could no longer compete. Jimmy helped him close it down, and when the inventory, fixtures and equipment were all sold, there was barely enough money left to pay all the bills. He was behind on his house payments, and the savings and loan company foreclosed on it, leaving him with no place to go. Jimmy and Eleanor took him in. He slept on the couch in the living room.

The year 1935 wasn't any better for the economy, and in August of that year the college's budget was cut so severely that they had to lay Jimmy off. With five mouths to feed and only a part-time job, Jimmy was beginning to feel a lot of pressure. Christmas that year was tough. They managed to buy small toys for the children, and they had a nice Christmas dinner, but gifts for the adults were non-existent. Jimmy went out in the country and cut down a small cedar tree, and they decorated it with popcorn strings and paper cut-outs of bells and Christmas trees that they colored with crayons.

Spring of 1936 didn't change things much. Safeway increased Jimmy's hours some to help cover vacations for the full-time butchers and help out on big sale days, but the Hardestys were beginning to fall behind on their rent. Jimmy's dad was starting to get very forgetful, but he loved to entertain the children. He would make paper cut-outs and little toys and gadgets out of out of scraps of lumber that he picked up at the lumber yard. He even made little Jimmy a toy he called a tractor out of an empty thread spool, a match stick, a button and a rubber band. Little Jimmy played with it by the hour. He would wind the match stick and set the toy on the sidewalk, and it would crawl along like a miniature tractor.

By early June, the elder Hardesty had started wandering away from the house, and Eleanor would have to take the children in tow and go looking for him. He was getting to be quite a worry. There was an old folks home run by the county out on East 50 highway that took in indigent elderly for free, but Mr. Hardesty didn't qualify because he still had relatives to take care of him. Eleanor Hardesty was getting desperate.

* * * * *

Jimmy walked home for lunch that hot June day. His dad brought an old pick-up truck with him when he moved in, but it quit running and was parked in the garage. It was the one he used to deliver meat when he was in the butcher business, and there was no money to fix it up. When Jimmy walked up the driveway to go in the back door to the kitchen, his dad and little Jimmie were sitting on the back steps. The old man was rocking back and forth. Little Jimmie was clinging to his arm, not saying a word. He didn't even greet his dad like he usually did. Jimmie sensed that something wrong. He opened the screen door enough to squeeze by his dad and went into the kitchen.

There was no lunch prepared, and the breakfast dishes were stacked in the kitchen sink. Jimmy got weak in the knees and started to sweat. He heard little Ellie's cry from the bedroom, and he started to tremble. The scene in the bedroom was unimaginable. Eleanor was lying crosswise on the bed, her legs dangling over the side. There was blood splattered on the opposite wall, along with hair and parts of her scalp and brain. The old double-barreled shotgun that was given to him by his dad was on the floor beneath her feet. She had apparently loaded the gun, cocked it while sitting on the bed, placed the barrel under her chin and pulled the trigger with her toe. Her shoes and socks were by the bed.

Little Ellie had pulled herself up to the bed and was patting her mother's leg and saying "Ma-ma, Ma-ma." She had apparently gone around to the other side of the bed and had tried to reach her mother there, as her face and blond curls were smeared with her mother's blood.

Jimmy almost fainted. He stood there for a moment, then reached down and picked up the old shotgun. He walked deliberately out to the kitchen and sat down. He cocked the other barrel, placed it under his chin and pulled the trigger.

The first blast had concerned some of the neighbors, and three of them walked outside and looked around, but seeing nothing out of place, had gone back inside. The second blast brought them back out along with two more from up the street.

The neighbor who lived just west of the Hardestys said, "Something's wrong, I'm going to call the police."

* * * * *

Darlene had just settled down at her desk when the phone rang.

"Police department," she chirped. She had decided that they needed a little cheer around the station, and she was going to do her share. Her mood didn't last long.

"I think there has been a shooting!"

"Who is this?" Darlene sensed something was terribly wrong.

"I'm Mrs. Yeager, and we heard gun shots!"

"Who are we?"

"Me and the rest of the neighbors!"

"Where do you live?"

She gave Darlene her address, and the address of the Hardesty house.

"I'll send someone right over, please just stay where you are."

Darlene jumped up and ran back to Buck's office. "Chief, I think there has been a shooting over on North Street!"

Buck was sitting at his desk with his head in his hands. Darlene could tell he had been crying. Suddenly he looked up. "Where is Clarence?"

"Out on patrol."

"What address on North Street?"

Darlene gave him the address, and he grabbed his straw hat and started for the back door. "Get hold of Clarence, and send him to that address as soon as he can make it," he said over his shoulder as he went out the door.

It was five blocks to the address on North Street, and Buck ran all the way. There was a small crowd on the sidewalk in front of the Hardesty home, and Mrs. Yeager ran up to Buck and told him what she knew. Buck was gasping for breath as he walked up to the back steps where the old man and little Jimmy were still sitting. The boy clung to his grandfather's arm as the old man rocked back and forth.

Buck squeezed through the screen door, trying not to disturb the pair. The sight in the kitchen almost made him throw up. He got that terrible feeling in the pit of his stomach again. Jimmy was lying on his side on the kitchen floor, surrounded by a pool of blood. There was blood and hair splattered on the ceiling and kitchen table. He heard Ellie crying in the bedroom and went to investigate.

He found her sitting on the floor near her mother's feet, smeared with blood. She was crying, and when she saw Buck she held up her arms to be picked up. Suddenly there was Ann Marie wanting him to hold her, and with his eyes welling up, he reached down, picked her up and hugged her close to his chest.

Buck went out through the front door carrying Ellie, just as Clarence pulled up in front of the house in the patrol car. Lester Phipps and Mutt Bridges were right behind him in the ambulance. Darlene had found Clarence having lunch at the Tip Top Cafe and told him what Buck said. She then hung up and called Lester. She told him that there had been a shooting over on North Street, and they would probably need an ambulance. Buck handed Ellie to Mrs. Yeager and went back into the house with Clarence and Lester. They removed Eleanor's body first, and Lester and Mutt took her to the morgue in the ambulance, then turned around and went right back for Jimmy's body.

Just as the ambulance arrived for the second body, Ann drove up in the Studebaker. She heard the ambulance go by and found out from Darlene what had happened. She went straight to Mrs. Yeager and took little Ellie from her. She started to take her to the car, when she saw Jimmie and his grandfather sitting on the back steps. Buck came out and explained to her what had happened.

She said "Honey, let me take the children home with me. I'll clean them up and feed them lunch."

"What about their grandfather? He doesn't seem to know what's going on."

"Let me take him, too. I'll take him out to the county home. Poor man. He's just lost his son and daughter-in-law, and probably doesn't even know it."

Buck was greatly relieved. He was worried about the children. He was glad Ann had come to get them. "Good, I'll be home as soon as I'm finished up here, I may be late, sweetie." Buck suddenly realized that Ann seemed her usual confident self again. He smiled and went back in the house. He was feeling better.

Ann loaded the children and their grandfather into the car and drove out to the county home. They were full, but when Ann explained what had happened, the woman in charge said she would make room for him somehow. She and her husband took him into the dining room and fed him lunch. Later that evening, Buck showed up with his clothing, and they made a bed for him in the men's dorm.

Ann took the children to the apartment over the police station. The first thing she did was give little Ellie a bath and wash her hair. Jimmie was by her side the whole time and didn't take his eyes off his sister. Ann took a box off the shelf in Ann Marie's closet. This was the first time she had been in Ann Marie's bedroom since the funeral. She had saved some of Ann Marie's clothing as she grew up and kept them in the box. She took out a yellow sun dress, some panties and a pair of white sandals. After she dressed Ellie, Ann brushed her hair and put a yellow ribbon in her pretty blond curls. She reminded Ann so much of Ann Marie at that age. She took the children to the kitchen and fed them lunch.

Buck and Clarence had been busy at the Hardesty house. With the aid of the neighbors, they stripped the bed and burned the sheets in the barrel in the back yard. Clarence stuffed the mattress into the trunk of the patrol can and took it down to the junk yard for salvage. While some of the neighbors scrubbed the bedroom and kitchen from ceiling to floor, Mrs. Yeager gathered the children's and the old man's clothing and put them in grocery sacks. Buck put them in the patrol car when Clarence got back.

The courthouse clock struck 5:00. Buck looked at his watch and realized that he hadn't had any lunch, and it was almost dinner time. He locked the house and thanked the neighbors for their help. He asked them to keep an eye on the house as a precaution against looters or curiosity seekers, and they all agreed.

Buck asked Clarence to take him by the apartment to check on Ann to see if she needed any help. She was doing fine. She and Darlene had gone down to the basement of the police station and recovered Ann Marie's old high chair and stroller that had been stored there years ago, and Ann had gone shopping with the children. She bought some diapers for Ellie, a pair of shorts and a striped tee shirt for Jimmy at Woolworth's, and had stopped at the grocery store where she picked up the ingredients for an Irish stew and some strawberry ice cream for dessert. She had the children down for a nap while she busied herself with dinner.

Buck was thrilled to see her so happy. "Clarence and I are going to take Mr. Hardesty's clothes out to the home, and I'll be home for dinner."

"Bye, honey, I'll see you in a few minutes."

Buck was whistling a tune as he bounced down the back steps to the parking space where Clarence was waiting for him in the patrol car.

The next day Buck and Harry went to the county judge and got Mr. Hardesty committed to county home permanently. The same day, Buck got custody forms from the prosecuting attorney's office, and he and Ann filled them out that night.

8

THE TRIAL

WHEN WILLIE CATES died, the out-of-town Klansmen left Warrensburg in a hurry, including White Shirt. They knew the sheriff and police would be hot on their trail. That left Charlie Shanks and a few of his drinking buddies to carry on their activities. They drove by Ed Wheeler's house late one night, but when big Ed came out on his porch with his 12-gauge shot gun, they took off in a hurry. They had already lost one pick-up truck that way.

Rudolph had talked to all of the prosecution's witnesses and was sure that he could discredit them on the witness stand. Milton's defense was looking pretty good, and with the trial coming upon the 22nd, he was almost ready.

Milton was holding up well. His parents visited him on the day of Willie's funeral and promised to be back for the trial. Rudolph wrote them regularly to keep them posted on his preparations for the trial.

Buck and Ann got temporary custody of Ellie and Jimmy until the Circuit Clerk could contact their living relatives to see if any of them wanted to take the children. They were ready to go to court if necessary to try to get permanent custody. In fact, they had seriously discussed adopting both of them.

* * * * *

Monday morning, June 15, Buck was sitting at his desk studying his notes on the Wilson murder, when Darlene buzzed him to pick up the phone.

"This is Chief Pettit, what can I do for you?"

It was a woman's voice. She spoke so low that he could hardly understand her.

"There are some things you need to know," she whispered.

"Who is this?"

"That's not important. What is important is that you are holding the wrong man in that murder case."

"Who should we be holding?" he asked.

She hung up.

Buck flipped the switch hook several times, and the operator came on.

"Who is this?" he asked.

"Chief, this is Ruby, didn't you recognize my voice?"

"Oh, yeah, sorry, Ruby. Where did my last call come from?"

"Just a minute, I'll check." There was a short wait. "It came from a phone booth in the administration building on campus."

"Thanks, Ruby." Buck hung up and went up front.

Clarence was sitting on the edge of Darlene's desk sipping a cup of coffee. Buck motioned for him to follow him outside.

"Drive me out to the campus as quick as you can," he said as he slid into the passenger side of the patrol car. He filled Clarence in on the mysterious phone call on the way to the college.

Clarence pulled the patrol car up in front of the administration building, and they both got out. They walked up to the receptionist's desk, and Buck introduced himself and Clarence to the young lady working there.

"Did anyone use that phone in the past few minutes?" he asked, pointing to the phone booth in the corner by the front door.

"I didn't notice anyone, sir, but I've been busy studying and might have missed seeing them if anyone did."

"Have many people been in here this morning?"

"Actually, I haven't seen anyone this morning since I came to work at 9:00. We're between semesters now, and there just aren't many students on campus. I missed one of my final exams on account of illness, and they are letting me take it tomorrow, so I have been studying for it. I'm sorry."

Buck thanked her and walked over to the phone booth and looked in. The phone book was open to the page with city office numbers. Someone had underlined the Police Department number with a fountain pen.

Buck and Clarence drove around the campus a couple of times before driving back to the station. Buck didn't know who he was looking for, but felt like he would recognize whoever it was if he saw her.

She called again on Thursday with the same message, this time from the phone booth in the train station waiting area. Again, there were no witnesses to the caller. Buck felt sure she was telling the truth, and that she knew who actually killed Margaret Wilson, but when he asked her who the killer was, she hung up.

Buck hoped she would continue calling. He knew that if she did, he would eventually get some vital information from her. Either that, or someone would see her make the call and identify her. Then he could bring her in for questioning. That was his only hope for solving the case at this time, as he didn't have any clues strong enough to make an arrest. He still believed strongly that Milton was innocent, but the trial was next Tuesday.

* * * * *

Tuesday, June 23, was the third day of summer, but that fact didn't seem to register on the citizens of Warrensburg. They had been experiencing summer weather since mid-April. A cool front moved through over the weekend, but since there was no moisture in the air, all it brought was dry wind and dust. The temperature did drop from the mid-90s to the upper 80s, which was some relief from the heat.

Judge Whitfield got to the courthouse early. He didn't know for sure what Milton's trial would bring, and he wanted to review the hearing transcript in his chambers one more time before it began. He had been following the newspaper accounts of the Klan activities in the area and was still worried that they would try to disrupt the trial somehow.

By 9:00, when the courtroom doors were opened, there were about 50 people waiting in line to get in. Twenty-four were colored folks from the Roy community near Slater. They came in a caravan of five cars, with George and Thelma Stevenson, along with their two daughters leading the way. They all sat in the section behind the defense table. Also in that section were Buck Pettit and Lois Huff. Dub had given Lois the day off at her request, but Ann Pettit was too busy with the Hardesty children to attend. There were a few local colored in attendance also, including Jennie Cates and Ed Wheeler.

On the other side of the aisle, behind the prosecution table, were four newspaper reporters, including Ross Ludlow from the *Warrensburg Star Journal,* about 30 white citizens, and a couple of local men suspected to be Klan. Judge Whitfield had allowed them in after they had been searched by the Sheriff's Deputies. Charlie Shanks was being held in the witness room, so there were no Klan demonstrations outside the courthouse.

Gerald Essex, the prosecuting attorney, and his assistant, Jim Sartin, were leaning on the rail that separated the gallery from the prosecutor's table, talking to the reporters. Gerald was wearing another new suit. This time it was a white linen double-breasted one. He wore a gold and black silk rep tie with a white linen hankie in the breast pocket. Buck guessed that the tie was left over from an alumni banquet, since Gerald was a University of Missouri grad, and gold and black were their colors.

Rudolph and Buck greeted the Stevensons when they came in, and were visiting with them and their friends. Harry Foster was waiting at the side door by the jury box. He was ready to bring Milton in as soon as things settled down and everyone was seated. He motioned for Rudolph and Gerald to take their seats, opened the door and signaled for his deputies to bring Milton in. Once again, Harry left the handcuffs off the prisoner. Milton smiled at his family, turned and sat down beside Rudolph.

"Oyez, Oyez, Oyez," the bailiff intoned. "The Circuit Court of Johnson County, State of Missouri, the Honorable Judge Emerson Whitfield presiding, will now come to order. All rise." Everybody stood.

Judge Whitfield took his seat at the bench. He rapped his gavel. "Please be seated," he said. The judge had a law degree from Yale and a stern demeanor. He wasn't going to put up with any foolishness.

He began his instructions to the court.

"This is a court of law, and we have a very serious case to try. All participants will exercise the utmost decorum at all times. To you folks in the gallery, there will be no cheering, applause or outbursts of any kind. If there are, the offenders will be escorted out of the courtroom by the bailiff, and not allowed to return."

Turning to the jury, he said, "To you members of the jury, I will expect you to pay close attention to these proceedings. You have been furnished with pads and pencils. You may take notes to refer to as you see fit. I see 12 able citizens sitting before me in the jury box. I expect you to render a verdict based solely on the facts of the case as presented in this courtroom. I want you to close your ears and minds to any outside influence. The only things concerning this case that should influence you are the facts that will be brought out in this courtroom. I will give you further instructions when these proceedings are over and you are ready to deliberate. Do you understand these instructions?"

They all nodded.

"Are the attorneys ready?" Both sides indicated that they were. "Mr. Essex, you may start with your opening remarks to the jury."

Gerald slid his chair back and stood up. He adjusted his tie and looked around the courtroom for full effect. He picked a yellow pad up from the table and strutted over in front of the jury box. The jury consisted of seven men and five women, all white. That was typical of juries in Johnson County in 1936.

He rocked up on his toes to appear taller, and in a dramatic tone began his opening remarks. "Ladies and gentlemen of the jury, the prosecution will prove to you without a shadow of a doubt, and with irrefutable evidence, that the prisoner at the bar is guilty of murder as charged in the indictment."

Buck leaned over to Lois and whispered, "I wonder what old movie that line came from?" Lois smiled and nodded.

Gerald strutted and gestured and pounded his fist on the rail in front of the jury box as he related how the witnesses he would call to testify would absolutely and without question prove that this heinous crime had indeed been perpetrated by the accused.

Harry stood by the side door with his arms folded in front of him, getting the full effect of this drama, and thinking to himself, *What a ham. He probably thinks he'll get an Academy Award for this performance.*

Gerald talked for about 20 minutes, and the jury members were starting to shift in their seats. The longer he talked, the redder his face got. Finally, he stopped, walked over and dramatically dropped his pad on the prosecution table and sat down. He sat there with his head down as though he were exhausted and was waiting for the applause.

Judge Whitfield nodded at Rudolph, who got up and patted Milton on the back as he walked behind him on his way to the jury box. He leaned on the rail and looked each one of them in the eye, then in a low, steady voice, talked to the jury as though he was standing on their front porch. His slight German accent piqued their interest.

"First of all, I would like to thank you folks for taking time out of your busy schedules to serve on this jury. I know that some of you had to take time away from your jobs and businesses. That you ladies with small children had to find someone to care for them, and that all of you have been inconvenienced one way or another by serving here today. This trial is important, and I want to thank again for your service."

Rudolph looked down at his shoes for a moment. Then, putting his hands in his pockets, he looked up at the jury and began his remarks.

"There are basically two kinds of evidence in a trial like this. Direct evidence and circumstantial evidence. Direct evidence would be the case if someone actually saw the defendant put his hands around the victim's neck and choke her to death. That witness could testify that the defendant was guilty because of first-hand knowledge. On the other hand, if someone thought he saw the defendant go into the building where the victim was working, come out later and leave, without witnessing the actual crime, that would be circumstantial evidence."

"Sometimes defendants are convicted on purely circumstantial evidence, but there must be a preponderance of such evidence by very reputable witnesses, or evidence tying the accused to the crime that is indisputable. If there is a reasonable doubt in your minds as to the quality or nature of this type of evidence, then you must acquit the defendant. I know I can depend on you honest folks to make the right decision."

Rudolph nodded to the judge and walked back to the defense table. The whole speech took less than three minutes. There was silence in the courtroom for about a half a minute. The jury looked relieved that they were not going to be subjected to another long speech.

* * * * *

The judge was caught off guard, so he banged his gavel. "Let's take a 15-minute recess. Court will convene again at 10:55. Only a few people in the gallery left to go to the restrooms. The judge went back to his chambers to look at his notes and sip a cup of coffee.

Buck went up to the rail and talked to Rudolph. He congratulated him on his opening remarks and asked him if Clarence had gotten to him about the truck. He nodded yes and smiled confidently.

At exactly 10:55, the bailiff announced the end of the recess. "All rise," he shouted, loud enough for the people in the hall to hear. Judge Whitfield mounted the steps to the bench and rapped his gavel.

"Mr. Prosecutor, you may call your first witness." He disliked Gerald so much he couldn't bring himself to call him by his given name.

Gerald stood up and studied his yellow pad for a few seconds, as if he were trying to make up his mind which witness to call from a long list. Actually, all he had were the same three he called during the hearing. They were a little better coached this time, however. "The prosecution calls Mr. Charles Shanks." Gerald was obviously trying to add a little prestige to his witness.

Charlie Shanks was a bit more humble than he was at the hearing. The loss of his truck, and the fact that most of the Klan had deserted him, made him less combative.

Gerald strutted up to the witness chair in his white linen suit. "Mr. Shanks, will you please tell the jury what you saw on the evening of Friday, May 15th of this year?"

Charlie related how he had been sitting on his front porch drinking a glass of buttermilk, when he saw the defendant go behind the school building and come back out pushing Margaret Wilson's body in a two-wheeled cart, with her leg sticking out. How he watched him push the cart on down the alley and turn north on Chestnut Street.

"Did you get a good look at the person pushing the cart?" Gerald asked.

"Yes, sir, I surely did." Charlie had been well-coached.

"And is that person in this courtroom today?"

"Yes sir, that's him right there!" Charlie said, pointing to Milton.

Gerald smiled at the judge. He was well pleased with how things were going so far. "That's all I have for this witness, Your Honor," he said confidently.

Judge Whitfield looked over at Rudolph. "Does the defense have any questions for this witness?" he asked.

"Yes, Your Honor, we do have a few." Rudolph stood and slowly made his way to the witness chair. He pursed his lips and studied his note pad. "Mr. Shanks, where did the cart come from?"

He caught Charlie napping. Charlie had done so well relating all that he had seen the night of the murder, that he had relaxed and let his mind wander a little.

"Uh, what do you mean, cart?"

"I mean the cart you allegedly saw the defendant push down the alley. You stated that you saw him walk behind the school and come out later pushing a cart. Where did the cart come from?"

"Uh, it was just there. Somebody must have left it there."

"Okay, Mr. Shanks, someone just left it there. We'll go along with that for the time being. You also stated that you got a good look at the alleged murderer, is that true?"

"I sure did!" Charlie was holding his temper in check pretty well.

"Okay, Mr. Shanks, what was he wearing?"

"Uh, what do you mean?"

"I mean the clothing he had on. You got such a good look at him, what was he wearing?"

"Uh, a shirt and pants."

"What color were they?"

"You mean the shirt and pants?"

"Yes, the shirt and pants, if that's what he was wearing!"

"I couldn't tell."

"Why couldn't you tell?"

"Because it was too da—" Charlie caught himself before he could say "dark."

"Because it was too dark, Mister Shanks?"

"No, dammit, because I can't remember!" Charlie was getting frustrated, and he knew why. It was because of that damn Jew lawyer.

"Okay, Mr. Shanks, we'll let it go at that for now. Mr. Shanks, did you know Willie Cates?"

It was as though someone lit a fire under Charlie Shanks. His face got red, and he started sweating profusely. "Hell, no, I didn't know that damn nig—" Charlie caught himself again, as he realized there were a number of colored in the room.

Bam! The judge's gavel came down hard. "There will be absolutely no profanity in this courtroom, do you understand?" he said, pointing his finger at Charlie Shanks. Charlie looked down at his hands; they were starting to shake.

The judge pointed at Rudolph. "You may continue," he said.

"Mr. Shanks, were you at the Cates home about midnight on Saturday, May twenty-third? Remember Mr. Shanks, you're under oath."

"Hell, uh," he caught himself again. "No, I was not!" he said emphatically.

"What if I could produce witnesses that saw you there that night, what would you say to that, Mr. Shanks?"

Charlie was starting to lose his self-control. "I'd say they're all a bunch of damn liars!" he said, almost shouting.

Bam! Down came the gavel. "One more outburst like that, and I'll hold you in contempt of court!" Judge Whitfield said, pointing his finger at Charlie.

Gerald Essex jumped to his feet. "I object, Your Honor!" he said loudly.

Judge Whitfield peered at him over his glasses. "Are you objecting to me admonishing your witness? Because if you are, you're out of order."

Gerald's face was red. "Na . . . no," he stammered, "I was objecting to the line of questioning by the attorney for the defense. He's badgering the witness."

"Objection overruled, you may continue," the judge said, nodding at Rudolph.

Gerald sat down, muttering to himself, his face getting redder by the minute.

"You claim you weren't there that night because the witnesses are liars, is that what you're saying, Mr. Shanks?"

"Yes!" He had reduced his answers to one syllable.

"How would you know the witnesses are liars, if you haven't been told who they are yet, Mr. Shanks?"

"Because all them nig—uh, colored folks are liars."

"Okay, Mr. Shanks, we'll let it go at that. Mr. Shanks, do you own a pick-up truck?"

Charlie's face blanched almost white. "Uh, yes."

"Where is that truck now, Mr. Shanks?"

"I loaned it to a friend."

"Please answer my question, Mr. Shanks. Where is the truck now?"

Charlie sensed that he had been caught in a lie, but he couldn't back down now. "I think it's in Kansas City," he said.

"What is it doing in Kansas City, Mr. Shanks?"

"I loaned it to Joe Versano, and he took it to Kansas City on business." He knew that White Shirt would back him up if necessary.

"When was that, Mr. Shanks?"

"About three weeks ago."

"Do you mean to say that your truck has been gone for three weeks and you don't know where it is?"

No answer from Charlie.

Rudolph walked over to the defense table and picked up a sheet of paper. "Mr. Shanks, this is a certified letter from the Missouri Motor Vehicle Department in Jefferson City. It lists the motor number of the Ford pick-up truck you bought six years ago from the local Ford dealer. Your Honor, I would like to enter this piece of evidence as Defense Exhibit A."

"Bailiff, have the clerk enter the evidence as Defense Exhibit A."

Charlie was trying to look disinterested.

"We found your truck, Mr. Shanks. Would you like to know where?"

Charlie didn't answer. Rudolph glanced over at the jury; they were on the edge of their seats, paying close attention.

"We found your truck in Murphy's pasture, Mr. Shanks, burned to a crisp. Were you trying to destroy evidence, Mr. Shanks? Because if you were, that's called obstruction of justice, and that's against the law."

Gerald jumped up. "Objection, Your Honor," he shouted. "Mr. Shanks is not on trial here!"

"Overruled." Judge Whitfield was just as interested in Charlie's testimony as the jury.

"I don't know nothin' about that," Charlie said as if he were disinterested in the whole line of questioning. He was starting to sweat profusely, and his hands were shaking.

"Mr. Shanks, that truck was used in the murder of Willie Cates. We have witnesses to that terrible event. In fact, one of the witnesses shot out the back window and the left tail light of your truck and blew out a tire. Do you remember that, Mr. Shanks?"

"Objection! Mr. Shanks is not on trial here!" Someone could have lit a cigarette off Gerald Essex's face.

"Sustained! Mr. Shanks, you don't have to answer that question, and the jury will disregard it. It should not become any part of your deliberations." Judge Whitfield would liked to have heard the answer to the question himself, but thought it would be unfair to the witness.

Rudolph went back to the defense table and picked up a long item wrapped in newspaper. He unwrapped it and showed the charred remains of the 22 rifle Clarence had given to him. He walked back to the witness stand.

"Your Honor, I would like to enter this gun as Defense exhibit B."

"Bailiff, have the gun entered as Defense exhibit B."

Rudolph continued, "Mr. Shanks, do you recognize this rifle?"

"No."

"You should, it came from your burned-out truck Mr. Shanks."

"It's not mine." Charlie was limiting his replies to as few words as possible. He was afraid he would completely lose his temper and give everybody in the room a good cussing. Between the Jew lawyer and all the colored in the room, he was getting very near that point.

"Are you sure. Isn't this the gun you used to shoot out the front window of the jail?"

"Objection!" Gerald started to approach the bench, but was waved back by the judge.

"Overruled, answer the question, Mr. Shanks."

"No, it was not!" Charlie was barely under control.

"That's all the questions I have for this witness, Your Honor." Rudolph had made his point. He knew that once a question had been asked, it stuck with the jury. It's hard to put the toothpaste back in the tube. The jury would remember.

"The witness may step down." Judge Whitfield looked up at the clock that hung over the clerk's desk. It read 12:15. "This is a good time to take a break in these proceedings for lunch," he said. "This court is recessed until 1:30."

* * * * *

The whites went for the local restaurants, some to Dub's, some to Walker's and some to Hearts and other restaurants close by. The out-of-town colored, foreseeing problems, brought picnic lunches and were directed by the local Negroes to the Howard School, where they parked their cars on the playground and ate. Buck took Rudolph to his apartment, where Ann fixed tuna salad sandwiches for the five of them.

151

Even little Ellie liked tuna salad. There was cold milk for the children and iced tea for the adults to drink, with bread pudding for dessert.

Buck complimented Rudolph on his conduct of the case so far. They both filled Ann in on the morning's proceedings. At 1:15, they walked back over to the courthouse and took their seats in the courtroom.

At exactly 1:30, the bailiff stood up. "All rise," he intoned in his loud voice.

Judge Whitfield took the bench and looked over the courtroom to see if everyone was in their proper place. When he had assured himself that all was in order, he nodded at the prosecuting attorney.

"Mr. Essex, you may call your next witness."

For the next 20 minutes, Gerald questioned his two other witnesses, the lady from over on Gay Street who said she saw Milton pushing the cart up Old Town hill, and the man who said he saw Milton push the cart into the dump area.

Rudolph let them complete their testimony, then took each one in turn and completely destroyed their testimony by questioning their ability to see well enough at that time of the evening to tell Willie Cates from Milton Stevenson. By the time he finished with them, it could have been Christopher Columbus, for all they knew. He chose not to put any witnesses for the defense on the stand. His logic was that since the trial had gone so well and the jury seemed sympathetic to his client, that introducing more witnesses would only cloud the issue. Besides, he didn't want to take the spotlight off Milton and put it on some unknown person. He wanted the jury to keep thinking about how innocent Milton was when they went into the jury room to deliberate. When he finished, it was 2:30.

Judge Whitfield was amazed that the trial had moved along so quickly. Murder cases usually took at least two days, sometimes much longer. He had expected more objections and orations from the prosecuting attorney. He surmised that the surprising skill of the defense attorney had simply taken the starch out of him. He hammered his gavel.

"We will now take a 15-minute recess. When we come back at 2:45, I will expect the opposing attorneys to be ready to give their closing arguments to the jury."

This announcement took Gerald by surprise. He wasn't ready to give his closing argument. He expected the trial to last much longer and had neglected to give much thought to his summation. Now he had 15 minutes to come up with one, and the thought unnerved him considerably. He tried to get the judge's attention to ask for a continuance, but Judge Whitfield was on his way to his chambers, and although he saw Gerald waving his arms, he chose to ignore him.

On the other hand, Rudolph was happy with the announcement by Judge Whitfield. He had the feeling that the jury was sympathetic to his client at this time, and he was more than ready to give his closing argument. This was the most important case he had been involved in, in years, and he had put in a lot of time on it. He smiled confidently at Milton's family as he walked up the aisle to go to the men's restroom. They smiled back.

Gerald grabbed Jim Sartin's arm before he could leave the courtroom. "You're going to have to give the closing argument," he said with panic in his voice.

"What the hell for?" Jim was stunned. "You've been in charge of the prosecution of this case the entire time. You give the closing argument!"

"I can't, I'm sick."

"You're sick all right, if you think I'm going to pull your chestnuts out of the fire." Jim started off.

"Oooh!" Gerald moaned and, holding his stomach, left the courthouse, walked up the street to the hospital and checked himself in at the emergency room.

* * * * *

At 2:45, the bailiff stood. "All rise," he said.

Judge Whitfield, prompt as usual, mounted the bench. He looked over the courtroom to see if everything was in order. "Please be seated. Is the prosecuting attorney in the courtroom?" he asked. Word had gotten to him quickly that Gerald Essex had checked himself into the emergency room at the hospital with a stomach ache.

Jim Sartin reluctantly rose to address the judge. "Your Honor, Mr. Essex is not able to attend this portion of the trial. He's ill, Your Honor."

"I'm sorry to hear that. Who will be giving the closing argument for the prosecution?" Judge Whitfield knew Gerald Essex well enough to know that this was a ruse to cover the fact that he was not prepared to give the closing argument. He had pulled things like this before in his court.

"I will, Your Honor. I'm the assistant prosecuting attorney."

"Proceed."

Jim rose reluctantly and approached the jury box. He reviewed the case for the jury. He tried to reinforce the prosecution witnesses as best he could, knowing in his mind that it was a losing cause. The defense had done a brilliant job of discrediting them.

When he finished his summation, he thanked the jury for their service to the judicial system by serving on the jury and sat down, knowing full well that if the defendant were acquitted, he would get the blame.

Judge Whitfield nodded at Rudolph. "You're next, counselor."

Rudolph slowly rose from his seat and approached the jury. Once again, he took the time to look each one in the eye.

"A young man's life is at stake here. You have the power to free him, return him to his lovely family, or condemn him to be executed in the electric chair. Putting all prejudices aside, you must judge this case by the evidence presented in this court and nothing else. You have listened to the witnesses testify. You must decide if they were telling the truth, or if young Milton here [he went over and put his hand on Milton's shoulder] was telling the truth when he denied committing this heinous crime.

"There has not been one shred of direct evidence introduced into this trial. No one actually saw the crime committed, so there was no one to point a finger at young Milton here and say, 'You did it, because I saw you do it.' There were only witnesses who thought they saw him near the crime scene. It was almost dark when the crime was committed. There was no way that any of the witnesses who testified here today could have told the difference between Willie Cates and Milton Stevenson at that hour with any certainty and, ladies and gentlemen, you must be certain. If there is a reasonable doubt in your mind that Milton did this terrible crime, then you must acquit him. You must acquit him! Thank you for your kind attention and for your service to your community and the great state of Missouri." He nodded soberly to the jury and sat down. It was 3:30.

* * * * *

Judge Whitfield was pleased. This would be one of the shortest murder trials in Missouri history. The trial went about the way he had planned when he bound Milton over for trial. He knew that the prosecution's case was weak.

It had been a while, but he had seen Rudolph work a jury before. In his mind, he felt Milton would be acquitted because of the lack of evidence and the way Rudolph had discredited the prosecution's witnesses. But he also knew that if Milton was not acquitted, or if he had not been brought to trial to prove his innocence, the white community in the state would never leave him alone. He would be haunted with threats and perhaps even violence against him the rest of his life.

He banged his gavel. "Ladies and gentlemen of the jury, you will now be taken to the jury room to deliberate this case. The first thing you must do is elect a foreman, who will lead you through these deliberations. You must find the defendant either guilty or not guilty of first degree murder as charged in the indictment. This is a big responsibility, but I know that you good citizens are up to the task. I don't want you to contact anyone outside of the jury room for any reason other than to go to the restrooms. If you have a question concerning this trial, have your foreman write it on a piece of paper and address it to me. The bailiff will deliver it to me for consideration. You are not to read any newspapers or listen to any radio stations while deliberating this case. Don't talk to anyone about this case until after the verdict has been rendered. I don't want any outside influence to taint this jury. Does everyone on the jury understand these instructions?"

They all nodded yes, and the bailiff led them out of the courtroom. Harry Foster took Milton to the holding cell, and the judge left the bench, but for a while no one in the courtroom gallery moved. It was if they were afraid that if they left the courtroom, they would lose their seat and wouldn't be able to get back in. No one wanted to miss the verdict. The courtroom was hot, even with all the windows open. The ceiling fans didn't help much.

Finally Rudolph got up and walked back toward the doors. Buck got up and followed him. When they went out the double doors, Irv was standing in the hall. The deputy in charge of the door wouldn't let him in the courtroom, so he had stood in the hall trying to peek through the cracks in the doors and straining to hear the proceedings.

"Mr. Eisenstein, sir, how did it go?" he asked.

Buck chimed in. "He did very well, son. We should have a verdict pretty soon now."

Rudolph was mopping his brow with his hankie. "I was pleased with the way things went, but you can never tell about a jury; they can fool you." He turned to the deputy on the door. "We'll be on the east steps. Would you call us if the jury comes in with a verdict?"

The deputy nodded, and they walked down to the east side and sat on the wide stone banisters of steps in the shade of the courthouse. A little breeze came up and helped ease the heat. After a few minutes, Lois Huff came walking across the courthouse lawn carrying a tray with several glasses of iced tea, compliments of Dub's Cafe.

"Would you folks like some iced tea?" she asked, smiling, knowing full well what the answer would be. They each took a glass and thanked her profusely. Lois set the tray down and took a glass for herself. They sat talking about the trial as the courthouse clock struck 4:00.

Suddenly, Lois had a thought. "Mr. Eisenstein, do you think Milton would like a glass of tea?"

"That's a good thought, Lois, but the sheriff and his people are taking good care of him. I'll tell you what, though, would you mind getting some tea for the Stevensons, Milton's parents and sisters? They've been in that hot courtroom all day, and they are under a lot of stress."

"Not at all, but how can I get it to them? They won't let me take into the courtroom, will they?"

"No, I'll go tell them to come down here. I'll be right back." Rudolph rose and went back into the courthouse. Just as he started up the steps to the second floor, the deputy who guarded the doors came running down.

"Mr. Rudolph!" he shouted, "the jury is in."

Rudolph rushed back outside to tell the rest, and they all ran back up to the courtroom, including Lois who left the tray on the banister.

* * * * *

The courtroom filled up quickly as word went out. It was abuzz with murmurs as the people speculated about the verdict.

"All rise!" the bailiff shouted, so he would be heard above the din in the courtroom. Judge Whitfield took the bench.

"Be seated!" The judge had to shout to be heard, too, because there was so much chatter in the room. He pounded his gavel several times to quiet the crowd. "The sooner you folks get quiet, the sooner we can bring the jury back in!" he said in a loud voice. They settled down quickly when Harry Foster walked out in front of the gallery and motioned for quiet.

Judge Whitfield nodded to the bailiff, and he brought the jury in and seated them. "Will the jury foreman please stand up?"

The foreman was a man in his 60s, retired from the college as a math instructor. He had been unanimously elected foreman. One reason might have been that when he stood, he was about six feet four and probably intimidated the rest of the jurors by sheer size.

"Has the jury reached a verdict?" Judge Whitfield asked. You could have heard a pin drop, it got so quiet.

"We have, Your Honor."

"So say you one, so say you all?" the judge asked.

"Yes, Your Honor, it is a unanimous verdict." Obviously, the foreman was familiar with courtroom phrases. That's another reason why he was elected foreman, most likely.

"Will you hand it to the bailiff, please?" The bailiff took it and handed it to the judge, who looked at it, and without a sign of emotion handed it back to the bailiff. The bailiff took it back to the foreman. "Will the foreman please read the verdict?"

The court clerk asked the obligatory question. "In the case [she gave the case number] of the State of Missouri versus Milton Stevenson of the charge of murder in the first degree, how do you find?"

The foreman hesitated just a moment for effect. He must have been a frustrated thespian. The silence was deafening. He cleared his throat, "We the jury find the defendant not guilty."

A whoop went up from the colored in the room, and not a few of the whites. Judge Whitfield banged his gavel over and over, until he finally got some semblance of order.

"I want to thank the jury for serving on this case and for your verdict. You are excused. Bailiff, you may release the prisoner."

The colored folks from the Roy community gathered around Milton and every one of them gave him a big hug. They shook Rudolph's hand until he thought his arm would fall off. Milton told them of Irv's role in securing such a good attorney, and they went looking for him to thank him. The courthouse clock struck five as the last of them were filing out. Most of them were standing on the courthouse lawn waiting for George Stevenson to give the signal to load up and head for Saline County. By 5:30 they were all gone. The janitor locked the courthouse and went home.

* * * * *

Buck went back to the station tired, but happy, after seeing Milton and his family off on their journey home. The only cloud on the horizon was the fact that there was still a murderer out there who needed to be caught. He was so deep in thought that he barely spoke to Darlene when he walked past her.

"Chief!" she yelled at him. "What did you think about the trial?"

He wheeled around, then went back and sat on the corner of her desk. "It couldn't have gone better," he said, smiling from ear to ear.

"I know, wasn't it great? You look tired, you had better go see your family, I think they're waiting supper on you."

Buck started to the back when the phone rang. Darlene called at him to pick it up. He walked into his office and picked up the receiver. It was that woman again.

"Congratulations, everybody knew the colored boy didn't kill that teacher." She spoke in a low voice, as usual, almost a whisper. "Now you can concentrate on catching the person who really did it."

"And who might that be, Miss uh . . . uh?"

She didn't fall for his little ploy. "Never mind who this is, but you'll be surprised when you do catch him."

"Can you give me a clue?"

She hung up. Buck sat there for a few minutes and thought about what she said. She gave him a couple of clues unthinkingly. One, it definitely was a man, and two, it was someone he hadn't thought of before. She said he would be surprised when he actually figured out who it was. In that event, she must know about his interviews with Russell Wilhelm.

The phone rang again, and again Darlene yelled for the Chief to pick up. It was Freda from the telephone office. "That call came from a phone booth in the drugstore on the corner of Pine and Holden."

"Thanks, Freda."

"Shall I ring that number?"

"No, she's very good at timing her calls, so there won't be any witnesses. I'll check with the store personnel later. Thanks anyway." He hung up.

The courthouse clock struck 6:00 as Buck walked up the steps and into another world. Ann had dinner on the table and was amusing the children while they waited on him. Little Ellie was in Ann Marie's old high chair, dressed in pink with a pink ribbon in hair. She looked so pretty that Buck's heart skipped a beat. It had been years since they had a little girl in the house, and he almost cried. She reminded him of those wonderful years in that big old house on Broad Street.

Ann had Jimmie on her lap and was teaching the children nursery rhymes. She had resurrected Ann Marie's toy piano from the basement and was pecking out tunes on it as they sang.

"Little Bo Peep has lost her sheep and doesn't know where to find them."

Even Buck joined in on that one.

* * * * *

Tuesday, July first, was pay day for Buck. The city paid its employees every two weeks, on the first and the fifteenth. He went by the city offices about 10:00 in the morning and picked up his check. That way, he got it a couple of days sooner and saved the city the three cents it took to mail it.

As he walked down to Breckenridge State Bank to deposit it, he thought about the mysterious phone calls he had received. In the back of his mind, he kept thinking he had heard that voice before, but just couldn't place it. Russell Wilhelm was coming out of the bank just as Buck started in the front door.

"I guess you'll be coming to visit me again, now that the colored boy has been acquitted," he said in a jocular way.

"I guess so," Buck said. He wasn't kidding. He needed a suspect. He went into the bank and got a deposit slip from the holder on the counter and started filling it out. He kept hearing that woman's voice. He looked around the bank. There were only two other customers in the bank besides himself; both were men. "I must be losing my mind," he said to himself. He went to the teller's window and made his deposit.

Just as he was starting to leave the window, Elizabeth Breckenridge came out of her husband's office. "Hi, Chief," she chirped. "Warm enough for you?"

"You're kidding, of course?" Buck asked as he held the door open for her.

"Yes, of course, I'm kidding," she laughed over her shoulder, as she walked down the street to her car. It was a new Chrysler Highlander coupe with leather upholstery. Elizabeth seemed to get most anything she wanted. At 31, she was 18 years younger than her husband. Everyone in town, at one time or another, had wondered how that came about.

Buck stood there in front of the bank for a moment, then headed back up Holden Street to the station. He was shaking his head and muttering to himself, *That voice, I keep hearing that voice.*

When he got back to the station, he found a thank you note from Margaret Wilson's parents on his desk. The postman had just brought the morning mail. Back in May, about a week after the murder and three days after Margaret's funeral, they drove to Warrensburg to clean out her room. They stopped by the station to thank Buck and all the people who had been so kind to them. Buck gave them Margaret's purse and apologized for not getting it to them sooner. They went by and thanked Lester Phipps, then left town.

It was a nice letter, thanking everyone for their kindnesses and apologizing for taking so long to write. They were grateful for the money that was in the purse. Mr. Wilson got his corn planted with help of neighbors, and they were feeling better.

Buck pinned the letter up on the bulletin board in the break room. He studied his notes on the Wilson case for a while, then went upstairs for lunch.

* * * * *

While he and Ann were having lunch with the children, the phone rang. It was Rudolph Eisenstein.

Ann answered the phone. "Ann," he said, "I have some good news for you and Buck."

Ann knew what he was going to say. "We're going to get to adopt the children!" she interrupted. She was so excited, her heart was pounding.

"I think so, but it's not definite yet, although the prospects are very good. I included the letters from Eleanor's brother and sister renouncing any claim to the children with the application for adoption, and the state is looking very favorably on it."

"Oh, I'm so excited!" she exclaimed, "Let us know as soon as you hear for sure, and come have dinner with us this evening, please!"

Rudolph begged off. Work piled up on his desk during his defense of Milton, and he needed to catch up. "I'll be glad to take you up on the dinner invitation some other time, but I'm real busy tonight." He hoped he hadn't hurt their feelings.

Ann was disappointed. "Sure," she said, "there will be other invitations. We would just like to show our gratitude some way. You have done such a good job for us, and we want you to know it."

"I know, Ann, I surely do, and I'll call you the minute I hear anything, bye." He hung up.

Ann filled Buck in on the conversation, and the news lifted his spirits. He and Ann were really getting attached to the children, and the thought of having them for good excited them.

"Do you know what would be fun?" she asked. "Saturday is the fourth. If you can get the day off, why don't we pack a picnic basket and take the children to the Swope Park Zoo in Kansas City for the day?"

"That sounds like fun to me." Buck liked the idea. "I'll take the day off, let's plan on it."

* * * * *

That afternoon, Buck was sitting at his desk pondering the Wilson murder, when it suddenly dawned on him where he heard that voice before. She tried to disguise it, but it was her. It had to be; it was Elizabeth Breckenridge, but what in the world did she have to do with the Wilson case, and why was she so sure Milton didn't do it?

That's why he heard the voice in the bank this morning. She was there, in her husband's office talking to him. He heard her through the door. He wasn't hearing things, she was actually there. He remembered talking to her by their swimming pool, when he and Clarence went to their house to ask about the fountain pen. It was her. "Now what?" he asked himself.

* * * * *

Elizabeth Breckenridge was Elizabeth Cole when she came to work at the bank. Born in Holden, Missouri, she came to Warrensburg in 1922, right out of high school to further her education. She worked one year at the Rexall Drug Store behind the soda fountain. Her parents would help her some, but she would have to work to get through college. She loved history and planned to major in it at CMSC, with a minor in English.

She roomed in a house over on South Street for three dollars a week and walked to work. She was paid $6 a week and got her lunch free at the store. Some days that's all she ate all day. With only $2 a week for food and clothing, she still managed to put a dollar a week in the bank toward her tuition. In a year, with some help from her parents, she planned to enroll at the college.

Elizabeth (Beth to her friends) was an attractive young lady, with long auburn hair and brown eyes. Her slender build and naturally sultry voice made her especially attractive to the boys, but she was no fragile doll. The week before she left for Warrensburg, she broke off with her boyfriend and told him firmly not to follow her, as she would be too busy to date much. She told him she was sorry, but she had plans for her future, and they didn't include him.

Actually, she told three boys the same thing. She was popular with the boys and dated all three, but one more than the others. Holden is only 15 miles from Warrensburg, and she didn't want them running back and forth and disrupting her plans for the future. She wanted a chance to meet other boys from other places and to broaden her horizons.

Raised on her folks' dairy farm, she knew what hard work was. She was used to getting up at 4:00 a.m. to hand-milk cows. She knew how to cool the milk, separate it if necessary, bottle it and deliver it from door to door. There was no pasteurization in those days on small farms, so all the equipment and empty bottles had to be carefully sterilized. She knew how to do that, too.

She had two older brothers, a younger brother and a younger sister. They all did their share to help make the dairy profitable. The Cole Dairy was a mainstay in Holden's economy, and in a town that small it was important for the citizens to have a dependable source of fresh milk. The restaurants, the schools, the townspeople all depended on Cole's Dairy.

Elizabeth was the first of her siblings to leave home and seek a life away from the dairy. Naturally, her parents were disappointed, but they knew in their hearts that this pretty bird would one day leave the nest. They all gathered at the bus station that June day in 1922 when she boarded the bus for Warrensburg.

One day in July 1923, she was in the Breckenridge Bank making her weekly deposit when Tom Breckenridge approached her and asked her if she would like to work in the bank. She was stunned. She had never thought about applying for work at the bank. She had no experience, and although she was a good student in high school and could type 40 words a minute, she thought the bank only hired college grads, or at least college students.

"Ya, yes, I would, very much," she stammered.

Tom took her into his office, asked her a few questions about herself and got her an application for employment. He was a handsome man of 38, married and with two teen-age sons in high school. One was a senior and the other a junior. Beth was flattered that he had noticed her.

"Fill that application out and bring it in tomorrow. We'll talk about hours and salary then," he said, smiling broadly. He was very pleasant and didn't seem bothered at all that Beth was only 19.

Beth thanked him and almost ran back to the drugstore where she worked. She wouldn't mention the job offer to anyone until she was certain she had been hired at the bank. She was afraid that she would be let go immediately at the drugstore, and if the bank job fell through, she would be unemployed. She couldn't afford that. It would throw her plans for the future out of whack.

Beth started work at the bank in mid-July, after giving the drugstore a week's notice. They let her stay for a week to train her replacement.

At first, she was given menial tasks, typing, running errands and making coffee for the rest of the employees. This suited her. The pay was better, and she enrolled in night classes at the college. She worked from 9:00 to 4:00 at the bank and went to school from 6:00 until 10:00. She was happy.

In January 1924, one of the tellers was promoted to job of secretary for Tom Breckenridge, and Beth was promoted to teller. She really liked the job. She was accurate with figures, and usually her window balanced to the penny at closing time. It also meant more money. At $12 a week, she could afford to dress nicer, and even toyed with the idea of buying a used car so she could visit her folks more often. She decided to put that off for a while. She liked saving money better.

* * * * *

In the summer of 1925, tragedy struck at the bank. Tom Breckenridge's wife accidentally drowned in the family swimming pool. The boys were both at summer camp, and it was the maid's day off, so there were no witnesses. Tom had lunch at the Lion's Club that day, and when he went home at 4:00 for his afternoon cocktail, he found her floating in the pool, fully dressed.

There was some suspicion surrounding the death, but with no witnesses, the coroner ruled it accidental. Tom appeared to be devastated by her death, but quickly recovered. That fall, both boys went off to college and never returned to the family home.

Tom became the most sought-after bachelor in Warrensburg, an unofficial title he seemed to revel in. It meant invitations to all kinds of parties and gatherings. If he had any romantic interests, he was very discreet. He joined the Kansas City Club, an exclusive gathering place for the elite of Kansas City and surrounding counties. They had guest rooms so out-of-town dignitaries could spend the night. It was rumored that Tom had a lady friend in Kansas City, but he denied it. Still the rumor persisted.

He had settled into something of a routine. Nine to 3:00 at the bank, Lions Club on Wednesday, golf on Saturday mornings and a trip to Kansas City on Saturday afternoon. He usually returned home on Sunday morning in time to sit on a front pew at the First Christian Church.

If he went to a banker's convention or out-of-town meeting, he always took his secretary with him to take notes. At least, that's what he told the people at the bank. He insisted they always stayed in separate rooms.

By the fall of 1928, things had settled down at the bank. The death of Tom's wife was pretty much forgotten. Beth had enough college hours to be classified as a second semester senior and would get her B.S. degree in June. She lacked 15 hours to graduate, and by taking eight hours in the fall semester and seven in the spring semester, she would barely qualify for her degree.

She planned to write her theses after Christmas. That would give her plenty of time to complete it by June of 1929. The History of Dairy Farming in Missouri was to be the subject of her theses, and she had already done her research. She just needed to get it down on paper.

She was happy and still had no serious boyfriends. Her old boyfriend from Holden had tried to rekindle a romantic relationship, but she discouraged him so that he finally gave up and married another girl. She would occasionally go to a movie on a Saturday night with one of the male students from the college, but that was as far as it went.

She did have several dates with one on the younger professors at the College, but when rumors about an impending wedding started spreading around the campus, she broke it off. She got the reputation of being cold toward men, and although she was undoubtedly one of the most beautiful women in Warrens-burg, men quit asking her out.

She wasn't cold, just ambitious and driven. She wanted to be the first in her family to get a college degree. Then she wanted to teach history, perhaps even on a college level. At 25, she figured she still had plenty of time for romance in her life.

* * * * *

Just before Christmas 1928, Tom's secretary quit her job and left town quite suddenly. Some eyebrows went up, but she didn't return. She was Beth's best friend at the bank, so Beth tried to get in touch with her to no avail. Her telephone had been disconnected, and she left no forwarding address at the bank. Beth even went by her apartment one day after work and talked to her landlady.

"Did she give you any idea where she was going?" Beth asked.

"No, she didn't, and she seemed very upset."

"How did she go, did someone pick her up?"

"Yes, a taxicab came by just before midnight, and I think he took her to the train station."

"Did she leave anything? Any letters or clothing, anything?" Beth had expected a note or some kind of clue as to her destination.

"Would you like to see her apartment?" her landlady asked.

"Yes, I would." Beth was determined to find out more about her friend's departure. The landlady gave her a key and she went up the stairs.

It was a one-bedroom furnished apartment on the second floor of an enormous house on east Grover Street. Beth walked in and looked in all the drawers, even in the kitchen. She checked the closet and found a sweater and a pair of slacks that Beth figured had been purposely left behind for lack of space in her suitcase. She was about to give up when she looked in the waste basket in the kitchen. There was a counter check from the bank crumpled up in the bottom with a telephone number written on the back of it. She put it in her coat pocket, gave the key back to the landlady, thanked her and left.

* * * * *

The bank had its Christmas party that year as usual, but there was a pall over the entire affair that no one could explain. Perhaps it was the fact that Mr. Tom Breckenridge's secretary was absent and no one knew where she had gone. They drew names and exchanged gifts, and Tom was a little more generous with their Christmas bonuses than the year before, but the spirit of Christmas had been dimmed.

One day in January of 1929, Tom called Beth into his office and shut the door. Beth was baffled. She had no idea what he would say or do. She had told no one about the phone number she found, so it couldn't be about that.

Tom motioned for her to sit in the chair next to his desk. "How long have you worked here at the bank?" he asked.

Her heart skipped a beat. "Uh, about five and a half years," she said, her heart pounding. *Was he going to fire me?* she asked herself.

"Do you like working at the bank?" he asked.

Oh, oh, here it comes, she thought. "Yes, sir, I do," she finally managed to say.

"How would you like to be my secretary?" he asked.

A hundred questions went through her mind before she answered. "Da—do you think I can do the work?" she sputtered, stalling for time.

"Of course, you can," he assured her. "You can type, can't you?"

"Yes, sir, and I can file and take dictation, although I'm a little rusty. It might take me two or three weeks to get my speed back."

"Okay, tell you what you do," he said. "You go home tonight and think about it and I'll talk to you about it again tomorrow." Beth thanked him and went back to her teller cage.

That night she skipped her classes at the college to do some serious thinking. She asked herself a number of questions. Did he really like her work, or was he setting her up for something else? She worried about what happened to his previous secretary. Would she be expected to go to meetings with him? Would this job open up other positions at the bank for her?

Finally she grabbed her coat and purse and walked to the drugstore on the corner of Holden and Pine. She got three dollars' worth of change at the cigar counter and went to the phone booth back by the soda fountain. She took the phone number, on the back of the counter check, out of her purse. Ruby at the telephone office had done some checking for her. It was a St. Louis number.

"Long distance for St. Louis, Missouri, please," she told the operator. When the long distance operator came on the line, Beth gave her the number.

The phone rang on the other end on the line, and a very pleasant voice answered.

"Sacred Heart of Mary Maternity Home, Sister Mary Katherine speaking," she said sweetly.

"Maternity home?" Beth asked.

"Yes, dear, how may I help you? Are you in trouble?"

"No, I'm just looking for a friend," she said.

"Is she expecting?"

"I think so."

"I'm sorry, dear, but we don't give out the names of our expectant mothers," the nun said.

Beth thanked her and hung up. "Wow," she said to herself, "I need to work things out. She went to the college library to do some deep thinking. She picked a table in the back, hidden from the front door, where she could be alone. There were only three other students in the library at that hour, scattered around the reading room. She looked through one of the waste baskets and found a sheet of notebook paper with very little writing on it. She turned it over and took a pencil from her purse.

She listed all the questions that were troubling her. Was Tom Breckenridge the father of his former secretary's child? If so, why not an abortion? Had he given her money for an abortion, perhaps to be performed in Kansas City, only to have her decide to have the child and flee to St. Louis? Did he know where she was? If Beth went to work as his secretary, would she be expected to be his mistress, too?

When she finished, she had a whole page of questions, with no answers. She sat and studied the page for a few minutes, then folded it and put it in her purse. She had made up her mind.

She would accept the job as Tom's secretary, but she wouldn't sleep with him unless he married her. She would study the banking business carefully. She would attend out-of-town banking meetings with him, but would insist on separate hotel rooms. She would not go partying with him and his banking friends after hours. That would only lead to trouble, and ruin her reputation. She had a definite plan in mind. It would take time, but in the long run, would be worth it.

* * * * *

Beth graduated in June of 1929 with a B.A. in history. Later the same month, she married Tom Breckenridge. Beth had teased him along for over five months, until he finally consented to marry her. It was a small wedding at the Breckenridge home, with a poolside reception afterward. Just some of Tom's business friends, a few out-of-town bankers and Beth's family.

There was no big honeymoon planned. Beth wanted to take a trip to New York by train in the fall to do some shopping, and they would call that their honeymoon. Tom did take her to Kansas City over the weekend following the Friday wedding. He wanted to show his "trophy wife" off to his high-rolling friends at the Kansas City Club. They were dazzled by her beauty and told him so. Tom was pleased and had a good time. Beth smiled and cooed and flirted. She was a hit at the club. They had no idea what was in her mind. Beth had a plan.

* * * * *

That fall, the stock market crashed, and banks began to close. By June of 1933, nearly half of the nations banks either were closed voluntarily or were forced to close by the federal government because of insolvency. Tom Breckenridge was scared. He didn't think Breckenridge State Bank could make it. Farmers were starting to default on their loans, which left them short of cash. They had used up most of their reserve, and people were starting to withdraw their savings for fear that the bank would fail.

On March 6, 1933, two days after President Roosevelt's inauguration, he declared a banking holiday, suspending all bank transactions for two weeks. Breckenridge Bank was closed. On March 9, Congress passed the Emergency Banking Relief Act. Only banks that were members of the Federal Reserve System were allowed to reopen immediately after the banking holiday.

The Secretary of the Treasury was empowered to recall all gold and gold certificates nationwide and was also authorized to determine which banks would be allowed to open after the national banking holiday. It also forbade gold hoarding and gold export, with a stiff fine and jail time for offenders.

* * * * *

Tom came to Beth on March 10th and told her to type up a notice on bank stationery that the bank was closed for good and tape it to the front door. He was going to tell the employees that they no longer had a job.

Beth was furious. "You're not going to close this bank!" she stormed.

"We're out of money!" he yelled back.

"What about your money, our money, the family money, let's use it. It will only be for a few months. The government is going to lend money to banks that they feel can make it, and we can make it!"

"Come with me," he told her, and started to the rear of the bank. She followed him, still fuming. He took her down the stairs to the basement under the bank. It was only the second time she had ever been down there. It was used for storage mostly. There were some dusty file cabinets full of old records. Piles of cardboard boxes full of more records. There was a long oak table covered with old ledger books dating back to the mid 1800s. He led her to the far end, to a door locked with a heavy hasp and a big brass padlock. He unlocked the door and turned on the light.

In the dim light of a single light bulb dangling from the ceiling, Beth saw two steamer trunks in the middle of the small room. Tom opened one of them. It was nearly full of gold. All kinds of gold. Gold coins of every denomination, even bars of gold bullion.

"What's left of the family fortune is in these two trunks," he said.

Beth was flabbergasted. "Where did all this come from?" she asked.

Tom told her the story of how his great, great, great-great grandfather, Sebastian Breckenridge, the Earl of Wickingham, received a grant of a large tract of land in Virginia from the king of England. How he had prospered as a tobacco farmer and left a fortune to his five sons, one of whom migrated to Kentucky. He in turn left his fortune to his only son, who came to St. Louis, Missouri, where he built warehouses along the river and imported all kinds of goods from Europe, which were sold at a very good profit.

He passed his fortune and businesses to his sons. Eventually, one of the Breckenridge men (Tom's grandfather), came to Warrensburg and opened up a hardware store. He never trusted banks and kept most of his money in gold. Finally, when he had accumulated more gold than was practical to store at home, he opened his own bank, and it prospered. When Tom inherited the bank from his father, he was told about the gold. It was Tom who built the room at the bank and stored it there.

Tom didn't believe in hoarding gold and invested most of the profits from the bank in stocks and bonds. The rest supported his lavish lifestyle. When the crash came, he was wiped out in the market. He had chased such stocks as AT&T, Westinghouse, Singer Sewing Machine and RCA all the way to the top, buying big blocks on margin. When they came tumbling down along with the rest of the market, it took his and the bank's entire fortune to cover his margin calls.

Their house, cars and this gold was all they had left in the world.

"There must be a million dollars in gold in these two trunks," Beth gasped.

"No, but about half that amount," Tom said.

Beth was really excited. "Tom, do you realize that if there is a half million in gold here, that our bank is safe? Our total deposits are only $360,000 in round numbers. There is enough here to cover all of our deposits and still have money to lend!"

Tom was amazed at Beth's grasp of the bank's condition. He had no idea what the bank's total deposits were. It was obvious that he hadn't been very close to the business end of the bank. He left that up to his vice-president and head cashier, Bill Worsham. He spent most of his time investing the bank's profits and doing public relations, like the Lion's club and playing golf. But Beth knew. She had worked closely with Bill the past ten years and knew more about the bank than anyone, including Bill.

"We've got to get this gold out of the country now," Tom was adamant.

"No, Tom!" Beth was just as adamant. "It's illegal to own gold now. Haven't you studied the new Emergency Banking Relief Act? We have to turn it into the Treasury!"

Tom had heard of the Act, but he hadn't studied it. He figured if they could get the gold out of the country, possibly to Switzerland, and open a numbered account, they could just give up the bank and live off the money from the gold. When he told Beth his plans, she hit the ceiling. He had never seen her like this.

"What about our depositors?" she screamed. "Do we just screw them out of their life savings? What about our reputation? Doesn't your good name mean anything to you?" She was livid.

They yelled at each other for 15 minutes. This was their first real argument in four years of married life. When Tom wouldn't be moved, she used another ploy.

"Okay," she said calmly. "You take the gold and run. I'll turn you into the FBI, and you won't even make it out of Missouri. According to the new Act, there's a ten-million-dollar fine and ten years in prison for violators. I'll see you in a federal pen."

"You're not serious?"

"I have never been more serious, and furthermore, I'll call the newspaper and tell them about the girlfriends you've had over the past four years—the ones I wasn't supposed to know about, including the one in Kansas City. And what about your son in St. Louis? How old is he now? Three, I think he is, isn't he?"

Tom was crestfallen. He had no idea Beth knew all these things.

* * * * *

Breckenridge State Bank opened March 14 for business as usual. The gold had been secretly taken to the Federal Reserve Bank in St. Louis by FBI couriers, and Breckenridge State Bank was credited with $508,742 in Federal Reserve funds and made a member of the Federal Reserve System. Everything was legitimate. Beth and Tom Breckenridge could hold their heads up in the community.

There was a small run on the bank when it first reopened, but when people saw that the bank wasn't going to fold, deposits started coming in again.

By July 1934, the bank was doing well, but there was no doubt among the business leaders in Warrensburg who ran the bank. Tom was allowed to approve loans and hire and fire the employees, but Beth made the big decisions.

* * * * *

The courthouse clock struck 3:00 just as Buck picked up the phone and called the bank. When he asked for Elizabeth Breckenridge, he was told that she had left the bank for the day. He called the house. The colored maid called Beth to the phone.

"This is Elizabeth Breckenridge," she said sweetly, "who am I speaking to?"

"This is Chief Pettit, Mrs. Breckenridge. I'd like to talk to you in private, if I may." He was absolutely sure it was her now.

"Well, there's no one here now, but my husband will be home soon, and then there's Doretha, our maid. Where would you suggest we talk, Chief?" She knew something was up.

"Why don't we meet in the college library? There's a table way to the back that's seldom used, we could talk there."

"I'll be there in 30 minutes, Chief." She hung up.

Buck took the Studebaker. He didn't want people to see a police car sitting near the library. He had just sat down when Beth walked in. He watched her walk back to the table. She had obviously changed clothes. She was not in her bank garb. She had on a yellow, green and red-flowered print silk blouse with silk slacks in solid green that matched the blouse. She wore white leather sandals with medium heels. Her dark auburn hair was pulled back and tied with a scarf that matched her blouse. Her finger and toenails were painted in matching red. She was strikingly beautiful.

Buck was trying to keep a low profile so nobody would notice him, and here she comes like a fashion model walking down the runway. He was surprised there weren't half a dozen college men trailing along behind her. If it wasn't July, there probably would be. He stood up to greet her.

"Hi, Chief," she cooed. "I hope you haven't been waiting long. I had to take a few minutes to change. I was in my work clothes when you called." She tossed her white linen clutch on the table.

"I just got here myself," he said pulling a chair out for her. They sat down.

"It has been a rather exciting summer, hasn't it?" She had a very beguiling smile. "I sure was glad to see that colored boy acquitted, weren't you?"

"Yes, I was; now I need to find the one who really did it." He hoped she got the drift of his statement and was suspecting that he was on to her game. He didn't want any more cat-and-mouse games; he wanted to know what she knew.

"You're not suggesting that I know who did it, are you?"

"I'm not suggesting anything, Mrs. Breckenridge, but I do recognize your voice as the one who has been calling me for the last month telling me that Milton didn't do it. What was the purpose of your calls, if you weren't suggesting you knew who actually did it?"

"My goodness, Chief, you can't possibly think that I would protect a murderer, can you?"

"Please don't play games with me, Mrs. Breckenridge. Tell me what you know. I need to catch a killer."

At the word "killer," her mood changed. "I know some things that I just can't tell. It might even mean my life. You'll just have to keep on looking, I'm sorry." She got up and walked out.

Buck was stunned. He knew she wanted to tell him who the killer was, but held back. He sat there for a few minutes thinking after she left. *Oh, she knows who did it all right,* he thought to himself. *It must be someone she knows real well, but who's she protecting?* He thought about that. Her husband? Someone at the bank? Could she be having an affair with someone? All these things were on his mind as he drove back to the station.

* * * * *

On Independence Day, July 4, 1936, the Pettits drove to Kansas City. Buck drove the Studebaker, with Ann holding Ellie on her lap and Jimmie in the back seat. They left Warrensburg a little after 8:00 in the morning and were at the Swope Park Zoo by 9:45. They took the children through the zoo, and at noon Ann spread a quilt on a grassy spot near where they parked the car and spread their picnic lunch.

There was fried chicken, potato salad, baked beans and chocolate cake for desert. There was a gallon thermos full of lemonade with ice cubes floating in it. Ellie had cut enough teeth to really be able to chew on a chicken leg. They laughed and sang little songs, swatted flies and had a great time. They didn't stay for the fireworks, as it would have made them too late getting home. That night Buck stood in the doorway to the children's room as Ann said their prayers with them and tucked them in. Buck smiled; Ann was her old self again.

* * * * *

Tuesday, July 7, was another hot one. Buck sat at his desk studying his notes on the Wilson murder case. He had four pocket-sized notebooks filled out and was working on a fifth. He ran across an entry he made on May 22. He was talking to Amos, the janitor at Reese School. When asked if he had seen any cars parked near the school, Amos told him he saw a big blue one parked along the east side of the school right at dark. When he locked up to go home, it was gone. So was Margaret Wilson.

Buck stuck his head out of his office door and yelled at Darlene. "Darlene, when Clarence calls in, tell him to come get me. We need to make a short trip." Fifteen minutes later, Clarence pulled up in front of the station and stuck his head in the door.

"Tell the Chief I'm here," he told Darlene and went out and sat in the patrol car and waited for Buck.

"Let's go out and talk to Russell Wilhelm again," Buck said as he slid into the passenger seat of the patrol car.

They found Russell with a crew baling hay. Fortunately, they were close to the road as Clarence and Buck drove by, and Buck spotted him among the rest of the farmers. Very few farmers owned a hay baler in those days, so they would cut the hay, rake it into wind rows and call a crew with a baler to come bale it for so much a bale, or on the shares. Clarence pulled over and honked the horn. Russell looked up and saw the patrol car. He motioned for the crew to go on with their work and walked over to the fence, pulling his leather gloves off as he walked. He spoke as soon as he got close enough for them to hear.

"Hi, Sheriff, you want to help us bale some hay? We could use another hand," he said facetiously.

Buck grinned. "I'm afraid I'm a little out of practice," he said. "Besides, I didn't bring my overalls."

"Don't worry about the overalls, I've got an extra pair at the house," Russell said as he crawled through the barbed wire fence. "What's on your mind, Sheriff?" he asked. He appeared calm, but his knees felt like they were about to buckle.

Buck didn't beat around the bush. "I was going through my notes on the Margaret Wilson case and found where Amos Swenson, the janitor, said he saw a dark blue car, a lot like yours, parked by the school as he was about to lock up and go home the night she was killed. Said he saw it out the window from the second floor. When he got outside, it was gone. Was that your car, Russell?"

"Oh, no, Sheriff. Like I said, I just drove by the school, I didn't stop."

"Are you sure? You know we caught you lying about this before."

"I'm sure, Sheriff, honest."

"Do you still own that dark blue Packard sedan?"

"Yes, sir, it's still out in the barn covered with a tarp."

"I may bring Amos out here to look at it, or better yet, I may have you bring it to the station in town, so Amos can see it."

"Any time, Sheriff, just give me a call, or come out. I'll be glad to show it to him, I've got nothing to hide."

Buck thanked him; there was no need to be mean or abrasive. Clarence started to drive off when Russell yelled at Buck and Clarence hit the brakes.

"When you call, Sheriff, just tell me you want to talk to me, or that you're coming out. No need to go into any details. I'm on a party line, and you know how fast rumors can spread around here."

"I know exactly what you mean," Buck said. He waved and they drove off.

"What do you think? Is he lying or not?" Clarence asked as he turned the car around and headed back to town.

"I still think he's telling the truth, but we've got to keep trying. Call Amos Swenson and set up a time for him to view the car."

* * * * *

Saturday, July 11, the nominating committee of the Missouri State Police Chiefs Association was having a meeting in Sedalia to nominate a slate of officers for their new fiscal year starting October 1. Buck was on the committee and was expected to be there for the dinner meeting at the Bothwell Hotel. The letter said, "Cocktails at 6:00 p.m. and dinner at 7:00. Nominating meeting from 8:00 'til 9:00, and after that they would adjourn to the Bothwell Lounge downstairs for more drinks."

Buck asked Ann if she would like to go with him, but she declined, citing the need to be with the children. She insisted the children were still too insecure to trust with a babysitter, and Buck agreed.

He dreaded going. He was not a big drinker, and some of these meetings turned into drunken orgies. He was determined to sneak out right after the nominations. He didn't want to hurt anyone's feelings, but he just didn't enjoy that kind of revelry. He would much rather be at home with his family.

As soon as the meeting was over and the men started drifting downstairs to the lounge, he slipped out and headed to the parking lot. He started the engine in the Studebaker and was ready to pull out when a yellow '35 Cadillac convertible with the top down swerved into the lot off Fourth Street and parked in a slot just three cars down. Buck thought he recognized at least one of the two people in the car. He turned the motor off and slouched down in the seat. The cars were parked facing an alley that ran beside the hotel. Buck figured they would pass behind him on their way into the hotel, which fronted on Fourth Street.

He heard a woman giggling and laughing, and there was no mistaking that voice. He heard the doors slam on the Cadillac, and shortly the two people walked behind the Studebaker arm in arm. They had obviously been drinking. When they turned the corner to go into the hotel, Buck got a good look at them.

What do we have here? he thought to himself. *Beth Breckenridge and the good Doctor Plunkett. So, Tom's wife is having an affair with Larry Plunkett, his best friend and golfing buddy. That's interesting.* He waited a few minutes, then went into the front desk. Flashing his police badge to the clerk on duty, he said, "Hi, I'm Chief Pettit, from Warrensburg. I'm here for the meeting, and I thought I just saw some friends of mine come in here. I would like to say 'hello' to them. Could you tell me if you have a Doctor Plunkett registered here?" Buck was hoping he registered under his own name.

The clerk checked his records. "No, I'm sorry, there is no Doctor Plunkett registered here," he said. "I have a Doctor Lou Preston and his wife, but no Pucketts. In fact, Doctor Preston is the only doctor we have staying here right now."

"How about an Elizabeth Breckenridge, or Beth Cole, or Elizabeth Cole?" Buck asked. The clerk checked again. He was starting to get suspicious.

"No such names in our records," he said rather sarcastically. "We can't give out room numbers, you know."

"I know," Buck said. "Thanks anyway." He walked back out to his car and drove away.

As he drove back to Warrensburg, he tried to make sense out of what he had seen. Obviously, Beth and Larry had registered as man and wife. Doctor Lou Preston and wife, in all probability, were Beth Breckenridge and Larry Plunkett. Where was Tom tonight? Out with another of his little sweeties?

Beth has always been known around Warrensburg as a straight arrow. The bank customers came first. If there was an error, she always came down on the side of the customer. She was honest and could always be depended on. She was well thought of by the business community, and there was never a hint of infidelity on her part. On the other hand, there were always rumors floating around about Tom's indiscretions.

Buck had some leverage with Beth now. He hated himself for thinking it, but now he had the means to force Beth to reveal who she thought the murderer of Margaret Wilson was. She knew; he just had to get it out of her.

9

GOTCHA!

ON MONDAY, JULY 13, Buck called the Breckenridge Bank and asked for Beth. The secretary told him to hold for a minute, and when she came back on, she said Beth was busy with a customer and would call him back. She didn't call back. He called again on Tuesday and got the same response. Beth didn't call back on Tuesday either.

Buck called Beth again on Wednesday, and when he got the same treatment, he called Rudolph Eisenstein. He asked Rudolph if it would be all right if he came by his office for a little chat. It was another scorching summer day, and Rudolph had a better idea.

"Meet me at the Rexall Drugstore," he said, "and I'll buy you a Coca Cola. My office is like an oven."

They found a table to the back, and over a Coke, Buck told Rudolph all he knew about the Wilson murder case, about the mysterious phone calls and his conversation with Elizabeth Breckenridge The last thing he told him was about seeing Beth and Larry Plunkett at the hotel in Sedalia. Buck trusted Rudolph, and over the past two months they had become good friends. What he told Rudolph wouldn't go any farther, he was sure of that. What he really wanted was Rudolph's advice.

"Do you think I have enough evidence to go to the prosecuting attorney and ask for an indictment?" he asked.

Rudolph sat and fanned himself with the menu he found sticking between the sugar dispenser and the napkin holder on the table. Finally, he said, "I think the best thing to do would be to try to get a Grand Jury impaneled. Then, if Beth Breckenridge refused to testify, they could subpoena her, but you've got to find out what she knows before you do anything.

"Do you think I'd be within my rights to bring her down to the station and grill her a little without getting rough? She knows who did it, I just need to get her to tell me who it was."

"No, it would be okay for you to do it, but she's pretty influential in business circles around town, and you'd probably ruffle some important feathers."

"What do you think I should do? I don't want to get Gerald Essex mixed up in it, he's such an idiotic boob."

Rudolph chuckled at Buck's remarks. "Why don't you just go down to the bank and ask to see her? It's always harder to refuse someone to their face than over the phone. You might even catch her out on the floor, then it would be easy to approach her."

"Rudolph, once again, I'm indebted to you," Buck said, getting out of his chair. "Let me get the Cokes. He paid for the Cokes at the register on the way out and walked down Holden Street with Rudolph as far as the Breckenridge Bank, where they shook hands and parted. "Thanks again for your advice," Buck said as Rudolph started on down the street.

"Wait 'til you get my bill," Rudolph laughed over his shoulder.

* * * * *

Buck walked into the bank, and as luck would have it, Beth was at one of the teller windows talking to a customer. Buck waited patiently until she was through, then approached her. Beth spoke first.

"Hi, Chief," she said pleasantly, completely disarming him. "What can I do for you?"

"Uh, I'd like to talk to you for a few minutes, uh, privately," he said, rather hesitantly.

"Right now?" she asked.

"Yes, I would."

"Okay, just follow me." She went through a private door and up a stairway to a balcony overlooking the banking floor. Half of the balcony was used as a conference room, and the other half was Beth's private office. She closed the heavy oak door. The wall facing the banking floor was glassed in. She could see the entire banking floor from her office, but it was soundproof, so they could talk. She pointed to an upholstered chair in one corner facing her desk. "Sit down, Chief," she said.

Buck sat down and took his notebook out of his shirt pocket and opened it. Before he could say a word, Beth started explaining why she hadn't returned his calls.

"Chief, I'm sorry I didn't return your calls, but we have had federal bank examiners in here since Monday. They came in unannounced and just left for lunch five minutes ago. They'll be here until Friday, I'm afraid. We have worked every night 'til 10:00. They're going through every book, every file, every drawer and every record. They've even been down in the basement going through all our old records stored down there."

"I just want to talk to you for a few minutes. I need to have some questions answered."

"I know what you want, Chief, and I'll be glad to talk to you after the examiners leave. What we have to discuss will probably be upsetting to me, and I don't want that to happen until after these men leave. Can you wait until Saturday? I would be most grateful."

"How often do these examiners come?" Buck was curious.

"That's the problem, we never know when they will come. Not that we have anything to hide, but it doesn't give us any time to arrange our schedule or prepare for them in any way. They just come in and take over. It's all part of that new banking law passed in 1933. You know, during the banking crises. Chief, I swear, I'll call you the minute they leave town."

Buck was beginning to feel better about Beth. "Okay, I'll wait for your call," he said as he stood up and headed for the door.

"Thanks, Chief," she said, relieved.

As Buck walked out the door, he glanced into the conference room. The table was strewn with files and ledgers. There were two adding machines, one on each end of the big conference table, and two waste baskets filled with used tapes from the machines. *Yup,* he surmised, *they had auditors all right.*

Over lunch with Ann and the children, Buck brought Ann up to date on the case. "Do you think she will tell me who did it?" he asked.

"I think she will, honey. I think she wants to unburden herself, just not right now."

Buck thought so, too.

* * * * *

180

Friday, July 17, was set aside for municipal court day. The city had a courtroom set up over the grocery store next to city hall. The office of municipal judge was a part-time position and didn't pay much, so the local lawyers took turns running for the job. That way they never had an opponent, either in the primary or the general election, therefore, didn't have any campaign expenses. That was important, because the job only paid $20 a month.

The court was for local arrests made and tickets issued by city police for speeding, public drunkenness, shoplifting, domestic disputes and other misdemeanors. They also heard juvenile cases. Buck was in court most of the day, and he was glad when he heard the courthouse clock strike 5:00. So was the judge. They were both tired from all the tedium.

They were just finishing up the last case, and when that case was decided, the judge rapped his gavel. "Court adjourned," he announced. Clarence took the prisoner off to the jail. He was a colored man who had gotten drunk and urinated on the sidewalk in front of Walker's Cafe the previous Saturday night. His main problem was that he had almost urinated on Clarence's shoe. Clarence and his family had just finished dinner at the cafe and were coming out the door when the act occurred. An arrest was made immediately.

Buck walked down the street toward the police station. It was hot, and he was tired. Ann was coming across the square from the general direction of Woolworth's and yelled at him. She had been shopping for the children and was pushing Ellie in Ann Marie's old stroller, with little Jimmie walking along beside her holding on to her dress tail. Buck stopped and waited for them. Darlene heard them coming and held the screen door open.

"Mercy, it's hot!" Ann exclaimed. "Darlene, if you'll watch the children for a couple of minutes, I'll run upstairs and fix us some iced tea."

Buck said, "I'll watch them," and he took Jimmie on his lap. The boy immediately tried to pull Buck's watch out of his pocket.

"This one's mine," Darlene said as she took little Ellie out of the stroller.

As they were sitting around Darlene's desk drinking iced tea, the phone rang. Darlene answered it and immediately motioned to Buck that it was for him. Buck went back to his office and picked up the receiver. It was Beth Breckenridge.

"Chief, I'm free now," she said. "The examiners left about 4:30 for St. Louis. Where would you like to meet?" "Where would best suit you?" he asked.

"Well, you could come to the bank, but I'm so tired, it would be better if you came to the house. I need to change clothes and fix something for us to drink. Let's see, it's about 5:30 now. Why don't you come over about 7:00? The maid will be gone, and Tom has supposedly gone to the mayor's house for a poker game, so we can talk privately."

"Seven it is, I'll see you then, bye." Buck hung up and went back up front.

"It was Elizabeth Breckenridge, wasn't it?" Darlene asked.

"Yes, and I'm to meet her at her house at 7:00. I wish I could take someone with me, but I'm afraid she wouldn't talk openly if I did. I need to get her to talk."

"My, my, what will the neighbors think?" Ann teased.

* * * * *

At 7:05, Buck swung the Studebaker into the Breckenridge driveway and guided it all the way back to the garage. He parked between the big four-car garage and the swimming pool. There were lots of trees and shrubs to hide it from the neighbors' prying eyes.

He got out and closed the car door as quietly as possible. Instead of going back up the driveway to the front of the house, he went through the back gate of the swimming pool and walked around the edge of the pool to the patio. Beth was sitting at a round table with a large yellow umbrella over it, tilted to shade it from the setting sun.

"Hi, Buck, come sit down," she said, motioning to the chair across from her. She looked tired. "What would you like to drink?" she asked.

"Nothing right now," he said, as he pulled the chair out and sat down.

"Are you sure?" she asked. "I have cold beer in the refrigerator, or I could mix you a highball."

"Do you have any red wine?" Buck asked. He didn't want to seem anti-social, considering the purpose of the meeting.

"Let's see, I have a bottle of rosé that's cold, but no red."

"The rosé will be fine" he said.

When she got up to get the wine, Buck was taken by the stunning white satin lounging pajamas she had on. It was obvious by the absence of any panty lines that she had nothing on under them. *Get thee behind me, Satan,* he thought to himself.

They sat and sipped in silence for a couple of minutes. Beth was the first one to talk.

"I've been doing a lot of thinking since our last conversation. What I'm about to tell you might ruin my life forever, or it might not, but I've got to take that chance. I just can't keep this to myself any longer. I think Tom killed Margaret Wilson."

"Your husband Tom? What on earth makes you think that?" he asked as he took out his notebook and started taking notes.

"Because he lied about that fountain pen you and Clarence brought out here right after the murder. I can't abide lying and cheating, and he has done both since our marriage. When you asked him about the pen, he told you it disappeared from his desk the afternoon of the murder. It didn't; he had it with him when he came home from the bank that afternoon."

"How can you be sure?"

"I came home from the bank the Friday afternoon of the murder about 4:00, and he came home shortly after that. Clarice, that's our maid, served us iced tea on the patio. It was warm, and a little too early to drink hard liquor. As you probably know, there is a phone jack here on the patio, and I brought the phone from the kitchen out here just in case. Clarice leaves at 5:00 on Fridays, so we usually eat out, but she always puts sandwiches in the refrigerator for us just in case.

"Well, we sat out here and read the afternoon paper and drank iced tea 'til about 6:30. Tom switched to scotch and tonic a little after 5:00. About 6:30, the phone rang, and I answered it. It was Larry Plunkett, and he asked for Tom. While they were talking, Tom asked me for a piece of paper to write on, so I dashed into the kitchen and brought out the note pad we keep on the counter by the phone. When he hung up, he told me Larry had invited him to a poker game at the mayor's house, and left."

"Is that when you saw the pen?"

"Yes, he made some notes with it, and then stuck it in the breast pocket of his suit coat."

"Are you sure it was the same pen?"

"Chief, there is only one pen like that in the entire world, and yes, I'm sure. I had that pen made especially for him at Tiffany's last Christmas. I even had his initials engraved on it. It was the same pen all right."

"Wow," Buck was astonished. "What did he have to say about the trial? Was he willing to let an innocent boy go to prison, or even the electric chair for something he did?"

"Yes, you see, Chief, it's all about him. He is so selfish that he doesn't care about anybody but himself. Oh, I know he puts on a good front, especially at the bank, but when push comes to shove, he only thinks about himself."

Beth told Buck about the gold hoard, and how he wanted to get it out of the country illegally, with no regard for the bank or their employees. How she threatened to tell the FBI and coerced him into turning the gold over to the Federal Reserve. "Chief, he has hated me for that for the past three years. He never forgave me, and to this day, we don't have any kind of a man-and wife relationship, except at the bank. We didn't have much before, but now, nothing. We even sleep in separate bedrooms. Oh, he has his girlfriends, I know that, but it doesn't bother me any more."

They sat in silence for a few minutes. Finally, Buck spoke. He couldn't resist asking her.

"What about Larry Plunkett?"

"What about him?" she asked.

"Are you having an affair with him?"

"No, absolutely not!"

"How about last Saturday night at the Bothwell Hotel in Sedalia?"

"My God, Chief! Are you having me followed?" Beth's face was getting red.

Buck explained to her about his meeting and about coming out of the hotel and seeing her and Larry go in. He didn't tell her about checking with the desk clerk and finding a Dr. Lou Preston registered, the only doctor in the hotel at that time.

"I couldn't help but see you two drive into the parking lot in Larry's yellow convertible," he said.

Correction

"Let me tell you how that happened. Last Saturday morning, Tom played golf with Larry as usual. After golf, they came out to the house and I fixed them some lunch. They each had a couple of drinks, then Larry went home.

"After Larry left, Tom went upstairs, showered and changed clothes and left in the Packard about 4:30 for Kansas City. He likes to rub elbows with those high rollers at the Kansas City Club. I was sitting out here by the pool, just as we are now, when the phone rang. It was Larry. He wanted to come by for a drink."

"What time was that?" Buck interjected.

"It was about 6:00. I wasn't too happy about it, but he insisted, so against my better judgment, I told him to come over. He got here about 6:15."

"Was he drunk?"

"Not quite, but getting that way. We had a drink here by the pool, and he insisted on taking me for a ride in his new convertible, and I went with him. Chief, I swear, that was the only time I have ever cheated on Tom. It was a combination of too much wine and not having been with a man for so long. I hope God will forgive me for that one indiscretion."

"Then what happened?"

"I made Larry put the top up on the convertible before we left the house, in case one of our neighbors saw us. I didn't want them to think we were going for a joy ride. They know Larry's car, and they know that he and Tom are best friends, so I figured they would think it was a routine thing. When we got to Knobnoster, we stopped at that beer joint on the highway, and Larry bought some beer and put the top down. We each drank a beer on the way from there to Sedalia."

"What time did you get to Sedalia?" Buck asked. He remembered that it was about 9:30 when he saw them at the hotel.

"It was about 9:15. We drove around for a few minutes, then he suggested we get a hotel room. I admit I was getting a little horny, so I took him up on it. I guess that's when you saw us."

"So you registered as Doctor and Mrs. Lou Preston and went up to the room?"

Beth laughed. "It looks like we could have been a little more creative then that, I mean, using his same initials. I'll bet you didn't have any trouble spotting us in the hotel register."

Buck didn't answer that.

"Buck, I don't even like the man, much less have an affair with him. After it was over, I was lying there in bed, regretting everything I had done, so I got up and made him bring me home." She took a sip of her wine and thought for a moment.

"Getting back to the night of the murder," she said, "I found out later that the phone call from Larry was a set-up to get him out of the house. There was no poker game. I think Tom left here and went by Reese School to try to make out with Margaret Wilson, and when she rebuffed him, he killed and raped her. He's used to getting his way with women, you know."

Buck was busy writing in his notebook. He couldn't believe what he was hearing. "How much does Larry Plunkett know about the murder?" he asked.

"I don't know. I don't think he knows about Margaret Wilson, but he's Tom's best friend, it's possible. I do know this—when he bought that new Cadillac, Tom loaned him the money at two percent, which is half our normal rate. He probably would have loaned it to him interest free, were it not for the bank examiners."

Buck studied his notes. Finally, he said, "I'll have a tough time getting an indictment against Tom, with just the pen as evidence, for two reasons. One, the defense can say that anybody could have been in possession of the pen. You would have to testify against your own husband to put the pen in his possession at the time of the murder; then it would be your word against his. Two, the law says you don't have to testify against your husband, but you can if you want to. He will put an awful lot of pressure on you not to testify. Could you stand that?"

"I think so, Chief. I've had just about all of his philandering I can take, not to mention the way he treats me."

"Has he ever hit you?"

"No, but he has come close a time or two. It's the things he says to me and the way he acts around me. He has always looked down on me, because he comes from old money, and I don't, and he can be real sarcastic about that. Not around the bank, just here at home, and sometimes around friends. He doesn't love me, he just tolerates me. It all goes back to when I stood up to him when he wanted to run off with all that gold. We got along pretty good until then."

"Do you think he would do anything to you if he found out, for example, that you have been talking to me?"

"He knows that if he did anything to me, he would have to kill me. I've got too much on him. I could destroy his reputation around town, and that would crush him."

Buck looked at his watch; it was 8:30. He stood up and extended his hand to Beth. "I have to go, but I really appreciate the information you have given me. Let's keep all this under our hats for a while. I need more time to come up with some more evidence. The pen is good, but I'm afraid it just isn't enough."

Beth shoved her chair back and stood up, still holding Buck's hand. She gave it a squeeze. "You don't what a relief it is to get all this off my chest. My conscience has been giving me fits. I know it will be rough, but I will testify against Tom if I have to. Good night, Chief." She turned and walked into the house.

Buck got into his car and drove toward the street with his headlights off. The lights went on in Beth's bedroom upstairs and cast just enough light on the driveway for Buck to see the dark outline of a man dart up the driveway and disappear around the front of the house. He sped up, but by the time he got to the front of the house, he was gone. Buck turned on his headlights and toured the neighborhood for a few minutes in a vain attempt to find him. There was no moon and too many trees and shrubs to hide behind. He started getting that sick feeling in the pit of his stomach again. He prayed nothing would happen to his star witness as he drove back to the station. Thoughts of Willie Cates went through his mind, and he chilled at the idea of something similar happening to Beth Breckenridge.

He parked the Studebaker in its usual spot behind the station and went in the back door. Clyde Burroughs was sitting at Darlene's desk minding the phone and reading the newspaper. He looked up as Buck walked in from the back.

"I thought you were upstairs with Ann and the kids," he said.

"No, I've been out talking to a witness." He didn't say who; he wanted to keep that secret for a while. He was confident Darlene and Ann would keep his secret, but the fewer who knew about Beth, the better. He did need Clyde's help though. "I've got an assignment for you for tonight," he said. "Instead of answering the phone here at the station, I want you to patrol South Holden Street, from the campus on south for a few blocks. Just circle around and keep your eyes open for a man dressed in dark clothing, especially around those big houses across from the campus."

"What's up, Chief?" Clyde asked. He didn't mind doing patrol. In fact, he liked it better than sitting around the station.

"Oh, there have been reports of a Peeping Tom in that neighborhood, and I promised the ladies that live around there I would have someone patrol the area for a few nights. Be sure your flashlight has fresh batteries and the spot light on the patrol car works good. I want a description of him if you can spot him. Better yet, catch him if you can."

"Who's gonna answer the phone in case there is an emergency?"

"Just switch the ring from down here to upstairs. I'll answer it up there. If there's a real emergency, I'll go in the Studebaker. Buck went upstairs to share this evening's conversation with Ann and get her opinion. The children were in bed, so Buck and Ann sat at the kitchen table and talked 'til almost midnight.

* * * * *

Saturday evening, Buck and Ann were lying in bed trying to sleep. It had been another hot summer day, and even with the windows open and a big oscillating fan on the dresser blowing air across the bed, it was still too hot to sleep. They heard the courthouse clock strike 11:00, and Ann got up to check on the children. Buck went out to the kitchen to get a drink and was just sitting down at the table when the phone rang. He jumped to answer it so it wouldn't wake the children.

"Hello." Buck didn't want to identify himself until he found out who was calling.

"Chief?"

"Clyde, is that you?" Buck knew who it was by his voice.

"Yeah, Chief, I caught your Peeping Tom! You're not going to believe who it is."

"Who?"

"He's a private investigator from Kansas City. I caught him on the banker's patio looking in their kitchen window. Mrs. Breckenridge was in the kitchen at the time, and it scared the daylights out of her when I nabbed him."

"Where are you now?"

"At the county jail. I brought him down here to book him. Are you coming down?"

"Not right now, did you check his identification?"

"Yes, he's a licensed private detective from Kansas City."

"Is he armed?"

188

"Yeah, he had a gun in a shoulder holster, but he has a license for it, too. I asked him who he was working for, but he wouldn't talk to me. You want to talk to him?"

"Yes, put him on."

"Hello, this is Joe Campano, who am I talkin' to?"

"Joe, this is Police Chief Buck Pettit. Tell me what you were doing sneaking into people's backyards and peeking into their windows this time of night."

"I wasn't sneakin', I was on business."

"What kind of business?"

"I can't say, it's private."

"Can't say, or won't say?" Buck wasn't in any mood to argue.

"I'm not talkin'."

"Fine with me, put the officer back on."

There was a slight pause. "This is Clyde."

"Clyde, book this guy for criminal trespassing, and throw him in the tank. I'll be down to talk to him in the morning."

"Sure thing, Chief." He hung up.

Buck was at the jail at 8:15 Sunday morning dressed for church. He was determined he wasn't going to waste much time on Joe Campano. If he didn't want to talk, Buck was going on to church with Ann and the children, and he could wait until Monday. If he didn't talk then, he could wait in jail until Tuesday. The deputy on duty brought Joe to the interrogation room.

Buck pointed to a chair. "Sit down, Joe, you and I are going to talk, and I don't have much time. Tell me, who are you snooping for?"

"I can't say, it's private business."

"Not in my town. It's not private business when you are arrested on someone's property peeking in their back window. You've been charged with criminal trespassing. You can talk to me now, or I'll take you before a judge Monday morning and have you bound over to circuit court. The lady you were peeking at is very upset. Now, tell me one more time, who do you work for?"

Joe was not relishing another night in the Johnson county jail. "I am employed by the Mid America Investigative services," he said.

"That old dog won't hunt, Joe, I want to know who employed you to snoop on Mrs. Breckenridge."

Joe sat there and stared at his hands folded on the table.

Buck waited about three minutes, then nodded at the deputy. "Take him back to the tank, Al," he said, and started to get up.

"No, wait a minute." Joe was beginning to see the light. "This has to be very private."

Buck motioned for the deputy to leave the room. Joe pulled his chair a little closer to the table and leaned toward Buck. "You've got to promise me you won't repeat this to anyone," he half-whispered.

"I can't do that, you may have to testify in court." Buck was getting impatient.

"Dammit, he'll kill me!"

"Who'll kill you?"

"Tom Breckenridge."

"Tom Breckenridge hired you to spy on his wife?"

"Yes, about a month ago, he came to me and said he would buy me one of those expensive German cameras, you know, the kind that can take pictures in low light without a flash, and pay me $50 to get some pictures of his wife cheating on him."

"Did you catch her cheating on him?"

"Not right away. I followed her for about a month and never saw a thing. Then a week ago yesterday, he called me at home and told me to drive to Sedalia and wait at the Bothwell Hotel, and I could get some pictures. Hell, that's a 90-mile drive, and my expense money was running out, so I argued with him for a while, but he said he would give me another 20 bucks if I got some pictures, so I went."

"Did you get any pictures?" Suddenly it dawned on Buck that that was the night he had seen Beth and Larry Plunkett at the Bothwell. Of course, he got some pictures. It was set up; Larry Plunkett was in on it.

"Oh, yeah, I got some dandies. Goin' in the hotel, comin' out of the room, leavin' in his pretty car. Damn tootin' I got some pictures."

"Where are they now?"

"In my car, locked up in the trunk.

"Where's your car now?"

"Parked down the street from the Breckenridge place."

Buck turned to the deputy. "Al, I want you to release this man in my custody for a while, and if he's telling the truth, I may let him go."

Al was agreeable. "Okay, he's your prisoner, just sign a release form to relieve me of any responsibility, and take him."

Buck drove Joe out Holden Street to his car. He glanced at his watch; he could still make church in time if he hurried. Joe opened the trunk of his '34 Chevy and took out a manila envelope. He opened it and handed Buck a hand full of 8x10 glossies. They were grainy, but you could sure identify the people in them. There was one of Beth and Larry Plunkett going into the hotel arm in arm, another of them leaving the hotel room in the middle of the night. He must have waited in the hall for about three hours to get that one. He had another one of them leaving the hotel parking lot in Larry's car. He purposely snapped the back of the car so you could read the license number.

He also had one of Buck's car parked in back of the Breckenridge home, and one of Buck and Beth sitting on the patio sipping wine. Buck held those two up in Joe's face with a quizzical look on his face.

"Hey," Joe said, "He told me to get pictures of his wife with other men, and there you were."

"I see you made two copies of each print, I want them for evidence."

"What'll I tell Tom?"

"Don't tell him anything. You've got the negatives, just make some more prints and act like nothing happened, but don't tell him I have copies, too. You did what he hired you to do; you got proof of her philandering. That's all he needs to know."

"What's in it for me?"

"You get to stay out of jail."

"What if I don't let you have these pictures? What if I don't cooperate, what then?"

"I still have an assistant chief who'll swear he caught you peeping in a lonely lady's window. The lady can testify, too. I can have you picked up in Kansas City and extradited to Warrensburg. You can still go to jail."

That convinced Joe. He gave Buck the pictures. Buck followed him back to the jail, where he picked up his personal property, including his gun, and left town. Buck drove back to the apartment, picked up Ann and the children, and they went to church. He didn't show Ann the pictures until that night after the children were in bed.

* * * * *

Monday, July 20, was a little cooler for a change. A front moved through the area during the night and cooled things off some. There was lightning and thunder, but only a few drops of rain, and the county was already seven inches short of normal for the year. The radio in the Pettits' apartment predicted a high of 85 for the day. Buck kissed Ann and the children and descended the stairs to his office. He sat at his desk and went over his notes for a while, then unlocked the middle drawer of his desk and took out the manila envelope with the pictures in it. He checked to make sure the fountain pen was still there, then closed and locked the drawer. The courthouse clock struck 10:00. He picked up the phone and called the Breckenridge Bank. He asked for Elizabeth Breckenridge and had to wait for a few minutes until she was finished with a customer.

"Elizabeth Breckenridge speaking," she chirped. That's the main reason the townspeople liked Beth; she was always so pleasant with everyone.

"Mrs. Breckenridge, this is Buck Pettit." Buck suspected that the telephone operators sometimes listened in on conversations, so he kept this conversation on an impersonal basis.

Beth got his signal, "What can I do for you. Chief?" she asked.

"You know that Peeping Tom the ladies in your neighborhood have been complaining about?"

"Yes."

"Well, we picked up a suspect Saturday night, and I would like for you to come down to the station to sign a complaint," Buck lied.

"When, Chief?"

"Right now, if you can."

"It will be half an hour before I can get there, will that be all right?" Beth sensed the urgency in Buck's call, but didn't want to arouse suspicion.

"Yes, that will be fine. Just tell whoever is on the desk that you have an appointment with me, and I'll see you in half an hour." Buck hung up. *This will work out fine,* he thought. *Darlene won't be in 'til noon, and Clarence is up front drinking coffee. I'll have him answer the phone while Beth and I talk. No one will suspect anything.*

Beth walked into the station at 10:40, and Clarence showed her back to Buck's office. This was the first time in all her years in Warrensburg that she had been inside the police station. Buck stood and greeted her, then motioned for her to sit down. He took the pictures out of the envelope, handed them to her and watched her jaw drop as she went through them.

Finally she said, "Larry is in cahoots with Tom, isn't he? He deliberately lured me to that hotel, knowing full well that there would be a photographer there."

"I'm afraid so," Buck said sympathetically. "What's his game?"

"He wants me out of the way. He wants complete control of the bank."

"Do you think he's building a case for divorce?"

"That's exactly what he's trying to do, but it won't work."

"Why is that?"

"Well, for starters, Tom is incapable of running the bank. He doesn't have the banking ability to make it go. As you probably already know, I've been the real force behind our success ever since the new banking laws went into effect in 1933. I've been studying the banking business ever since Tom and I were married. I'm the one who attends all the banking seminars and classes to keep up on all the rules and regulations, as well as the best banking techniques and marketing strategies. When we go to banking meetings in Kansas City and St. Louis, Tom parties while I attend classes. We went to a week-long banking seminar in Washington, D.C. last year, and Tom stayed drunk the whole time, while I attended classes."

"Why would he want control of the bank, if he knows he can't make a go of it?"

"He hates banking. His father forced him into it to keep it in the family. He wants control of the bank so he can loot it and transfer the money to numbered Swiss bank accounts. Then he would take bankruptcy, sell the house and move to Switzerland. He tried to do that in 1933, and I stopped him. He's hated me ever since."

"How would divorcing you help him? Doesn't he own the controlling shares of stock already?"

"No, that's the catch. When we reorganized after the banking holiday in 1933, I made them give me 26% of the stock, and he got 26%. Between the two of us, we own 52%, or controlling shares."

"Who owns the rest of the stock?"

"Various businessmen around town. The seven board members besides Tom and myself own some of it. Your friend, Rudolph Eisenstein, and his brother, the dentist, own a number of shares. If we have a messy divorce and Tom can prove that I am unfaithful, he could get the court to award all the stock to him. You know how courts are about women in business."

"I need to talk to Larry Plunkett to see if I can get him to own up to his role in this unsavory plot."

"Don't do that, Chief. He would just go to Tom, and Tom would make it that much harder on me."

"There's always Joe, the detective. He sure knows what they have been up to."

"Now there's an idea, Chief. I've got some money stashed around in different places that Tom doesn't know about. Why don't I offer Joe some money to follow Tom around and take some pictures of him and all his little cuties?"

"That's a great idea," Buck said as he looked through his desk and found the business card Joe gave him Sunday morning. He handed the card to Beth with a big grin on his face. Beth dropped the card in her purse and stood up.

"Are you through with me, Chief," she asked.

"Yes, but be sure and watch your back."

"I'll let you do that, they tell me that's my best side," she said laughingly as she walked up toward the front of the station. She nodded at Clarence on the way out and walked back to the bank.

That night Tom had another "poker game," and while he was gone, Beth found the key to his gun cabinet in the den. She gave it to him one year for Christmas, so she knew where the key was kept. She opened it and selected a 25-caliber automatic hand gun. It was the one she learned to shoot with when they were first married and belonged to a gun club in Kansas City. She took it and a box of cartridges, put them in the glove compartment of her car and locked it.

* * * * *

Saturday afternoon, July 25, Joe Campano called the Kansas City Club and asked to speak to Tom Breckenridge. Per their arrangement, Joe was never to go there. He was to call the club and leave a message for Tom and wait at his office for a return call. Always on Saturday afternoons after 4:00. That's when Tom would most likely be there. If he had something for Tom, he was to mail it to a box in the main post office. Joe mailed the pictures last Tuesday.

He waited in his office until after 7:00. He was hungry and thought about going to a rib joint over on Troost for a beer and some ribs. That's the thing he missed most about being divorced, having someone to go out with on Saturday nights. The phone rang just as he was walking out the door. He went back and picked up the receiver.

"Hello." He never identified his detective agency after hours.

"Joe? This is Fred." Even though Kansas City had dial phones, an operator could still listen in if she wanted to, so Tom used a code name. "You got some good pictures," he said. "I was really surprised when I saw the P.C. in one of them."

"Yeah, that was a bonus."

"I want you to do another set-up. I need all the evidence I can get before I make my move. I'll call you when I'm ready. There's another $20 in it if it turns out as good as the last one. I'll let you know." He hung up before Joe could answer.

Joe decided he didn't like Tom. He didn't like snakes, and to Joe, Tom was a snake. He didn't like his condescending attitude either. Following husbands who were cheating on their wives was one thing, but a beautiful woman like Tom's wife didn't deserve to be set up like that. Maybe he would get more pictures, and maybe he wouldn't. After all, he had already earned the camera and 50 bucks. The extra 20 did little more than cover his expenses. The extra fast film he used came from a studio that specialized in sports pictures, and it was expensive. He'd think about it over some ribs and a beer.

* * * * *

Monday morning, July 27, Buck was working at his desk when Darlene buzzed him to pick up the phone. It was Rudolph.

"Buck?" he asked. He seemed excited.

"Good morning, counselor, what can I do to make your life more pleasant?"

"You sound like you're in a good mood for a police chief, did you just hit a jack pot or something?"

"I am in a good mood. I thought I would never be happy again after Ann Marie died, but now Ann and I have two beautiful children to live for, and life is good again."

"That's why I called. The mail just came, and the adoption has been approved. All we have to do now is go before the judge, have him sign the papers, have them notarized, and the children are yours, now and forever."

Buck was ecstatic. "That's great news, I'll go tell Ann now, she'll be so pleased."

"I'll set up an appointment with the judge and call you as soon as I know the date and time."

"Wonderful! Why don't you have dinner with us tonight? We can open a bottle of wine and celebrate." Buck and Rudolph had become good friends since the Stevenson trial, and they both cherished that friendship.

"Why don't we wait until the papers are signed and everything is legal? That will give Ann some notice and me a chance to pick out some wine. I want to buy the wine to show my appreciation for the way things have gone. It will be Friday at the latest, probably sooner, I'll let you know."

"Thanks for the good news." Buck hung up and raced up the steps to tell Ann.

* * * * *

Tuesday morning about 10:00, Beth left the bank and went down to the train station to use the pay phone. She made sure nobody followed her, and when no one was looking, she ducked into the phone booth and closed the door. She took Joe Campano's card out of her purse and gave the operator the number.

"Mid America Investigative Services, Joe speaking."

"Joe, you don't know me, but my name is Elizabeth Breckenridge, and I need your services. She pretended she hadn't even seen the pictures, much less heard his name."

Joe was surprised. How did she get his name and number if she didn't know him. Was this some kind of set-up? Was her husband trying to pull something on him, or was it just a coincidence?

"How did you get my number?" he asked.

"The Warrensburg Police Chief and his wife Ann are good friends of mine, and when I saw the Chief the other day, I told him I needed some investigative work done, and I asked him if he could recommend someone. I don't know where he got it, but he gave me your card with your phone number on it." She didn't think a little white lie would hurt, with so much at stake.

The explanation seemed to satisfy him. The Chief had been kind of rough on him, and maybe now he is just trying to throw some business his way. "What kind of work you want done?" he asked.

"Mr. Campano, do you mind if I call you Joe?" she asked. You can call me Beth, if you like."

Joe was flattered that such a pretty lady would want to be on a first-name basis with him. Her charm was working. "Why, uh, no, ma'am," he stammered.

"Good," she cooed. "I suspect my husband is seeing other women, and I would like proof of that. Can you help me?"

"Yes, I can, that's what I do for a living." He had finally regained his composure.

"Good, his name is Tom Breckenridge, and he lives in Warrensburg, Missouri. Do you want our address?" she asked, knowing full well he already had it.

"No, ma'am, I can look in the phone book if I need it."

"Joe, you're very efficient," she said sweetly. "You might also find him at the Kansas City Club on Saturday afternoons." She knew he already had all the information he needed on Tom, but acting innocent was part of her little plan.

Joe hated to bring it up, but he needed to be paid. "Mrs . . . . er, Beth, I charge $20 a day, plus expenses for my services." He lied, his base rate was $10 a day, but here was this sweet, innocent little banker's wife who probably had plenty of money, asking for his help, and he just couldn't resist the temptation.

"That sounds fair." She knew she was being gouged. Over half of the wage earners in the country earned less than $20 a week, let alone a day. "I'll wire you a hundred dollars as a retainer, and you can bill me weekly. Will that be all right?"

It was more than all right. Joe just about passed out. The highest retainer he had ever received previously was the $50 her husband had given him. "Yes, that'll be fine, send it Western Union, and I'll pick it up at their local office." He hung up.

The Western Union office was in the train station, so Beth went to the window and wired the money, then went back to the bank. Joe got it that afternoon.

* * * * *

Things started getting progressively worse between Beth and Tom. Their relationship had been strained ever since the bank holiday in 1933, but by early August 1936 they were hardly speaking, even at the bank. Beth tried, but got no response from Tom, even on important business matters. Beth attributed it to the pictures Joe took at first, but then figured that if he and Larry had set it all up to get evidence of her infidelity, he should be happy, not so dour. She worried that he was up to something new, something more sinister.

Friday afternoon, August 8, about 3:00, Beth got a call at the bank from Joe. He told the girl who answered the phone that he was a relative and needed to talk to her about a family matter. Concerned, she answered the phone in her office. "Hello, this is Elizabeth, who am I speaking to?" she asked.

"This is your Uncle Bill in Kansas City. How have you been, honey?" Joe got a small thrill out of calling her "honey."

Beth recognized Joe's voice immediately. "Hi, Uncle Bill, how are you?" she said familiarly.

"I'm fine, honey [he loved saying that word to her]. I have some pictures your mother wanted me to send to you. I took them at a family get-together at Swope Park last month. You weren't there, so I thought I would make copies and send you some."

"That would be great, Uncle Bill." Beth really laid it on. She would have made a good actress. "Where are you now?" she asked.

"Well, you see, that's the thing, I'm on my way to Jefferson City, and I don't have much time. Could I just drop them off someplace?"

"Where are you calling from?"

"I'm at a place called the Tip Top Cafe, out here on Highway 50. There is a police officer in here drinking coffee, and I thought I would ask him directions to the bank and bring the pictures to you. They're in a sealed envelope. I don't have much time," he repeated. He was trying to give Beth as much information as possible without arousing suspicion, in case someone was listening in on the conversation.

"I have a better idea," Beth caught on to his style of coding his speech. The mention of a police officer meant he had to be very careful what he said. The sealed envelope meant he could leave it with someone other than Beth. "Why don't you write Police Chief Pettit's name on the envelope, and give it to the police officer? He'll take it to the police station and I can pick it up there."

"Would the Chief be interested in your family?" In other words, what if he opens it?

"Oh, the Chief knows my family well, and would probably like to see some pictures of them." She knew Clarence wouldn't dare open the envelope, and she didn't care if the Chief saw them. In fact, she was going to show them to him anyway.

"Sounds fine to me," Joe said. He wrote Buck's name on the envelope and asked Clarence to deliver it to the Chief for him. Clarence took the envelope, tossed into the passenger side of the front seat and drove off. Joe watched the patrol car until it turned south on Holden Street, then got in his car and drove back to Kansas City.

* * * * *

Buck opened the envelope and leafed through the pictures. It seems like Tom had two girlfriends and was seeing both of them on a regular basis. According to the letter in with the pictures, he had one stashed in a room at the Martin Hotel in Warrensburg, and one that met him almost every Saturday night at the Kansas City Club.

Just after the courthouse clock chimed 4:00, Beth drove up in front of the police station and went in. Darlene motioned her on back to Buck's office where he was still sitting at his desk. He motioned for Beth to sit down while he unlocked the middle drawer of his desk. He took out the envelope and slid it across to her. He watched her face as she went through them. No emotion, she just shook her head and put the pictures back in the envelope.

"Will you keep them for me?" she asked. "I'm afraid Tom might find them and really get angry with me for thwarting his little scheme to smear me."

"They'll be locked up in my desk until you need them," he promised.

Beth thanked him and drove home. Tom was sitting by the pool sipping a Scotch-on-the-rocks when she came in. She poured herself a glass of wine and joined him.

"Where are the pictures?" he asked.

199

A cold chill went up her back. *How did he find out so soon?* she asked herself. "What pictures?" she inquired.

"The ones Joe brought you this afternoon," he said sarcastically.

"Joe?"

"Yes, Joe! Didn't you think I would recognize his voice? That was cute, the way you two tried to fool me."

"You listened in on my phone?" Beth's fear was turning to anger. "How did you manage that?"

"Simple," he said. "Do you remember that on Wednesday of last week I said the phone in my office wasn't working, and I called the phone company? Well, my phone was okay. I just wanted the telephone man to run an extension line from your phone down to my office with a little red light that came on when you picked up your receiver. You didn't even notice that I had two phones on my desk. I slipped him a few bucks to keep his mouth shut, and that was that. If you hadn't been cheating on me, none of this would have been necessary, you know."

Beth hit the ceiling. "Me cheating on you! You set me up with that slimy friend of yours so you could get some pictures to smear me with. Well, what goes around comes around, Mr. Big Shot Banker!"

"It takes two to tango," he said sarcastically.

"Yes, it does, and I'm not proud of what I did, but you knew I was vulnerable. We haven't slept together in three years, while you've been having two at a time, it seems, and that's been going on for a lot longer than three years!"

Beth was furious. She ran out the back door and around the pool to the garage, opened the stall where her car was parked and backed out. She drove over to the apartment house on South Street, where she lived when she first came to Warrensburg, and got out. The same landlady still owned the house, though she was a widow now. She and Beth had become good friends over the years. Beth knocked on her apartment door and waited. The woman, now in her 60s, opened the door and smiled broadly when she saw Beth.

"Hi, hon," Beth said, holding out her hand. The woman took her hand and patted it, a wide grin on her face. She swung the door open wide.

"Come in, child," she said. Beth was 32, but Maud still called her child. "My beautiful, beautiful child, what can Aunt Maud do for you?"

"I need a room, Aunt Maud." She was no relation, but Beth called her Aunt, out of respect. In those days, you never called an older person by their first name, just as you wouldn't call a parent by their first name. It was called courtesy and respect.

"A room?" she gasped. "What on earth do you need a room for? You have one of the most beautiful homes in town."

Ann explained to her what happened—that she had had a fight with Tom and she just needed a place to go to cool off. "Aunt Maud, I'm not moving out, I just need a place where I can go to think and get my mind straight. I may not ever stay in it overnight, but if I need to, I'll have it, do you understand?"

"Yes, child, I do understand, and I won't tell a soul that you have rented a room from me. Most of the students are gone for the summer, and you can have your old room back if you want."

"Thank you, Aunt Maud, you've always been so kind to me. Let me give you a week's rent right now, and I'll bring a few of my things over later, if that's okay."

"That's just fine child, the rent is $3 a week, same as always. You can drive up the alley and park in back if you want. Just come in the back door and go up the back stairs. That way, you can have some privacy." Maud figured Beth wouldn't want people to see her coming and going.

"You are so understanding." Beth gave her a hug and left.

She drove by the police station. Buck was upstairs having dinner with his family. Darlene was still on duty, so Beth visited with her for a few minutes. The courthouse clock struck 6:00, and Beth automatically looked at her watch.

"Darlene, I didn't know it was getting so late. Don't bother the Chief now, just have him call me at the bank tomorrow morning, please." She left the station and drove home.

The blue Packard was gone when Beth got home. She figured Tom was with his little cutie at the Martin Hotel. She went upstairs and carefully selected two changes of clothing, including lingerie and hosiery. Two pairs of shoes, some cosmetics, nightwear and personal items such as toothbrush and comb. She packed all of the items in an overnight bag and took it down and locked it in the trunk of the Chrysler. Tomorrow, she would withdraw $300 from a personal account at the bank and lock it in the glove compartment with her hand gun. She went to the kitchen and found the sandwiches in the refrigerator that the maid had left and ate one, along with a glass of milk, went upstairs, took a bath and went to bed.

In the summer, Beth slept on the sleeping porch at the back of her bedroom. There were two big sleeping porches on the back of the house, one for each of the large bedroom suites, and they were separated by a wooden partition that was painted to match the bedrooms. Two sides of the porch were screened to let in the evening breeze flow through. By opening the transoms above the doors to the bedrooms on the front side of the house, just across the hall and leaving the big transom over the double doors to the master bedroom suite open, usually enough air movement was created to sleep comfortably. Especially with the ceiling fans on.

Beth was lying on top of the sheets, listening to the night noises. The sun had just gone down, and the tree frogs in the shrubbery around the pool were calling for their mates. A mockingbird in the big sycamore tree back by the garage was singing his repertoire. Beth wondered why they were the only species of songbird that sang at night. She heard a great horned owl hooting in the distance. She could picture him swooping down, silently gliding on his powerful wings and catching a rabbit or field mouse in his talons. She even thought she heard the lowing of cattle out in the pasture. Her mind drifted back to her happy days on the farm. She didn't know if she would ever be happy again. Finally, she drifted off to sleep, dreaming of her childhood on a dairy farm.

* * * * *

Beth's big shock came on Tuesday morning, August 18. At 10:15 two FBI agents from the Kansas City office came in the bank with a warrant for her arrest, handcuffed her and took her to the Johnson County jail. Beth looked over her shoulder as they marched her out the front door and saw Tom in the doorway of his office with a smirk on his face, as if to say "Gotcha, didn't I?"

She was allowed to call an attorney. She knew a number of them, but the only one she could think of under such duress was Rudolph Eisenstein. He rushed right up to the jail. The jailer took him to the interrogation room and brought Beth in from her cell.

"What's all this about?" he asked Beth.

"I don't know for sure," she said. "I couldn't get much out of the two agents who arrested me, I think I'm being charged with embezzlement."

Beth was pale, and her hands were shaking. "Will you represent me? Can you get me out of here?" she asked.

"Yes, I'll represent you," he said, "and I think I can bail you out, as soon as I can find out the particulars of the case. In the meantime, I don't want you to talk to anyone until I see to you again, understood?"

"Yes, but please hurry, I'd like to get out of here as soon as possible."

"I'm going up front to talk to the sheriff and see if I can get a copy of the arrest warrant. I need to find out what's been going on. Since it's obviously a federal case, it may take a couple of days to get you out. I don't think a local judge can set bail on a federal case, so we may have to go to Kansas City for a bail hearing."

"Oh, my," Beth sighed. "He has really done it to me this time."

"What do you mean? Do you think Tom is responsible for your arrest somehow?"

"I know he is, and when you get to the bottom of this mess, you will find his fingerprints all over it. I don't know how, but I know he's in on it some way."

"Do you have any funds available to you for bail and other court expenses that may occur?" Rudolph asked. He knew he would have to post bail sooner or later, and he wanted to be ready.

"Yes, I have some funds in other banks that I have access to. Oh!" she just thought of something.

"What's wrong?"

"They grabbed me while I was down on the floor of the bank, and my purse is still on my desk, or at least I hope it is. My car keys are in it, and two check books from out-of-town banks. I don't want my car sitting on the street. Could you pick up my purse and get my car for me, and could you stash it some place safe? There's over $300 in cash in my purse. I was going to lock it in the glove compartment of my car. I know that sounds like a lot of money to be carrying around, but I felt like something like this might come up."

"Yes, I'll do that, but I need to go right now. I'll come back to see you as soon as I know anything." He called for the jailer to take Beth back to her cell, and went up to talk to Harry Foster.

Harry didn't know much either. He said the federal agents brought Beth in about half an hour ago, showed him a federal arrest warrant, and told him to lock her up. He showed Rudolph the booking sheet, where he had entered her into the county records. The charge was embezzlement of funds from a federally insured bank. He said the agents told him to keep her for a couple of days while they went to a federal judge and got a hearing date set, then they would take her to Kansas City.

* * * * *

"Is Judge Whitfield in town?" Rudolph asked.

"Yes, I just came from his office not an hour ago."

"Thanks," Rudolph said, and he rushed out the door.

Rudolph was 73, and not in the best of shape, but he hurried down to the bank. Breathlessly, he asked a teller to take him to Beth's desk. All she did was go get Tom. Tom knew Rudolph from the trial, so no introduction was necessary. He came out on the floor of the bank and asked Rudolph what he wanted, in a rather sarcastic tone.

"I'm here to pick up your wife's purse," Rudolph informed him.

"Sorry, I can't give it to you," was his reply.

Rudolph was ready for him. "Your wife is in jail on a trumped-up charge, and you won't even give me her purse, much less go comfort her in her time of need!" he said in a voice loud enough for everyone in the bank to hear. There were several customers in the bank, and heads turned their way. "You should be ashamed," Rudolph continued, "I guess I'll have to go to the judge and get a court order for you to release the woman's own purse," he said in an even louder tone.

Tom turned on his heels, stomped upstairs and retrieved Beth's purse. He practically threw it at Rudolph, then went into his office and slammed the door.

* * * * *

Rudolph walked as fast as he could up Holden Street to the courthouse, clutching Beth's purse. He struggled up the steps to the judge's chambers and asked the clerk if he could see Judge Whitfield. The clerk knew Rudolph and was only gone a few seconds when she reappeared and motioned Rudolph to go on back to the judge's chambers.

Rudolph sat in a big chair opposite the judge and panted for a couple of minutes. Judge Whitfield had sympathy for him, because he had climbed those stairs many times himself, and he was several years younger than Rudolph.

"I need your help, Your Honor," he finally managed to say. "I have a client in the county jail who has been arrested on a federal warrant. Can you set bail in a federal case so I can bond her out?" Rudolph filled him in on the circumstances surrounding Beth's arrest.

The judge leaned back in his high-backed swivel chair and laid his hands in his lap, fingers interlaced. He rested his chin on his chest for a moment, looking a lot like he was napping. Finally, he looked up. "I can't help you, but there is someone in town who probably can."

"Who would that be?" Rudolph asked, his breathing almost back to normal.

"Do you know Judge Earnest Hoffman?"

"No, Your Honor, I don't know a judge by that name."

"Well, actually, he's a retired circuit judge from Platt County. He served on the bench up there for years and decided to retire and move here to live with his daughter and son-in-law. His wife died about three years ago, and he wanted to be close to family."

"How can he help my client?" Rudolph asked.

"Well, the first of June the Attorney General in Washington appointed him a U.S. Magistrate for a three-county area, Johnson, Henry and Lafayette. There wasn't much about it in the papers, because it's only a part-time job."

Rudolph was puzzled. "Is a magistrate the same as a judge?" he asked.

"Not exactly, but almost. A federal judgeship is a step above a magistrate. They can do some things that he can't, but I think he can set bail. Let me call Judge Hoffman and ask him."

"Shall I wait?" Rudolph asked.

Judge Whitfield picked up the phone and took the receiver off the hook. "Yes, this shouldn't take long." He motioned for Rudolph to stay seated.

"Hello, this is Judge Whitfield at the courthouse. Who am I speaking to?" he asked. "I know it's the operator, but which operator?" Judge Whitfield didn't have much patience. "Ruby?, Okay, Ruby, do you have a number for Judge Hoffman? He lives with his daughter over on College Street, I think. Yes, I know I should have asked for information, but can't you look the number up for me?" There was a two-minute pause. "Number

885? Thank you, Ruby, you just moved up a notch on my Christmas list." Judge Whitfield was not without a sense of humor. "Now, will you ring it for me, please?"

The judge's daughter answered and got her father to the phone.

"Judge Hoffman? This is Judge Whitfield at the courthouse. How are you, sir?" he asked. "Fine, sir, I'm well, too, thank you. I have a question for you concerning federal law, if you don't mind. No, sir, it's not very complicated. I just want to know if you have the authority to set bail for a person arrested on a federal warrant and incarcerated in this county? No, sir, it's not murder, but it is a serious offense. All right, we'll wait for you." He hung up. "His daughter is going to bring him down here right now to look at the warrant and discuss it with you."

Rudolph called the jail and asked Harry to bring the warrant to the courthouse, while they waited. Judge Hoffman looked it over, and after discussing the events surrounding the arrest, he performed his first act as U. S. Magistrate and set the bail at $3,800, the amount Beth was accused of embezzling.

* * * * *

Beth wrote a check for the $380, and a bail bondsman guaranteed the rest. She and Rudolph walked down Holden Street to her car, and she drove him to the back of her apartment on South Street. She pulled into a space under a huge oak tree by the back porch, and they sat and talked for a while.

She told him about the bank examiners, how they stayed for a week and left without telling her anything. She told him about her escapade with Larry Plunkett and the pictures Joe took. She told him how Tom had tapped into her phone and found out about the pictures he had taken of him. She didn't hold back, she trusted Rudolph, so she told him everything.

Rudolph sat for a few minutes and mulled it all over in his mind. Finally, he said, "Do you think Tom might have alerted the Federal Reserve that his wife might be embezzling from your own bank?"

"I think he alerted them that he suspected some embezzling going on at the bank, and they just happened to catch me."

"Do you think he is smart enough to have planted some documents in the records at the bank that would incriminate you?"

"No, but he has friends who are."

Rudolph thought about that for a minute, then said, "I'll tell you what I think is going to happen. A federal judge is going to set a hearing date to hear the evidence the federal prosecutor has against you, and if he thinks there is enough evidence, he will set a trial date. The bond you posted today should carry you through to the trial, unless the prosecutor can convince the judge that you are a flight risk. That shouldn't happen if you show up for the hearing on time. The judge does have the power to raise the bail bond if he wants to, so be prepared to come up with some more money in case he does, so you can stay out of jail. If you do go to jail, it will be in Kansas City, and you don't want that to happen."

"What can we do in the meantime to fight these charges?" Beth asked.

"I don't want you to do anything but lay low. Don't go into the bank and aggravate Tom, as tempting as it may be, and don't go home. Do you have anything to wear, or will you have to send someone to the house for some clothes?"

Beth told him about the overnight bag in the trunk and about renting the room. She also told him about the gun in the glove compartment. Rudolph was upset about the gun and made her give it to him.

"I don't want any fire arms involved in this matter at all.

Someone could get killed, and I don't want it to be you. I'll turn the gun over to Chief Pettit," he said. "It looks like you are in pretty good shape, as far as having a place to go, so I won't worry about that." He saw tears welling up in her eyes. He patted her on the arm. "Don't worry, we'll get you out of this mess. Tell you what, tomorrow I'm going to Kansas City to the FBI office, and possibly the U.S. prosecutor's office to look at the evidence they have against you. Would you like to ride with me?"

"Yes, I would," she said. "Let's take my car, it needs some miles on it, and besides, it would be safer with us than parked here."

"Okay, two things. One, would you drive me to the police station so I can turn this weapon over to Buck? And two," he said looking at his watch, "it's nearly 1:00, so would you allow me to buy you some lunch?"

* * * * *

When they got to the police station, Buck was upstairs having lunch with Ann and the children. Darlene insisted they stay while she went upstairs to tell Buck they wanted to see him. When Buck heard who it was, he insisted they come up and have lunch with them. Rudolph tried to refuse, but neither Buck nor Ann would hear of it.

"We're just having ham and cheese sandwiches," Ann said, "but there is plenty." She fixed them each a sandwich with potato chips and dill pickles and a glass of iced tea.

While they ate, Beth and Rudolph filled them in on the situation. Buck agreed to hold the gun for Beth until it was all over. When they left the station, Beth dropped Rudolph off at his office, promising to pick him up Wednesday morning at 7:00, and drove to the college library where she could be alone to think. At 8:00, she drove to the back of the apartment house, took her bag out of the trunk and went in the back door. She had not eaten since lunch, but she was not hungry, and didn't want anything. Her room was actually an efficiency apartment with its own bath and a tiny kitchen. She took a bath and went to bed.

* * * * *

Rudolph was waiting for Beth at 7:45 when she drove up in front of his office. He tossed his leather file case in the back seat and got in. They drove out of town quickly, trying not to be noticed. They stopped at a little roadside diner on Highway 50 in Lees Summit and had coffee. Rudolph laid out his itinerary for Beth.

First, they would go to the Federal Courthouse and talk to the judge about the evidence needed from the bank examiners to be used in Beth's defense, and how best to obtain it. Then to whatever office that had control of the evidence to get copies.

"I would like to get a copy of the bank examiners' report to the Federal Reserve, along with all supporting documents, if possible," Rudolph said.

Beth didn't reply; she was too frightened to know what to do. She was just glad she had Rudolph to do her thinking for her while she was so mixed up. She didn't touch her coffee; she stared at her cup until Rudolph was ready to go. Rudolph laid a dime on the counter and they left.

The big multi-story courthouse in downtown Kansas City was built in 1930, and still looked new. It was actually the Jackson County courthouse, but the federal government had leased space in it for their offices on various floors. Rudolph looked at the directory in the lobby and punched a button on one of the elevators. They got out on the floor where federal judges and prosecutors had their offices and approached the lady behind the counter.

"We would like to talk to the federal judge," Rudolph said to her, setting his leather bag on the floor beside him.

"Which one?" she asked. "We have three."

Rudolph explained to her that he was there to get information about a pending hearing, and whichever judge was free could probably help him.

"Are you a lawyer?" she asked.

"Yes, ma'am, and this is my client, Mrs. Breckenridge. We're from Johnson county." Rudolph liked to keep strangers off guard with his politeness, and it usually paid off.

"Just a minute," she said and picked up her phone. "Number 826," she told the operator. After a brief pause, "Les, this is Helen on the desk. Can you meet with an attorney from Johnson County? He needs some information on a pending hearing, can you help him?" She listened for a minute. "Okay," she said and hung up. She pointed to her left down a long hall. "Lester Green can help you now; he's in room 826."

"Is he a judge?" Rudolph asked.

Helen smiled and said, "No, he's the courts manager. He sets the dockets, calls the juries and generally runs the courts. He can tell you what you want to know better that any of the judges."

Rudolph thanked her profusely, and he and Beth started off down the hall. Room 826 was almost at the end of the hall. He knocked, and a booming voice yelled, "Come in."

* * * * *

Les Green was an imposing figure. A man of about 40, over six feet tall, with black hair and a sharp prominent nose that reminded Rudolph of Dick Tracy in the comics. He offered his hand to them.

"Hi, I'm Les Green. What can I do for you folks?" he said. His voice was loud, but friendly.

Rudolph shook his hand. "Hello, I'm Rudolph Eisenstein, and this is my client, Elizabeth Breckenridge." He motioned toward Beth.

The big guy shook Beth's hand. She cringed at his grip, but managed to smile one of her prettiest smiles.

"Sit down, folks, and tell me what I can do for you," he said, motioning toward the two chairs facing his desk.

Rudolph told him why they were Kansas City—that his client had been arrested for embezzling funds from a federally insured bank. That the bank was controlled jointly by his client and her husband, and that Mrs. Breckenridge was sure her husband had forged her signature on some document that was responsible for her arrest. He mentioned that the bank had been audited by a team of bank examiners the week of July 13th through the 17th. He also told Les that his client was out on a $3,800 bond, at least until the hearing.

Les sat and listened carefully to Rudolph, and when he was through, shook his head. "Well, I don't think you will get much information to help your client from the prosecutor's office. They're a bunch of young jackals all out to make a name for themselves. They're out for convictions, so they can go on up the ladder."

"What about discovery?" Rudolph asked. "I'm entitled to see any evidence against my client, so I can build our case."

"Well, here is the way it works in the real world of government politics." Les lowered his voice as if someone might be listening outside the door. "These guys down the hall, including the judges, were all appointed by the current Attorney General and approved by the current senate. It looks like the President will easily be re-elected for a second term this year, along with all his incumbents in Congress, plus a lot more. These guys feel like they will have at least four more years to work on a better job in this administration, so they are after convictions. Bottom line is, they won't be very cooperative."

"Are you saying I won't be able to get the information I need?" Rudolph was getting anxious.

"No, it can be done, but you'll have to use a little finesse."

"What do you mean 'finesse'?" Rudolph asked.

"Play one against the other. The prosecutor against the FBI, the judge against the prosecutor, the FBI against the judge, get the picture?"

I'm a holdover from the Hoover administration, and that's the way I have survived the last four years. When this administration took over, they tried to make an errand boy out of me, to get me out of the court system, so they could put their boy in. In six months he had everything so messed up that they had to call me back in to straighten things up. I've been here ever since."

* * * * *

Rudolph got the picture. Les could be very valuable in getting what he wanted. "Can you help me get the documents I need?" he asked.

"Let me make a couple of phone calls," he said, picking up the phone. "FBI office, please," he told the operator. After a pause, "Let me talk to John O'Toole," he told the clerk who answered the phone. John was the chief agent in the Kansas City office.

"John O'Toole here."

"John, this is Les in the court manager's office. I heard some of your agents arrested a woman in Warrensburg yesterday on a warrant from your office. Is that correct?"

"Why do you want to know?" he asked, as if he was afraid someone would try to usurp his authority.

"Well, I'm always under pressure to keep everything on schedule up here, and if she is going to have a hearing, I need to get it on the docket," he lied.

"Oh, yes, we did arrest a woman, and she'll need a hearing.

"Is there a lot of evidence to present? How long a hearing do I need to schedule?"

"No, the only evidence we got from the bank examiners were four documents, but that's all we'll need to convict her."

"Oh, why is that?"

"Because they are very incriminating. There was a forged deed on a piece of property used for collateral on a loan. There was a faked appraisal on the property and a loan application signed by the woman."

"I thought you said there were four documents."

"There were; there was a cashier's check drawn on the bank for $3,800 signed by the woman we arrested. It was cashed somewhere and returned to the bank by the Federal Reserve Bank in St. Louis."

"Where are those documents now?" Les asked.

"In the U.S. Prosecutor's office up on your floor. Hey, why are you so concerned about those documents? You don't have anything to do with them. Why don't you mind your own damn business?" He hung up.

Les was grinning when he hung up the phone. "My, my, he's touchy today," he said. He picked up the phone and called the secretary for the three federal judges. "This is Les Green, let me talk to Judge Matthews, please."

A short pause, "Judge Matthews speaking."

"Judge Matthews, this is Les Green. I've assigned a hearing on an embezzlement case to your docket [another small lie], and I need to get copies of the evidence against the accused from the prosecutor's office for the defense attorney so he can prepare his case. The defendant and her attorney are in my office right now, and they are from out of town, so I need to expedite things if I can."

"Are you expecting problems from the prosecuting attorney?" he asked.

"No, sir, but can I have them call you if there is any question?"

A federal judge knows the importance of both sides in a case having equal access to the evidence so there can be a fair hearing. "No, I don't mind them calling me if there is any question about furnishing copies of the evidence to the defense attorney. I'll be glad to back you up on that."

"Thanks, Judge. Les hung up, this time with an even bigger grin on his face. "See how that's done?" he asked. "Now let's go down the hall to the prosecutor's office."

* * * * *

The prosecutor's offices were way down the hall at the other end of the building. Les led them past Helen at the reception desk to a set of double doors on the left. They opened up into a large reception area where several secretaries were busy at typewriters. At the desk nearest the door, a pleasant—looking, slightly plump, middle—aged woman with red hair sat shuffling through a pile of official-looking papers. She looked up and smiled, "Hi, Les, what's on your alleged mind?" she joked.

"Don't be sarcastic with me, sweetie, or I won't run off to Hawaii with you, like we'd planned."

"That's okay, there's an FBI agent down on four that will take me, and he's a lot better-looking than you."

"Is Carl in?" he asked. Carl Driscoll was the chief prosecutor.

"Yes, but he's in a mood," she warned. She buzzed his line. "Mr. Driscoll, Les Green is out here to see you, and he's with some people. He say's it's important." She winked at Les. "I'll send him right in," she said. She turned to Les, "Mr. Fickle Manager, you know where his office is, he's waiting for you." She smiled as she nodded in the direction of Carl's office, then went back to shuffling her papers.

They went through the reception area to a hall on the right that led to a large corner office. Carl Driscoll was waiting for them with his door open. He frowned at Les, but his face brightened into a big smile when he saw Beth. He may have been a grouch, but like most men, he admired beauty. They all went in and took their seats. Carl leaned back in his big leather chair, trying to impress Beth.

"Now, what's this all about?" he queried, giving Les a stern look. "It's 11:30 now, and I have an important luncheon meeting, so let's be brief."

Les explained that Rudolph was Beth's attorney, and that Carl's office had some evidence backing up an arrest warrant that Rudolph needed to copy.

"You know better than that, Les. We don't turn our evidence over to anybody, much less an opposing attorney," he snorted.

"Oh, but you must," Les corrected. It gave him much pleasure to inform an important lawyer about the law. After all, he only had a business degree. "Haven't you heard about Discovery?"

"What on earth is that?"

"It's a statute that says attorneys on both sides of a case must share evidence with each other."

"What the hell for?" he snorted. "Excuse me, lady," he nodded toward Beth.

"So a defendant can get a fair trial," was Les' answer.

"Well, I'm not going to give up my evidence, I don't care what the statute says."

Les remained calm, in spite of the ranting of this bumbling idiot, who obviously used political clout to get where he is. "Why don't you call Judge Matthews," he suggested. "I was talking to him about this very thing just a few minutes ago. You know, he's a stickler about conducting fair trials."

"Why don't you call him, you're so damn smart? Excuse me again, lady."

Les smiled and picked up the phone on the corner of Carl's desk. "Operator, this is Les Green, will you please ring Judge Matthews' office for me?" He waited for a few seconds. "Judge Matthews, this is Les Green, will you please explain to the Chief Federal Prosecutor why it is important that he let the opposing lawyer in an embezzling case have access to his evidence concerning that case?" There was a pause. "Thank you, sir." He handed the phone to Carl and watched as he listened and squirmed.

A red-faced Carl slammed the phone down and glared at Les. "I'll show the evidence to you, but you can't take it out of my office!" he snarled.

"Do you have a camera and a photographer who can photograph the documents for her attorney?" Les asked pleasantly.

"No!"

"If we can't take the documents out of your office, how do you propose we copy them?" Les was firm in his tone. In 1936, photocopiers such as Xerox were non-existent.

"That's your problem," Carl snorted.

Les had had enough. "Why don't we let Judge Matthews settle this?" he suggested, and reached for the phone.

* * * * *

The arrangement agreed to was this. A deputy prosecutor would accompany Rudolph and his client, with the documents, to a photography studio down on Main Street, where they would be photographed. The deputy could then return the documents to the federal prosecutor's office. The cost of the photography work was to be borne by the defendant.

The photography studio was over a Woolworth store near the intersection of Twelfth and Main. It was a large commercial studio that took up the entire second floor. They specialized in photographing documents and enlarging them. They had no problem with the order, and since it was a rush order from the feds, they had the prints ready in less than an hour. Rudolph had them make four 12x14 prints of all four documents, and a 24x48 print of the loan application and the cashier's check. He would need them for a trial, should one be necessary. Rudolph whistled at the price. Forty-eight dollars was a lot of money for the pictures, he thought. Beth assured him that it was in line for a rush job.

It was shortly afternoon when Rudolph and Beth got out of the photographers, so they walked down to the Forum Cafeteria for lunch, Rudolph carefully carrying the big cardboard tube the pictures were sealed in. After lunch, they retrieved Beth's car from the parking lot and drove home. Rudolph discussed his defense with Beth as she drove.

Beth was certain the signatures on the documents were not hers. A pretty good forgery, but a forgery nonetheless. Rudolph would build his case on that fact.

* * * * *

On Thursday, Rudolph received notice of the hearing to be held in Kansas City on Monday, August 24, at 10:00 a.m. The hearing went just as Rudolph had expected. Carl Driscoll and his staff presented their evidence, consisting of the four documents in their possession, and demanded a trial date be set. Rudolph didn't have time to get his case together, as it required corresponding with some handwriting experts and lining up witnesses. Beth pleaded "not guilty," and Judge Matthews set the trial for Monday, September 15, 1936.

Rudolph busied himself getting ready for Beth's trial. He had some contacts in New York and Chicago from his days of practicing law in those cities, and he called in some favors. A lawyer in New York who went to the same synagogue as Rudolph lined up a handwriting expert to look at the loan application and cashier's check, and to testify in the trial, if necessary. Rudolph sent him copies of the two documents, along with samples of Beth's handwriting to study. He was to call Rudolph as soon as he reached a conclusion. Rudolph didn't try to influence him in any way, not that he didn't trust Beth, he just wanted straightforward answers.

He located another handwriting expert in Chicago and forwarded the same documents and samples to him with the same instructions. He waited nervously for their replies.

The summer of 1936 dragged on in Warrensburg. Buck and Ann got the final adoption papers on the children and had a little celebration afterward with friends. The football team at the college were the first ones back on campus for the fall semester to start their practices. They were expected to have a good team and would probably vie with Southwestern State for the conference championship. Irv continued to caddy golf and carry papers part-time so he could buy school clothing and supplies.

Beth didn't go near the bank. Although she was one of the principal stockholders, Tom made it clear that she was not welcome. He couldn't get enough votes from the board to fire her, but he could sure make it miserable for her if she came in and tried to work. He busied himself spreading gossip around town that she was a thief and a slut who slept

GOTCHA!

around. Beth couldn't face her friends, so spent most of her time alone. She spent a lot of time in the college library, reading the *Wall Street Journal,* law books and books on banking. She had the utmost confidence that Rudolph would clear her of the charges against her, and she wanted to be ready for the time when she went back to the bank to take her rightful place as its president. She felt that Tom had forged the evidence against her, and when she was vindicated, he would go down. Sometimes, she would walk across South Street, look down on the football field, which was in sort of a bowl, and watch the football players practice. It reminded her of her high school days in Holden.

* * * * *

On Friday, August 28, Rudolph got a call from the handwriting man in New York. There was no question in his mind, he said, that the documents were forged, and that he would be happy to testify before a jury to that effect. Rudolph's heart skipped a beat. This was exactly the news he was hoping for. He didn't come cheap. His fee was $25 a day from the time he left New York until the time he got home, plus hotel, transportation, cab fare and meals. Rudolph agreed and sent him a check for a hundred dollars as a retainer.

Monday, August 31, Rudolph got a letter from his man in Chicago. He was a language professor at the University of Chicago. It turns out that he had been a patient of Wilhelm, his brother, and Wilhelm had not charged him for the dental work he did on him, as a professional courtesy. Therefore, he would not charge a fee for his services and would pay his own way to Kansas City for the trial. That was good news for Rudolph, but the best news was that after exhaustive study of the documents, he was positive the signature of his client had been forged.

Rudolph couldn't contain himself. He went looking for Beth. He found her at the college library and told her the good news. They celebrated with a Coke at the Rexall store.

It was still two weeks until the trial, and Rudolph had his preparation finished. He just needed to prep his two star witnesses, and he would do that the day before the trial in the suite he had reserved at the Phillips Hotel.

He turned his thoughts to who did the actual forging of the documents. Was it Tom Breckenridge? He didn't think so. Oh, he planned it all right,

216

but someone else forged the documents. Another thing bothered him. Tom must have suspected that Beth was talking to the police, or he wouldn't have rigged a way to listen in on her phone conversations. He had an accomplice somewhere, either in the Police Department or somewhere else. He doubted anyone in the Police Department would tip Tom off. Then it hit him. The telephone operators often listened in on conversations, especially the supervisor so she could rate the other operators on their ability to handle calls. Buck said the calls were made in the daytime. That meant Ruby McCullum.

Rudolph called his friend Buck at the police station and told him about the good news from New York and Chicago. Buck was happy to hear that Beth didn't do anything wrong. He didn't think she had, but still he had a few doubts. He was getting to know Beth better each day. Then, Rudolph broached the subject of Ruby. "How did Tom know that Beth was calling you, unless someone at the telephone company told him?" he asked.

"You may be on to something," Buck mused. "I have often suspected that the operators listened to conversations they weren't supposed to. You know, they can be fired if they're caught."

"I know, but that doesn't mean they don't do it. I would be very interested in how Tom found out about Beth's calls."

"Me, too."

"Let's keep our eyes and ears open and see what we can come up with, and I'll check with you later. We have some time to work on it, but right now I just want to concentrate on getting Beth exonerated."

"I'll do some checking around, and call you if I come up with anything, bye." Buck hung up.

* * * * *

It was all set up. Rudolph had reserved a two-bedroom suite for the handwriting experts to share, and two single rooms, all on the same floor at the Phillips. Not a plush hotel, but nice. Rudolph and Beth would drive to Kansas City on Saturday afternoon, and check into the two single rooms so they could get a good night's sleep. On Sunday morning at 7:45, Beth would pick Abe Goodleman up at Union Station. He was coming in on an overnight sleeper from New York. At 11:00 she would pick up David Mueller at the Municipal Airport. He was coming in from Chicago on a 7:30 flight via TWA.

They would have lunch in the suite, catered by room service, then they would all have dinner together in the hotel dining room. That way, they would have all Sunday afternoon to go over Rudolph's notes for the trial. Special attention would be given to what the two handwriting experts could expect in the way of questions from the prosecuting attorney. Both men were prepared to stay up to three days if necessary, but Rudolph thought he could get them on the stand the first day of the trial. After their testimony, both men could catch cabs to their respective transportation, and go home.

Rudolph had one more detail to take care of before the trial. He went to the bank and asked for a loan application from their files from a paid-off note, one that Beth had signed as the loan officer. When Tom refused to give him one, he marched right up to the courthouse and got a subpoena from Judge Whitfield, and took Harry Foster with him back to the bank. This time, they reluctantly gave him one. Rudolph went back to his office, put it in an envelope, addressed it to the photographer in Kansas City, and mailed it. Four days later, a big round cardboard tube came in the mail with a 24x48 blow-up of the application. He then went to a frame shop and had all three of the 24x48's mounted on cardboard. He was ready.

* * * * *

Saturday, September 12, Beth and Rudolph drove to Kansas City, getting there about 3:00 in the afternoon. After checking in at the hotel, they met in the coffee shop and discussed the next two days' events. Rudolph was a careful planner and had allowed for all kinds of contingencies. If Abe missed his train or it was delayed, or David's flight from Chicago was delayed, he would put them on the stand a day or two later. If the prosecution introduced any new evidence that he hadn't seen, he might have to ask for a continuance. He went over all his plans with Beth until she was as familiar with them as he was. The exhibits he had made were locked in the trunk of Beth's car, ready to go to the courthouse Monday morning. They had dinner in the hotel dining room and went to bed before 9:00. Beth had to get an early start Sunday morning.

By 5:00 Sunday afternoon, the two handwriting experts were very familiar with the case and were more convinced than ever that the documents were forged.

According to information that Rudolph had gathered, the name, Noah Rodgers, on the loan application was fake, and the address given turned out to be a grocery store in Holden, Missouri. The building on the deed was, in fact, a real building at 31st and Troost in Kansas City, being leased by a Katz Drug Co. store, a dentist and a small gift shop. The only problem was, in checking with the Jackson County Assessor's office, Rudolph found out that the building wasn't owned by Noah Rodgers, but by a group of Kansas City investors who had owned it for a number of years. The appraisal was by a firm nobody had heard of, so it too was a forgery. That left the cashier's check. Both experts agreed that the signature of the bank officer who signed it, i.e., Elizabeth Breckenridge, was an obvious forgery. The signature was traced, not signed. Same for the signature on the loan application. The defense team was ready.

* * * * *

By 10:00 Monday morning, September 14, 1936, the federal courtroom was ready. Rudolph and Beth sat at the defense table, while Carl Driscoll and two of his cohorts were at the prosecution table. Rudolph's two expert witnesses were in the witness room.

Beth turned and looked the gallery over. She didn't recognize many faces. Her dad and mom were sitting a few rows back on the defense side. She didn't suppose there would be many there from the bank, especially on a Monday, which was usually a busy day.

Then she spotted Tom sitting on the prosecution's side, almost on the back row. He was sitting with his newest secretary, holding hands. They were so busy looking at each other and giggling that they didn't notice Beth looking at them. She turned back in disgust.

A federal marshal, acting as bailiff for the court, stood up and demanded, "All rise!" Everyone stood as Judge Matthews took the bench. Les Green had carefully assigned this case to Judge Matthews, for reasons best known to him.

The trial was anticlimactic for Rudolph and his client. They had worked hard gathering information and exhibits and preparing their brief. They were ready.

On the other hand, Carl Driscoll and his crew seemed bored and preoccupied. They conveyed the impression that their case was in the bag and all they had to do was present the evidence to the jury, and it was over.

His opening statement was boring, and soon the jury began to look around. He talked for 20 minutes, going over everyone's duty in the federal justice system and where it all fit into the scheme of things. He was obviously trying to impress the jury with his knowledge and experience in these matters. When he finally got around to the case at hand, he seemed to have forgotten what he wanted to say. He stuttered and stammered for a few seconds, and finally said, "And that's why you should find the defendant guilty as charged in the indictment." Red-faced, he sat down.

When the judge motioned to Rudolph, he stood and contemplated his notes for a minute. Then, as was his usual demeanor, sauntered over to the jury box with his thumbs hooked in his vest pockets like a country lawyer just in from the sticks. He studied his shoes for another minute and then gave a stirring five-minute talk on how bad things sometimes happen to good people. He praised Beth's record at the bank, denounced the accusing documents as out-and-out forgeries, and intimated that he knew who had actually forged the documents. He said that he thought it was the duty of the FBI to catch the guilty party and not harass an innocent person. Rudolph knew that judges are usually pretty lenient with opening statements, so he felt he could get away with that part of his statement. No one slept through his talk, and when he took his seat, the murmurs started again.

Judge Matthews banged his gavel for quiet. He nodded to the prosecution and said, "Call your first witness."

The only witness they called was the head of the audit team that did the examination at the Breckenridge Bank. All he testified to was the trail the evidence took after they found it at the bank. He had turned it over to the Federal Reserve Bank in St. Louis, with the recommendation to prosecute. They turned it over to the FBI, who arrested the perpetrator. The FBI then turned it over to the Federal Attorney's Office in Kansas City. Rudolph didn't even bother to cross-examine the witness; it would just confuse the jury.

When Rudolph's turn came, he passed out the 12x24 copies of the documents, one each to the judge, the prosecutor, and one set for the jury to pass around, and had them entered into the court records as evidence. All the prosecutor did was hold up the documents one at a time and explain to the jury what they were and how they proved that the defendant was an embezzler. The jury hadn't even gotten a close look at them. The jury was obviously delighted to get a chance to see the documents close up.

"The defense will prove that the documents you have before you are all forgeries. There is no Noah Rodgers. The address he allegedly gave was false, the property assessment was by a company that doesn't exist, and the signatures of defendant on the loan application and cashier's check were forged."

The team at the prosecution table was starting to fidget. They looked at each other, as if to say, *Why didn't we have pictures made of the documents and present a stronger case?* They hated to lose, and it wasn't looking too brilliant for them at the moment.

Rudolph produced an affidavit from the county clerk of Johnson County showing that there was no registered voter in Johnson County by the name of Noah Rodgers. He had a letter from the Missouri Real Estate Commission stating that there was no real estate appraisal company by the name given on the appraisal in question. Both were entered into evidence.

Rudolph then nodded to the bailiff, who by pre-arrangement brought three folding easels into the courtroom and set them up. He then brought in the 24x48 enlargements Rudolph had given to him, and placed them on the easels. They were mounted on cardboard, so they stood up where the jurors could see them. One was of the canceled loan application, showing Beth's real signature. The other two were of the loan application and the canceled cashier's check, supposedly cashed be Mr. Rodgers. They were copies of the originals held by the prosecution.

He then called his first witness, Dr. David Mueller, professor of languages at the University of Chicago, and a recognized expert on handwriting. Rather than question him for the jury, he asked the judge's permission to just allow the witness to leave the witness box and point out the differences on the exhibits between the real and forged signatures.

Dr. Mueller did a marvelous job of pointing out the difference between a natural, free-flowing signature and one that had obviously been traced. When blown up the way they were, the traced signatures showed a waviness that the real signature did not. He also pointed out some differences in the letters that, even though they had been traced, were slightly different because the person doing the tracing had injected their own personality into the tracing. Dr. Mueller was a polished speaker, and even though it was a boring subject, he kept the jury's attention. He was scoring points with the jury.

When Dr. Mueller was finished, Judge Matthews asked the prosecution if they wanted to cross-examine the witness. There was a long pause while the three men at the prosecution table looked at each other, as if trying to decide who should answer the judge. Finally Carl stood up and said, "No, Your Honor," and sat down, obviously disgusted with his team.

It was nearly noon when Dr. Mueller finished his testimony, and Judge Matthews recessed the court for lunch. The court would reconvene at 1:30. Rudolph, Beth and the handwriting experts went to a small hamburger joint near the courthouse for lunch. They were a bit more relaxed after the morning session. Carl took his crew back to their offices and ordered in sandwiches so they could rethink their strategy. It was obvious to him that they were not doing well at all.

* * * * *

At 1:30 sharp, the court reconvened.

By most legal standards, it is accepted that if you have three independent witnesses, all testifying to the same thing, then it is true. Rudolph put Abe Goodleman on the witness stand, and he did an equally good a job of convincing the jury that the documents were forged. That left the third witness. Rudolph called Beth to the witness stand.

Beth was dressed in a tailored white long-sleeved blouse and a black skirt. Her long auburn hair was pulled back in a chignon on the back of her head, and she wore very little jewelry, just plain gold loop earrings, a bracelet to match and her wedding rings. Oh, yes, she wanted people to know she was still married to the president of the Breckenridge State Bank, especially the young twit sitting next to her husband. She wore very little make-up, but in spite of her modest attire, her natural beauty shone through and was duly noted by the jury, especially the male members. She was sworn in and seated in the jury box.

Rudolph approached the jury box slowly; he wanted the jury to get a good look at this sweet innocent woman before he interrupted their thoughts. Finally, he cleared his throat and asked, "Mrs. Breckenridge, how long have you been associated with the Breckenridge State Bank?"

"Thirteen years," she said softly.

"Thirteen years," Rudolph repeated. "Mrs. Breckenridge, you'll have to speak a little louder, so the jury can hear you. What is your job there, Mrs. Breckenridge?"

Beth looked directly at the jury. "I'm senior vice-president and public relations manager," she said in a voice usually reserved for the bank's best customers.

"Are you a stock holder in the bank?"

"Yes, sir, I own 26% of the bank's stock."

"Are you adequately paid for your services, Mrs. Breckenridge?"

"I was until this past August 18th."

"What happened then, Mrs. Breckenridge?"

"I was arrested."

"On what charge?"

"Embezzling funds from the bank."

"From your own bank?"

"Yes, that's what the FBI said when they arrested me."

"What is your relationship with Mr. Breckenridge?"

"He's my husband."

"How long have you been married?"

"Ten years."

"Do you have any children?"

"We don't, but Mr. Breckenridge has two grown sons by a previous marriage. He didn't want any more children."

"Do you want for anything?"

"What do you mean?"

"Do you have a nice home, a car, plenty to eat and wear?"

"Yes, sir, we have done well."

"Why would you want to steal from your own bank, if you couldn't improve your life by doing so?" Rudolph glanced at Carl Driscoll. He seemed about ready to object, but changed his mind.

"I didn't steal from the bank. Those documents they are using against me are all forgeries. I did not sign that loan document, nor did I issue that fake cashier's check."

Rudolph paused for a moment to let her statement register with the jury. He continued, "Mrs. Breckenridge, how many people in the bank are authorized to approve loans and sign cashier checks?"

"Just three—myself, Mr. Breckenridge and Bill Worsham, our vice-president and head cashier. Bill Worsham is only authorized to approve loans when both Mr. Breckenridge and I are out of town, and then only up to $500."

"Who would benefit the most if you were sent to jail for a long time?"

"Why, my husband, of course."

"Why is that?"

"Because, if I am forced to leave the bank for over three years, my stock reverts to my husband automatically. That would give him 52% of the outstanding stock, and control of the bank."

"Is that provision written in the bank's bylaws?"

"No, sir, it is written in the new state charter that was issued in 1934, when we reorganized after the new banking laws went into effect."

"Is your husband in attendance here today?"

"Yes, sir, he is sitting in the back of the courtroom," she pointed to Tom, "alongside his newest fling."

Carl jumped to his feet, "Objection," he shouted, "her husband is not on trial here!"

Two things happened simultaneously. Tom and his "secretary" ducked out the front door (back) of the courtroom, and Judge Matthews banged his gavel.

"Sustained," the judge frowned at Rudolph. "The jury will disregard the last remarks by the witness and her attorney."

"That's all the questions I have for this witness, Your Honor." Rudolph was pleased with Beth's testimony.

Judge Matthews nodded at Carl, "You may cross-examine the witness, Mr. Driscoll," he said.

Carl didn't want this witness on the stand any longer than absolutely necessary. He rose and said, "No cross-examination at this time, but the prosecution reserves the right to question the witness at a later date." Beth left the stand, and the bailiff took down the exhibits.

* * * * *

Judge Matthews looked at Rudolph, "Does the defense have any more witnesses at this time?" he asked.

Rudolph stood and looked down at his notes on the table for a moment. Finally, he looked up and said, "Your Honor, we could have called hundreds of witnesses to testify as to the integrity of the defendant. Her loyalty to the bank and her loyalty to her husband, but we prefer to let her 13 years of faithful service to the bank she loves and her unstained record during that time speak for itself. Your Honor, the defense rests."

He sat down, and it was deathly silent in the courtroom for a moment. People in the courtroom couldn't believe it was over so soon; then the murmuring started. Carl and his crew put their heads together. The question was whether they should question the defense witnesses and try to refute their testimony, or ask for a continuance in the trial to get some more witnesses of their own. They decided they would probably lose in either case.

Carl stood, nodded to the judge and said, "The prosecution rests, Your Honor."

Judge Matthews looked at his watch. It was 3:10 p.m. He contemplated his notes for a moment, and said, "We have time to start the closing arguments, and perhaps, by staying a little past our regular time, we can finish this trial today. That would save the taxpayers a good deal of money. The court will recess for 15 minutes, and when we come back, I want the opposing attorneys to be ready to give their closing arguments." He banged his gavel, and the courtroom began to clear.

* * * * *

At 3:25 p.m., Judge Matthews banged his gavel, and the crowd began to quiet down. He gave them another minute, and when the courtroom wasn't quiet enough to suit him, he banged it again, and the room went silent. He pointed to Rudolph and said, "Since the prosecution went first with the opening statements, the defense will go first with their closing argument." He pointed at Rudolph.

Rudolph slowly pushed his chair back and stood. His 73 years were beginning take their toll. He was tired. Beth looked up at him and smiled, as if to say, *"You can do it, old friend. You've been great up to now, just one more hill to climb."* Rudolph smiled back and took a sip of water from the glass on the table. He wiped his forehead with his hankie on his way to the jury box, leaned on the rail and looked each one of the jurors in the eye.

Finally, he said, "It's been a long hot day, and I know you folks are tired. So am I, so I won't bore you with a long-winded speech." Immediately, the jury sympathized with him and, therefore, his client.

"Ladies and gentlemen," he continued, "this young woman is innocent. We have proved to you without a doubt that the accusing documents are forgeries. The question that now remains is who perpetrated this dastardly deed on this young woman, whose record of 13 years has been spotless?" Rudolph was from the old school of orators, and sometimes got a little too dramatic, but the jury loved it. His faint German accent only enhanced his credibility with them.

"Was it some nameless, faceless villain?" he continued, "I don't think so. I think it was someone close to her, someone she trusted, someone who for reasons yet unknown, violated that trust, tried to put her in prison, and ruin her reputation. Who stood to gain the most if Mrs. Breckenridge went to prison for an extended period of time? I'll let you decide the answer to that one. There is one thing that I do know, however, and that is that this woman is innocent, and you must acquit her, or a grave injustice will be done. Ladies and gentlemen, you must acquit her! Thank you for serving on this panel." He walked back to the defense table and sat down. His speech took less than five minutes. The jury was grateful.

Judge Matthews nodded at Carl, "Your turn, Mr. Prosecutor," he said.

Carl and his cohorts had been caught in the middle of a huddle when Rudolph finished his speech, and it took Carl a minute to gather his thoughts. Finally, he stood, picked up his yellow pad from the table and walked over to the jury box.

"Ladies and gentlemen of the jury," he began, "the documents we presented to the court are real and true. They were discovered during an unscheduled audit of the Breckenridge State Bank, by examiners sent by your government to do just what they did, detect fraud." Then he made a big mistake. He went into a long dissertation about why bank examiners came into being. He told them it was because of the banking laws passed by the Congress of the United States to stop fraud and to put the country's banking system back on a sound footing. He cited statistics on the amount of deposits in U.S. banks from 1933 to 1936. He told of the number of fraud cases that had been tried in federal courts around the country, thus saving depositors from losing their life savings. On and on he went, trying to prove to the jury how smart he was and, therefore, because he was so smart, he should win this case.

It was having the opposite effect on the jury. They were bored and started squirming in their seats. It was hot in the courtroom, and they wanted to start their deliberations. They started fanning themselves and looking at the clock on the wall behind the clerk's desk. The two lawyers at the prosecution desk were trying to signal Carl to cut it off, but on he droned. Finally, at 4:45, he thanked the jury and sat down.

Judge Matthews then gave his instructions to the jury. Among other things, he said he hoped they were prepared to stay late, because he would like for them to continue deliberating until they had reached a verdict. If they went past 6:00, he told them they would be furnished a meal and would be allowed 30 minutes to eat it in the jury room. If by 10:00 p.m. they had not reached a verdict, they would be sent home and would start again tomorrow at 10:00 a.m. They were not to talk to anyone about the case outside of the jury room and were not to read any newspapers or listen to the radio outside of the jury room. The bailiff led the jury out of the courtroom, and Judge Matthews went back to his chamber.

Rudolph was spent. It had been a tough two weeks leading up to the trial. He and Beth sat at the defense table for a few minutes as people filed out of the courtroom. Rudolph had no idea how long the jury would be out. He asked Beth if she would like to go for a cup of coffee. She said she would rather just wait in the courtroom for at least an hour, to see what happened.

David and Abe came in and sat with them. David had picked up two newspapers from the stand down in the lobby. *The Kansas City Star* had a small article on the trial in section B. *The Journal Post* had an article on the front page below the fold, but neither paper had pictures accompanying the article. The big headlines in both papers were about the Spanish civil war and Nazi Germany's involvement.

They moved to a long bench in front of the rail separating the trial participants from the gallery, where they could spread out and be more comfortable. Beth's parents came up and sat on the other side of the rail so they could visit. Rudolph had never met her parents, and he enjoyed visiting with them. They planned to stay until about 10:00 p.m., and if the verdict wasn't in by then, they were going to have to drive back to Holden so they could get up at 4:00 a.m. to help with the milking. Milking 38 cows by hand twice a day was quite a chore.

At 6:00, a meal was catered to the jury from a nearby restaurant, and at 6:30 they settled in for more deliberating. At 8:15, the foreman signaled to the bailiff that they had reached a decision, and he, in turn, notified Judge Matthews, who was still in his chambers. Word went out via the deputy marshals that the verdict was in and would be announced soon. Not many people returned for the verdict. Most had gone home for the evening. There were two reporters and Beth's parents, of course, but not many of curiosity seekers who like to hang around courthouses. Rudolph and Beth went back to the defense table. Carl and his crew came up from his offices as soon as they got word.

* * * * *

"All rise," the bailiff intoned, and Judge Matthews slowly walked up the steps to the bench. It had been a long, hot day, and he was getting weary. He looked over the courtroom, as was his custom, to see if everyone was where they were supposed to be. He banged the gavel and declared the court back in session. "You may be seated," he said. He turned to the marshal in charge, "Bailiff, you may bring the jury in now." Even his voice sounded tired.

The bailiff led the jury in, and they took their seats in the jury box. Rudolph looked at their faces as they filed in, to see if he could get some clue as to how they might have voted. He didn't detect anything at all and was beginning to worry about the verdict.

"Will the foreman please stand?" he asked.

"Forewoman," a middle-aged school teacher said as she got up.

"My apologies," Judge Matthews said, "have you reached a verdict?"

"We have, your honor."

"Is it unanimous?"

"It is, Your Honor."

"Please hand it to the bailiff."

She handed the slip of paper with the verdict on it to the bailiff, who in turn handed it to Judge Matthews. He looked it over and handed it back to the bailiff, who took it to the foreman.

"Will the forem—excuse me, the forewoman, please read the verdict?"

She put her reading glasses on and scanned the sheet in her hand. "As to the charge of embezzlement of funds from a federally insured bank, we the jury, find the defendant not guilty."

Carl Driscoll was on his feet in an instant. "Your Honor, I move to have the jury polled!" he said in a loud voice. He hoped one of the jurors might change his or her mind if they were polled in open court.

"Motioned denied," the judge said in a equally loud voice. "It is a unanimous decision, and nothing can be gained by polling the jury at this point. The jury is dismissed with the thanks of this court, you may go home now." He banged his gavel. "This court is adjourned." He left the bench.

Carl and his crew left the courtroom in a huff. He was not used to losing in his court. Beth gave Rudolph a big hug, who as tired as he was, was grinning from ear to ear. Her parents came up and congratulated both of them. Her dad shook Rudolph's hand and thanked him profusely. He couldn't remember having ever met a real live Jew before, but he sure liked this one.

Rudolph gave a brief statement to the reporters, and they all left the courtroom. Beth said good-bye to her parents in the parking lot, and they made her promise she would come home for Thanksgiving. She and Rudolph got in her car for the drive home. Beth drove; she knew downtown Kansas City better than Rudolph.

Besides, he was very tired, and she was afraid he might fall asleep at the wheel if he drove. It was 9:00, and downtown traffic was slow at that hour on a Monday, so they made good time and were soon on Highway 50 headed toward Lee's Summit.

Beth hardly said a word until they got out on the open highway. Finally, she turned to Rudolph and said, "I don't know what to do now."

Rudolph, who was starting to nod, was startled when she spoke. "Uh, what do you mean?" he asked.

"I mean about going to work. Since I've been cleared of the embezzling charge, I can go back to work at the bank, but Tom will make it so miserable for me that it's going to be awfully hard."

"You're a 26% owner, and I haven't read or heard anything about you being fired by the board from your position at the bank. You have as much, or more, say-so at the bank than Tom. What if you showed up at work tomorrow, and just went about your business without having any contact with Tom, would that work?"

"I'm afraid not. Everything I did, or said, Tom would go along behind me and countermand it. It would be confusing for everybody in the bank, including the customers. It just wouldn't work."

Rudolph closed his eyes, put his hands in his lap and thought for a minute. Finally, he said, "Why don't you go by the house tomorrow while he's at work and get the rest of your clothes and what other things you might need and take them over to your apartment. If you don't have room for all of your clothing at the apartment, take the rest to your cleaners, they'll store them for you, especially things like your fur coat. Or maybe your folks can drive over from Holden for a couple of hours in the afternoon and help you. It's only 15 miles, and I'll bet they would be glad to help. They could take some of your things home with them for safekeeping, if you don't have enough room in your closet."

He thought for a few more minutes and said, "As far as going back to work, why don't you just take a vacation from now until the first of the year? That's three and a half months. That's time enough for Tom to get things really messed up at the bank.

"That will also give me time to work on some of the board members. My brother and I have quite a few shares of stock in the bank, and I am personally acquainted with most of the board. I could start gathering proxies from stock holders, and by January we could have enough votes, so that by adding your 26%, maybe we could oust Tom as president and kick him out of the bank completely."

That idea appealed to Beth, all except taking the part about taking a three-and-a-half-month vacation. She wasn't used to taking vacations. "What would I do with myself for three and a half months?" she asked.

"Enroll at the college and take some courses besides banking. Something that would stretch your mind. English Literature, Greek Philosophy, offer to help coach the football team, things like that."

Beth chuckled; she knew he was just trying to cheer her up.

Rudolph continued, "Why don't you take a real vacation? Sail to Europe and spend a few weeks in England and France, go to Rome and Paris, have some fun?"

Beth didn't think going to Europe by herself would be much fun. "I like your idea of gathering up stock proxies. I think it is a good one," she said. "I'll probably take your advice and stay away from the bank until January 2nd. I'll spend some time at the college library, but I don't want to enroll in any classes. I may start on a book that I've been wanting to write—a history of banking in the United States from the early 1600s until 1934. What do you think?"

This time it was Rudolph's turn to chuckle.

10

CHRISTMAS IN WARRENSBURG

BETH KEPT HER promise and stayed away from the bank. She did go down once when Tom was out of town and picked up some personal things she kept in her office. There was an umbrella hanging on the back of the door that she thought she might need, some framed pictures of her family hanging on the wall, plus a couple standing on her desk, a flashlight that belonged in her car, and most of all, a portable typewriter that was a Christmas gift from her parents last year. She gathered it up and took it to her apartment. On her way out of the bank, two of the tellers sort of hinted to her that they would like to talk to her privately, but she didn't encourage it. There would be time for that later.

She cleaned her room out at the house on the Thursday after the trial. Her youngest brother, Sam, came over from Holden with a pick-up truck and helped her carry it out. Beth laid a clean sheet in the bed of the truck, and the clothing and personal items she didn't have room for in her apartment, they laid in the truck and covered them over with another sheet. Sam had brought a tarp with him, and he covered the bed of the truck with it, then tied it down so it wouldn't blow off. Beth put the rest of her things in the trunk of her car.

Beth gave Sam a big hug and kissed him on the cheek. "Thanks a million, little brother," she said. "I won't forget this. Give Mom and Dad a big hug for me." Sam was only 17, and the kiss from his sister embarrassed him. His face got red and he mumbled something about her being welcome, then got in the truck and drove off. The clothing and

231

other personal things would be stored in a vacant upstairs bedroom in the big farmhouse near Holden.

Beth spent most of her time, while waiting for the first of the year, in the college library with her portable typewriter, catching up on her correspondence and writing an untitled novel.

Buck and Ann busied themselves with Ellie and Jimmie. Ann was giving Jimmie piano lessons, and little Ellie would sit on the floor and try to play on Ann Marie's toy piano while Jimmie was practicing. Ann was in cat heaven. She still loved the memory of Ann Marie, but also adored these two little children. Buck felt the same way. The only cloud on his horizon was the fact that he was sure in his mind that Tom Breckenridge killed Margaret Wilson, but he didn't have enough evidence to arrest him. The fountain pen would help, but he needed another, bigger clue that would prove he did it. Tom called him twice and asked for his pen back, but each time Buck refused. He needed to keep it for that day in court when he could use it as evidence to help convict him.

There was a rumor around town that Harry Foster and Lois Huff were getting serious about each other. She was seen on several occasions taking fresh baked pies to the jail after she got off work at Dub's Café. Harry, who was raised a Baptist and had always attended the Haver Hill Baptist Church a mile from his home out in the country, had recently joined the First Baptist Church in town. A fine baritone, he had volunteered for the choir. Just by coincidence, Lois attended the First Baptist Church and sang alto in the choir. Someone even reported seeing them holding hands in the balcony of the Star Theater one Saturday night.

Aunt Belle got a surprise visit from George, Thelma and the children at Thanksgiving. They brought a baked turkey with all the trimmings, two pecan pies and a sweet potato pie. Aunt Belle had planned to spend the day with a neighbor lady, who was a widow like her. They had planned to kill one of her neighbor's chickens and bake it for dinner. Thelma suggested that she invite her neighbor to eat with them, which she did. They spent the night with Aunt Belle, and on Friday after breakfast, Milton went by the jail, to once again thank Harry for all he had done for him. Harry was tickled to see him. He even called Buck and Rudolph and told them Milton was in town. Ten minutes later, they were all in Harry's office reminiscing about the events of the past summer. They could joke about it now, but back then it was real serious.

After promising to come see them again, Milton walked back to Aunt Belle's house, and right after a lunch of turkey sandwiches, the Stevensons loaded up the car and headed back to Saline County.

Irv and his family had a big Thanksgiving. Katie's only sister, Harriett, came all the way from Newcastle, Indiana, with her husband and son, on the Wednesday before Thanksgiving. She and Katie baked a big turkey with all the trimmings. The round oak table in the Hodges kitchen wouldn't accommodate everybody, so Irv, his cousin Vernon and LeRoy ate off the wash bench on the screened-in back porch. The weather was mild, so nobody minded. That afternoon, Irv went over to Aunt Belle's to say hello to Milton. It had been over five months since they had first met under the Hodges kitchen. They both laughed about that meeting.

* * * * *

Things at the Breckenridge State Bank were not going well. Without Beth there to meet and greet customers and manage the bank's personnel and operating expenditures, they were starting to lose money. Tom began to act as if his was the only bank in town. He would get rude with farmers who came in to borrow money and lost some of the bank's oldest customers that way.

Just down the street was another bank, run by a shrewd banker and businessman, who coincidentally had the same first name as Tom Breckenridge. He and his family also lived in a big fine home on South Holden Street, not far from the Breckenridge mansion. The other Tom was active in local charities and his church. He served on the Chamber of Commerce Board and gave freely of his time to the Scouts and other organizations, things that Tom Breckenridge did not do. Tom Breckenridge was too busy throwing parties at his big house on south Holden and chasing women. The Breckenridge State Bank began losing customers to the other bank.

It didn't happen all at once, but when the Breckenridge State Bank was a week late mailing out their Christmas Club checks, it began to accelerate—people were depending on those checks to do their Christmas shopping. The bank had to dip into their loan reserve to cover the checks, something that was illegal. Tom hoped the federal bank examiners wouldn't pull another audit of the bank's books until he could pay the reserve fund back.

* * * * *

Christmas of 1936 wasn't much better than the past five Christmases had been. The nation still suffered from nearly 25% unemployment. A lot of factories were still closed, but government crop subsidies were keeping most of the farmers' heads above water. They weren't getting rich, but at least most of them could pay their bills. The hours were long and the work was hard, but there was hope, always there was hope.

The Warrensburg Chamber of Commerce and the Merchants' Association got together and decorated downtown with evergreen garlands across the streets and a big statue of Santa Claus on the southeast corner of the courthouse lawn. The Santa Claus was 12 feet tall and sat on a base that was six feet tall, making the entire structure 18 feet tall overall, an imposing sight to the children. The merchants bought it used, from a company in Kansas City that specialized in such things, so they weren't out a lot of money. The front of the base had a small window with a cloth screen over it, and children were encouraged to tell Santa what they wanted for Christmas. A volunteer inside the base would talk to them without being seen. It was a hit with the children.

On Saturday, November 28, the Christmas season was kicked off with a parade at 10 a.m. They marched down Holden Street from Gay Street, all the way south to the campus, a distance of about eight blocks. The day dawned with a fine mist falling, and the merchants feared the parade might be rained out, but almost as if on cue, the sun came out and the day turned out to be a cool, crisp fall day, ideal for a parade and the football game that night at the college stadium.

The Mule Marching Band led off with baton twirlers in their cute costumes and a strutting drum major. Then came a tractor pulling a hay wagon with the First Christian Church Choir sitting on hay bales, singing Christmas carols. Next came the Smith Cotton High School Marching Band from Sedalia. After that, another tractor pulling a flat bed wagon with a live nativity scene, sponsored by the First Baptist Church, complete with live sheep and a real baby in the manger. Harry Foster played one of the wise men, but hardly anyone noticed it was him because of the false beard and long robe he wore.

There were two other bands from neighboring schools; then came the big attraction, Santa riding on a fire truck, waving at the children, with two of his elves, one on either side of the truck, throwing candy to the crowd lining both sides of the street.

* * * * *

A light snow began falling the day before Christmas, just enough to give the town a Christmas look. It clung to the branches of the spruce and cedar trees, and made the lawns look like white blankets. At 6:00 p.m., the merchants locked their doors and went home to their families.

Ann's parents had invited her and her family to their big house on south Holden Street for a Christmas Eve celebration. There would be lots of snacks and drinks, and about 8:00 they would open presents. After that, they would gather around the big grand piano in the drawing room and sing Christmas carols, to Ann's accompaniment on the piano. Buck's family was invited, too, but they were entertaining Buck's two sisters and their families at their house. Buck and Ann promised to go by Christmas Day with the children for a visit and to exchange presents.

Lois Huff, along with her mother and ten-year-old son, spent Christmas day with Harry Foster at his farm north of Warrens-burg. While the women cooked dinner, Harry took Lois' son, Caleb, rabbit hunting with the new 410-gauge shotgun he got him for Christmas. Harry carried his trusty double barrel 12gauge, and between them they got four rabbits. It was Caleb's first hunting experience, so Harry showed him some safety precautions that he must always observe with a gun, and then let him fire a few times at a tin can sitting on a stump to get the hang of it. Caleb was so excited when he shot his first rabbit that he ran back to the house waving the rabbit in the air for his mother to see.

While Lois and her mother were getting dinner on the table, Harry showed Caleb how to dress and skin a rabbit for cooking. After Christmas dinner, Harry got a bushel of potatoes and several Bermuda onions from his cellar and put them in the trunk of his patrol car, along with the rabbits, and they all took a ride into town. They drove down the lane to Willie Cates' house.

Jennie heard the car coming down the lane and met them at the kitchen door. She was leaning on her crutch with the children peeking out from behind her.

"Praise the Lord," she shouted as they unloaded the rabbits, potatoes and onions. "Willie always kept us in rabbits when he was livin', and now with him gone, we been missin' 'em. How'd you know they was our favorite food?"

Harry grinned as he carried them into the kitchen, "Because I was raised on rabbits," he said, "and I know they taste mighty good this time of the year. Miss Jennie, do you have flour to roll the rabbits in for frying?" he asked.

"Yes, suh, I surely do," she said as she hobbled over to the table to look them over. "Um, um, these are mighty fine rabbits." She was obviously taken by their generosity. "We's gonna have a fine Christmas dinner now, chillins'," she said, her lower lip starting to tremble.

Lois reached into her coat pocket. The Christmas card from Dub with the ten crisp one-dollar bills in it was still there. It was a week's wages for Lois, but she took the money out of the envelope and pressed it into Jennie's hand. "Merry Christmas," she said softly, as she hugged her tightly. During the drive back to the farm, the four of them sang Christmas carols, Lois' alto notes a perfect match to Harry's baritone.

Irv went out to a field near Warrensburg a week before Christmas with an axe and cut down a wild cedar tree. He carried it home and rigged a bucket of sand for a base, which Katie covered with an old sheet she was saving for rags. Irv, LeRoy and Kathy took turns hanging what ornaments they had on it. Mostly, they were tree decorations sent to them by an old friend of Katie's who lived in White Plains, New York. They had been dear friends since their teens, but that's another story. Her name was Pearl, and her husband was chief financial officer for a big company that produced roofing material that went into just about every home that was built in those days. They were very well off, but Pearl never forgot her old friend, Katie. Every Christmas she sent a big box with clothing for the children, games, and yes, even Christmas decorations.

On Christmas day, Katie cooked a chicken in a big aluminum pot, and when it was just right, she spooned homemade dumplings into the broth surrounding the chicken and let it simmer until time to eat. She baked cornbread and opened a jar of green beans she had canned the past summer. She added some salt pork and onions for flavor and put them on the back of the stove to simmer, but her real culinary skills lay in her pies and cobblers. She opened two jars of home-canned cherries and made a big cobbler for desert. She was ably assisted by her husband, Nate, who, when they were first married, took a fling at selling aluminum cookware and was handy around the kitchen. That, in fact, was where the big aluminum pot for the chicken came from, a testimony to the quality of the cookware he sold. Her children were all there, including Louis and Chuck, who were home on a Christmas pass from CCC camp. They all sat down to eat, and as Nate asked the blessing on the food, Katie's thoughts were, "Yes, we are indeed blessed."

Beth went home for Christmas. They all got up early to open gifts on Christmas Day, which was no chore for a family in the dairy business. She helped her mother prepare dinner, and when they all gathered around the table, her dad asked her if she would like to ask the blessing on the food. Beth was embarrassed; she had never done that before. There was a moment of silence, when her kid brother Sam spoke up. "I'd like to say the blessing, if you don't mind," he said, and without hesitation, he offered a lovely little prayer he had learned at Sunday School. Beth was ashamed; once again her little brother had bailed her out.

That afternoon around 3:00, Beth went for a walk out in the pasture to think things out. She got as far as the creek that separated the pasture from a walnut grove, when she heard footsteps and someone panting as if out of breath. She turned, and Sam ran up to her with a big smile on his face.

"You mischievous rascal," she said as she put her arm around his shoulder, and they walked down the creek to the fence and back to the house.

George and Milton drove to Warrensburg the day before Christmas and took Aunt Belle home with them, where she stayed through New Year's. They had a special Christmas dinner in her honor at the church, and the entire Roy community attended. Aunt Belle was happy beyond measure.

Rudolph and Wilhelm Eisenstein put a menorah up in their apartment over the print shop, where they quietly celebrated Hanukkah. They hadn't been in a temple since leaving Germany, but they still believed in the old Jewish ways.

Tom Breckenridge spent Christmas in Kansas City with one of his girlfriends. He would get a surprise for New Year's. Christmas of 1936 turned out pretty well for Warrensburg, after all.

11

CAT AND MOUSE GAMES

WHEN BETH WALKED into the bank on Monday, January 4, 1937, there were some surprised looks. She was dressed for work and went straight up to her office. She dusted her furniture, sharpened a couple of pencils and went looking for Bill Worsham. "Bill, I would like to see the balance sheet for December 31st, Please," she said, in as nice a voice as she could muster.

"Beth, I'm not supposed let you look at any of the bank's records," he said.

"By whose orders?" Beth asked.

"By Tom's," he said sheepishly.

Beth took a deep breath; she didn't want to cause a scene. "Bill, I'm still senior vice-president and a principal stockholder in this bank," she said in a soft but firm voice, "and I still have the bank's best interests at heart. I think I'm entitled to look at the records, don't you?"

"Beth, it's not up to me, why don't you talk to Tom?" he asked.

"There was no light on in his office when I came. Is he even in the bank?"

"No, ma'am, he usually doesn't come in on Mondays until about 11:00." Bill was uneasy.

Beth could tell that he wanted to say more, but was too afraid.

She thanked him and walked out on the floor. She couldn't believe the difference in attitude everyone seemed to have, compared to her last visit just three and a half months ago. The tellers had their heads down and wouldn't even look up. There was only one customer in the bank, and she just came in for a free calendar. Beth went back up to her office and got her purse. She went downstairs, walked out the front door and went down to Rudolph's office on Pine Street.

The publicity of the two trials he had been involved in the past three months as a defense lawyer had increased Rudolph's business considerably at a time when he really didn't want new business. He was 73, and was thinking about retiring. He longed to travel. He had no desire to go back to Germany because of the Nazi persecution of the Jews. Letters from family and old friends there warned him and his brother, Wilhelm, not to come back.

He did long to see some old friends in New York and Chicago that he and his brother had kept in touch with, and he had always wanted to visit California, especially San Francisco. He was day-dreaming over a pile of files on his desk when Beth walked in. He was pleasantly surprised and immediately got to his feet and extended his hand. He could tell by the look on her face that she was not happy.

"Beth, what a nice surprise," he said. "Sit down, my dear," he said, motioning to the chair beside his desk. He and Beth had talked several times during the past three and half months, but only over the phone, and never openly about Rudolph's project in her behalf, because of the suspected operator problem. It was time to talk about it face to face.

Beth told him about her problem at the bank this morning. "Do you have enough proxies lined up for us to make our move?" she asked.

Rudolph unlocked the lower right-hand drawer of his desk and pulled out a 9x12 manila envelope. In it were proxies for all of the stockholders in the bank, except Tom's, Bill Worsham's and a few shares owned by out-of-town stockholders that hadn't returned the proxies he sent them. The proxy form was written by Rudolph and printed in secret by the print shop on the first floor of their building. Through the Secretary of State's office in Jefferson City, Rudolph had obtained a list of the bank's stockholders, their addresses and the number of shares they owned. Most of them lived in Warrensburg.

During the months of November and December, he had carefully approached the ones in town and showed each of them their proxy. It had their name on it, the number of shares they were voting, and the statement that they were voting in favor of a stockholder's proposal to oust Tom Breckenridge as president of the Breckenridge State Bank because of his ineptness as the bank manager, resulting in losses of customers and, therefore, losses of profits, during the past several months.

"There are nine board members, and they all own stock," he said, "and how they vote their stock is very important. I have talked to all of them except you, Tom, Bill Worsham and Larry Plunkett."

Beth spoke up, "Tom's and my shares will cancel each other out."

"That's true," he continued, "so we'll have to depend on the rest of the board to help us carry this thing. Bill owns 3,000 shares, and Larry has 2,000. Add those to Tom's 26,000, and they have a total of 31,000 shares of the original issue of 100,000."

"That's assuming that Bill and Larry will vote with Tom," Beth added.

"Oh, I get the feeling they will, don't you?" Rudolph asked.

"Bill may not; Tom has been pretty hard on him," Beth said.

Rudolph scratched his head. "I'm still a little confused about how the bank stock was re-issued after the reorganization in 1934. Could you go over that again for me?"

"Let's see," Beth pondered, "we issued 100,000 shares of new stock at one dollar par value, and we traded the new stock for the old bank's stock at the rate of one share of the new for ten shares of the old. The old stockholders felt cheated, but that was the only way to save the bank. The old stock was worthless anyway. This way, at least they got something for it. We wrote off all of the old bad debt on the books and started with a clean slate."

"That's why I found so many stockholders listed in the records at Jefferson City. They had been holders of the old stock. How was the rest of the new stock handled?"

"First, I went around to people with influence and money and asked certain ones to serve on our board. The stipulation was that if they wanted the prestige of serving on a bank board, they would have to own stock in the in the corporation, to show their good faith. My request was that they buy at least 500 shares of the new stock at the par value of one dollar. I got six outside people; by that, I mean people outside the bank, to agree to buy the stock and serve on the board. They each bought 1,000 shares, except J.W. Christian and Larry Plunkett, who bought 2.000."

"How was the rest of the new stock handled?"

"Well, I insisted that Tom and I retain control of the bank, so we were issued 26,000 shares each, which make up 52% of all the stock. I knew that Tom was cheating on me at the time, so I had the stock evenly divided between us. That way, he couldn't divorce me and take it all. I'm sure glad we did it that way now. We issued 3,000 shares to Bill Worsham, as a bonus, because he was such a valuable employee. The rest, we sold at one dollar a share to anyone we could. That gave us enough money to keep going until our loan payments started generating enough cash flow to pay our bills, and have some left over to loan out.

Rudolph thought for a minute, "Then you, Tom and Bill make up the rest of the board, nine members in all?"

"That's right, but do you know what?" Beth just had an exciting thought.

"What?"

"The board is supposed to meet sometime between September 1st and December 31st each year to elect new officers for the coming year, and I don't think that was done last year."

Rudolph's eyebrows went up, "What are the implications of that?" he asked. "Is it in the by-laws?"

"Yes, it's in the by-laws, and it means that the board has 30 days to correct the situation, or Tom is no longer president and chairman of the board. After 30 days in the new year, any stockholder can call for referendum to elect a new board, which in turn must elect a chairman and appoint new officers. If we can keep this quiet for 30 days, we have a real shot at getting Tom out!" Beth was really getting excited now.

"Where should we go from here?" Rudolph asked.

Beth could hardly contain herself, "Just hang on to that list of stockholders and the proxies; we'll be needing them in 30 days."

Rudolph took a sheet of paper out of his upper left-hand drawer. "Beth, I hate to bring this up, but I've been out some expenses, you know, postage, long distance phone calls and the trip to Jefferson City. I have it all itemized here if you would like to see it."

Beth looked at the sheet. "You shouldn't regret billing me for work I asked you to do," she said. She wrote him a check for the amount, thanked him, and went back to the bank. She almost broke into a song on her way back, she was feeling so much better.

* * * * *

The 30 days went by fast for Beth. She ignored Tom entirely. Twice, he tried to make small talk, but Beth knew he was just trying feel her out to see what she was up to. She didn't even give him a hint, which upset him, because he had been getting inquiries from some of the stockholders about a proxy they had received in the mail. He suspected Beth was trying to oust him as president and chairman of the board, so he told the ones that called to just tear up the proxy and throw it away. Some did, and some didn't. Not every stockholder liked Tom. His father had been popular with them, and that's why they hung on to their stock, but Tom's popularity was slipping fast.

For one thing, he canceled the regular quarterly board meetings. At the July meeting, right after the bank examiners left, he told them that the meetings were a waste of time, and if he deemed it necessary, he would call one. There hadn't been one since, which was a violation of the bank's by-laws and federal banking laws. Beth knew the by-laws and was just waiting for the 30 days to pass so she could call a referendum. Not one of the six outside directors had contacted Tom. They suspected what Beth was up to, and while they talked among themselves, no one talked to Tom about it. The bank was starting to lose money, and they knew why. They wanted Beth back in charge.

Beth's presence in the bank had an effect on the other employees, however. A whole different attitude was beginning to permeate the bank. Although Tom wouldn't let Bill, or anyone else for that matter, show her any of the bank's records, Beth pretended that she didn't mind. She went around the bank humming to herself and would often position herself by the front door and greet customers as they came in. She would inquire about their children and other family members, smiling sweetly all the time. She went to Woolworth's five-and-dime store and bought penny suckers out of her own pocket and would give them to children as they left the bank with their parents. The tellers were actually starting to smile again. The customers loved this personal touch.

At least twice a week, she would confer with Rudolph at his office. He was preparing a letter to mail out to all stockholders on Friday, January 29, calling for a stockholders' referendum meeting on Wednesday, February 17, at 10:00 a.m. in Dockery Hall on the campus of CMSC. The purpose of the meeting was to elect a new nine-member board of directors for the Breckenridge State Bank. Enclosed was a list of recommended candidates, which was nothing more than a list of the current members, except omitting Tom's and Larry Plunkett's names and adding Rudolph Eisenstein and Judge Emerson Whitfield's to it. The stockholder had the choice of attending the meeting or checking the box approving the candidates and mailing it back. The letter was signed by Elizabeth Breckenridge, holder of 26,000 shares of stock.

Rudolph had talked to all parties involved, and all had agreed to serve. He also made arrangements with the college to use their basketball gym for the meeting. He had no idea how many would attend. There were over 1,100 stockholders of record, some owning as few as five shares.

The current board could have met and ousted Tom, but Beth knew he wouldn't accept their decision and would fight it. This way, if the majority of stockholders voted in a new board, and then he was ousted, the decision would have teeth in it. Besides, Beth wasn't sure how the outside members of the board would vote until Rudolph had spent the month of January talking to them individually. To a man, they were for Tom's ouster.

The by-laws called for the stockholders to be notified at least two weeks before the meeting, and Beth knew there would there would be hell to pay when Tom got his letter the end of January, but she felt she could handle it as long as he didn't get violent.

* * * * *

Monday morning, February 1, at 10:55, Beth was sitting at her desk reading the morning paper, when she heard Tom come stomping up the stairs to her office. He flung the door open and stared at her with his hands on his hips. His face was red, and he was steaming mad.

He walked over and slammed the proxy letter on Beth's desk. "What the hell is this?" he hissed through his teeth.

"It's a letter calling for a stockholders' referendum," she said calmly. "It's required by law."

"You don't have the authority to do this!" he shouted.

Beth was ready for him. She unlocked the middle drawer of her desk and took out a copy on the bank's by-laws, plus a copy of the 1934 banking law. She had underlined the clause about stockholders being able to call a referendum. With shaking hands, she pointed it out to him.

"Why?" he screamed.

"I think you know why," she said as calmly as she could. "I need to be a part of this bank, too, and you have shut me out."

"You cheap slut," he said through clinched teeth, as he smacked her across the face with the back of his right hand. Beth fell backward out of her chair and hit the floor with a thud. Bill Worsham, whose office was on the ground floor, heard the noise and came running up the stairs. When he saw Beth on the floor and Tom standing over her, he lunged at him and planted a shoulder in the middle of his back. The force of the blow sent Tom sprawling over Beth's desk. At that moment, Bill hit the back of Tom's head with the palm of his right hand, slamming it into the top on the desk, almost breaking his nose.

As most bullies do, when faced with any real opposition, Tom ran. Although Bill was ten years older than Tom, he stood his ground and threatened to hit him again. Tom ran down the stairs and out the back door of the bank, slamming it after him. Bill helped Beth up. Her lower lip was cut and starting to swell. Bill handed her his handkerchief, and she wiped the blood away.

"I'm sorry, Beth," he said. "I should have warned you. He's been like this for months, but don't worry, I won't let him hit you again."

"That's okay, Bill," she said, wiping more blood from her lip. "He has only hit me once before in our 12 years together, and both times the bank was in a crisis and I needed to do something bold. Did you get your letter today, too?"

"I did, and you can count on me."

* * * * *

Tom stayed away from the bank much of the next two weeks, which was good, because it gave Beth time to go over the books and plan what she could do to help the bank get on its feet, if she won the election. He only stayed a few days at the house on south Holden, spending most of the time at the Kansas City Club drinking.

Wednesday, February 17, dawned cold and crisp. A six-inch snow that fell the first week of the month had all but vanished. The weather in the morning newspaper predicted the temperature could reach as high as 45 degrees by 3:00 p.m.

Dockery Hall was ready. The college crew had set up 300 chairs in theatre fashion on the gym floor, facing a raised platform. There was a lectern on the platform, and the mike and speakers were in place. Beth stood on one side of the double doors and Rudolph on the other, checking identification as the stockholders came in.

By 10:00, Beth counted 116 stockholders, mostly locals. Rudolph quickly went through the proxies that had been mailed in and could account for 86,519 shares. They needed 50,001 to win. Deducting Tom's 26,000 shares, if 10,519 shares accounted for were voted against the proposal, it would fail. It was going to be close.

At 5:10, Rudolph closed the doors and locked them. Beth mounted the platform and introduced herself to the crowd. She thanked them for making to effort to attend the meeting and promised them it would be worthwhile. She introduced the current members of the board with the exception of Tom and Larry Plunkett, who were absent. She then introduced Rudolph and Judge Whitfield as prospective members of the board. She said she wanted to talk to them for just a few minutes; then the current board members would pass among them and collect their voting sheets to be tallied along with the ones that were mailed in.

"I am currently the senior vice-present of the Breckenridge State Bank," she said. "I was active in the operation of the bank until last August 18th, when I was arrested on false embezzlement charges. I was acquitted of those charges on September 14th. The documents used to indict me were proven false. In other words, someone wanted me out of the way. In my absence, my husband took over operation of the bank, and now it is in a crisis. We are not taking in enough money from loan payments and fees to cover the costs of running the bank. My husband has been dipping into our reserve account to cover payrolls and pay the utilities. This is illegal, according to the federal banking laws. If that money is not replaced soon, the Federal Reserve System and the Justice Department could close us down and possibly send someone to jail. That money has to be there to cover any loans that might be defaulted. It's the law.

"I have a plan to take care of the situation, but first I need your confidence and your vote so I can get the job done. You all have ballot sheets given to you when you came in, listing your name and the number of shares you own. There are two boxes on the bottom of the sheet. One marked yes, and one marked no. If you want me to take back control of the bank and fix the problem, I would appreciate a yes vote. If you want the bank to continue doing what it's doing now, then vote no. We put a pencil on each chair. We want you to mark your ballots now, sign them and stay for a few minutes while we tally the votes. There will be coffee and doughnuts in the lobby when we adjourn."

As the stockholders were marking their ballots, there was a loud banging on the double doors to the gym. No one answered, so it got louder and more fierce. Then two fists started banging on the doors, so loud that it was disturbing everyone in the gym. Beth, Rudolph and three of the board members ran back to see who it was. Rudolph unlocked the doors and opened them.

There stood Tom and Larry Plunkett, obviously drunk. Tom staggered in the door, one side of his shirt tail hanging out of his pants.

"We're here to vote our stock!" he shouted, waving his letter. "We have a right to be here, dammit, I own 26,000 shares, and Larry here owns 2,000, and by God, we're going to vote 'em." He spotted Beth and lunged toward her. "You bitch, you're the one that started all this," he screamed.

Several of the men tried to grab him, but he shook loose. "Get your hands off me, you sons-a-bitches," he yelled, and started after Beth who was running up toward the podium. An older man sitting on an end seat stuck his cane out and tripped him as he went by. He fell flat on his face. Several men jumped on top of him and held him down. Beth stopped and went calmly back, reached down and grabbed the sheet from his hand.

"We'll be happy take your vote," she said, "Will you be voting yes or no?"

Tom started cussing her out, but one of the men stuffed his handkerchief in Tom's mouth, while Rudolph went out to the lobby and called the police on a pay phone. All this time Larry stood in the doorway weaving on his feet with a silly grin on his face. Beth walked back and snatched his proxy sheet from him and took it up to the podium. She went to the microphone.

"Ladies and gentlemen, she said. "There has been a slight disturbance, but I want you to continue marking your sheets, and we'll collect them in just a minute."

The sheets were gathered up, and while they were tallying them, Clarence and Buck came and took Tom and Larry to the jail and threw them into the drunk tank. They were charged with public drunkenness.

By 12:30, with the help of two adding machines and four members of the board helping, a total was reached. Beth won by over 10,000 votes. Apparently a lot of the stockholders changed their minds after Tom caused such a ruckus. Seeing him drunk was quite a shock, especially to some of the older stockholders.

The by-laws dictated that a week's notice must be given before a board meeting could be called, so a meeting was scheduled for the next Wednesday, February 24. They met in the bank's boardroom, and Beth was elected chairman of the board unanimously. She was then appointed president of the bank by a unanimous vote. Bill Worsham was selected as senior vice-president, and Rudolph was selected as secretary/treasurer. The rest of the offices, such as vice-president and head cashier, were left open until Beth had time to study the staff and make recommendations. Everyone breathed a sigh of relief.

12

JUSTICE

BETH WASTED NO time getting the bank back on the right track. Tom had been charging a lot of travel and entertainment expenses to the bank, and there were checks written for supplies that were never delivered. She stopped all that immediately. The second thing she did was kick off a Christmas Savings Club contest among all the employees. The one who brought in the most deposits each week would get two free tickets to the Saturday night double feature at the Star Theater.

The third thing she did was run a big ad in the *Star Journal* offering free checking accounts, with the bank paying for the new customer's first 200 printed checks. She also ran ads offering automobile and appliance loans at competitive interest rates and personal signature loans up to $100.

Her plan started bringing in more deposits almost immediately. By the end of March, deposits and loan payments were again exceeding salaries and expenses. Beth tightened the banks overhead even more. No long distance phone calls were allowed, unless cleared by Beth. A letter cost three cents to mail, and long distance phone calls were over a dollar for three minutes. She had them turning off lights in the restroom and lunchroom when not in use. By April, the bank was making a profit, and Beth started putting money back into the reserve account.

* * * * *

Tom came back into the bank the day the board was meeting to elect a chairman. It was 10:00 in the morning, and he had already had too much to drink. He tried to enter the board room, but was rebuffed by all the members of the board. Two of the bigger men on the board escorted him to the front door, and as they were shoving him out onto the street, he screamed, "This is my bank! My grandfather started it, and by God, I'm going to run it! You'll be sorry, all you sons-a-bitches!" The men gave him one last shove, and he staggered off down the street.

Tom tried to keep somewhat of a schedule. Although he no longer went to the bank, he would get up in the morning, shave and shower and dress as though he were. Clairece, the maid would fix his breakfast, and then busy herself cleaning and doing laundry. She generally managed to avoid him during the day. She was getting afraid of him. His demeanor was getting nastier by the day. After breakfast, he would read the morning paper and start sipping Scotch. Sometimes he only had one, but when he was extremely upset, he might have three or four before lunch.

On Wednesdays, he would try to stay sober so he could have lunch with the Lions Club, and on Saturday mornings he still played golf with Larry Plunkett. After golf they would go out to Tom's house for sandwiches that Clairece would leave in the refrigerator before she left for the day. After sandwiches, Larry usually went home, and Tom would shower and change clothes then drive to Kansas City for fun and frolic. He would usually drive back to Warrensburg on Monday morning. The rest of the time he would sit around the house and mope, plotting how he would get even with Beth and the members of the board. Sometimes he would drive his car around town, spying on Beth, or Rudolph or anyone else he could blame for his plight.

In March, Clarence pulled him over twice in the patrol car for weaving all over the street. He knew Tom had been drinking, but he had no way to test him, and if he arrested him, it would just be his word against Tom's. He did, however, issue him a warning ticket each time and told him the third time he stopped him he would throw him in the drunk tank. Tom took his words seriously, and tried not to drive when he had too much to drink.

One night in mid-April, Tom tried to sneak into the apartment house where Beth lived. It was about 11:00 p.m., and Beth was in bed. Aunt Maud heard the front door open and opened her door a crack to get a look. This was a normal practice of hers, as all her tenants were women and she was very protective of them. She always left the light on in the hall, and she saw Tom creeping up the stairs with what appeared to be a baseball bat in his hand. She ran back to her bedroom and called the police.

Clyde Burroughs was there in his patrol car in less than five minutes. Aunt Maud was watching for him, and met him on the front porch in her nightgown and robe. Clyde started up the stairs with his flashlight in one hand and his 38-caliber police special in the other. When he got to the first landing, Tom came plummeting down the stairs and ran right into Clyde, knocking him against the wall. As he ran down to the stairs to the ground floor, he tripped and fell flat; his baseball bat went flying. In a second, Clyde was on top of him and cuffed his hands behind him. He was still a little stunned when Clyde dragged him to his feet.

By this time, everyone in the house was awake. The ones on the second floor were looking over the balcony rail. The rest were huddled next to Aunt Maud.

Beth walked down the stairs, and when she saw it was Tom, she walked over, picked up the bat and handed it to Clyde. "I think this belongs to my husband," she said, looking Tom in the eye. "You might need it for evidence."

Clyde took Tom to the county jail. Clyde and the jailer on duty scratched their heads as what to charge him with. Finally, they settled on prowling; it was the only charge they thought would stick. They locked him up, and Clyde went back to the station to fill out his report. Two of the sheriff's deputies went over on South Street and got Tom's car. They parked it in the basement of the jail.

* * * * *

Saturday, May 15, was the first anniversary of Margaret Wilson's death, and Buck still didn't have enough evidence to arrest Tom Breckenridge. He had wracked his brain and followed every lead he could think of, but still no luck. It bothered Buck that a killer was still walking the streets of Warrensburg. Almost every day he would take the fancy fountain pen out of his middle drawer and look at it, as if it might somehow tell him what he needed to know. He constantly reviewed his notes, and he, Clarence and Harry Foster would get together over coffee about once a week to discuss the case. He was starting to get discouraged.

* * * * *

Irv got up at 7:00 a.m., his usual time for a Saturday, unless he was substituting for LeRoy on his paper route. On those days, he got up at 5:30. Friday was the last day of school, and Irv was looking forward to the three months of summer vacation. He had caddied for Tom Breckenridge several times already this spring and had made a little money to help out with groceries and other household expenses. He was proud of being able to help the family out.

Everyone in the household was gone by the time he got up, so he fixed his usual breakfast of oatmeal, toast and a glass of milk. LeRoy had already run his paper route, and the morning *Kansas City Times* was on the kitchen table. Irv scanned the headlines, then turned to his favorite comic strips, "Gasoline Alley" and "L'il Abner."

By the time he got to the golf course, Brad was already there sitting on the caddy bench sipping a Nehi cream soda. Four other caddies were already out on the golf course with players. Katy tried to keep her children from drinking soda pop. She told them the sugar in them would rot their teeth, and besides, five cents was a ridiculous price to pay for what was basically flavored water. Irv got a drink from the water hose and sat down next to Brad.

At 9:55, Tom Breckenridge's blue Packard pulled up the drive with Larry Plunkett in the front passenger seat. When they pulled up in front of the clubhouse, the boys rushed over to get their clubs out of the trunk. While Tom and Larry were in the clubhouse signing in, Irv and Brad busied themselves washing balls and wiping the club faces off.

It was a good round of golf. The temperature stayed in the mid-70s, and despite the fact that both men had been drinking, they played a respectable round. Irv only lost one ball, and it was hit in grass so high, it was impossible to find. After 18 holes, the men were ready to go to Tom's house for more drinks. Irv and Brad put the men's clubs in the trunk of the Packard and waited while the two of them went into the clubhouse to get change to pay their caddies. They each got the usual 50 cents for 18 holes of caddying, plus a 25-cent tip.

As the boys started down the drive to Pine Street, Tom yelled at them. He opened the right rear door of the Packard and motioned for them to get in.

"Hop in," he said, "I'll give you a ride to town."

What prompted him to do that, no one has been ever been able to figure out, but it turned out to be the biggest mistake of his life.

The boys climbed in, and Tom slammed the door. He climbed behind the wheel, and they started for town. As they turned onto Pine Street, he turned his head and said, "You boys are the first ones to ride in the back seat. I've had this car for almost three years, and no one has ever ridden back there before, how does it feel?"

"Great," Brad said as he ran his hands over the soft velour of the seat cushion.

"Yeah, great," Irv said. He ran his hands over the seat and back. He had never seen anything as fancy and plush as this. As he ran his hands over the seat cushion one more time, his left hand felt something hard. Curious, he ran his hand into the crack between the cushion and back. Something was wedged into the crack. *How could that be,* he thought, *if no one had been in these seats before?* He pulled the object out far enough to see what it was and almost fainted. It was the heel of a woman's shoe. He sat there for a few seconds, so dazed he couldn't move. Finally he pulled it out enough to see the rest of it. *It was Margaret Wilson's other shoe!*

Quickly he shoved it back into the crack and sat there, his hands shaking, pale as a ghost. When they got to Warren Street, Tom stopped and let them out. Brad went on up Pine Street to the Vernaz drug store to get a candy bar. Irv managed to walk over to the Skelly service station on the corner and sat down on a chair under the canopy.

"That's my chair you're sittin' in, fella," the station operator said as he walked out from behind the building.

"I'm sorry," Irv said, and tried to get up.

"Whoa there," the operator said, and pushed Irv back into the chair. "You look like you're about to pass out."

"I . . . I guess I got too hot," Irv said.

"Just sit there a minute," the man said. He went inside and got a clean rag and ran some cold water on it from the hose used to fill radiators, and put it on Irv's forehead. "Are you all right?" he asked after a few of minutes. Irv was feeling better. He stood up and gave the rag back to the man and thanked him.

Irv walked up the hill to the police station as fast as his wobbly legs would take him. When he got he got there, he opened the screen door, walked over to the bench along the wall and collapsed. Darlene came over and looked him over. Sensing something was wrong, she tried to calm him.

"You're the Hodges boy, aren't you?" she asked.

"Yes, ma'am," Irv managed to say. Just then, the courthouse clock struck one-thirty.

Darlene had a hunch what might be, at least partially, wrong with him. "Have you had any lunch today?" she asked.

"No, ma'am," was the answer.

"I thought as much," she said, "why aren't you home having lunch with your family?"

"I . . . I need to see the Chief," he stammered.

"What about?" she asked.

"Please, ma'am, it's important," he said.

"Yes, I can see it is, wait here," she cautioned him and started to the back to get Buck.

Buck was still upstairs having lunch with Ann and the children. He was late getting back from a car wreck out on Maguire Street, so was an hour late for lunch. Darlene knocked on the kitchen door. Buck came to the door, and invited her in. When she told Buck that Irv Hodges wanted to see him and that it was urgent, he remembered that he told Irv to come see him if he ever heard anything concerning the Margaret Wilson murder case nearly a year ago. It was Irv who found the fountain pen at the crime scene.

Buck excused himself and followed Darlene down the stairs to talk to him. Irv was still sitting on the bench trembling. Buck took him back to his office and sat him down. Darlene followed them back, and whispered in Buck's ear. Buck nodded yes, and she went back up the stairs to the apartment.

"Well, young man, what can I do for you?" he asked as kindly as he could.

"Uh, Chief, sir," Irv was still very nervous, "you told me to come to you if I ever found out anything about Miss Wilson."

"I sure did, son, I remember it well. Do you have anything for me?"

"Yes, sir, I do, but if Mr. Breckenridge ever found out I told you, he would hurt me bad."

"Well, son, we'll make this our little secret, just between you and me. Would that be okay?"

"Yes, sir."

"Okay, what is it you have to tell me?"

"I found the other shoe."

"Miss Wilson's other shoe?" Buck's heart skipped a beat. He'd been waiting a year to hear those words.

"Yes, sir."

"For heaven's sake, where?"

"In the back of Mr. Breckenridge's car." Irv told Buck how Tom had offered him and Brad a ride to town from the golf course, how he came to find the shoe, and that he left it in the car.

"Are you sure it was Miss Wilson's shoe?" Buck was really getting excited.

"Yes, sir, I'm sure."

Buck thought for a minute. Finally he said, "I have the other shoe stored in the basement, along with some other things from the case. Would you come downstairs with me and take a look at it to be sure?"

"Yes, sir." Irv got up and followed Buck to the basement.

Buck unlocked a four-drawer file cabinet and opened the second drawer from the top. Right on top of a box containing Margaret's clothing rested the shoe. Buck had been down there several times in the past year to look at it. He showed it to Irv.

"Are you sure what you saw was the mate to this shoe," he asked again.

"Yes, sir, I'm sure."

Buck's heart skipped another beat. They went back upstairs to his office. Buck sat him down and took the chair next to him. In hushed tones he said, "We have to keep this very quiet until I can take action. If word gets out that we know the shoe is in his car, Mr. Breckenridge could destroy the shoe, and there would go our case. Do you understand how important this is? I mean, we can't tell anyone. I can't tell my wife, and you can't even tell your mother. Understood?"

"Yes, sir."

"Good, let's shake on it." They shook hands.

Just as they finished their little talk, Ann and Darlene came down the steps from the apartment carrying a plate with a cold roast beef sandwich on it, a dish of Jello with oranges and bananas in it, and a glass of cold milk. They took Irv back to the break room where he ate every bite. He went home feeling much better.

* * * * *

Monday morning, Buck found out from the circuit clerk that Judge Whitfield was holding court in Clinton that day. He went down to the jail and got Harry Foster to drive him to Clinton in his patrol car. At Buck's insistence, Harry turned on his red light, and they made the 30-mile trip in 30 minutes. Usually people drove under 50 miles per hour on Highway 13, but twice during the trip, Harry got up to 65 in the '35 Ford V-8. On the way down, Buck filled Harry in on finding the shoe. He wanted Harry to go with him to arrest Tom.

Harry parked on the square in a space reserved for sheriff's cars. They went in to see Judge Whitfield, but he was already in court. Buck talked the deputy guarding the door into passing an urgent message to the judge that Buck needed to see him at once. Judge Whitfield called for a 15-minute recess in the proceedings and met them in his chambers.

When Buck told him about finding the shoe, the judge was elated. He knew how hard Buck had worked on the Wilson case. He had his clerk fill out the needed search warrant and signed it immediately. On the way back to Warrensburg, Buck outlined his plan. He would get Clarence to drive him out to the Breckenridge mansion with the warrant. Harry was to meet them there in case they needed back-up. They pulled up behind Clarence's patrol car in front of the police station and parked, just as the courthouse clock struck 10:00. Clarence was inside sitting on the corner of Darlene's desk, sipping a cup of coffee. Buck motioned him outside.

After telling Clarence of the plan to arrest Tom Breckenridge, they drove out South Holden Street to the mansion, only to find out that Tom hadn't gotten back from Kansas City yet. The maid opened the door when they knocked and informed them that he usually got home about 11:00 on Mondays.

Out at the curb, they devised a plan. Harry would drive on out Holden Street for about a block and turn around facing north. Buck and Clarence would park at the corner of Ming and Holden Streets, facing east. When Tom went by in the big blue Packard, Clarence would fall in behind him in the patrol car. When he pulled in his driveway, Clarence would pull in behind him and block the driveway. The back was all fenced in; there was no other way out. Harry would then pull up in front of the mansion with his motor running, just in case Tom tried to run away on foot. Desperate men do stupid things sometimes.

At 11:08, Tom went by the corner where Buck and Clarence were parked, and they followed him home. He pulled into the driveway and drove all the way back to the garage area. Clarence and Buck walked up to him as he was getting out of his car.

"Tom Breckenridge, I have a warrant to search your car," Buck said, holding the warrant out for Tom to see.

Tom was flabbergasted, he had no idea that he was under suspicion for anything.

"Give me the keys," Buck continued, "we'll probably have to impound it to search for clues."

Tom refused; after all, he was Tom Breckenridge, and these men were servants of the people. He proceeded to lock the car and headed for the gate to the swimming pool area. Clarence quickly stepped in front of the gate.

"We're serious, Mr. Breckenridge," he said, frowning at Tom. Tom tried to push him aside.

Buck grabbed him by the left arm and clamped a handcuff on it, then reaching around from behind, he grabbed Tom's other wrist and pulled his hands behind and finished cuffing him. "You're under arrest for obstructing justice," he said. He almost said, "For murder, but he hadn't found the shoe yet."

Tom went off like a cannon. He had obviously been drinking. He got red in the face and started cussing them at the top of his voice. "I'll sue the Police Department for this!" he yelled. "Do you know who I am?"

Harry came down the driveway at that time, and he and Clarence held on to Tom, while Buck fished through his pockets for the car keys. Buck unlocked the back doors to the Packard and opened them. He found the shoe just where Irv said it was. Tom was as amazed as anybody when Buck held up the shoe.

Harry took Tom to the jail with Clarence following him to make sure there was no trouble. Buck drove the Packard to the jail also, where it was impounded in the basement garage. Buck then took the shoe to the police station and locked it up in the basement file cabinet with the other one. It was nearly noon when he called Rudolph and gave him the news.

Rudolph immediately got hold of Beth and told her. She was so happy she could hardly talk. After all these years, Tom was finally going to have to account for the things he had done and the way he had treated the people around him. "I wonder if Larry Plunkett was involved in Margaret

Wilson's murder?" she asked, more of herself than of Rudolph. That night Buck slept better than he had in months.

* * * * *

On Tuesday afternoon, May 18, Buck met with Jim Sartin, assistant prosecuting attorney, and Judge Whitfield in the judge's chambers, and after presenting the evidence he had against Tom, an indictment for first degree murder was issued against him. Just as the meeting was breaking up, three attorneys from Kansas City marched into the courthouse and demanded to see the Judge Whitfield.

The judge's chambers were too small, so he agreed to meet them in the circuit court room. Buck and Jim stayed to listen and observe. They didn't want their prisoner walking free on bail, by any means. The three men in their dark suits and white shirts came in, and Judge Whitfield seated them at the defense table. He wasn't in his robe, so he pulled up a chair and sat in front of them.

"Now, what can I do for you?" he asked. He knew exactly what they wanted.

One of the men stood up. He apparently he was the lead attorney. A tall man in his late 50s with a deep baritone voice, he cleared his throat. "We represent Mr. Tom Breckenridge and are prepared to post bond for his release," he said.

"Bail denied!" Judge Whitfield said, almost before the lawyer had finished talking.

"How can you say that? Your Honor?" he asked. "We haven't even presented our case yet."

Judge Whitfield didn't hesitate. "Gentlemen," he said, "I'm sorry you made an unnecessary trip down here, but let me make this clear. This is a first degree murder case with strong evidence against your client. There will be no bail!"

The tall man started to speak again, but Judge Whitfield repeated his words before the man could say anything, "There will be no bail." The judge sensed he was being a little too harsh on these out-of-town lawyers, so he lowered his voice. "If you gentlemen want to wait here for a few minutes," he said, "I'll go look at my calendar and give you an arraignment date, and you can present your case then."

257

They nodded their approval, so the judge went back to his chambers and came back a few minutes later with a date for them. "The prisoner will be arraigned this Friday, May 21, in this courtroom, at 11:00 a.m. The late hour should give you plenty of time to drive down here from Kansas City," he said as he handed the tall guy a slip of paper with the information on it.

* * * * *

The arraignment the following Friday was a mere formality. All the prosecution had to prove was that there was enough evidence to support the indictment. With the fountain pen and shoe as evidence, and Beth and Irv as witnesses to connect them to the crime, Judge Whitfield ruled that there was sufficient evidence to support the indictment, and set a date for an evidentiary hearing for Wednesday May 26.

Tom's lawyers pleaded him "not guilty," then moved for a month's extension, but Judge Whitfield was in no mood to delay the proceedings, and denied their motion.

Tom didn't let out a peep during the arraignment. His lawyers had done a good job of convincing him that he was being held on very serious charges, and that any outbursts in the courtroom could hurt his chances for acquittal. That, plus the fact that he was unable to get any booze to drink in jail and was suffering from withdrawal symptoms, made him seem docile. In fact, he was feeling sick to his stomach and trembling so on the inside that it took all his concentration to keep from throwing up.

* * * * *

Wednesday, May 26, was a beautiful day. A cool front had moved through Johnson County during the night, and they got some much needed rain. Gerald Essex was out of town on a fund raiser to support his unannounced run for the office of Attorney General of the State of Missouri. Lately, he was spending more time in Kansas City, Jefferson City, Springfield and St. Louis than he was in Warrensburg. That left the burden of the Breckenridge case on his assistant, Jim Sartin, which was not all that bad. Jim was actually a better lawyer than his boss.

The hearing was scheduled to start at 10:00, and although it was only a hearing and not a trial, it attracted a larger than usual crowd. School was out, and some of the teachers who knew Margaret Wilson were there. A number of people who knew of Tom Breckenridge, but didn't know him personally, were there out of curiosity.

By 9:30, the three lawyers from Kansas City were at the defense table with Tom, going through their evidence and their list of witnesses. The judge had limited witnesses to three from each side, so they had to pare their list down to what they considered were the three most effective for their case. Tom seemed a bit more animated than on his last visit to the courtroom.

Jim Sartin, at Harry Foster and Buck Pettit's insistence, had hired Rudolph Eisenstein to assist him in the prosecution. It didn't take much coaxing. Jim knew he needed help, and he had witnessed Rudolph's courtroom skills first-hand. They were at the prosecution table going over their notes. Their three witnesses were Beth, Buck and Amos Swenson, who were already in the witness room awaiting their call to the stand.

At precisely 10:00 a.m., the bailiff called for order and Judge Whitfield took his seat on the bench. He reminded the opposing attorneys that this was not a trial, but a hearing to determine if there was enough evidence against the accused to bind him over to circuit court for trial; therefore, he would allow the attorneys a little more latitude in their arguments.

Jim Sartin went first, and after he had called his three witnesses, it became apparent that he had a strong case against the defendant. He also alluded to the fact that there were other witnesses he could call who would bolster the state's case, but he was limited by Judge Whitfield's ruling concerning witnesses. He assured the court that he would call more witnesses at the actual trial. He entered the fountain pen and both of Margaret Wilson's shoes into evidence. This was done at the judge's request so that the defense team would have a chance to examine them.

The tall man on Tom's team, an attorney by the name of Oscar Levinthall, gave the defense's side of the story. He was an eloquent speaker with a deep baritone voice, which captured the attention of everyone in the courtroom. It was a shame he didn't have a case to present. He called three of Tom's poker buddies to the stand to tell what a great guy he was, and that he had been playing poker with them at Doctor Plunkett's house the night of Margaret Wilson's murder. Dr. Larry Plunkett was conveniently separated from his wife, and she had taken their two children to Higginsville to live with her parents. The fact that he lived alone in his house and there was no wife or children there that night to corroborate the poker story was not lost on Judge Whitfield.

Both sides were essentially finished by noon. Judge Whitfield recessed the hearing until 1:30 for lunch, telling the lawyers to be prepared to give what closing arguments they might have at that time.

By 2:30 they were through, and Judge Whitfield didn't hesitate. He announced that he was binding the accused over for trial in circuit court, and that the trial would be held on Tuesday, July 6, in this same courtroom.

Once again, Oscar Levinthall moved for a continuance, but Judge Whitfield's reply was, "You have six weeks to prepare for trial, counselor. That should be enough, motion denied." He banged his gavel. "Court adjourned," he said, and left the courtroom.

* * * * *

The summer of 1937 was not as hot in Warrensburg as the three previous summers, and although the depression was still in full bloom and the economy was actually slipping a little lower, people's hopes were still high that the country would soon recover from its economic morass. After all, it had been with them for seven years already.

Some things were actually booming. The junk yards around the country were selling as much scrap iron as they could get their hands on. It was all going overseas to Germany and Japan. New housing starts were starting to pick up a little. The Federal Housing Authority was pumping more money into home mortgages, and with interest rates very low, it was making it as cheap to buy a house as to rent one. The only hitch was the fact that not many people had money for the required down payment.

Ann busied herself with vacation Bible school. She and three of her friends from church had volunteered to teach the children for the two-week school. It was held in the basement of the church, and naturally Ann chose to teach the pre-schoolers so she could work with Jimmie and Ellie. Buck approved and even went by the church several times to help out with projects, such as building the set for the play the children presented for their mothers on the last day of school.

More and more rumors were circulating around town about the affair between Harry Foster and Lois Huff. They sang together in the church choir, went to movies together, and Harry was coaching the baseball team Lois' son played on. She was seen on more than one occasion taking a piece of Harry's favorite pie by the jail, and sometimes staying as long as 30 minutes. She always told the folks who asked, and there were those who asked, that she just stopped by to visit her friend Elsie Reed, who worked in the office at the jail. Also, there was last Christmas, when she was rumored to have spent the entire day with him at his farm. No mention was ever made of the fact that her mother and son were there also. It was scandalous.

Nothing was said, nor did anyone notice that Larry Plunkett was visiting Tom at the jail almost daily. Larry would always bring Tom something he needed. First, Tom complained about constipation, so the jailer let Larry bring him a pint bottle of castor oil every day for nearly two weeks, until even the jailer thought that was a lot of castor He did notice that Tom was becoming a lot more active, though, and talked a lot more. He figured the castor oil must have done the trick.

Next, Tom complained that the water at the jail was making him sick and asked if it would be all right if Larry brought him some special water that he filtered at home through a very special charcoal filter to take out all of the impurities. The jailer guessed it would be all right, if he was allowed to inspect it before Larry gave it to Tom. Larry brought a quart Mason jar full of what looked like water the very next day. Larry held it up for the jailer to inspect, but when he tried to screw the lid off, Larry snatched it back. He convinced the jailer that if he opened it, it would let in a lot of germs and other contaminates, and that's what was making Tom sick. The jailer let him give it to Tom. What would it hurt? After all, Tom seemed to be getting more like the Tom he knew, and the orange juice he asked for every day was good for him, too. He let it go.

Irv and his friend Brad still caddied golf, although they missed caddying for Tom Breckenridge and Larry Plunkett. Mostly they missed the generous tips.

Beth busied herself at the bank. She tried to put Tom out of her mind and dreaded having to testify against him. Not that she was afraid of him; she just didn't like being around him. She toyed with the idea of moving back into the big house, but decided not to until she knew how Tom's trial would turn out. She cut Clairece's hours back to two days a week. All she needed to do now, with Tom gone, was dust and vacuum once a week, defrost the refrigerator and sweep the walks and porches. There were no meals to fix, except her own lunch, and no laundry. Beth just wanted the house to look lived in. She knew that Clairece and her invalid husband needed the money, so she didn't cut her pay, and she promised Clairece that if she moved back in she would need her full-time again.

Rudolph had more to do than he really wanted. His business at the office had picked up to the point that he was having to turn clients down. Also, he had agreed to help with the prosecution of Tom Breckenridge, which was taking up a lot of his time. He didn't complain. If the truth were known, he rather enjoyed all the attention he was getting and, of course, the extra money didn't hurt any either.

* * * * *

The time for Tom's trial came around faster than most people expected. It was a sensational story for a small town like Warrensburg, and it even made headlines in the Kansas City and St. Louis newspapers. A well-known local banker was accused of sexually assaulting and killing a pretty young school teacher.

By 10:00 a.m. Tuesday, July 6, the courtroom was packed. The windows were open and the ceiling fans were humming, but the big room was still very hot despite the high ceilings. There were four lawyers from the Kansas City law firm of Lebrand and Cox, including the tall one with the deep voice, sitting at the defense table. Sitting with them, Tom seemed happy to be there. He smiled and waved at people he recognized in the courtroom. It was almost as if he were drunk, but that would be impossible since he had been locked up all this time. His lawyers didn't look too happy.

On the other hand, Jim Sartin and a very confident Rudolph Eisenstein looked very much at ease. They had spent a lot of time on the case and were ready.

"All rise," the bailiff intoned, and there was a shuffling of feet as everyone stood. "The circuit court of Johnson County, Missouri, the Honorable Emmerson Whitfield presiding is now in session."

Judge Whitfield in his long black robe, took the bench, and banged his gavel. "You may be seated," he said. He then admonished the gallery to be quiet during the trial, and told them he would not permit demonstrations of any kind. He asked the bailiff to bring the jury in, and the trial began.

The tall lawyer for the defense gave a passionate plea for Tom in his opening remarks to the jury. His deep resonate voice echoed through the courtroom. He referred to him as a compassionate citizen of the community, who gave freely of his time and money to help his fellow men. He made much of the fact there was not one single blemish on his record, and that he had been married to the same woman for 13 years. The three times Clarence stopped him for driving while drunk didn't count, of course, because Clarence had only warned him. If they had researched the police records, they would have found the three warning tickets Clarence wrote. Also, there was no mention made of the fact that he had not lived with his wife for nearly a year.

He alluded to the rumor going around town that the evidence against his client, i.e., the fountain pen and shoe, was trumped up by the Police Chief to solve a year-old crime, because he was under pressure from the city council, that the shoe was in the Chief's possession all along. How could he know that the rumor was started by a certain telephone operator who had a crush on the wealthy banker?

Jim Sartin let Rudolph give the prosecution's opening remarks. He knew that Rudolph was the better speaker of the two and had a better grasp of the facts surrounding the case, and although not as eloquent as the defense lawyer, he did have a way with jurors.

Rudolph stated that the evidence being presented by the prosecution was indeed true, and that a number of credible witnesses would be put on the stand to testify to that fact. The only time he strayed from the facts of the case was when he mentioned that the defendant did have a drinking problem and was known to get violent when drinking, ala the stockholder's meeting.

He also mentioned something that the whole town already knew, that Tom was a womanizer. Rudolph's theory concerning the murder was that Tom was smitten by the pretty Miss Wilson when she had been in the bank earlier that day to make a loan. From their conversation, he learned that she would be working late at the school that night. He went home after work about 4:00 and had a few drinks. The more he drank, the more he thought about Miss Wilson, and the more he wanted her. About dark, he drove to the school, went into her classroom and tried to make love to her. When she rebuffed him and started to scream for the janitor, he went into a rage and choked her to death.

The trial lasted three days. There were so many witnesses that Judge Whitfield finally had to call a halt. Beth, Buck, Harry Foster, Irv and Amos Swenson were among the prosecution's witnesses. The defense had scheduled 30 witnesses. They were all brought in to tell the jury what a swell guy Tom was. They had no witnesses as to the facts of the case, except one. Ruby McCullum, a telephone operator, testified that she accidentally overheard a conversation between Chief Pettit and Elizabeth Breckenridge, plotting to falsify evidence in the case. She said the fountain pen and shoe were both mentioned.

The jury evidently didn't buy the conspiracy rumor, because on the third day of the trial, at 6:15 in the evening, they returned a verdict of guilty of first degree murder. It was a unanimous verdict, but the tall guy on the defense team asked the judge to poll the jury. The theory was that if each juror had to stand and tell the court how he or she voted, there was always the possibility that one of them would change his or her mind, and a hung jury would result. Judge Whitfield had the clerk poll the jury, and one by one they all stood, looked Tom in the eye and voted guilty.

Tom didn't take the verdict too well. He thought all along he would be acquitted. It was late in the day, and he hadn't been to his cell in nearly ten hours. His happy-go-lucky attitude had worn off hours ago. Judge Whitfield set the next day, a Friday, at 10:00 a.m. for sentencing. He remanded Tom to the sheriff for custody, thanked the jury, and adjourned the court.

* * * * *

Back in his cell, Tom was walking the floor. His Mason jar was empty, and he needed to talk to his friend, Larry Plunkett. Finally, at 8:30, Larry arrived at the courthouse and asked to see Tom. He had gone by his house to get Tom some more filtered water to drink. The unsuspecting jailer let him in.

Tom took a big swig from the fruit jar and waited a couple of minutes for his nerves to calm down. Finally, he said, "Larry, you've got to get me out of here. Those bastards found me guilty. They're going to sentence me to prison tomorrow, for God knows how long, or maybe even give me the electric chair!"

"How long do you think you will stay here after the sentencing?" Larry asked.

"I don't know, probably not more than a week. We've got to figure something out now."

Larry stayed until almost 10:00. Twice the jailer told Larry it was time to leave, and twice he begged the jailer to let him stay a few minutes longer. The plan they hatched was this. Larry was to take his yellow Cadillac convertible to the local Chevrolet/Cadillac dealer Friday and trade it in on a new Cadillac sedan, preferably black, and have it serviced and ready to roll.

On Saturday when he came to visit, he was to bring a kitchen knife with at least a five-inch blade. To smuggle it into the cell, he would tuck it into his sock, on the inside of his leg, and fasten it in place with a rubber band. The jailer, when he patted Larry down before entering the cell, always patted him down on the outside of his legs, never on the inside. Also, he was to bring about 12 feet of cotton clothesline. He could wrap that around his waist, under his belt. Larry had a 36 waist, so four times around would do the trick.

About midnight Saturday, when the jailer made his rounds to check on him, Tom would complain that he had something in his eye, and that it was hurting him bad. When the jailer came into his cell to look in his eye, Tom would pull the knife and use it to disarm him. He would force the jailer to lie on his bunk, face down. If the jailer started to make any noise, Tom would hold the point of the knife to his back and threaten to kill him if he wasn't quiet. Using his own handcuffs, Tom would cuff his hands behind him and tie his feet together with some of the clothesline, then using the rest of the line, he would tie the jailer to the bunk so he couldn't get up. He would be gagged with his own handkerchief and necktie.

After that, it was simple. Tom would go down the stairs to the basement, out the door leading to Washington Street, and Larry would pick him up in the new car. Their route out of Missouri was well planned. Instead of taking Highway 50 west to Kansas City, they would take Highway 13 north all the way to Route 36. It was a narrow, winding road, but not patrolled by the state police nearly as much. Then west on 36 to St. Joseph, where they would hit Highway 71 which would take them all the way to Fort

Frances in Ontario, Canada. From there, it was Canadian Route 11 to Ottawa and Montreal, where Tom had some money stashed.

* * * * *

Friday, July 9, 1937 was a busy day for Larry Plunkett. He had no problem trading cars. The dealer was more than happy to take in a two-year-old car in as good shape as Larry's. He did however, ask $400 over the trade-in price of the convertible for the new black sedan. When Larry complained, he was told that convertibles were hard to move. Larry had the feeling that if it was the other way around and he was trading in a black sedan, that black sedans would be hard to move. By noon, they did have it serviced and ready to roll.

While the dealer was getting his new car ready, Larry went to the bank and closed out his accounts. He had a little over $300 in his business account and $44 in his personal account. He also had a letter from Tom authorizing him to take $500 from his account. Tom's reasoning was that if he closed out his account, the bank would be suspicious and alert the police. By taking out $500, they could claim it was to pay the expenses of his high-priced lawyers. He went from the bank back to the dealer and paid him the $400 on the new car and drove it away.

He went by Tom's house and picked up some of his clothing. He told the maid that Tom needed a few things to take to Jefferson City with him. She stood and watched him pack a suitcase, making sure clothes was all he took. She did allow him to take Tom's golf clubs out of the garage and put them in the back seat of the car. Later she had second thoughts. Why would Tom need golf clubs in prison? She didn't trust Larry Plunkett in any way. After Larry left, she called Beth and told her what had happened. Beth thanked her, then called Harry Foster and let him know.

His next stop was his house on west South Street. He bought the house in 1928, but it had depreciated so much the past seven years that he still owed more on it than the house would bring on the market. He wouldn't mind walking off and leaving it to the bank. His ex-wife had moved most of the furniture out when they divorced, so there would be no regrets in leaving what was left. He packed a suitcase and put it, his golf clubs and a small radio from the kitchen in the car. The golf clubs wouldn't fit in the trunk, so he put then in the back seat with Tom's.

He figured that whoever closed out his office could sell the equipment and pay any bills owed, such as back rent. He was ready to roll. As a second thought, he went back in the house and filled two quart fruit jars with vodka he had bought to keep Tom in good spirits. He also took a blanket off the bed to cover the golf clubs.

He stopped at Walker's Cafe and had a hot beef sandwich and a cup of coffee, then went up to the jail to visit Tom.

Tom was walking the floor of his cell when Larry got there. The contents of one of the fruit jars helped calm him a good deal. He had been taken to court at 10:00 a.m., and Judge Whitfield had sentenced him to life at Jeff City. He was more determined than ever to get out of the country. He was anxious to know what Larry had gotten done. Larry filled him in on everything he had accomplished that morning. As he related the things he had picked up, Tom checked them off in his mind.

Tom sat there for a minute thinking, then finally said, "The knife, did you get a knife?" he asked, "and what about the clothesline?"

"Damn," Larry said, "I knew I was forgetting something. I don't have any kitchen knives at home, or clothesline either, for that matter, I guess I'll have to go buy some."

"No, don't buy them, steal them," Tom said emphatically.

"Steal them?"

"Yes, steal them! You can get the clothesline from somebody's back yard, and you can steal a knife from Woolworth's when the girl isn't looking. That way, nobody will get suspicious and call the Sheriff."

He had no idea that Beth had done just that, but Harry Foster made a mistake in judgment. He figured Tom wouldn't try anything until Sunday when he would be at minimum staff in the jail.

Larry went down to Woolworth's. They closed at 5:00, so he had to hurry. He went by the candy counter and bought a pack of Wrigley's Spearmint gum. He looked around as he laid his nickel on the counter. There were only three counter girls on duty. The rest had already closed their registers and gone to the office to check out. It was 4:55 as he walked back to the hardware counter. He picked out a ten-inch boning knife, looked around, and when he saw no one was watching him, he slipped it into his right front pants pocket. About three inches of the blade stuck out, so he dangled his right arm to cover it. He strolled casually out the front door, all the time expecting the manager to grab him by the arm.

He was sweating when he got to the car, and his heart was racing. This was the first time in his life he had ever stolen anything.

He drove back out to his house and went out into the backyard. He looked both ways at his neighbors' yards. To the east of his house, three houses down, he spotted clothesline made of cotton cord. The rest of his neighbors had steel wire lines. He knew he didn't want that. After dark, he walked down behind the houses and cut a 12-foot length from it with the knife he had stolen from Woolworth's.

* * * * *

Saturday morning, Larry slept in. Why not, he was packed, the car was loaded, and he had only one thing left to do before picking Tom up at midnight, and that was to deliver the knife and cord to him. He planned to give him the other fruit jar full of 90-proof courage also.

He got up about 9:00 and shaved and showered. He put his shaving equipment, toothpaste and toothbrush in a small traveling bag and dropped it in the trunk of the Cadillac when he went out to the car. He drove down Washington Street and topped the gas tank off at the Skelly station on the corner of Washington and Pine Streets. Leaving the car parked at the station, he walked up to Walker's and had a platter of bacon and eggs with toast and coffee.

Surprisingly, he was feeling quite calm about leaving Warrensburg at midnight. He certainly didn't have anything or anyone to hold him here. After that night in Sedalia with Beth, he tried to get something started with her, but she let him know real quick that he had caught her in a weak moment and it would never happen again. She also told him that she knew he was part of a conspiracy to defame her so Tom could get control of the bank, and if she were a man, she would punch him in the nose.

At 2:00 p.m. he drove to Dub's Café and ate a hamburger, followed by a slice of home-made apple pie and coffee. He tried to flirt with Lois Huff, but she returned his ogle with a cold stare that almost froze the coffee in his hand. He was a nice-looking fellow, but as Lois told Harry later, "For some reason, he makes my skin crawl."

About 3:00, Larry left the car parked up on the square and walked the block and a half to the jail, carrying the fruit jar. The knife was stuck down in his left sock on the inside of his leg and held in place by a rubber band. The cord was wrapped around his waist, under his shirt, and held in

268

place by his belt. When he walked in the front door of the jail, the deputy on duty knew him and did a quick search of his body and escorted him back to Tom's cell. He didn't say anything about the fruit jar.

Tom was fit to be tied, and as soon as the jailer left he grabbed the fruit jar and took a big swig. He quizzed Larry about the preparations for the jailbreak. Larry assured him everything was ready and gave him the knife and cord. At ten minutes before midnight, Larry was to pull the black sedan almost up to the corner of Washington and Market Streets, on the east side facing south, and wait for Tom to come out of the basement door.

"Shouldn't I be facing north so we can have a straight shot out to Highway 50, then we can swing over to 13, and be on our way quicker?"

"Just do as I say, I know what I'm doing," Tom retorted.

Larry left about 4:00 and went out to his house to take a nap. He knew he would be driving all night. He dreaded it, as it had clouded up while he was in the jail, and a fine mist was starting to fall.

* * * * *

At three minutes until midnight, the jailer went back to check on Tom. He was being held in the same cell that had housed Milton Stevenson over a year earlier. It was one of only four private cells in the jail, usually reserved for women prisoners and juveniles. As he approached the cell door, he saw Tom sitting on the bunk holding a handkerchief over his left eye.

"What's wrong?" the jailer asked.

"I've got something in my left eye, and it hurts," Tom said. "Will you come in here and take a look at it for me, please?"

Something didn't smell right to the jailer. It was midnight, and he was one of only two deputies on duty until 7:00 in the morning. He took the cell key off the clip on his belt, had second thoughts and clipped it back on. "Sorry," he said, "It's against the rules. I'm not supposed to enter any of the cells unless someone's with me."

Tom was starting to panic. Larry was already waiting for him down on Washington Street. He had to make this work, or spend the rest of his life at Jeff City. "If I come over to the door, do you think you could get whatever is in my eye out by reaching through the bars?" he asked, edging

269

toward the cell door. The knife was stuck in the back of his trouser waist band where the jailer couldn't see it.

"I don't know," the jailer was getting wary. "The light in the hall here is pretty dim."

"Well, just take a look," he said, "I can't stand much more of the pain." Tom stuck his face close to the bars in the door.

The jailer moved closer to the door. Tom reached through the bars with his left hand and grabbed his belt. The jailer tried to resist as Tom pulled him as close to the bars as he could, and at the same time he reached behind with his right hand and pulled the knife out. Tom only meant to scare him with the knife, but when he went for his gun, Tom panicked. He thrust the knife into the man's stomach just below the rib cage on his left side, penetrating his heart. He gave a moan and slumped to the floor.

Tom reached between the bars of the door, pulled the key off the jailer's belt and unlocked it. He looked around quickly to see if there was anything he needed to bring with him. He decided to leave his cell just like it was, and opened the door. He had to push hard to shove the jailer's body aside so he could get out. No need to try to hide his body; already there was blood spreading in a puddle on the floor. He reached down, pulled the jailer's revolver from its holster and raced down the steps to the basement.

When he stepped out into the night, he looked toward Market Street and was surprised to see the streets were wet. He was starting to sweat, even though the temperature had dropped 15 degrees since mid-afternoon. His hands were cold, and his mouth was dry. When he didn't see the car, he looked the other way down Washington Street. No car. He started hyper-ventilating. When he looked back, he saw the black car easing across Market Street toward him with its lights off. He ran to it and jumped into the passenger seat.

When the car got to Culton Street, Larry started to turn left to go over to Highway 13 so they could head on out of town.

"Go straight!" Tom yelled at him.

"Straight?"

"Yes, I've got something I need to take care of before we leave town. Go on up to South Street!"

"Tom, leave her alone, we need to get out of town now," Larry screamed at him.

Tom stuck the barrel of the jailer's gun into Larry's ribs. "Damn it, do as I say, drive up the alley behind her apartment, and wait for me!"

* * * * *

Larry still had his lights off when he eased into the space behind the apartment house, right beside Beth's car. Tom got out, taking the car keys with him. He wanted to make sure Larry would be there when he got back. He walked around to the trunk, unlocked it and searched in the darkness until he found the tire iron that came with every new Cadillac. He shut the trunk as quietly as he could and walked to the screen door on the porch. Using the tire iron, he pried it open.

Aunt Maud was a light sleeper. She woke to the sound of a car driving up the alley behind her house. Then she thought she heard a door shut, and she was sure she heard someone opening the screen door to the porch. Quickly she slipped out of bed and donned her robe and slippers. Just as she unlocked the door to her apartment and peeked out into the hall, the back door gave way and someone went up the back stairs. She ran back to her bedroom where the phone was and called the police.

* * * * *

Assistant Chief Clyde Burroughs was sitting at Darlene's desk sipping a cup of coffee when the phone rang. "Police!" he snapped. He hated getting phone calls in the middle of the night, even though it was his job.

Aunt Maud was not the hysterical type. She whispered to Clyde that someone had broken into her house and was in it now. "Please come quick," she said, and gave him the address.

Clyde flipped the switch on Darlene's desk transferring incoming calls upstairs to Buck and Ann's bedroom, and rushed out the front door, locking it behind him. He jumped in his patrol car sitting at the curb and sped off. He didn't use his red light or siren for two reasons; there was no traffic at that time of night, and he didn't want to alert the intruder that he was coming.

Aunt Maud saw him pull up in front with his lights off and met him on the front porch. She told him the intruder was on the second floor, and she feared he was going to kill Elizabeth Breckenridge. Clyde drew his gun and started up the steps to the second floor. When he got to the top step, he heard someone prying on one of the doors. He could hear the wood cracking. There was just a ceiling night light on, so he felt around the corner until he felt the light switch and flipped it on. He stepped into the middle of the hall, and he and Tom spotted each other at the same time. Tom had laid his gun on the floor so he could operate the tire iron as a pry bar, so Clyde had the edge on him. As Tom reached for the gun, Clyde fired, hitting him in the left shoulder.

"Drop the gun!" he shouted, "or I shoot you again!"

Tom raised the gun, so Clyde fired again, hitting him in the same shoulder. Still clutching the gun in his right hand, Tom ran down the back steps and out the door. He slid into the passenger seat and handed the keys to Larry. "Let's get out of here," he shouted.

Larry started the car and backed out into the alley, just as Clyde came out the door. He spun the wheels on the cinders in the alley and sped off down toward Washington Street. Clyde ran through the house to the front door.

"Go check on Mrs. Breckenridge," he shouted to Aunt Maud as he ran out the door to his patrol car.

Larry lurched out of the alley and turned right. Washington Street was downhill all the way to the Missouri Pacific Railroad tracks, and Larry floored the accelerator. He was doing over 60 when he saw the headlight of the Colorado Eagle coming down the tracks. The Eagle was a crack express train that carried passengers and mail non-stop from St. Louis to Kansas City. It was doing over 60 miles per hour when it plowed into the black car, cutting it in half. The signal lights on Washington were working, but with the street wet from the rain, there was no stopping.

Clyde got to the crossing seconds after the crash. He got out of his patrol car and examined the wreckage of the car. The front half was on the north side of the tracks and the back half was on the south side. There were no bodies, just bits and pieces of flesh and bones scattered along the right-of-way.

The train was a mile down the tracks when it finally stopped. The station master called the police, and Buck showed up about 12:20 in the Studebaker. He sent Clyde to get Lester Phipps to come sort out the bodies, or what was left of them. The train came, backing slowly up the tracks. Buck walked down the tracks and met the engineer before he got to the crash site.

"I didn't see a thing," the engineer said. "What did we hit?"

"I'm not surprised," Buck said, "it was a black car, and he was driving with his lights off."

"Anyone hurt?"

"I'm afraid so. According to my assistant chief, there were two men in the car."

"Oh, my God, I'm so sorry," the engineer said, he was devastated. "What should I do?"

"Well," Buck said, "the crossing lights were working, the car was speeding with its lights off, and both men in the car were known to drink heavily. If I were you, I would just go on into Kansas City and fill out an accident report. If anyone has any questions regarding the accident, just have them contact me. My name is Buck Pettit." He handed his card to the engineer. The trainman thanked Buck and went back to his cab. The train was 30 minutes late getting into Union Station.

Buck stood there on the tracks waiting for the coroner. The crossing bells stopped ringing, and suddenly it was quiet. He sighed a big sigh of relief. The past year had been quite a strain. He was glad it was over. The courthouse clock struck 1:00.

EPILOGUE

W ARRENSBURG IS STILL there at the junction Highways 50 and 13 in mid-Missouri, a thriving city of over 17,000. Central Missouri State College is now Central Missouri State University, a vital institution of higher learning with about 10,000 students on campus. Some of the old limestone buildings of the original campus are still used.

The courthouse clock still chimes, and Shepard Park is still on North Holden Street. Reese School was torn down years ago, but Howard School still stands on west Culton Street. It is being refurbished by a group of dedicated citizens as a monument to the time when colored schools were separate, but far from equal.

Warrensburg's biggest asset is still its people. They're as warm and friendly and as willing to help each other as they were in 1936, when Ann and Buck Pettit adopted the Hardesty children, and Harry Foster adopted Lois Huff's ten-year-old when they were married.

When Ann's parents died within two months of each other in 1945, she and Buck moved into the big house on south Holden Street. Jimmy was 13 and Ellie was 11. What wonderful times they had playing in that big old house. Ann inherited her mother's grand piano, and she played as they danced and sang with their friends, especially on holidays like Thanksgiving and Christmas.

Jimmy played guard on the high school basketball team and graduated with honors in 1952. He was drafted into the army right out of high school and was wounded in Korea in 1953. He recovered from his wounds and received an honorable discharge from the army in 1954. He enrolled in the University of Missouri in the fall of that year to be near his sister, Ellie, who was enrolled at Stevens College, both in Columbia. They both graduated from college in 1958, and what a year that was for Ann and Buck. They attended both graduations, and Ellie's wedding in June, and another wedding in October when Jimmy married his high school sweetheart. Jimmy and his bride stayed in Columbia, so Jimmy could work as an assistant basketball coach and they could both work on their Master's degrees at MU.

Ellie married a Sedalia boy who graduated from the University of Missouri with Jimmy. In fact, he and Jimmy were good friends; that's how Ellie met him. They set up an apartment in Warrensburg, so she could get her Master's in music at CMSC and her husband could teach woodworking in the junior high.

* * * * *

Beth ran the bank after Tom's death, and was quite successful. After Tom's death, she got the fancy fountain pen back from the court and gave it to Irv, who gave it to his mother. She moved back into the big house on south Holden Street, and in 1939 at the age of 35 married a man from Holden whom she had dated before in her high school years. He had proposed to her after high school graduation, but she turned him down. He married another girl shortly after that, but she died in 1938 during the polio epidemic, leaving him with two teen-age children, a boy 16 and a girl 15. They moved in with Beth, and she adopted them, raising them as her own. She made a good mother.

In 1944, she ran for governor of Missouri and was defeated by a small margin. In 1948 she was elected to congress and served two terms from her district, and in 1952 she was elected to the Senate on President Eisenhour's coattails, one of only two women in the Senate. She served her state well for three terms and retired from the Senate in 1970 at the age of 66. She lived out her years in the big house on south Holden Street with her husband. She was a highly respected banker and mother.

* * * * *

Harry Foster and Lois Huff married in June 1938. Lois and her son, along with her mother, went to live on the farm north of Warrensburg. Harry adopted the boy and turned an old smokehouse just behind the farm house into a small cottage for his mother-in-law. After graduation from CMSC, Lois taught at the country school across the road from the farm. She loved it. She didn't get to teach her son though; he started to junior high in town the year they were married. The boy didn't mind; he got to ride to school every morning in a sheriff's patrol car. Sometimes when no cars were around, Harry let him run the siren and turn on the red light. Harry retired from the Sheriff's department in 1950 and lived on the farm with his family until he died in 1966 at age 81.

* * * * *

Rudolph and Wilhelm Eisenstein retired to Florida in 1946, where they lived out their years in a retirement village near Sarasota.

Clarence became Police Chief at Buck's retirement, a job he deserved.

Russell Wilhelm did finally marry a school teacher. He was chairman of the rural school district that included his farm, and while interviewing a pretty young CMSC graduate for the job of teacher for their school, he fell in love. They were married the next spring, and surprisingly it turned out to be a good marriage. As it turned out, she was raised on a farm in Henry County and loved the rural life. They had four children.

* * * * *

Milton Stevenson enrolled in Lincoln University, an all-colored school in Jefferson City, in 1937 at the age of 16. He was so far ahead of the other freshman students that he only stayed one year. In 1938, he moved his credits to Howard University in Washington, D.C., graduating in 1941 with a Master's degree in psychology. He also had a bachelor's degree in languages, having mastered both French and German. After a year of teaching languages in the Washington, D.C. school system, he was drafted into the army and assigned to the O.S.S. (the forerunner of the C.I.A.). In 1944, he parachuted into northern Italy behind the German lines to link up with Italian Partisans, and was successful in sabotaging the German Army to the extent that his group helped shorten the war in Italy. After the war, he and an army buddy established a building contracting company, and in 1986 he retired from it to write and produce plays.

Gerald Essex ran for the office of Attorney General for the state of Missouri in 1938, but was defeated by a wide margin in the Democrat primary. He wound up practicing law with a private firm in Kansas City.

* * * * *

As for the three boys who found the body of Margaret Wilson:

Irv Hodges' family moved to Kansas in the spring of 1941. His father was successful in a bid to paint some military buildings being constructed in Salina. After graduating from Salina High School in the spring of 1944, he enlisted in the Navy. While he was in the Navy, his parents moved to Sedalia, Missouri, where his mother had inherited a house and some land southwest of town from a great aunt. After two years in the Navy, he was honorably discharged and enrolled in CMSC under the GI bill.

While attending college, he worked part-time at a department store in Sedalia on weekends. It was part of a large regional chain of stores. He liked the manager of the store, and the manager liked him. Irv was bored with college and wanted to get started on a career, so in 1946 when the store manager offered him a full-time job as a management trainee, he jumped at it. While in Sedalia, he met and married Sarah, an air brush artist who specialized in painting black and white photographs to look like color photography. This was years before color photography was cheap enough for the masses, so Sarah did very well. There were artists who colored photographs in oils and watercolors, but there was no comparison in the quality; therefore, while the other artists were charging $5 to color an eight-by-ten portrait, Sarah charged $25 and had customers standing in line for her work. It was tedious work though, and it often took her a week to finish a portrait.

They met at a bowling alley in November of 1948. Sarah bowled with a group of young people from her church, and Irv came in to practice. He bowled with his store's team in a merchants' league. It was love at first sight, and in February of 1949 they were married. Sarah put her air brushes away and stayed home to care for the four children that were born of this union. They lived in several cities around the Midwest as Irv completed his training. In 1979 he was assigned to manage one of the company's larger stores in a beautiful Southern city that they both loved. With their children grown and gone from the nest, Irv retired in 1986.

* * * * *

Johnny O'Reilly graduated from Warrensburg High School in May 1944 and enlisted in the Marine Corps in June. Although he was only 17, he begged his parents to sign the papers necessary for his enlistment, and they finally relented. He was severely wounded on Okinawa. He was helping to take some high ground that was necessary for the defense of the area needed to unload troops and supplies. He died in a tent hospital on the beach. His memory lives on.

* * * * *

Robert McKnight graduated from Warrensburg High School with Johnny in 1944 at the height of World War II. He enrolled in a pre-med curriculum at the University of Missouri, and because doctors were in such short supply, he was given a high draft number. So many doctors were in the service of their country, at least the younger ones, that some retired physicians went back to their practices to help out until the war was over.

Robert graduated from MU in 1948, and because of his high grades, was accepted as a med student at Washington University in St. Louis. After graduating from medical school in 1951 and completing his internship and residency in family practice at Barns Hospital in St. Louis, he moved to a small town in southern Missouri and set up practice. While in residency in St. Louis, he married a nurse, and they eventually had two children. Three years later, in 1957, he talked another doctor, a classmate at Washington University, into joining him, and they opened a small clinic, which they operated successfully until they both retired in 1991 and sold their clinic to a group of doctors in Springfield.

* * * * *

There are many more stories to tell about those hot summers during the great depression of the '30s, but they will have to wait for another time.